There suddenly glided across their vision forms – of every conceivable shape, i.e., those resembling corpses of human beings and animals, with bloodless faces, glassy eyes and stiff limbs – some apparently just dead and others in an advanced state of decomposition, all possessed and propelled by Impersonating Elementals; phantoms of actual earthbound people – misers, murderers, etc., several of whom approached the trio and tried to peer into their faces.
'For heaven's sake keep off!' Kelson shrieked, as the vibrating form of an epileptic imbecile, with protruding blue eyes and pimply cheeks, came up to him, and thrust its face into his.
'This is a bit thick,' Hamar said, vainly attempting to elude the phantom of a short, stout woman with a big head and purple face, who, putting out a large black, swollen tongue, leered at him.
'Curse you! d—n you!' Curtis screamed, throwing out his hands in a vain endeavour to beat off the phantoms of two idiot boys who were trying to bite him with their loose, dribbling mouths. 'A little more of this and I shall go mad!'

The Dennis Wheatley Library of the Occult

Dracula
BRAM STOKER

Moonchild
ALEISTER CROWLEY

The Werewolf of Paris
GUY ENDORE

Carnacki the Ghost-Finder
WILLIAM HOPE HODGSON

Studies in Occultism
HELENA BLAVATSKY

The Sorcery Club
ELLIOTT O'DONNELL

SPHERE BOOKS LIMITED
30/32 Gray's Inn Road, London WC1X 8JL

First published in Great Britain
by William Rider & Son Ltd 1912

Published by Sphere Books 1974

Introduction copyright © Dennis Wheatley 1974

TRADE
MARK

This book is sold subject to the condition that
it shall not, by way of trade or otherwise, be lent,
re-sold, hired out or otherwise circulated without
the publisher's prior consent in any form of
binding or cover other than that in which it is
published and without a similar condition
including this condition being imposed on the
subsequent purchaser.

Set in Intertype Baskerville

Printed in Great Britain by
Hazell Watson & Viney Ltd
Aylesbury, Bucks

ISBN 0 7221 6505 6

CONTENTS

	Introduction by Dennis Wheatley	7
1	How they first heard of Atlantis	9
2	The Black Art of Atlantis	17
3	Learning to sin	29
4	The Tests	39
5	The Initiation	46
6	The First Power	57
7	San Francisco Ladies and Divination	72
8	Two Dreams	82
9	Love at First Sight	89
10	How the Dreams were interpreted	97
11	Leon Hamar calls on the Martins	103
12	The Great Challenge	113
13	The Modern Sorcery Co. Ltd. give a Gratis Performance	124
14	Shiel to the Rescue	132
15	How Hamar, Curtis and Kelson entered the Astral Plane	139
16	Hamar makes Advances	147
17	The Course of True Love	154
18	Stage Three	160
19	A Series of Misadventures	168
20	The Stage of Hauntings	179
21	The Selling of Spells	187
22	The Persecution of the Martins	194
23	Love	200
24	The Subpœna	207
25	Curtis in a New Role	214
26	In Hyde Park at Night	220
27	The Right Girl to marry	228
28	Whom will he marry?	234
29	The End and 'The Beyond'	242

INTRODUCTION

THIS book by Elliott O'Donnell (1872-1966) was first published in 1912. I met the author only once, and that was at a small dinner party in, of all places, the Admiralty. Many years were to pass before those splendid apartments of the First Sea Lord were to be occupied by Earl Mountbatten, but, by a curious coincidence, his mother-in-law, Lady Mount Temple, was our hostess that evening.

I did not particularly take to O'Donnell, so did not pursue the acquaintance, but there can be no doubt about it that he had a very wide knowledge of the occult. He wrote many books, both fiction and non-fiction, on the subject and it is our intention to include the best of them in this series.

Unlike the majority of novels about the supernatural, to begin with the three principal characters not only know nothing about the occult, they regard everything to do with it as utter nonsense.

It starts in San Francisco during the great slump of the early 1930s. Three clerks have been turned off and out of work for weeks. One of them, Leon Hamar, accidentally damages a book and is forced into buying it. To his disgust he finds it is on Atlantean magic. He reads passages of it with the utmost scepticism, but the three friends are literally starving, so it's a case of 'let's try anything once'.

After a week or so performing preparatory acts laid down in the book and passing various tests, they go out from San Francisco by night to Muir Woods, a national reserve. I visited it some years ago and found it of surpassing grandeur. In its 400-odd acres many of the giant redwood trees are over 200 feet high and 2,000 years old.

There the three perform an Atlantean magical operation. To their amazement and terror it calls up a demon, with whom they enter into a pact. During each three-month period for the following twenty-one months they will be given, for three months only, certain supernatural powers. If during the whole period they live together in harmony and none of them marry, at the end of the twenty-one months all the powers granted to them during the seven three-month periods will be theirs for the rest of their lives. The powers given them during these periods include divination, thought reading, leaving one's body, making oneself invisible, being able to breathe under water, taming wild beasts and understanding their language, inflicting diseases, creating plagues of insects, curing any ailment, transforming humans into vampires or werewolves, complete domination over women's affections and numerous other manifestations achievable only by invisible influences.

The major interest of the story therefore lies in the use that can be made of these magical powers bestowed by Satan, and the difference of the natures of the three men who form the Sorcery Club.

Naturally, they soon grow rich. Then, finding San Francisco too small for their operations, they move to London. There, among other activities, they give performances as conjurors and are able to perform such fantastic tricks that they nearly bankrupt Maskylen and Devant. But they can make use of each occult power – such as becoming invisible – only for three months, and for infringing the law they are still liable to arrest by the police. But by far the worst danger they are up against is failure to fulfil the condition of maintaining harmony between them. And here their leader, Leon Hamer, is faced with a terrible task, for one of his companions is a confirmed drunkard and the other ungovernably attracted to women.

It is this struggle between mental weakness due to physical desires and the wiles of Satan that is the high spot of this intriguing story.

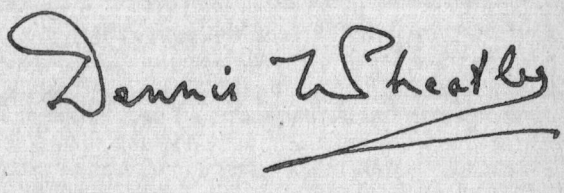

THE SORCERY CLUB

CHAPTER 1

HOW THEY FIRST HEARD OF ATLANTIS

RAIN is responsible for a great deal more than the mere growth of vegetables – it is a controller, if a somewhat capricious controller, of man's destiny. It was mainly, if not entirely, owing to rain that the French lost the Battle of Agincourt; whilst, if I mistake not, Confucius alone knows how many victories have been snatched from the Chinese by the same factor.

It was most certainly rain that drove Leon Hamar to take refuge in a second-hand bookshop; for so deep-rooted was his aversion to any literature saving a financial gazette or the stocks and shares column of a daily, that nothing would have induced him to get within touching distance of a book save the risk of a severe wetting. Now, to his unutterable disgust, he found himself surrounded by the things he loathed. Books ancient – very ancient, judging by their bindings – and modern – histories, biographies, novels and magazines – anything from ten dollars to five cents, and all arrayed with most laudable tact according to their bulk and condition. But Hamar was neither to be tempted nor mollified. He frowned at one and all alike, and the colossal edition of Miss Somebody or Other's poems – that by reason of its magnificent cover of crimson and gold occupied a most prominent position – met with the same vindictive reception as the tattered and torn volumes of Whittier stowed away in an obscure corner.

Backing still further into the entrance of the store for a better protection from the rain, which, now falling heavier and heavier, was blown in by the wind, Hamar collided with a stand of books, with the result that one of them fell with a loud bang on the pavement.

A man, evidently the owner of the store, and unmistakably a Jew, instantly appeared. Picking up the book, and wiping it with a dirty handkerchief, he thrust it at Hamar.

'See!' he said, 'you have damaged this property of mine. You must either buy it or give me adequate compensation.'

'What!' Hamar cried, 'compensation for such rubbish as that? Why all your books together are not worth five dollars. Indeed I've seen twice as many sold at a sale for half that amount. You can't Jew me!'

The two men eyed each other quizzically.

'Perhaps,' the owner of the store observed slowly, 'perhaps some of your ancestors were once Yiddish. In which case there ought to be a bond of sympathy between us. You may have that book for a nickel. What, no! Your cheeks are hollow, your fingers thin. A nickel is too much for you. I will take your chain in exchange.'

'And leave me the watch!' Hamar retorted, with a grim smile. 'You are a philanthropist – not a storekeeper.'

'I should leave you nothing!' the Jew laughed. 'There's no watch there! See!' and he pointed to the concave surface of the watch-pocket. 'I noticed its absence at once. It's been keeping you alive for some days past. I'll give you four dollars on the chain – and you may have the book!'

'The book's no good to me!' Hamar grunted. 'The money is. Here! hand me over the four dollars and you can have the chain. It's eighteen carat gold and worth at least ten dollars.'

'Then why not take it to some one who will give you ten dollars!' sneered the Jew. 'Because you know better. You're no greenhorn. That chain is fifteen carat at the most, and there's not a man in this city who would give you more than four dollars for it.'

'Very well, then!' Hamar said sulkily. 'I agree. No! the money first.'

The Jew dived deep down into his trouser pocket, and, after foraging about for some seconds, produced a handful of greasy coins, out of which he carefully selected the sum named.

Hamar, who had been watching him greedily, grabbed the coins, bit them with his teeth, and rang them on the counter. With an air of relief he then slipped his watch-chain into the outstretched palm before him, remarked upon the fact that the rain had suddenly ceased, and prepared to take his departure.

'Here's the book!' the Jew ejaculated, whilst his face became suffused with a smirk. 'Don't go without it. Now! there's no knowing but what we may not have further dealings with one another. I'm a money-lender – I've a place downstairs – I take all sorts of things – all sorts of things. On the strict Q.T. mind. Sabez!'

In another moment Hamar found himself standing on the wet pavement, nursing the four dollars in his waistcoat pocket with one hand, and mechanically clutching the despised volume with the other. Had he ever acted upon impulse, he would most certainly have hurled the book into the gutter; but on second thoughts he came to the conclusion that it would be better to dispose of it less obtrusively.

It was now evening, and having tasted nothing since mid-day, he realized, for at least the hundredth time that week, that he was hungry. The touch of the dollars, however, only made him smile. He could eat his fill for twenty-five cents and yet live well for another four days. And, besides, he still had a tie-pin and a fur coat. He might get a dollar on the one and two, if not two and a half, on the other; which would carry him through till the end of the week when something else might turn up – something which would not involve too hard work and would just keep him clear of jail. He turned sharply down Montgomery Street, crossed Kearney Street, and slipped noiselessly through the side doorway of a restaurant, in a suspicious-looking alley, not a hundred yards distant from the gorgeously illuminated Palace Hotel. Here, within five minutes, he was served with as good a meal as one could get in San Francisco for the money – and if the table linen was not as clean as it might have been, the food was not a whit the less excellent for that. At least so Hamar thought; and it was not until there was nothing left to eat that he left off eating. When he thought no one was looking in his direction, he popped the despised book under his chair and rose to go. Before he had gone ten yards, however, one of the waiters came running after him.

'Hi, sir, stop, sir!' the fellow cried. 'You've left something behind!' And in spite of Hamar's denials the officious menial persisted the book was his. In the end Hamar was obliged to submit. He took the book, and rewarded the waiter with curses.

Hamar next tried to dispose of it down the area of a Chinese laundry; but a policeman saw him, and he only escaped being taken up on suspicion, by parting with a dollar. This was the climax. He did not dare make any further attempt to dispose of the book, but, with bitter hatred in his heart, tucked it savagely under his arm, and made direct for his room in 115th Street.

To his annoyance – for under the circumstances he preferred to be alone – he found two men sitting in front of his empty hearth. They were Matt Kelson and Ed Curtis; both of whom had been his colleagues at Meidler, Meidler & Co., in Sacramento Street, and like himself had been thrown out of work when the firm had 'smashed'. Since that affair Hamar had studiously avoided them. It was true he had once been as friendly with them as he deemed it politic to be friendly with any one; but now – they were out of employment, and in danger of starvation. That made all the difference. He did not believe in poverty encouraging poverty, any more than he believed in charity among beggars. He had nothing to share with them, not even a thought; and resolving to get rid of his quondam friends as soon as possible, he confined his welcome to a frown.

'Hulloa! what's the matter?' Kelson exclaimed. 'When a man frowns like that, it usually means he is crossed in love.'

'Or has an empty stomach, which amounts to the same thing,' Curtis interposed. 'Come – let the sun loose, Leon! We've good news for you! – haven't we, Matt?'

Kelson nodded.

'What is it, then?' Hamar grunted. 'Have you both got cancer?'

'No! We've come to borrow from you!'

'Then you've come to the wrong shop! I'm about done, and unless something turns up mighty quick I shall clear out.'

'For good?'

'I don't count on being a ghost nor yet an angel,' Hamar said; 'when we've done here, I reckon we've done altogether!'

'I shouldn't have thought suicide was in your line,' Curtis remarked. 'More Matt's. I should have credited you with something more original.'

'Original!' Hamar snarled. 'I defy any man to be original when he hasn't a cent, and his stomach contains nothing but air. Give me money, give me food – then, perhaps, I'll be original.'

'You don't mean to say you're cleared out of grub!' Kelson and Curtis cried in chorus. 'We've come to you as our last hope. We've neither of us tasted anything since yesterday.'

'Then you'll taste nothing again to-day – at least as far as I'm concerned,' Hamar jeered. 'I tell you I'm broke – haven't as much as a crumb in the room; and I've pawned everything, save the clothes you see me in!'

'And yet you can buy books – unless – unless you stole it!' Curtis said, eyeing with suspicion the volume Hamar had thrown on the table.

'Buy it! Not much!' Hamar cried quickly. 'It's one I've had all my life. Belonged to my grandfather. I took it with me to-night to see what I could raise on it.'

'And no one would have it? I should guess not,' Kelson said, drawing it towards him. 'Why it's got a new label inside – S. Leipman! I know him. He's slick even for a Jew. This looks as if it belonged to your grandfather, Leon. If I'm not real mistaken you bought the book to-night. There's something in it you thought you could make capital of. Trust you for that. Now I wonder what it was!'

'You're welcome to see!' Hamar sneered. 'Perhaps you'd like some water!'

'Water! Why water?'

'Well, instead of tea or whisky to help digest the book. Besides, it's the only thing I have to offer you.'

'Look here, Leon,' Curtis interrupted; 'what's the good of behaving like this? We are all in the same boat – starving – desperate. So let us lay our heads together and see if we can't think of something – some way out of it.'

'A Burglary Company Limited, for instance!' Hamar sneered. 'No! I'm not having any. I've neither tools nor experience. The San Francisco police handle one roughly, so I'm told, and hard labour isn't to my liking.'

'There are other things beside burglary!' Curtis said in tones of annoyance. 'We might work a fake.'

'If I work anything of that sort,' Hamar said hastily, 'I work alone. Think of something else.'

'I tell you Matt and I are pretty well desperate,' Curtis cried, 'and if we don't think of something soon, we shan't be able to think at all. We've tried our level best to get work – we've answered every likely and unlikely advertisement in the papers – and all to no purpose. So if Providence won't help us we must help ourselves. Robbery, burglary, fakes, anything short of murder – it's all the same to us now – we're tired of starving – dead sick of it. We would do anything, sell our very souls for a meal. My God! I never imagined how terrible it is to feel so hungry. You appear to be interested, Matt. What is it?'

'Why, look here, you fellows!' Kelson said slowly. 'This book is all about a place called Atlantis that is said to have existed in the Atlantic Ocean between America and Ireland, and to have been deluged by an earthquake owing to the wickedness of its inhabitants. They practised sorcery.'

'Practised foolery,' Hamar said. 'It's tosh – all tosh! Wickedness is only a matter of climate – and there's no such thing as sorcery.'

'So I thought,' Kelson replied; 'but I'm not so sure now. The author of this book writes darned sensibly, and is apparently at no loss for corroborative testimony. He was a professor too. See! Thomas Henry Maitland, at one time Professor of English at the University of Basle in Switzerland. There's an asterisk against his name and a footnote in very old-fashioned handwriting – the 's's' are all 'f's,' and half of the letters capitals. Listen—

"Thomas Maitland, despite the remonstrances of his friends, visited Spain. By order of the Holy Inquisition he was arrested, May 5, 1693, on a charge of practising sorcery, and burned alive at the Auto da Fé, in the Grand Market Square, Madrid; having in the interim been subjected to such tortures as only the subtle brains of the hellish inquisitors could devise. On receipt of a message from him, delivered in his supernatural body, we attended his execution, and can readily testify that he suffered no pain, although the torments endured by those around him were pitiable to behold.

(*Signed*) GEORGE RICHARD POOL,
Physician;
and
ROBERT JAMES FOX,
Merchant.

Citizens of Boston, Massachusetts;
August 1, 1693.' "

'Rot!' Hamar said savagely; 'don't waste time reading such bunkum.'

'It may be bunkum, but if it takes away his mind from his stomach let him go on.' Curtis interposed. 'It's very obvious you haven't arrived at our pitch of starvation yet, Leon, or you would welcome anything that would make you forget it even for a moment. Let's hear some more, Matt! Go on, tell us something. How to make coyottes out of paraffin paint, or convert a Sunday pair of pants into a glistening harem skirt! Anything that won't remind us of food.'

Thus encouraged Kelson slowly turned over the pages of the book. 'I see it was printed and published for – I presume that means by – A. Bettesworth and J. Batley in Pater-noster-Row, London, England, in 1690. Basle, London, Boston, Madrid! The author seems to have had wandering on the brain. By the by, Leon, with your features you could easily work off a fake as "the Wandering Jew." There's money in it – people will swallow anything in that line now.'

'I don't see how it would profit you anyhow,' Hamar snarled. 'Leave my features alone and go on with your reading.'

Kelson chuckled – here was one way at least in which he could occasionally get even with Hamar. Hamar's features were Yiddish, and the Yids were none too popular in California.

'Oh, all right!' he said; 'if the subject is so painful I'll try and avoid it in future; but it's odd how some things – for instance, murder and noses – will out. Let me see, what have we here? "Discovery of ancient books, manuscripts, etc., relating to Atlantis." Apparently, Thomas Maitland, when shipwrecked on an island, called Inisturk, off Mayo, in Ireland, found a wooden chest of rare workmanship – he had seen, he says, similar ones in Egypt and Yucatan – containing some very ancient books – curiously bound, and some vellum manuscripts, which after an infinite amount of labour, he managed to translate. The books, he says, were standard histories, biographies, and scientific works on occultism – all published in Banchicheisi, the capital of Atlantis – and the manuscripts, he affirms, had been transcribed by one Coulmenes, who believed himself to be the only survivor of a tremendous submarine earthquake that had destroyed the whole of Atlantis. The manuscripts included a diary of the events leading up to the catastrophe – even to the meals! How about this? – "Sunrise on the day of Thottirnanoge in the month of Finn-ra. Breakfasted on cornsop, fish (Semona, corresponding to salmon), fruit, and much sweet milk."'

'For God's sake, don't!' Curtis groaned. 'Skip over that part. The very mention of grub makes the gnawing pain in my stomach ten times worse.'

'You're different to me then!' Hamar grinned; 'I love to think of it. My word, what wouldn't I give to be in Sadler's now. Roast beef – done to a turn, eh! As only Sadler knows how! Potatoes nice and brown and crisp! Horseradish! Greens! Boiled celery! Pudding under the meat! Beer – What, going?'

Curtis had risen from the table with his fingers crammed in his ears. 'There's a fat splice of the devil in you to-night, Leon!' he panted. 'I've had enough of it. I'm off. Come on, Matt. If you want us, you know where to find us – only if we don't get something to eat soon – you'll find us dead.'

CHAPTER 2

THE BLACK ART OF ATLANTIS

For some time after Kelson and Curtis had left him, Hamar lolled back in his seat, lost in thought. Thought, as he told himself repeatedly, should be the poor man's chief recreation – it costs nothing; and if one wants a little variety, and the walls of one's rooms are tolerably thick, one can think aloud. Hamar often did, and derived much enjoyment from it.

'I'm convinced of one thing,' he suddenly broke out; 'I'd rather be hungry than cold. One can, in a measure, cheat one's stomach by chewing leather or sucking pebbles, but I'll be hanged if one can kid one's liver. It's cold that does me! A touch of cold on the liver! I could jog along comfortably on a few dollars for food – but it's a fire, a fire I want! The temperature of this room is infernally low after sunset: and half a dozen coats and three pairs of pants don't make up for half a grateful of fuel. Hunger only makes me think of suicide – but cold – cold and a chilled liver – makes me think of crime. Yes, it's cold! Cold that would make me a criminal. I would steal – burgle – housebreak – cut the sweetest lady's throat in Christendom – for a fire!

'There! that little outbreak has relieved me. Now let me have a look at the book.'

He dragged the volume towards him, and despite the feeling of antagonism with which it had inspired him, and despite the cynical attitude he had, up to the present, adopted towards the supernatural, he speedily became engrossed. On a few leaves, somewhat clumsily inserted between the cover and first page of the book, Hamar read an account, presumably in the author's own penmanship, of how he, Thomas Maitland, after being shipwrecked, had remained on Inisturk Island for a fortnight before being rescued, and had spent the greater portion of that time in examining the books, etc., in the chest he had found – his only food – shell-fish and a keg of mildewy ship's biscuits.

He was taken, so the account ran, by his rescuers, on the barque *Hannah,* to London, where he lived for five years. His lodgings were in Cheapside, and it was there that he compiled his work on Atlantis, having obtained his subject matter from the Atlantean books he had managed to bring with him, and which, after an enormous amount of perseverance and labour, he had translated into English. Though these books were subsequently destroyed in a big fire that demolished the entire street, luckily for him, he had sent his MS. to the publishers, Messrs. Bettesworth and Batley, a week or so before the conflagration broke out; so that he was, at any rate, spared the loss of his own arduous and invaluable work.

The publishers did not accept the MS. at once. At that time there were very severe laws in operation against anything savouring of witchcraft and magic, and as the manuscript dealt at length with these subjects, and in a manner that left no doubt whatever that he, Thomas Maitland, had practised sorcery extensively, Messrs. Bettesworth and Batley were forced to consider whether it would be injurious to them to publish it. Mrs. Bettesworth was eventually consulted – as indeed she always was, on extraordinary occasions – and her interest in the MS. being roused, she decided in its favour. Within a week of its publication, however, it was suppressed by law; all the copies saving three presentation ones to the author, which he successfully concealed, were destroyed; Messrs. Bettesworth and Batley were put in the stocks on Ludgate Hill and fined heavily, and he, Thomas Maitland, was ordered to be arrested, flogged and imprisoned.

'But,' wrote Maitland, 'I was not to be caught napping. My previous adventures and hairbreadth escapes had rendered me unusually wary, and perceiving a number of people, among whom were two or three sheriff's officers, approaching my house, I at once interpreted their mission, and climbing through a trap-door leading on to the roof of the building, nimbly made my way to the end of the row, and slipping down a waterpipe easily eluded my enemies. London, however, being now too hot to hold me, I booked passage on board the *Peterkin,* a Thames trading vessel of some eighty tons, and sailed for Boston. My flight had been so hasty that I brought very little with me – nothing in fact except the clothes I stood in – a stout winter suit of home-spun brown cloth, a cloak, and a pair of good, strong leather leggings – a purse of fifty sovereigns (all I had), a knife, pistol and two copies of my precious book, the third copy, alas! I had left behind in my hurry.'

After giving a few unimportant details as to his life on board ship, Maitland went on to say:

'Owing to a succession of storms the *Peterkin* was driven out of her course, and after narrowly escaping being dashed to pieces on the Florida reefs, Lat. 24½° N., Long. 82° W., we ran ashore with the loss of only two lives – the second mate and cabin boy – on the Isthmus of Yucatan, close to the estuary of a river.[1] Here we were forced to spend nearly a year, during which time I made several journeys of exploration into the interior of the continent. In the course of one of my rambles amid a dense mass of tropical foliage, I suddenly found myself face to face with a gigantic stone Sphinx, which I at once recognized and identified. It was Tat-Nuada, an Atlantean deity, elaborately described in one of the burned books. Much excited, I set to work, and, after clearing the base of the idol of fungi and other vegetable growth adhering to it, discovered a superscription in Atlantean dialect to the effect that the image had been set up there by one Hullir – to commemorate the destruction of Atlantis, of which catastrophe Hullir believed himself and his family, *i.e.* his wife Ozilmeave and daughters, Taramoo and Nikétoth, and the crew of his yacht, the *Chaac-molré* (ten in number), the sole survivors.

'Here, then, to my unutterable joy, was strong corroborative evidence of the great disaster narrated in detail in the manuscripts I had found in Inisturk Island. The existence of Atlantis was now thoroughly substantiated. On all sides of me I stumbled across further evidences of these early settlers. Here, standing in bold outline on a slight eminence was a stone edifice adorned with symbolical carvings of eggs, harps, mastodons, triangles, and numerous other objects, all of which were capable of interpretation, and indicated that the building was a temple to some god.

'I was much struck by the extraordinary similarity in many of the things I saw – notably in the sphinx, idols and symbols – to many I had seen in Egypt, and to some extent in Ireland, and I at once set to work to draw up a careful analogy between the language of those countries.

'The word Branchicheisi[2] I found to contain the Celtic ban, a barrow; and Coptic isi, plenty; whilst I recognized in

---

[1] The river referred to by Maitland is the river Lagartos, which was then (1691) unnamed.

[2] For chiche compare the ancient Maya or Yucatan word Chicken-Itza (*i.e.* name of town in Yucatan where excavations are now taking place – 1912).

the words Coulmenes,[1] the Celtic Coul, a man's name, *i.e.*
Finn, son of Coul; in Thottunanoge, the Coptic Thoth, *i.e.*
name of ancient Egyptian deity, and Erse Tirnanoge, the
name of the wife of Oisin, the last of the Feni; in Chaac-
molré[2] the Coptic deity, ré; in Ozilmeave,[3] the Celtic
Meave, a girl's name; in Taramoo,[4] the Celtic Tara, a girl's
name; and in Nikétoth,[5] toth, the Erse technical form of
feminine gender; and comparing the alphabets I traced a
very striking likeness between the Atlantean—

    △ (a) and the Gaelic or Erse △
    □ (B) and the Coptic □
    D (d) and Erse D
    3 (g) and Erse 3
    ᴐ(T) and Coptic ᴐ

and many of the other letters. To the Atlantean
ψ(C), ○(O), ʃ(E), ᒡ(Z),[6]
I could, however, find no likeness.

'From all these similarities, *i.e.* in architecture, symbols,
letters, and words, I could come to no other conclusion than
that there was some strong connecting link between Atlantis
and ancient Ireland and Egypt.

'Assuredly this great link could not have been merely due
to stray survivors of the great catastrophe! Was it not much
more probable that the earliest inhabitants of Ireland and
Egypt had originally migrated from Atlantis, carrying its
language, and ways and customs with them? Moreover,
since the Atlanteans were so deeply versed in magic and
everything appertaining to the occult, this migration would
account for the mysticism that has always been so closely

[1] For Menes compare Mayan Menes, wise men.
[2] Compare Mayan Chaac-mol, a leopard.
[3] Compare Ozil, Mayan for well-beloved.
[4] Moo, Mayan for Macaw.
[5] Niké, woman's name in Mayan.
[6] Recent (1912) discoveries of statues in Easter Island still
further corroborate the sinking of Atlantis.

The Atlantean character ψ resembles the Easter Island ψ (C)
   "   "   ○   "   "   "   "   ○ (O)
   "   "   ʃ   "   "   "   "   / (E)
   "   "   ᒡ   "   "   "   "   ᒡ (Z)

It will be noticed that all the Atlantean characters are distinguished by additional curling strokes.

associated with Egypt and Ireland, and for the psychic faculty so strongly observable in the inhabitants of these two countries.

'I was highly satisfied – I had proved much and my discoveries had upset many of the theories advanced by the modern sages. I could now positively assert that the wisdom of the world came not from the East but from the West. It was to the golden West – to Banchicheisi, capital of Atlantis, that humanity owed its knowledge of the sciences and arts, and of all things good and evil. Eden, if Eden existed at all, was not in Asia, it was in Atlantis; and the Deluge, that is recorded in the Hebrew Bible, and is traditional in the histories of nearly every tribe and nation, was none other than the mighty inrush of the ocean over Atlantis, due to some abnormal submarine earthquake.

'Of what eventually became of the Atlanteans whose relics I had so opportunely alighted upon, I could only surmise.

'The last record I found was on a tablet set up by Nikétoth. On this she spoke of the death of Hullir and Ozilmeave, of the inter-marriage of the crew of the *Chaacmolré* with native women; of the consequent growth of the colony; and of her determination to leave it, and, accompanied by a chosen few, to push her way further inland.[1]

'The anxiety of my comrades to leave the continent, perforce put an end to my explorations, and in the beginning of the year 1692 – exactly ten months after our landing – the *Peterkin* was refloated.

'This time nothing happened to impede our progress, and in April of the same year, we sighted Boston. Here I remained for some months, making many new friends, and studying magic and sorcery. But the love of travel had laid so strong a hold on me that I again took to a roving life. I set sail for Spain in November 1692; landed at Corunna, and made my way to Madrid, where I arrived on January 1, 1693.'

For the rest, Hamar had to turn to Messrs. Fox and Pool's addendum, *i.e.* the footnote that Matt Kelson had read aloud.

---

[1] In all probability she was the founder of Chicken-Itza, the capital of Yucatan.

Hamar was now inclined to regard the book in a very different light. What he had read seemed to him to be set down in too simple, straightforward, and, at the same time, detailed a manner to be other than true. Up to the present he had not believed in ghosts and witches, for the very simple reason that – like all sceptics – he had never inquired into the testimony respecting them. He had pooh-poohed the subject, because everyone he knew pooh-poohed it, and also because it had never seemed worth his while to do otherwise. But provided he thought it would pay him, he was ready to believe in anything – in Christianity, Mahommedanism, Buddhism, Theosophy, or any other creed; and granted the book he had in his hands was really written by Maitland, and Maitland was *bona fide* (which Hamar saw no reason to doubt), and granted, also, that Maitland was sane and logical – which from his writing he certainly appeared to be – then there was a certain amount in the volume that in Hamar's opinion was 'a find.' Needless to say, he referred to the magic of the Atlanteans – the art through the practice of which they had got in touch with the Powers that could endow them with riches. The actual history of Atlantis – once he was satisfied there had been such a place – did not interest him. He skimmed through it quickly, and I append a brief summary, only, for the benefit of more intelligent and disinterested readers.

The Atlanteans were the oldest intelligent race in the world – they existed contemporaneously with Paleolithic man, with whom their mariners and explorers came in contact, and about whom their novelists wrote the most delightful stories, just as Fenimore Cooper and Mayne Reid, in these days, have written the most delightful stories about the Red Indians. In religion they were polytheists; they believed that, in the work of Creation, many Powers participated; that some of these Powers were benevolent, some malevolent, whilst others – neither benevolent nor malevolent – were merely neutral. To the benevolent creative Powers they attributed all that is beautiful in the world (*i.e.* certain of the trees, plants, flowers, animals, insects, and pleasing colours and scents); all that is fair and agreeable in the human being, such as affection, love, kindness, the arts and sciences – in a word all that in any degree affected the welfare of mankind; and to the malevolent creative Powers they attributed all that was noxious in creation; all that was harmful to man, and detrimental to his moral and physical progress (*i.e.* diseases, and all savage and filthy passions); all races of low intelligence, viz. Paleolithic and Neolithic man – and all those born with black or red skins (those colours being particularly significant of the malignant Occult Elements); all destructive animals; (*i.e.* reptiles such as the teleosaurus, steneosaurus, etc.; birds, such as the pterodactyl, vulture, eagle, etc.; mammals, such as the cave lion, cave tiger, etc.; fish, such as the shark, octopus, etc.); and all ugly and venomous insects.

These earliest records show that at one time the physical and superphysical world were in close touch; all kinds of spirits – trolls, pixies, nymphs, satyrs, imps, Vagrarians, Barrowvians, etc. – mixing freely with living human beings; but that as the population increased and civilization evolved, superphysical manifestations became more and more rare, until finally they became restricted to certain conditions dependent on time and locality.[1]

Up to this period there had been no state religion – no temples in Atlantis. If any one wished for a particular favour from the Occult Powers – for example, from the Rabsés, the Occult Powers of music; the Brakvos, the Occult Powers of medicine; or the Derinas, the Occult Powers of love, they retired to some secluded spot and held direct intercourse with these Powers. The idea of praying to an invisible being – who might or might not hear them – never entered their minds; they were far too matter of fact for that – and it was not until superphysical manifestations had become confined to a very select few, that the plan of erecting public buildings in spots frequented by the spirits, so that all who wished could assemble there and communicate with them, was proposed and put into operation. In these buildings, however, the spirits did not choose always to appear to order – sometimes they quitted the spot where the edifice had been erected; sometimes they would only appear there periodically; and sometimes, out of perversity, they would appear when least expected. But whether occult manifestations really took place in these buildings or not, those assembled to see them were persuaded by those in charge of the building, who saw thereby an opportunity of

---

[1] Types of Elementals still to be met with in certain localities (vide *Byeways of Ghostland,* published by Rider & Son).

making money, that the spirits were actually there; and in due time these buildings became known as temples, and their showmen as priests. Every temple was dedicated to an individual spirit – one to the Spirit Bara-boo; another to the Spirit Karaboro, and so on; whilst in the absence of genuine spirit manifestations, prayers, incantations and rituals, invented by the priests, always attracted a large concourse of people to these temples, and finally proved a greater source of attraction than the spirits themselves.

It was to gain favours from the Occult Powers that donations from the public were at first invited, then demanded; and the priests in this manner accumulated vast fortunes. Later on, too, there sprang up, in connection with these temples, colleges for the training of young men – invariably selected from the wealthy classes – to the priesthood; and from the parents of these youthful aspirants large fees, which in course of time became exorbitant, were extracted, thereby furnishing another source of revenue to the priests. The most famous colleges for the training of priests in Atlantis were those of Bara-boo-rek[1] at Keisionwo, Karaboro-rek and Diniangek, and Ballygarap-rek at Tijimin.

It was in the reign of Barrahneil,[2] fifty-first sovereign of the Dynasty of Shaotak, that the evocation of spirits (from which modern spiritualism takes its origin) commenced. Barrahneil was most eager to see a superphysical manifestation. Being of a somewhat poetical turn of mind he was particularly enamoured of fairies, and in the hope of seeing one, constantly frequented their favourite haunts, *i.e.* woods, caves, and lonely isolated habitations. But all to no purpose – they never would manifest themselves to him. At last, he lost patience. Against the advice of his oldest and most trusty counsellors, and accompanied by one or two of his favourite courtiers, he went to an excessively lonely spot in the heart of a desert, and besought spirits – spirits of any sort – he did not care what – to manifest themselves. To his surprise – for he had grown extremely

1 Compare Egyptian ré.
2 Maitland raises the question as to whether Barrahneil was the ancestor of Niall of the Nine Hostages. Of this there is every possibility, since many Atlanteans undoubtedly escaped to Ireland, carrying with them the knowledge of Black Magic – to which might be traced the Banshee and other family ghosts.

sceptical – an Occult form, half man and half beast,[1] materialized. It informed them that it was Daramara, *i.e.* in Atlantis, the Unknown – that it had no beginning and no end, and that it would remain an impenetrable mystery to them during their existence in the physical sphere, but would be fully revealed to them when they passed over into Malanok – one of the superphysical planes. On this, and on several subsequent occasions, when it manifested itself to them, it gave them instructions with regard to evocation, and described to them the tests they must undergo before they could aquire the great powers the Unknown was able to bestow on them, namely, (1) second sight; (2) divining other people's thoughts and detecting the presence of waters and metals; (3) thought transference, *i.e.* being able to transmit messages, irrespective of distance, from one brain to another without any physical medium; (4) hypnotism; (5) the power to hold converse with animals; (6) invisibility, *i.e.* dematerializing at will, (7) walking on, and breathing under, water; (8) inflicting all manner of diseases and torments; (9) curing all kinds of diseases; (10) converting people into beasts and minerals; (11) foretelling the future by palmistry, pyromancy, hydromancy, astrology, etc.; (12) conjuring up all manner of spirits antagonistic to man's moral progress, *i.e.* Vice Elementals – Vagrarians, Barrowvians, etc.

Taking every care to observe the greatest secrecy, Barrahneil caused a full account of these interviews with Daramara, together with all the instructions the latter had given him, to be transcribed in a book, which he called *Brahnapotek*[2] – or the *Book of Mysteries*; and which he kept sealed and guarded in a room in his palace.

During his lifetime no one held communication with Daramara saving himself and his friends, but after his death the secret of Black Magic leaked out; countless people sought to acquire it, and ultimately the practice of it became universal. But the Atlanteans little knew the dangers they were incurring. The spirits they conjured up – though at first subservient, that is to say, mere instruments – at length obtained complete dominion over them – the whole

[1] Probably a Vice Elemental.
[2] All subsequent works dealing with Black Magic were founded on it.

race became steeped in crime and vice of every kind – and so horrible were the enormities perpetrated that, fearful lest Man should be entirely obliterated, the benevolent Occult Powers, after a desperate struggle with the malevolent Occult Powers, succeeded, by means of a vast earthquake, in submerging the Continent and hurling it to the bottom of the Atlantic Ocean, where, what remains of it, now lies. The catastrophe took place in the reign of Aboonirin, twentieth sovereign of the Dynasty of Molonekin – three thousand years after the reign of Barrahneil.

So ran the history of Atlantis, or at least all of it that need be quoted for the elucidation of this story. That Black Magic – the Black Art of the Atlanteans was by no means dead – Hamar felt convinced, and if Maitland could resuscitate it – why could not he? At any rate he might try. He could lose nothing by giving it a trial – at least nothing to speak of – the outlay on chemicals would be a mere song – whereas, on the other hand, what might he not gain? He eagerly perused the tests – the tests he must impose upon himself before he could get in touch with the Unknown, and acquire the magic powers – which, according to Thomas Maitland, were copied from the original *Brahnapotek*, and including a preface, ran as follows:
(*Preface*) 'It is essential that the person desirous of being initiated into the Black Art – the Art of communicating with the Unknown (Daramara) in order to acquire certain great powers, should dismiss from his mind all ideas of moral progress, and wholly concentrate on the bettering of his material self – on acquiring riches and fame in the physical sphere. His aspirations must be entirely earthly, and all his affections subordinate to his main desire for wealth and carnal pleasures. Having acquired this preliminary psychological stage, for one clear week he must give himself up entirely to the breaking of all conventionalities of morality with which society is hedged in. He must practise every kind of deception – lie, cheat and steal, and go out of his way to seek an opportunity to avenge any personal injury; and if his mind is earnestly and wholly concentrated on acquiring knowledge of the Black Art no bodily mishap will befall him. During this time of probation he must will himself to dream, at night, of all the deeds he has in mind to do, during the day; when he will know, by his visions, to what extent he is

progressing. At the end of the week he must apply the tests to see if he is in a ripe state to proceed.

'The tests—

No. 1. At midnight, when the moon is full, place a mirror, set in a wooden frame, in a tub of water, so that it will float on the surface with its face uppermost. Put in the water fifteen grains of bicarbonate of potash, and sprinkle it with three drops of blood, not necessarily human. If the reflection of the moon in the mirror then appears crimson, the test is satisfactorily accomplished.

No. 2. At midnight, when the moon is full, take a black cat, place it where the moonbeams are thickest, sprinkle it with three drops of blood, not necessarily human, and rub its coat with the palm of the hand. Sparks will then be given out, and if those sparks appear crimson the test is satisfactorily done.

No. 3. Take a human skull – preferably that of some person who has met an unnatural end, pour on it a single drop of fresh, human blood – place it on a couch, and go to sleep with the back part of the head resting on it. If you are awakened, at the second hour after midnight, by hearing a great commotion close at hand, and the room is then discovered to be full of crimson light, the test is satisfactorily fulfilled.

No. 4. Take half a score of the berries of enchanter's nightshade,[1] two ounces of hemlock leaves in powder, and one ounce of red sorrel leaves. Heat them in an oven for two hours, pound them together, in a mortar, and at midnight boil them in water. As soon as the contents begin to bubble, remove them from the fire and stand them in a dark place; and if the experiment is to prove satisfactory, three bubbles of luminous green light will rise simultaneously from the water and burst.

[1] Closely allied to deadly nightshade, and known in botany as *Circæa*. It is found in damp, shady places and was used to a very large extent in mediæval sorcery.

No. 5. In the above preparation after the test described, soak a hazel twig, fashioned in the shape of a fork. On meeting a child hold the fork with the V downwards in front of its face, and if the child exhibits violence and signs of terror, and falls down, the experiment is successful.

No. 6. Take a couple of handfuls of fine soil from over the spot where some four-footed animal has recently been buried. Put it in a tin vessel, mix it with three ounces of asafœtida and one drachm of quassia chips, to which add a death's-head moth (*Acherontia atropos*). Heat the vessel over a wood fire for three hours. Then remove it and place it on the hearth, rake out the fire and make the room absolutely dark. Keep watch beside the vessel, and if, at the second hour after midnight, any strange phenomena occur, the test will be known to have been satisfactorily executed.

'(*Addendum*) If any of these tests fail the candidate must wait for six months before giving them a further trial, and he must occupy the interim by training his thoughts in the manner already prescribed. But if, on the other hand, the tests have been successfully performed, he can proceed with the rites appertaining to the Black Art.'

Hamar had read so far when, with a gesture of impatience, he closed the book. 'What a fool I am!' he exclaimed, 'to waste my time with such stuff! . . . But Maitland writes in such a devilish convincing way! Jerusalem! Any straw is good enough for the drowning man, and if witchcraft and sorcery with motors dashing by every second and the whole air alive with wireless and telephones, is a bit beyond my comprehension, what then? All I care about is money – and I'll leave no stone unturned to get it. If it were possible for man to get in touch with Daramara – the Unknown – Devil, or whatever else it chooses to call itself – I'll call it an angel if it only gives me money – twenty thousand years ago – why shouldn't it be possible to get in touch with it now? Anyhow as I said before, I'll have a try. As far as the preliminary stage is concerned, I fancy I'm pretty well fixed. My mind is occupied right enough with things of this world – I don't give a cent for anything belonging to another – and if only I had half a dozen souls, I'd sell them right away now, for less than twenty thousand dollars – a damned sight less. As for these tests – foolish isn't the word for them – but it won't cost much just to try them. . . . Now, according to Thomas Maitland, the ceremony of calling up the Unknown stands a far greater chance of success if there are three human beings present . . . but, of course, if there is any truth in this business, I'd rather keep the secret of it to myself. However, if I try alone, the Unknown might not come to me, and then I shall have had all the trouble of going through the tests for nothing! . . . Ah! now I see! If the other two get more of the profits than I think necessary – I can make use of my newly acquired Occult Power to – to dissolve the partnership! Ha! ha! I could – I could trick the Unknown if it comes to that. Trust a Jew to outwit the Devil! I'll just look up Kelson and – Curtis.'

CHAPTER 3

LEARNING TO SIN

Messrs. Kelson and Curtis did not live in Pacific Avenue where the Popes hold sway, nor yet in California Street where the Crockers are wont to entertain their millionaire friends. Where they lived, there were no massive granite steps flanked with equally massive pillars – such as herald the approach to Nob Hill palaces; no rare glass bow-windows looking out on to flower bedecked lawns; no vast betiled hall, with rotundas in the centre; no highly polished oak staircases; no frescoed ceilings; no tufted, cerulean blue silk draperies; and no sweet perfumery – only the smell, if one may so suddenly sink to a third-class expression – only the smell of rank tobacco and equally rank lager beer. No, Messrs. Kelson and Curtis resided within a stone's throw of the five cent baths in Rutter Street – and that was the nearest they ever got to bathing. Their suite of apartments consisted of one room, about ten feet by eight feet, which served as a dining-room, drawing-room, study, boudoir, kitchen, bedroom, and – from sheer force of habit, I was about to add bathroom; but as I have already hinted cold water on half-empty stomachs and chilly livers is uninviting;

besides, soap costs something. Their furniture was antique but not massive; nor could any of it be fairly reckoned superfluous. All told, it consisted of a bedstead (three six-foot planks on four sugar cubes; the bedclothes – a pair of discarded overalls, a torn and much emaciated blanket, a woolly neck wrap, a yellow vest, and the garments they stood in); a small round and rather rickety deal table; and one chair. Of the very limited number of culinary utensils, the frying-pan was by far the most important. Its handle served as a poker, and its pan, as well as for frying, roasting and boiling, did duty for a teapot and a slop-basin. They had no crockery. They had only one thing in abundance – namely, air; for the lower frame of the window having long lacked glass in it, a couple of pages of the *Examiner*, fixed in it, flapped dismally every time the wind came blowing down 216th Street.

They had not lived there always. In the palmy days of work, before the firm smashed, they had aspired to what might properly be called diggings; and, moreover, had 'digged' in respectable surroundings. It was the usual thing – the thing that is happening always, every hour of the day, in all the great cities of the world – starvation, through lack of employment. Civilization still shuts its eyes to everyday poverty. Who knows? Who cares? Who is responsible? No one. Is there a remedy? Ah! that is a question that requires time! Time for the politician, and time for the starving ones! Half the world thinks, whilst half the world dies; and the cause of it all is time – too much, a damned sight too much – time!

But Kelson and Curtis could not grumble. They had their room – bare, dirty and well-ventilated – for next to nothing. Fifty cents a week! And they could furnish it as they pleased. Fancy that! What a privilege! They were glad of it all the same, glad of it in preference to the streets; and probably, when asleep, they thought of it as home. But on leaving Hamar's, that evening, they had fully resolved to convert their little room into a cemetery. What else could they do? What can any one do who has no money and no prospect of getting any, and who has reached the pitch of acute hunger? He has passed the stage of wanting work, because, if work were offered to him, he would not be in a fit state to do it – he would be too weak. Too weak to work! What a phenomenon! Yes – to all those who have never missed a day's meals. To others – no! They can understand – and understand only too well – the really poor who have long ceased to eat, cannot work – they are beyond it.

When Curtis and Kelson staggered down the stairs of the house where Hamar lodged, they realized that unless something turned up pretty soon, it would be too late – they would be past the stage of caring for anything – too feeble to do anything but lie on the ground and pray that death would come quickly.

'Home?' Kelson inquired, as they emerged on to the pavement.

'Hell!' Curtis answered, and Kelson, taking it for granted that the terms were synonymous, at once headed for their garret.

'Don't walk so confoundedly fast,' Curtis gasped; 'this pain in my side is like a hundred stitches rolled in one. It fairly doubles me up. Ease down a bit, for heaven's sake!'

Kelson obeyed, and presently came to a dead halt before a dingy-looking restaurant. Both men leaned against the window and gazed wolfishly at the food. A warm, fœtid rush of air from under the grating at their feet tickled their nostrils and mocked their hunger with a mockery past endurance. Arranged on the window-sill was a miscellaneous collection of very smeary plates and dishes, containing an even more miscellaneous collection of food. A half-consumed ham, with more than a mere suspicion of dirt on its yellowish-white fat; some concoction in a bowl that might have been brawn made from some peculiarly liverish pig, or – from one of the many homeless mongrels that roam the streets at night; a pile of noxious-looking mussels, side by side with a glistening mass of particularly yellow whelks; a round of what purported to be beef – very fat and very underdone; some black shiny sausages, and a score or so of luridly red polonies. A similar assortment was to be seen on the counter behind which lolled an anæmic girl, in a dirty cotton blouse, and a much soiled sky-blue skirt.

A month ago such an exhibition would have been an offence in the fastidious eyes of Messrs. Kelson and Curtis; but now it was otherwise. Their stomachs would have refused nothing short of garbage.

'Matt!' Curtis's hands had left off clutching at his belt

and were now hanging by his side; the fingers twitching to and fro in a manner that fascinated Kelson. 'Matt! Is there any logic in our starving?'

'None, excepting that we haven't a cent between us!' Kelson rejoined.

'I know that,' Curtis went on slowly, 'but – I mean – why should we starve when all this grub is within two inches of us! It's unreasonable – it's intolerable.'

'Doesn't the smell of it satisfy you?' Kelson replied, attempting to force a smile, and failing dismally.

'D—n the smell!' Curtis cried. 'It's the ham I want. I'd give my soul for a good munch at it. And just look at that tea, too! Don't you see it steaming over there? What wouldn't I give for just one cup! Ten minutes more and it may be too late. The pain will come on again – and it will be very doubtful if I shall ever get home. I'm close on the stage when one begins to digest one's own stomach. Curse it! I won't starve any longer! Matt! she's in there all by herself!'

'So I've been thinking,' Kelson murmured, glancing uneasily up and down the street. 'Still, she's a girl, Ed!'

'That's just it!' Curtis whispered; 'it is because she is a girl. If she were a man, in our present condition, we shouldn't stand a chance. Come! It's this or dying in the gutters. It's our one and only chance. Let's go in – have a feed – take what we can and make a bolt for it. If she tries to stop us we can settle her right enough.'

'Without being too rough! There's no need to be too rough with her, Ed.'

'I shouldn't stick at much!' Curtis answered. 'Occasions like this don't admit of chivalry. Come along! It's the ham I'm after.'

Curtis shuffled forward as he spoke, and the next moment Kelson and he were standing in front of the counter.

The girl eyed Curtis very dubiously and it is more than likely would have have refused to serve him had he been alone. But her expression changed on looking at Kelson. Kelson was one of those individuals who seldom fail to meet with the approval of women – there was a something in him they liked. Probably neither he nor they could have defined that something; but there it was, and it came in extremely handy now.

'What do you want?' she inquired shortly.

'Ham!' Give me some of that ham over there, miss, and a cup of tea! Bread too!' Curtis cried eagerly. 'Do you know what it is to have a twist on, miss? I have one on now – so please give us a full twenty-five cents' worth.'

Kelson said nothing, but his eyes glistened, and the girl wondered as she passed him the polonies.

Both men ate as they had never eaten before, and as they would not have eaten now had they paid any attention to the advice of hunger experts. However, they survived, and when they could eat no more they leaned back in their chairs to enjoy the sensation of returning – albeit, slowly returning – strength.

Curtis was the first to make a move. 'Matt,' he murmured, 'we've about sat our sit. We'd better be off. You go and say a few nice words to the girl and make a pretence of paying. I'll secure the ham – there's still a good bit left – and anything else I can grab. The moment I do this, throw these chairs on the ground so that the girl will fall over them when she makes a dash for me, which she is certain to do. We will then head straight away for 216th Street. Don't look so scared or she will think there is something up. She has never taken her eyes off you since we sat down!'

'She's rather a nice girl!' Kelson said. 'I wish I didn't look quite such a blackguard – and – I wish I hadn't to be quite such a blackguard. Who'll pay for all this? Will she?'

'We shan't, anyway,' Curtis sneered. 'Come, this is no time to be sentimental. It was a question of life and death with us, and we've only done what any one else would do in our circumstances. The girl won't lose much! Are you ready?'

Curtis rose, and Kelson, who was accustomed to obey him, reluctantly followed suit. A look almost suggestive of fear came into the girl's eyes as they encountered those of Curtis, and she shot a swift glance at an inner door. Then Kelson spoke, and as she turned her head towards him, her lips parted in a sort of smile.

'Nice night, miss, isn't it?' Kelson said, halting half-way between the counter and the chairs. 'Aren't you a bit lonely here all by yourself?'

'Sometimes,' the girl laughed. 'But my mother's in the room there,' and she nodded in the direction of the closed door. 'And one can't be dull when she's about. She's that there active as a rule, there's no keeping her quiet – only just at present' – here she glanced apprehensively at Curtis – 'she's recovering from ague. Gets it every year about this time. Your friend seems to have kind of taken a fancy to our ham.'

Kelson glanced at Curtis and his heart thumped. Curtis's right hand was getting ready to spring at the ham, whilst his left was creeping stealthily along the counter in the direction of a loaf of bread. Kelson slowly realized that an acute crisis in both their lives was at hand, and that it depended on him how it would end. He had never thought it possible to feel as mean as he felt now. Besides, his natural sympathy with women tempted him to stand by the girl and prevent Curtis from robbing her. He was still deliberating, when he saw two long dark objects, with lightning rapidity, swoop down on the plates and dishes. There was a loud clatter, and the next moment the whole place seemed alive with movement.

A voice which in his confusion he did not recognize at once shouted – and seemingly from far away – 'Quick, you fool, quick! Fling down the chairs and grab those sausages!' Whilst from close beside him – almost, he fancied, in his ears – came a wild shriek of 'Mother! Mother! We are being robbed!'

Had the girl appealed to him to help her it is more than likely that Kelson, who was even yet undecided what course to adopt, would have offered her his aid; but the instant she acted on the defensive his mind was made up; a mad spirit of self-preservation swept over him – and dashing the chairs on the ground at her feet, he seized the sausages, and flew after Curtis.

Ten minutes later, Curtis and Kelson, their arms full of spoil, clambered up the staircase of their lodgings, and reeled into their room.

'Look!' Curtis gasped, sinking into the chair. 'Look and see if we are being followed!'

'There's no one about!' Kelson whispered, peering cautiously out of the window. 'Not a soul! I don't believe after that first rush across Rutter Street, any one noticed us. To leave off runing was far the best thing to do. You are a perfect genius, Ed. I wonder if this sort of thing – er – thieving – is dormant in most of us? I say, old fellow, I wish I hadn't looked at that book of Hamar's. Do you know, directly I took it up, an extraordinary sensation of cunning came over me; and I declare, when I put it down, I felt it would take very little to make me a criminal!'

'We're both criminals now – in the eyes of the law – anyway!' Curtis said. 'And now we've got so far there's no alternative but to go on! It's easier for a hundred camels to pass through the eye of a needle than for a clerk to get work, that's a fact. The markets are hopelessly overstocked – no one wants us! No one helps us! No one even thinks about us. The labouring man gets pity and cents galore – we get nothing! – nothing but rotten pay whilst we work, and when we're out of work, dosshouses or kerbstones. D—n clerks, I say. D—n everything! There's no justice in creation – there's no justice in anything – and the only people who prate of it are those who have never known what it is to want. Say, when shall we take the next lot?'

'When we're obliged, not before!' Kelson said. 'Or rather, you do as you like – and I'll do the same.'

'Well, I'm not going to commit suicide anyhow,' Curtis sneered. 'We haven't the money to buy poison – and I've no mind to drown myself or cut my throat – they're too painful! If we don't go on doing what we've done tonight, what are we going to do?'

'Trust to luck,' Kelson sighed.

'All right – you trust to luck – but I won't trust any more in Providence, and that's a fact,' Curtis retorted. 'We've been done enough. Now I'm for doing other people. Good-night.'

He tumbled into the makeshift bed as he spoke; and in a few minutes, worn out after the unwonted exertions of the evening, both men were fast asleep.

They were at breakfast next morning – real *déjeuner à la carte* – sausages, bread, water – and they were doing ample justice to it, when some one rapped at the door. For a few seconds there was silence. Their hearts stood still. Had they been followed, after all? Was it the police? Some one spoke – and they breathed again. It was Hamar.

'This looks like starving, I must say!' Hamar exclaimed, as he sniffed his way into the room and sat on the bed. 'Why, from what you fellows told me last night I thought you were cleared out. And here you are, stuffing like roosters! You look a bit surprised to see me, but you'll be more surprised, I reckon, when I tell you what brings me here. You remember that book?'

Kelson and Curtis nodded.

'Well,' Hamar went on. 'I read it after you left last night, and I've come to the conclusion that there's something in it that may be of use to us.'

'Us!' Curtis ejaculated.

'Yes! Us!' Hamar mimicked. 'It contains full particulars of how we can get in touch with certain Occult Powers – that can give us money or anything else we want!'

'Rot, of course!' Curtis said.

'You say that now. But, listen to me,' Hamar replied. 'Since I've read that book, I believe there's a lot more in Occultism than people imagine. You may recollect the name of the author of the book – Thomas Maitland. Well! to begin with, he impresses me as being truthful; and he not only believed in Magic but he practised it. If he hadn't gone into details I shouldn't think anything of it, but he's so darned thorough, and tells you exactly what you've got to do to get in touch with the Occult Powers and to practise sorcery. He learned it all from that old MS. he found, written by an Atlantean; and the Atlanteans, he says, were adepts in every form of Occultism. I tell you, this chap himself scoffed at it at first; and it was more out of curiosity, he says, than because he was convinced, that he began to experiment. He afterwards came to the conclusion that the Atlanteans were no fools. What they had written about the Occult was absolutely correct – there was another world, and it was possible to get in touch with it. Now, if Thomas Maitland was able to practise sorcery, why can't we? There was a gap of close on twenty thousand years between his time and that of Atlantis, and there's not much more than two hundred years between his day and ours. But, of course, if you're going to pooh-pooh the whole thing I won't trouble to tell you any more!'

'Well, Leon,' Kelson ejaculated, 'magic and sorcery do seem a trifle out of date, don't they? Could any one look out of the window at what is going on in the streets below, and at the same time believe in fairies and hobgoblins? Still, the book made a bit of an impression on me, so that I'm inclined to agree with you. Anyway, go ahead! Ed is agreeable, aren't you, Ed?'

Curtis gave a sulky nod. 'I'm not averse to anything that may put us in the way of a livelihood,' he said.

Hamar, somewhat appeased, briefly informed them of the tests and other preliminaries necessary for the acquirement of the Black Art, and without more ado proposed that they – the three of them – should form a Syndicate and call it the Sorcery Company Limited. 'To begin with,' he said, 'we might sell tricks and spells, and later on tackle something more subtle. Why, we could soon knock all the jugglers and doctors on the head – and make a huge fortune.'

'That is to say if it isn't all humbug!' Curtis observed.

'Well – do you or don't you think it worth trying?' Hamar cut in. 'You call me a Jew – but Jews, you know, have a tolerably cool head, and a keen faculty for business. They don't touch anything unless it is pretty certain to bring them in money. Will you try?'

'Y-e-s!' Curtis said slowly; 'I'll try.'

'And you, Matt?' Hamar queried. 'We must have three.'

'I don't mind trying,' Kelson replied. 'I expect it will be only a try.'

'That settles it, then!' Hamar cried. 'Now, we'll get to business. To begin with, we're all wholly occupied with things of this world – money chiefly!'

'Sometimes music!' Curtis said sententiously.

'And sometimes girls,' Kelson joined in. 'Music's a pose on Ed's part. I don't believe he really cares a bit for it. He's far too material.'

'Just what I want him to be!' Hamar laughed. 'Girls are material enough too – especially when you take them out to supper. Anyhow, money is our first consideration, isn't it?'

To this there was general assent.

'The preliminary requirement is fixed then,' Hamar said. 'Now for the week of wild oats! Lying, stealing, cheating – anything to counteract the code of Moses! Let's take them in turn. Lying won't trouble us much. Every one lies. Lying is the stock-in-trade of doctors, lawyers, sky pilots, storekeepers—'

'And dentists!' Curtis chimed in.

'And shop girls!' Kelson added.

'All women – rich as well as poor!' Hamar went on. 'Lying is woman's birthright. She lies about her age, her looks, her clothes – everything. With a lie she sends callers away, and when she is in the mood, entertains them with lies. Women are born liars, but they are not the only liars. In these days of keen competition every one lies – every editor, publisher, undertaker, piano-tuner, dustman – they couldn't live if they didn't. Moreover, lying is natural to us all. Every child lies as soon as it can speak; and education merely teaches him to lie the more effectually. Lying comes just as natural as sweating—'

'Or kissing,' Kelson interrupted.

'Or any of the other so-called vices,' Hamar continued. 'So we can manage that all right. As to cheating – having nothing to cheat with – according to instructions we've got to keep in with each other, so present company is excepted – we must pass over that. Now – how about thieving!'

'Never done any yet, so can't say,' Curtis exclaimed.

'Nor I either,' Kelson put in rather hurriedly.

'Well, I didn't suppose you had!' Hamar laughed; 'though, after all, more than half the world does thieve – all employers steal labour from their employés, all tradesmen steal a profit – the wholesale man from the middleman – the middleman from the retailer. Every Government thieves. Look at England – righteous England! At one time or another she has stolen land in every part of the world. But theft is an ugly word. When statesmen steal it's called diplomacy, when the rich steal it's called kleptomania or business, and it's only when the poor steal that stealing is termed theft. We who have every excuse – we who are starving – will be content with – that is to say – we will only *take* – just enough to keep us alive – a few lumps of sugar, a handful of raisins, or a loaf of bread. How about that?'

'I might manage that,' Curtis said. 'I might – but I don't want to get caught.'

'And you, Matt?'

'I don't mind stealing food so much,' Kelson said. 'In the face of so much wealth – and waste too – it seems a bigger sin to starve than to steal a loaf of bread.'

'The lying and stealing are fixed then,' Hamar laughed. 'What you have to do, too, is to make the most of every opportunity you can find of doing people – present company excepted – bad turns.'

'I don't see how – in our present condition – we can do

any one much harm,' Curtis remarked. 'We haven't even the means to buy a tin sword, let alone a bomb or pistol. If we wish them ill, perhaps, that will do instead.'

'Possibly – but don't be such an ass as to wish any one any good!' Hamar said. 'Do your best to carry out the injunctions I have given you, and we will meet here, this day week, to discuss the tests.'

CHAPTER 4

THE TESTS

SEVEN days later, Hamar again knocked at Curtis's and Kelson's door and walked in. A faint sigh of relief escaped him.

'I see we are all right so far,' he said. 'I wondered whether I should find you both flown, or lying stretched in the icy hands of death. Have you experimented?'

'We have,' Curtis said. 'We've done our best. In what way, we prefer not to say.'

'Perhaps there is no need,' Hamar replied, eyeing the mantelshelf which bore ample testimony to a full larder, and glancing at Curtis's feet which were encased in a pair of new and very shiny boots. (A handsome overcoat that was hanging on the door also attracted his attention; but that he had seen before, and concluded that it had been there on the occasion of his last visit.) 'But you had better dry up now, Ed,' he continued somewhat caustically, 'or there'll be no chance of forming the Sorcery Society; it will be dissolved before it's started. There's no need to ask if you've tried to carry out instructions as to thoughts. I see it – in your faces. I could never have believed one experimental week in badness would have made such a difference to your looks.'

'You told us to try hard!' Kelson murmured, 'and naturally we did. I reckon you've done the same by your expression. I should hardly have known you.'

'It shows pretty clearly,' Curtis said, 'what a lot of bad is latent in most people; and that the right circumstances only are needed to bring it out. Starvation, for instance, is calculated to bring out the evil in any one – no matter whom. But what puzzles me, is how we have escaped being caught!'

'That's a good sign,' Hamar said. 'It bears out what is written in the book. If you give your whole mind to doing wrong during this trial week you'll meet with no mishap. But you must be heart and soul in it. Hunger made us – hunger has been our friend.'

'What do you mean?' Curtis said.

'Why,' Hamar replied, 'if we hadn't been well-nigh starving we shouldn't have been able to carry out the instructions quite so thoroughly.'

'Have you, too, stolen?' Curtis queried.

'I have certainly appropriated a few necessaries,' Hamar said shortly, 'but I mean to stop now. We have higher game to fly at. Now, with regard to the tests. I have not been idle, I can assure you. I have secured all the requisites. The mirror and black cat I – well, er – to use a conventionalism that comes in rather handy – the mirror and cat – I picked up. The skull I borrowed from a medical I know – the moth – er – from some one's private collection – and the elderberries, hemlock and chemicals I obtained from a drug store man in Battery Street with whom I used to deal. The moon will be full to-night so that we may as well begin. Will you come round to my room at eleven-thirty?'

They promised; and Hamar, as he took his departure, again glanced at the handsome fur coat hanging on the door.

He was hardly out of hearing when Curtis looked across at Kelson. 'Do you think he recognized it?' he whispered. 'You may bet he did, and he had only just stolen it himself! However, it's his own fault. He told us to lie and steal, and we've done his bidding.'

'We have indeed!' Kelson sighed; 'at least you have. For my part I'd rather be content with food!'

'Well, I needed clothes just as much as food!' Curtis snarled. 'If I went about naked I should only be sent to prison – that's the law. It punishes you for taking clothes, and it punishes you for going without them. There's logic for you!'

Curtis and Kelson spent the rest of the day indoors; and at night sallied forth to Hamar's.

The solitary attic – if one could thus designate a space of about three square yards – which comprised Hamar's lodging – had the advantage of being situated in the top storey of a skyscraper – at least a skyscraper for that part of the city. From its window could be seen, high above the serried ranks of chimney-pots on the opposite side of the street, those two newly-erected buildings: William Carman's chewing gum factory in Hearnes Street, and Mark Goddard's eight-storied private residence in Van Ness Avenue; and, as if this were not enough architectural grace for the eye to dwell on, glimmering away to the right was the needle-like spire of Moss Bates's devil-dodging establishment in Branman Street; whilst, just behind it, in saucy mocking impudence, peeped out the gilded roof of the Knee Brothers' recently erected Cinematograph Palace.

All this and more – much more – was to be seen from Hamar's outlook, and all for the sum of one dollar and a half per week. When Curtis and Kelson entered, the room was aglow with moonlight, and Hamar and the black cat were stealthily regarding one another from opposite corners of the room. From far away – from somewhere in the very base of the building, came the dull echo of a shout, succeeded by the violent slamming of a door; whilst from outside, from one of the many deserted thoroughfares below, rose the frightened cry of a fugitive woman. Otherwise all was comparatively still.

'You're a bit early!' was Hamar's greeting, 'but better that than late. Everything is ready, and all we've got to do is to wait till twelve. Sit down.'

They did as they were bid. Presently the cat, forsaking its sanctuary, and ignoring Curtis's solicitations, glided across the floor, and climbing on to Kelson's knee, refused to budge. The trio sat in silence till a few minutes before midnight, when Hamar rose, and, selecting a spot where the moonbeams lay thickest, placed thereon the tub of water, in which – with its face uppermost – he proceeded to float a small mirror, set in a cheap wooden frame. He then calmly produced a pocket knife.

'What's that for?' Kelson inquired nervously.

'Blood!' Hamar responded. 'One of us must spare three drops. The conditions demand it – and after all the ham and sausages you two have eaten I think one of you can spare it best. Which of you shall it be? Come, there's no time to lose!'

'Matt has more blood than I have!' Curtis growled; 'but why not the cat?'

'It would spoil our chances with it for the other experiment,' Hamar said. 'It's a sulky, cross-grained brute, and would give us no end of trouble. Besides, it can bite. Look here, let's draw lots!'

Curtis and Kelson were inclined to demur; but the proposed method was so in accordance with custom that there really did not seem any feasible objection to raise to it. Accordingly lots were drawn – and Hamar himself was the victim. Curtis laughed coarsely, and Kelson hid his smiles in the cat's coat. A neighbouring clock now began to strike twelve.

'Look alive, Leon!' Curtis cried, nudging Kelson's elbow. 'Look alive or it will be too late. The Unknown is mighty particular to a few seconds. Let me operate on you. I've always fancied I was born to use the knife – that I've really missed my vocation. You needn't be afraid – there's no artery in the palm of your hand – you won't bleed to death.'

Thus goaded, Hamar pricked away nervously at his hand, and, after sundry efforts, at last succeeded in drawing blood; three drops of which he very carefully let fall in the tub.

'I wish it was light so that we could see it,' Curtis whispered in Kelson's ear. 'I believe Jews have different coloured blood to other people.'

Though Kelson was apprehensive, Hamar did not appear to have heard; his whole attention was riveted on the mirror, on the face of which was a reflection of the moon.

'I knew nothing would happen,' Curtis cried, 'you had better wipe your knife or you'll be arrested for severing some one's jugular. Hulloa! what's up with the cat?'

Hamar was about to tell him to be quiet when Kelson caught his arm. 'Look, Leon! Look! What's the brute doing? Is it mad?' Kelson gasped.

Hamar turned his head – and there crouching on the floor, in the moonlight, was the cat, its hair bristling on end and its green eyes ablaze with an expression which held all three men speechless. When they were at last able to avert their eyes a fresh surprise awaited them; the reflection of the moon in the mirror was red – not an ordinary red – not merely a colour – but red with a lurid luminosity that vibrated with life – with a life that all three men at once recognized as emanating from nothing physical – from nothing good.

It vanished suddenly, quite as suddenly as it had come; and the reflection of the moon was once again only a reflection – a white, placid sphere.

For some seconds no one spoke. Hamar was the first to break the silence. 'Well!' he exclaimed, drawing a long breath; 'what do you think of that!'

'Are you sure you weren't faking?' Curtis said.

'I swear I wasn't,' Hamar replied; 'besides, could any one produce a thing like THAT? The cat didn't think it was a fake – it knew what it was right enough. Besides, why are your teeth chattering?'

'Why are yours?' Curtis retorted; 'why are Matt's?'

'Shall we try the second?' Hamar asked.

'No!' Kelson and Curtis said in chorus. 'No! We've seen enough for one night. We'll be off!'

'I think I'll come with you,' Hamar said, 'after what has happened I don't quite relish sleeping here alone – or rather with that cat. Hi – Satan, where are you?'

Satan was not visible. It had probably hidden under the bed, but as no one cared to look, its whereabouts remained undiscovered.

With the coming of the sun, the terrors of the night wore off, and the trio separated. Hamar would on no account accept his friends' invitation to breakfast on the sausages and ham they had run such risks in procuring; he made hasty tracks for a snug restaurant in Bolter's Street, where he had a sumptuous repast for a dollar; and then slunk home.

Shortly before midnight all three met again, and at once commenced preparations for the second test. The question arose as to who should hold Satan. They all had vivid recollections of the cat's behaviour the previous night; consequently no one was anxious to officiate. Finally they drew lots, and fate settled on Curtis. An exciting chase now began. Satan, demonstrating his resentment of their treatment of him, at every turn, knocked over a water bottle, ripped the skin of Kelson's knuckles, and made his teeth meet in the fleshy part of Curtis's thumb.

'Hulloa! what are you up to?' Curtis savagely demanded, as Hamar thrust a cup at him.

'Hold your hand over it!' Hamar said sharply. 'Don't suck it! We want blood for this test and for the next.'

'I wish the brute had bitten you!' Curtis snarled; 'then, perhaps, you wouldn't be so precious keen on economics. You did right to name it Satan! and if it doesn't attract devils nothing will. I'm not going to touch it again. See if you can hold the beast by yourself, Matt! It seems to be less afraid of you than of either of us.'

Kelso called out: 'Puss!', and the cat at once came to him.

As it was now striking twelve, Hamar carefully shook three drops of Curtis's blood from the cup on to Satan's back, while he instructed Kelso to rub the animal's coat with the palm of the hand. Kelso cautiously obeyed. There was a loud crackling and a shower of sparks, of the same lurid red colour as the reflection in the mirror on the previous night, flew out into the enveloping darkness.

'That will do!' Hamar observed quietly. 'Test two is satisfactorily accomplished. We must be riper for Hell than we imagined. There is no need for you fellows to stay any longer. I can manage the third test alone.'

As soon as his colleagues had gone and he felt assured they were no longer within hearing, Hamar took a saucer from the mantelshelf, filled it half full of milk, and poured into it some colourless liquid out of a tiny phial labelled poison.

'Here pussy,' he called out, softly. 'Pretty pussy, come and have your supper! Pussy!'

And Satan, unable to resist the tempting sight of the milk, crept out of his hiding-place and quite unsuspiciously dipped his tongue into the saucer and lapped. Hamar, in the meanwhile, went to a box at the foot of the bed and produced a sack. Then he slipped on his boots and coat, and opening the door of a cupboard near the head of the bed fetched out a small spade.

He was now ready; and – so was pussy.

'That paves the way for test six,' Hamar observed; 'no one can say I am a waster – I make use of everything – and every one;' and so saying he tumbled the cat into the sack and hurried out.

Some half-hour later he had returned to his room, and was busily engaged making preparations for test three. Letting a drop of Curtis's blood fall on the skull, he put the latter under his pillow, and retired to rest. He had slept for little over an hour, when he awoke with a start. The muffled sound of hammering – as of nails in a coffin – was going on all around him, and occasionally it seemed to him that something big and heavy stalked across the floor; but in spite of the fact that the room was illuminated with a red glow – the same lurid red as had appeared in tests one and two – nothing was to be seen. The phenomena lasted five or six minutes and then everything was again normal. Hamar was so terrified that he lay with his head under the bedclothes till morning, and vowed nothing on earth would persuade him to sleep in that room again. But sunlight soon restored his courage, and by the evening he was quite eager to go on with the next test. He had some difficulty in persuading any one to allow him the use of an oven for so pernicious a mixture as nightshade and hemlock; but at last he over-ruled the objections of some good-natured woman – the mother of one of the office boys at his former employer's – and test four proved as successful as the previous three. The preliminary part of test five was also successfully accomplished; but in carrying out the second part of it, Hamar all but met with disaster. He was walking along Kearney Street with the specially prepared hazel twig carefully concealed beneath his coat, when just opposite Saddler's jewelry store, he came upon a child standing by itself. The nearest person being some fifty yards away, and no policeman within sight, Hamar concluded this was too good an opportunity to be lost. He whipped out the twig, and held it, in the manner prescribed, in front of the child. The effect was instantaneous. The child turned white as death, its eyes bulged with terror, and opening its mouth to its full extent it commenced to shriek and yell. Then it fell on the pavement; and clutching and clawing the air, and foaming at the mouth rolled over and over. People from every quarter flocked to the spot, and judging Hamar, from his proximity to the child, to be responsible for its condition, shouted for the police. The latter, however, arrived too late. Hamar, whose presence of mind had only left him for the moment, seeing a bicycle leaning against a store door, jumped on it and soon put a respectable distance between himself and the crowd.

That night the trio met once more in Hamar's room for test six. There was a wood fire in the grate, and on it a tin vessel containing the prescribed ingredients. Somewhat unpleasantly conspicuous amongst these ingredients were the death's-head moth, and the soil from Satan's grave. As soon as the mixture had been heated three hours, the vessel was removed, the fire extinguished, and the room made absolutely dark. Then the three sat close together and waited.

On the stroke of two every article in the room began to rattle, whilst out of the tin vessel flew a blood red moth. After circling three times round each of the sitters' heads, the moth flew back again into the vessel, and the silence that ensued was followed by a soft tapping at the window, and the appearance of something, that resembled a big tube filled with a thick, pale blue fluid, made up of a mass of distinct veins. This tube floated into the room, and passing close to the three sitters, who involuntarily shrank away from it, disappeared in the wall, behind them. A loud crack, as if the branch of a tree had broken, terminated the phenomena – the room again becoming pitch dark. But the three sitters, although they knew there would be no further manifestation that night, were too terrified to move. They remained huddled together in the same spot till the morning was well advanced.

CHAPTER 5

THE INITIATION

SAN FRANCISCO possesses one great advantage – you can easily get out of it. Leaving the pan-handle of the Park behind one, and following the turn of the cars, one passes through a pretty valley, green and fair as any garden, and dotted with small houses. An old cemetery lies to one side of it; where unconventional inscriptions and queer epitaphs can be traced on the half-buried stones, covered with a tangle of vines and weeds. Still moving forward one reaches Olympus, and climbing to its heights, one sees away below, in the far distance, the Coast Range – like a rampart of strength; the blue waters of the bay, sparkling and dancing in the sunlight – steamers flashing their path on its bosom; and tiny white specks scudding in the breeze. Below is the city, its houses, small, and closed in, like toy villages in

Christmas boxes; whilst the slopes around are green with fresh grass; and here and there are thick clusters of eucalyptus and pines. The ocean is partly hidden from view by a peak, which rises directly to the west, and is separated from that on which one is standing by a deep and thickly woded valley. Descending, by means of a narrow winding path, one passes through dense clumps of hickory, chestnut, mountain ash, and walnut trees, whose strong lateral branches afford ample protection from the sun, and at the same time furnish playgrounds to innumerable bright-eyed squirrels. Further down one comes upon gentle elms, succeeded by sassafras and locust – these, in their turn, succeeded by the softer linden, red bud, catalpa, and maple; and at the foot of the declivity, and in the bottom of the valley, wild shrubbery, interspersed with silver willows, and white poplars. Still following the path down the vale, in a southerly direction, one, at length, finds oneself in an amphitheatre, shut in on all sides by trees and bushes of a still greater variety; here and there, a gigantic and much begnarled oak; here, a triple-stemmed tulip tree of some eighty feet in height, its glossy, vivid green leaves and profuse blossoms presenting a picture of unsurpassed beauty and splendour; there, equally beautiful, though in marked contrast, a tall and slender silver birch. The floor of the amphitheatre is, for the most part, grass – soft, thick, velvety and miraculously green. The silence is such as makes it wholly inconceivable, that so vast a city as San Francisco can be little over six miles distant. Though one may strain one's ears to the utmost, nothing is to be heard but the occasional tinkling of a cow-bell, the lowing of cattle and the desultory note of birds. It is the perfect quiet which Nature alone can give; and it so impressed Hamar that he at once decided that this was the very spot essential for the ceremony of initiation into the Black Art.

The locality selected, the night had next to be chosen – and the conditions demanding that on the night of the initiation there must be a new moon, cusp of seventh house, and conjoined with Saturn, in opposition to Jupiter,[1] Hamar and his confederates had to wait exactly three

[1] This is a very sinister sign in astrology, denoting the presence of evil influences of all kinds. – (*Author's note.*)

weeks, from the date of the conclusion of the tests, before they could proceed.

Shortly before midnight, on the spot already described, Hamar, Curtis and Kelson met; and, after searching thoroughly amongst the trees and bushes in the vicinity of the amphitheatre to make sure no one was in hiding, they commenced operations.

On a perfectly level piece of ground a circle of seven feet radius was clearly defined. This circle was cut into seven sectors; and an inner circle from the same centre and with a radius of six feet was next drawn. In each part of the sectors, between the circumferences of the first and second circle, were inscribed, in chalk, the names of the seven principal vices (according to Atlantean ideas), and the seven most malignant diseases. Within the second circle, and using the same centre, was drawn a third circle, of five feet in radius, and in each part of the sectors, between the circumferences of the second and third circles, were written the names of the seven types of spirits most antagonistic to man's moral progress.[1]

Hamar had brought with him a sack – the same he had used to transport Satan's corpse – and from out of it he produced a half-starved tabby, that obviously could harm no one, owing to the fact that its head was tied up in a muslin bag and its four legs strapped together.

'It's a good thing there is no member of the Society for the Prevention of Cruelty to Animals anywhere near,' Kelson exclaimed, eyeing Hamar resentfully. 'Wouldn't a mouse or a rat have done as well?'

'No!' Hamar ejaculated, depositing the brute with a plump on the ground; 'the conditions are that the animal sacrificed must be a cat. I got the poorest specimen I could find, for I dislike butchering just as much as you do.'

'How are you going to do it?' Kelson asked.

---

[1] According to Atlantean ideas these spirits were:— Vice Elementals; Morbas (or Disease Elementals); Clanogrians (or malicious family ghosts, such as Banshees, etc.); Vampires; Barrowvians, *i.e.* a grotesque kind of phantasm that frequents places where prehistoric man or beast has been interred; Planetians, *i.e.* spirits inimical to dwellers on this earth that inhabit various of the other planets; and earthbound spirits of such dead human beings as were mad, imbecile, cruel and vicious, together with the phantasms of vicious and mad beasts, and beasts of prey. – (*Author's note.*)

Hamar pointed to a chopper. 'The conditions say with steel,' he said; 'only with steel, and I should bungle with a knife. You must look the other way. Now help me with the fire.'

Besides the cat, the sack contained a dozen or so bundles of faggots, well steeped in paraffin, several blocks of wood, a tripod, and a big tin saucepan.

With the wood, a fire was soon kindled in the centre of the circle; and the tripod placed over it. Two pints of spring water were then poured into the saucepan, and to this were added 1 ounce of oxalic acid, 1 ounce of verdigris, $1\frac{1}{2}$ ounces of hemlock leaves, $\frac{1}{2}$ ounce of henbane, $\frac{3}{4}$ ounce of saffron, 2 ounces of aloes, 3 drachms of opium, 1 ounce of mandrake-root, 5 drachms of salanum, 7 drachms of poppy-seed, $\frac{1}{2}$ ounce of asafœtida, and $\frac{1}{2}$ ounce of parsley. As soon as the saucepan containing these ingredients began to boil Hamar threw into it two adders' heads, three toads and a centipede.

'Where on earth did you get all those horrors?' Curtis asked, shrinking away from the bag which had held them.

'Here,' Hamar said laconically. 'It's extraordinary what a lot of nasty things there are amid so much apparent beauty. I say apparent, because Nature is a champion faker. You have only to rake about in these bushes and you'll find snakes galore, whilst under pretty nearly every stone are centipedes. Like both of you, who never by any chance poke your noses outside the city, I fancied snakes and centipedes were confined to the prairies. But I know better now. Besides, where do you think I found the toads? Why, in the cellars under Meidlers'!'

'What, our late governor's?' Kelson cried.

Hamar nodded. 'Yes!' he said; 'under the very spot where we used to sit. The water's a foot deep in that cellar, and if there are as many toads in the cellars of the other houses in the block, then Sacramento Street has a corner in them. I'm going to be executioner now, so look the other way, Matt!'

Kelson needed no second bidding; and sticking his fingers in his ears, walked to some little distance. When Hamar called him back, the deed was accomplished – the conditions prescribed in the rites had been observed – the tabby was in the saucepan on the fire, and its blood had been besprinkled on each of the seven sectors of the circle.

'We must now take our seats on the ground,' Hamar said; 'I'd better be in the centre – you, Matt, on the right, and you, Ed, on the left – allowing three clear feet between us.'

Hamar showed them how to sit – with legs crossed and arms folded.

For some minutes no one spoke. The wind rustled through the bushes and an owl hooted. Kelson, feeling the night air cold, drew his overcoat tightly around and the others followed suit. Then Curtis said—

'Do you really think there's anything in it, Leon? Aren't we fools to go on wasting our time like this?'

To which Hamar replied: 'Shut up! You were frightened enough doing the tests!'

From afar off, away on the shimmering bosom of the bay came the faint hooting of a steamer.

'That's the *Oleander!*' Kelson murmured.

'Rot!' Curtis snapped. 'How do you know? You can't tell from this distance. It might be the *Daisy*, or the *San Marie*, or any other ship.'

Kelson made no reply; Hamar blew his nose, and once again there was silence.

The effect of the moonlight had now become weird. From the trees and bushes crept legions of tall, gaunt shadows, and whilst some of these were explicable, there were others that certainly had no apparent counterparts in any of the natural objects around them. Even Curtis, in spite of his scoffing, showed no inclination to examine them too closely; but kept his face resolutely turned to the more cheery light of the fire. The soft, cool, sweet-scented air gradually acted as an anæsthetic, and Kelson and Curtis were almost asleep, when Hamar's voice recalled them sharply to themselves.

'It's just two!' he said. 'Sit tight and listen while I repeat the incantation, and for goodness' sake keep cool if anything happens. Remember we are here with an object – namely – to get everything we can out of the Other World.'

'Trust you for that!' Curtis sneered; 'but all the same nothing's going to happen.'

'I am not sure of that,' Hamar said, and after a brief pause began to repeat these words[1]—

---

[1] They are a literal translation of the Atlantean by Thos. Maitland, and are very nearly identified with forms of spirit invocation used in Egypt, Indian, Persia, Arabia, and among the Red Indians of North and South America. – (*Author's note.*)

> 'Morbas from the mountains,
> Where flow malignant fountains,
>   We are ready for you – Come!
> Vampires from the passes,
> Where grow blood-sucking grasses,
>   We are ready for you – Come!
> Vice Elementals pretty
> Give ear unto our ditty
>   We are ready for you – Come!
> Planetians, forms so fearful,
> We inform you, eager, tearful,
>   We are ready for you – Come!
> Clanogrians, things of sorrow,
> Postpone not till to-morrow,
>   We are ready for you – Come!
> Barrowvians, shades seclusive,
> Be not to us exclusive,
>   We are ready for you – Come!
> Earthbound spirits of the Dead
> Approach with grim and noiseless tread –
>   We are ready for you – Come!'

He then got up and, going to the fire, sprinkled over the flames six drachms of belladonna, three drachms of drosera and one ounce of nux vomica; using in each case his left hand. Returning to his former position he drew with the forefinger of his left hand, on the ground, the outline of a club-foot; a hand with the fingers clenched and a long pointed thumb standing upright; and a bat. At his request Kelson and Curtis carefully imitated the devices, each in the space allotted to him.

Hamar then cried: 'Creastie havoonen balababoo!'; which Hamar explained was Atlantean for 'devil of the damned appear!'

'He won't!' Curtis muttered, 'because he doesn't exist. There are devils – Meidler Brothers were devils – but there is no one devil! It's all—' He suddenly stopped and an intense hush fell upon them all.

A cloud obscured the moon, the fire burned dim, and the gloom of the amphitheatre thickened till the men lost sight of each other. A cold air then rose from the ground and fanned their nostrils. Something flew past their heads with an ominous wail; whilst from the direction of the fire came a hollow groan.

'The advent of the Unknown,' Hamar murmured, 'shall be heralded in by the shrieking of an owl, the groaning of the mandrake – there is mandrake in the saucepan – the croaking of a toad – we haven't had that yet!'

'Yes, there it is!' Kelson whispered – and whilst he was speaking there came a dismal croak, croak, and the swaying and crying of an ash – 'Hush!'

They listened – and all three distinctly heard the swishing of a slender tree trunk as it hissed backwards and forwards. Then, a cry so horrid, harsh and piercing that even the sceptical, sneering Curtis gave vent to an expression of fear. Again a hush, and increasing darkness and cold. Kelson called out—

'Don't do that, Leon.'

'I'm not doing anything,' Hamar said testily. 'Pull yourself together.' A moment later he said to Curtis, 'It's you, Curtis. Shut up. This is no time for monkeying.'

'You are both either mad or dreaming,' Curtis replied. 'I haven't stirred from my seat. Hulloa! What's that? What's that, Leon. There – over there! Look!'

As Curtis spoke they all three became conscious of living things around them – things that moved about, silently and surreptitiously and conveyed the impression of mockery. The hills, the valley, the trees were full of it – the whole place teemed with it – teemed with silent, subtle, stealthy mockery. The senses of the three men were now keenly alive, but a dead weight hung upon their limbs and rendered them useless. And as they stared into the gloom, in sickly fear, the firelight flickered and they saw shadows, such as the moon, when low in the heaven, might fashion from the figure of a man; but yet they were shadows neither of man, nor God, nor of any familiar thing. They were dark, vague, formless and indefinite, and they quivered – quivered with a quivering that suggested mockery.

Suddenly the shadows disappeared; the flickering of the flames ceased; and in the place of the fire appeared a seething, writhing mass of what looked like white luminous snakes. And in the midst of this mass sprang up a cylindrical form, which grew and grew until it attained a height of ten or twelve feet, when it remained stationary and threw out branches. And the three men now saw it was a tree – a tree with a sleek, pulpy, semi-transparent, perspiring trunk full of a thick, white, vibrating, luminous fluid; and that it was laden with a fruit, in shape resembling an apple, but of the same hue and material as the trunk. Spread out on the ground around it, were its roots, twitching and palpitating with repulsive life, and bare with a bareness that shocked the senses. It was so utterly and inconceivably unlike what Hamar, Curtis and Kelson had imagined the Unknown – and yet, withal, so monstrous (not merely in its shape but in its suggestions), and so vividly real and livid, that they were not merely terrified – they were stricken with a terror that rendered them dumb and helpless. And as they looked at it, from out the trunk, shot an enormous thing – white and glistening, and fashioned like a human tongue. And after pointing derisively at them, it withdrew; whereupon all the fruit shook, as if convulsed with unseemly laughter. Then they saw between the foremost branches of the tree a big eye. The white of it was thick and pasty, the iris spongy in texture, and the pupil bulging with a lurid light. It stared at them with a steady stare – insolent and quizzical. Hamar and his friends stared back at it in fascinated horror, and would have continued staring at it indefinitely, had not Hamar's mercenary instincts come to their rescue. He recollected that time was pressing, and that unless he got into communication with the strange thing at once, according to the book, it would vanish – and he might never be able to get in touch with it again. Thus egged on, he made a great effort to regain his courage, and at length succeeded in forcing himself to speak. Though his voice was weak and shaking he managed to pronounce the prescribed mode of address, viz.: 'Bara phonen etek mo,' which being interpreted is, 'Spirit from the Unknown, give ear to me.' He then explained their earnest desire to pay homage to the Supernatural, and to be initiated into the mysteries of the Black Art. When Hamar had concluded his address, the anticipations of the three as to how it would be answered, or whether it would be answered at all – were such that they were forced to hold their breath almost to the point of suffocation. If the Thing *could* speak what would its voice be like? The seconds passed, and they were beginning to prepare themselves for disappointment, when suddenly across the intervening space separating them from the Unknown, the reply came – came in soft, silky, lisping tones – human and yet not human, novel and yet in some way – a way that defied analysis – familiar. Strange to say, they all three felt that this familiarity belonged to a far back period of their existence, no less than to a more modern one – to a period, in fact, to which they could affix no date. And, although a perfect unity of expression suggested that the utterance of the Thing was the utterance of one being only, a certain variation in its tones, a rising and falling from syllable to syllable, led them to infer that the voice was not the voice of one but of many.

'You are anxious to acquire knowledge of the Secrets associated with the Great Atlantean Magic?' the voice lisped.

'We are!' Hamar stammered, 'and we are willing to give our souls in exchange for them.'

'Souls!' the voice lisped, whilst trunk and branches swayed lightly, and the air was full of silent merriment. 'Souls! you speak in terms you do not understand. To acquire the secrets of Black Magic, all you have to do is to agree that during a brief period – a period of a few months, you will live together in harmony; that you will make use of the powers you acquire to the detriment of all save yourselves; that you will never allow your minds to revert to anything spiritual; and – that you will abstain from – marrying.'

'And if we succeed in carrying out the conditions?' Hamar asked.

'Then,' the voice replied, 'you will retain free, untrammelled possession of your knowledge.'

'For how long?' Curtis queried.

'For the natural term of your lives – that is to say, for as long as you would have lived had you never been initiated into the secrets of magic.'

'And if we fail?'

'You will pass into the permanent possession of the Unknown.'

'Does that mean we shall die the moment we fail?' Kelson inquired timidly.

'Die!' the voice lisped. 'Again you speak in terms you do not understand. You may be sent for.'

'You say – in perfect harmony,' Hamar put in. 'Does that mean without a quarrel, however slight?'

'It means without a quarrel that would lead to separation. The moment you disunite the compact is broken.'

'What advantages will the secrets bring us?' Hamar inquired. 'Can we gain unlimited wealth?'

'Yes!' the voice replied. 'Unlimited wealth and influence.'

'And health?'

'So long as you fulfil the conditions of the compact you will enjoy perfect health. Will you, or will you not, pledge yourselves?'

'I am ready if you fellows are,' Hamar whispered.

'I am!' Curtis cried. 'Anything is better than the life we are living at present.'

'And I, too,' Kelson said. 'I agree with Ed.'

'Very well, then,' the voice once more lisped. 'Each of you take a fruit and eat it, and the compact is irrevocably struck. You cannot back out of it without incurring the consequences already named. Don't be afraid, step up here and help yourselves – one apiece – mind, no more.' And again it seemed to Hamar, Curtis and Kelson as if the tree and everything around it was convulsed with silent laughter.

'Come on!' Hamar cried, somewhat imperatively. 'Don't waste time. You've decided, and besides, remember this affair may turn out trumps. I'll go first,' and walking up to the tree he plucked a fruit and began to eat it. Curtis and Kelson slowly followed suit.

'I believe I'm eating a live slug, or a toad,' Curtis muttered, with a retch.

'And I, too,' Kelson whispered. 'It's filthy. I shall be sick. If I am, will it make any difference to the compact, I wonder?'

What the fruit really tasted like they could never decide. It reminded them of many things and of nothing. It was sweet yet bitter; it repelled but at the same time pleased them; it was as perplexing as the voice – as enigmatical. When they had eaten it they resumed their former positions on the ground, and the voice once again addressed them.

'The fruit you have consumed has created in you a fitness to make use of the powers about to be conferred. You have acquired the faculty of sorcery – you will be initiated by stages, into the knowledge and practice of it. These stages, seven in number, will cover the period of your compact, *i.e.* twenty-one months, and at the end of every three months

– when a fresh stage is reached – you will receive fresh powers.

'In the first stage, the stage you are now entering upon, you will receive the power of divination. You will be told how to detect the presence of water and all kinds of metals, and how to read people's thoughts.

'In the second stage – exactly three months from to-day – you will receive the gift of second-sight; the power of separating your immaterial from your material body and projecting it, anywhere you will, on the physical plane; and, to a large extent, you will be able to circumvent gravity. Thus you will be able to perform all manner of jugglery tricks – tricks that will set the whole world gaping. Profit by them.

'In the third stage you will possess the secrets of invisibility; of walking on the water; of breathing under the water; of taming wild beasts; and of understanding their language.

'In the fourth stage you will understand how to inflict all manner of diseases, and work all sorts of spells; such, for instance, as bewitching milk, causing people to have fits, bad dreams, etc. You will also know how to create plagues – plagues of insects, or of any other noxious thing.

'In the fifth stage you will possess absolute knowledge of the art of medicine and be able to cure every ailment.

'In the sixth stage you will acquire the power of producing vampires and werwolves from the human being, and of transforming people from the human to any animal guise.

'In the seventh and final stage you will be given the complete mastery of every art and science – including astrology, astronomy, necromancy, etc.; and for this stage is reserved the greatest power of all – namely, the complete dominion over woman's will and affections. The power of creating life, and of extending life beyond the now natural limit, and of avoiding accidents, will never be conferred on you. Neither shall you learn, not at least during your physical existence – who or what we are, or the secrets of creation.

'Each successive stage will cancel the preceding one – that is to say, the powers you have acquired in the first stage will be annulled on your arriving at the second stage, and so on. But if you carry out your compact faithfully – that is to say, if at the end of twenty-one months you are still united – all the powers you have held hitherto, in the different stages, temporarily, will return to you and remain in your possession permanently. Have you anything to say?'

'Yes!' Hamar answered; 'I fully understand all you have explained to us and I like the idea of it immensely. The fear of our coming to any serious loggerheads and of dissolving partnership doesn't worry me much – but I must say, it seems very remote – the prospect of gaining such tremendous powers – powers that will give us practically everything we want – save youth—'

'Youth you will never regain,' lisped the voice. 'And elixirs of life, surely you must know, are no longer sought after, by beings of the planet Earth. They are quite out of date. You will, of course, learn the most efficacious means of making yourselves and other people youthful in appearance.'

'Yes, but how shall we learn these secrets?' Kelson nerved himself to ask.

'They will be revealed to you in various ways – sometimes when asleep. You will receive preliminary instructions as to divination before this time to-morrow.'

'And meanwhile, we shall be in want of money,' Curtis remarked.

'No!' the voice replied, 'you will not be in want of money. Have you anything more to ask?'

No one spoke, and the silence that followed was interrupted by a loud rustling of the wind. The darkness then lifted; but nothing was to be seen – nothing save the trees and bushes, moon and stars.

CHAPTER 6

THE FIRST POWER

AFTER their rencontre with the Unknown, Hamar and his companions did not get back to their respective quarters till the sun was high in the heavens, and the streets of the city were beginning to vibrate with the rattle and clatter of traffic.

'It's all very well – this wonderful compact of ours,' Curtis grumbled, 'but I'm deuced hungry, and Matt and I haven't a cent between us. As we went all that way last night to oblige you, Leon, I think it is only fair you should stand us treat. I'll bet you have some nickels stowed away, somewhere, in those pockets of yours – it wouldn't be you if you hadn't! What do you say, Matt?'

'I think as you do,' Kelson replied. 'We've stood by Leon, he should stand by us. How much have you, Leon?'

'How much have you?' Curtis echoed, 'come, out with it – no jew-jewing pals for me.'

'I might manage a dollar,' Hamar said ruefully, as the prospect of a good meal all to himself, at his favourite restaurant, faded away. 'Where shall we go?'

Just then, Kelson, happening to look behind him, saw a young woman of prepossessing appearance ascending the steps of a dive in Clay Street. He was instantly attracted, as he always was attracted by a pretty woman, and something – a kind of intuition he had never had before – told him that she was a waitress; that she was discontented with her present situation; that she was engaged to be married to a pen driver at Hastings & Hastings in Sacramento Street; and that she had a mother, of over seventy, whom she kept. All this came to Kelson like a flash of lightning.

Yielding to an impulse which he did not stay to analyse, he gripped Hamar and Curtis, each too astonished even to remonstrate, by the arm, and, dragging them along with him, followed the girl.

The dive had only just been opened, and was being dusted and swept by two slatternly women with dago complexions, and voices like hyenas. It still reeked of stale drink and tobacco.

'What's the good of coming to a place like this?' Hamar demanded, as soon as he had freed himself from Kelson's clutches. 'We can't get breakfast here.'

'Matt's mad, that's what's the matter with him,' Curtis added in disgust. 'Let's get out.'

He turned to go – then, halted – and stood still. He appeared to be listening. 'What's up with you?' Hamar asked. 'Both you fellows are behaving like lunatics this morning – there's not a pin to choose between you.'

'They're playing cards, that's all,' Curtis said. 'Can't you hear them?'

Hamar shook his head. 'Not a sound,' he said. 'Just look at Matt!'

While the other two were talking, Kelson had followed the girl to the bar, and catching her up, just as she entered it, said in a manner that was peculiar to him – a manner seldom without effect upon girls of his class – 'I beg your pardon, miss, are we too early to be served? Jerusalem! Haven't I met you somewhere before?'

The girl looked him square in the eyes and then smiled. 'As like as not,' she said. 'I go pretty near everywhere! What do you want?'

'Well!' Kelson soliloquized; 'breakfast is what we are particularly anxious for – but I suppose that is out of the question in a dive!'

'Then why did you come here?' the girl queried.

'Because of you! Simply because of you,' Kelson replied. 'You hypnotized me!'

'That being so, then I reckon you can have your breakfast,' the girl laughed, 'though we don't provide them as a rule before nine. Indeed, the management have only just decided – this morning – on providing them at all.'

'How odd!'

'Why odd?' the girl questioned, taking off her hat and arranging her curls before a mirror.

'Why, that I should have happened to strike the right moment! Had I come here yesterday it would have been useless. As I said, you hypnotized me. Evidently fate intended us to meet.'

'Do you believe in fate?' the girl asked, shrugging her shoulders. 'I believe in nothing – least of all in men!'

'You say so!' Kelson observed, before he knew what he was saying. 'And yet you have just got engaged to one. But you've had a bad attack of the pip this morning, you have had enough of it here – you want to get another post.'

The girl ceased doing her hair and eyed him in amazement. 'Well!' she said. 'Of all the queer men I've ever met you are the queerest. Are you a seer?'

'No!' Hamar observed, suddenly joining in. 'He's only very hungry, miss. Hungry body and soul! hungry all over. And so are we.'

'Well, then, go into that room over there,' the girl cried, pointing in the direction of a half-open door, 'and breakfast will be brought to you in half a jiffy.'

'Who's that playing cards?' Curtis asked.

'How do you know any one is playing cards?' the girl queried with an incredulous stare. 'You can't see through walls, can you?'

'No! and I'm hanged if I can explain,' Curtis said, 'I seem to hear them. There are two – one is called Arnold, and the other Lemon, or some such name, and they are rehearsing certain card tricks they mean to play to-night.'

'That's right,' the girl said, 'two men named Arnold and Lemon are here. They were playing all last night with two of the clerks in Willows Bank, in Sacramento Street, and they cleared them out of every cent. You knew it!'

'No! I didn't,' Curtis growled, 'I don't lie for fun, and I'm just as much in a fog, as to how I know, as you are. Let's have breakfast now and we'll look up these two gents afterwards, if they haven't gone.'

'Your friend's a brute, I don't like him,' the girl whispered to Kelson. 'Let him lose all he's got – you stay out here.'

'Nothing I should like better,' Kelson said, 'it's a bargain!'

The breakfast was so good that they lingered long over it, and the bar-room had a fair sprinkling of people when they re-entered it. Leaving Kelson to chat with the girl, Hamar and Curtis, obeying her directions, found their way to a small parlour in the rear of the building, where two men were lolling over a card table, smoking and drinking, and reading aloud extracts from a pink sporting paper.

'It's a funny thing,' one of them exclaimed, 'we can't be allowed to sit here in peace – when there's so much spare space in the house.'

'We beg your pardon for intruding,' Curtis said, 'but my friend and I came in here for a quiet game of cards. We're farmers down Missouri way, and don't often get the chance to run up to town.'

'Farmers, are you?' the man who had not yet spoken said, eyeing them both closely. 'You don't look it. My friend Lemon, here, and I were also wanting to have a game – would you care to join us?'

'By all means,' Curtis at once exclaimed. 'What do you play?'

'Poker!' the man said, 'Nap! Don! But I'll show you something first, which, being fresh from the country, you've probably never seen before, though they do tell me people in Missouri are mighty cute.' He then proceeded to show them what he called the Bull and Buffalo trick, the secret of which he offered to sell them for ten dollars.

'I wouldn't give you a cent for it!' Curtis snapped. 'Any one can see how it is done.'

'You can't!' the man retorted, turning red. 'I'll wager twenty dollars you can't.' Curtis accepted the wager, and at once did the trick. He had seen through it at a glance – there appeared no difficulty in it at all; and yet he was quite certain if he had been asked to do it the day before, he would have utterly failed.

'Now,' he said, 'give me the money,' – and the man complied with an oath.

'Any more tricks?' Curtis asked complacently.

'I know heaps,' the man rejoined. 'There's one you won't guess – the seven card trick.'

He did it. And so did Curtis.

'Well, I'm—' the man called Lemon ejaculated. 'He's the dandiest cove at tricks we've ever struck. Try him with the Prince and Slipper, Arnold!'

Arnold rather reluctantly assented, and Curtis burst out laughing.

'Why!' he said, 'that's the simplest of all! See!' And it was done. 'You two had better come to an understanding with us or you'll not shine to-night. How about a game of Don?'

Lemon and Arnold agreed, but they had barely begun before Curtis cried out. 'It's no use, Lemon, I can see those deuces up your sleeve. You've some up yours, too, Arnold – the deuce of clubs and the deuce of hearts. Moreover, you can tell our cards by notches and thumb smears on the backs. I'll show you how.' He told the cards correctly – there was no gainsaying it. The men were overwhelmed.

'What are you, anyway?' Lemon asked; 'tecs?'

'Never mind what we are!' Curtis said savagely. 'We know what you are – and that's where the rub comes in. Now what are you going to pay us to hold our tongues?'

'Pay you!' Lemon hissed. 'Why, damn you – nothing. We're not bankers. All we've got to do is clear out and try somewhere else.'

'That might not be so easy as you imagine,' Hamar interposed. 'We would make it our business to have a scene first. Why not come to terms? We'll not be over exorbitant –

and consider the convenience of not having to shift your quarters.'

'Well, of all the blooming frousts I've struck, none beats this,' Lemon said. 'Fancy being pipped by a couple of suckers like these. Farmers, indeed! Why don't you call yourselves parsons? How much do you want?'

After a prolonged haggling, Hamar and Curtis agreed to take fifty dollars; and, considering their penniless condition, they were by no means dissatisfied with their bargain.

They were now ready to go, and looking round for Kelson, found him engaged in a desperate *tête-à-tête* with the young lady at the bar, who, despite her avowed lack of faith in mankind, counted half the room her friends. She promised Kelson that she would meet him at eight o'clock that evening; but as both she and he were quite used to making such promises and subsequently forgetting all about them, their rencontre resulted in only one thing, namely, in furnishing the three allies with the nucleus of the big fortune they intended making.

On finding themselves outside the dive Hamar, Curtis and Kelson first of all divided the spoil. Then they went to a clothes depot and rigged themselves out in fashionably cut garments; after which they took rooms at a presentable hotel in Kearney Street, next door to Knobble's boot store. Then, dressed for the first time in their lives like Nob Hill dukes, they paraded the pet resorts of the beau-monde – of the bonanza and railroad set – and making eyes at all the pretty wives and daughters they met, cogitated fresh devices for making money. As they sauntered across Pacific Avenue, in the direction of California Street, Kelson suddenly gave vent to a whistle.

'What the deuce is wrong with you?' Hamar exclaimed. 'Seen your grandmother's ghost?'

'No! but I've seen the inner readings of that lady yonder,' Kelson replied, indicating with a jerk of his finger a fashionably dressed woman walking towards them on the other side of the road. 'The deuce knows how it all comes to me, but I know everything about her, just the same as I did with the girl in the dive – though I've never seen her before. She is the wife of D. D. Belton, the cotton magnate, who lives in a big, white house at the corner of Powell Street – and a beauty, I can assure you. Supposed to be most devoted to her husband, she is now on her way to keep an appointment with the Rev. J. T. Calthorpe of Sancta Maria's Church in Appleyard Street, with whom she has been holding clandestine meetings for the past six months.'

'Whew!' Hamar ejaculated. 'You speak as if it was all being pumped into you by some external agency – automatically.'

'That's just about what I feel!' Kelson said, 'I feel as if it were some one else saying all this – some one else speaking through me. Yet I know all about that woman, just as much as if I had been acquainted with her all my life!'

'It's the first power,' Hamar said excitedly, 'the power of divination. It takes that form with you, and the form of card tricks with Ed – with me nothing so far.'

'But what shall I do?' Kelson cried. 'How can I benefit by it?'

'How can't you?' Curtis growled. 'Why, blackmail her! If it is true, she will pay you anything to keep your mouth shut. If once you can tell a woman's secret, your future's made. All San Francisco will be at your mercy – God knows who'll escape! After her at once, you idiot!'

'Now?' Kelson gasped.

'Yes! Now! Follow her to Calthorpe's and waylay her as she comes out. You can refer to us as witnesses.'

'I feel a bit of a blackguard,' Kelson pleaded

'You look it, anyway,' Curtis grinned. 'But cheer up – it's the clothes. Clothes are responsible for everything!'

After a little persuasion Kelson gave in, but he had to make haste as the lady was nearly out of sight. She took a taxi from the stand opposite Kitson's hotel, and Kelson took one, too. Two hours later, raising his hat, he accosted her as she stood tapping the pavement of Battery Street with a daintily shod foot, waiting to cross. 'Mrs. Belton, I think,' he said. The lady eyed him coldly.

'Well!' she said, 'what do you want? Who are you?'

'My name can scarcely matter to you,' Kelson responded, 'though my business may. I have been engaged to watch you, and am fully posted as to your meetings and correspondence with the Rev. J. T. Calthorpe.'

'I don't understand you,' the lady said, her cheeks flaming. 'You have made a mistake – a very serious mistake for you.'

For a moment Kelson's heart failed. He was still a clerk, with all the humility of an office stool and shining trousers'

63

seat thick on him, whilst she was a *grande dame* accustomed to the bows and scrapes of employers as well as employed.

Several people passed by and stared at him – as he thought – suspiciously, and he felt that this was the most critical time in his life, and unless he pulled through, smartly in fact, he would be done once and for all. If he didn't make haste, too, the woman would undoubtedly call a policeman. It was this thought as well as – though, perhaps, hardly as much as – the look of her that stimulated Kelson to action. He hated behaving badly to women; but was this thing, dressed in a skirt that fitted like a glove and showed up every detail of her figure – this thing with the paint on her cheeks, and eyebrows, and lips – artistically done, perhaps, but done all the same – this thing all loaded with jewellery and buttons – this thing – a woman! No! She was not – she was only a millionaire's plaything – brainless, heartless – a hobby that costs thousands, whilst countless men such as he – starved. He detested – abominated such luxuries! And thus nerved he retorted, borrowing some of her imperiousness—

'Do you deny, madam, that for the past two hours you've been sitting on the sofa of the end room of the third floor of No. 216, Market Stret, flirting with the Rev. J. T. Calthorpe, whom you call "Mickey-moo"; that you gave him a photo you had taken at Bell's Studio in Clay Street, specially for him; that you gave him five greenbacks to the value of one hundred and fifty dollars, and that you've planned a moonlight promenade with him to-morrow, when your husband will be in Denver?'

'Don't talk so loud,' the lady said in a low voice. 'Walk along with me a little and then we shan't be noticed. I see you do know a great deal – how, I can't imagine, unless you were hidden somewhere in the room. Who has employed you to watch me?'

'That, madam, I can't say,' Kelson truthfully responded.

'And I can't think,' the lady said, 'unless it is some woman enemy. But, after all, you can't do much since you hold no proofs – your word alone will count for nothing.'

'Ah, but I have strong corroborative evidence,' Kelson retorted. 'I have the testimony of at least two other people who know quite as much as I do.'

'Adventurers like yourself,' the lady sneered. 'My husband would neither believe you nor your friends.'

'He would believe your letters, any way,' said Kelson.

'My letters!' the lady laughed, 'You've no letters of mine.'

'No, but I know where the correspondence that has passed between you and the Rev. J. T. Calthorpe is to be found. He has sixty-nine letters from you all tied up in pink ribbon, locked up in the bottom drawer of the bureau in his study at the Vicarage. Some of the letters begin with "Dearest, duckiest, handsomest Herby" – short for Herbert; and others, "Fondest, blondest, darlingest Mickey-moo!" Some end with "A thousand and one kisses from your loving and ever devoted Francesca," and others with "Love and kisses *ad infinitum*, ever your loving, thirsting, adoring one, Toosie!" Nice letters from the wife of a respectable Nob Hill magnate to a married clergyman!'

The lady walked a trifle unsteadily, and much of her colour was gone. 'I can't understand it,' she panted; 'somebody has played me false.'

'As the Rev. J. T. Calthorpe is on his way to Sacramento, where he has to remain till to-morrow,' Kelson went on pitilessly, 'it will be the easiest thing in the world to get those letters. I have merely to call at the house and tell his wife.'

'And what good will that do you?' the lady asked.

'Revenge! I hate the rich,' Kelson said. 'I would do anything to injure them.'

'You are a Socialist?'

'An Anarchist! But come, you see I know all about you and that I have you completely in my power. If once either your husband or Mrs. Calthorpe gets hold of those letters – you and your lover would have a very unpleasant time of it.'

'You're a devil!'

'Maybe I am – at all events I'm talking to one. But that's neither here nor there. I want money. Give me a thousand dollars and you'll never hear from me again.'

'Blackmail! I could have you arrested!'

'Yes, and I would tell the court the whole history of your intrigues! That wouldn't help you,' – and Kelson laughed.

'Could I count on you not molesting me again if I were to pay you?' the lady said mockingly.

'You could.'

'Do you ever speak the truth?'

'You needn't judge every one by your own standard of morality – the standard set up by the millionaire's wife,' Kelson said. 'I swear that if you pay me a thousand dollars I will never trouble you again.'

The lady grew thoughtful, and for some minutes neither of them spoke. Then she suddenly jerked out: 'I think, after all, I'll accept your proposal. Wait outside here and you shall have what you want within an hour.'

'Not good enough,' Kelson said, 'I prefer to come with you to your house and wait there.'

The lady protested, and Kelson consented to wait in the street outside her house, where, eventually, she delivered the money into his hands.

'I've kept my word,' she said, 'and if you're half a man you'll keep yours.'

Kelson reassured her, and more than pleased with himself, made for the hotel, where the three of them were now stopping.

This was merely a beginning. Before the day was out he had secured two more victims. No woman whose character was not without blemish was safe from him – his wonderful newly acquired gift enabling him to detect any vice, no matter how snugly hidden. And this wonderful power of discernment brought with it an expression of mystery and penetration which, by enhancing the effect of the power, made the application of it comparatively easy. Kelson had only to glide after his victim, and with his eyes fixed searchingly on her, to say, 'Madam, may I have a word with you?' – and the battle was more than half won – the women were too fascinated to think of resistance.

For example, shortly after his initial adventure, he saw a very smartly dressed woman in Van Ness Avenue peep about furtively, and then stop and speak to a little child, who was walking with its nurse. Divination at once told him everything – the lady was the mother of the child, but its father was not her legitimate husband, W. S. Hobson, the millionaire mine owner.

When Kelson courteously informed her he was in possession of her secret – a secret she had felt positively certain only one other person knew, she went the colour of her pea-green sunshade and attempted to remonstrate. But

Kelson's appearance, no less than his marvellous knowledge of her life, and character dumbfounded her – she was simply paralysed into admission; and before he left her, Kelson had added another thousand dollars to his hoard.

That evening, close to the Academy of Science in Market Street, he saw a lady get out of a taxi and quickly enter a pawnbroker's. Her whole life at once rose up before him. She was Ella Crockford, the wife of the Californian Street Sugar King, and, unknown to her husband, she spent her afternoon at a gambling saloon in Kearney Street, where she ran through thousands.

She was now about to pledge her husband's latest present to her – a diamond tiara, one of the most notable pieces of jewellery in the country – in the hope that she would soon win back sufficient money at cards to redeem it.

Kelson stopped her as she came out, and in a marvellously few words, proved to her that he knew everything. Her amazement was beyond description. 'You must be a magician,' she said, 'because I'm certain no one saw me take my jewel-case out of the drawer – no one was in the room! And as I put it in my muff immediately, no one could have seen it as I left the house. Besides, I never told a soul I intended pawning it, so how is it possible you could know – and be able to repeat the whole of the conversation I had with Walter Le-Grand, to whom I lost so heavily last night? Tell me, how do you know all this?'

But Kelson would tell her nothing – nothing beyond her own sins and misfortunes.

'I have nothing to give you,' she told him. 'I dare not ask my husband for more money.'

'What, nothing!' Kelson replied, 'When the pawnbroker has just advanced you fifty thousand dollars. You call that nothing? Be pleased to give me one thousand, and congratulate yourself that I do not ask for all your "nothing."' And as neither tears nor prayers had any effect, she was obliged to pay him the sum he asked.

Flushed and excited with victory, and thinking, perhaps, that he had done enough for one day, Kelson took his spoils to a bank near the Palace Hotel, and for the first time in his career opened a banking account. As he was leaving the building he ran into Hamar, bent on a similar errand. The two gleefully compared notes.

'I thought,' Hamar said, 'my turn would never come, and that I must have done something to get out of favour with the Unknown; but as I was sitting in the Pig and Whistle Saloon in Corn Street drinking a lager, I suddenly felt a peculiar throbbing sensation run up my left leg into my left hand, and the floor seemed to open up, and I saw deep below me, in a black pit, a skeleton clutching hold of a linen bag, full of coins. I could see the gold quite distinctly – Spanish doubloons, none newer than the eighteenth century. I knew then that the Unknown had not forgotten me. "Look here, boss," I said to old man Moss – the proprietor, you know – "You're a bit of a juggins to go on working with so much money under here," – and I pointed to the floor.

' "I'm surprised at you, Hamar," Moss said, cocking an eye at me, "and lager, too!"

' "No, old man!" I said, "I'm not drunk. I'm sober and serious. You've got a cellar below here, haven't you?"

' "Well, and what if I have!" Moss retorted, drawing a step closer and running his eyes carefully over me. "What if I have! There's no harm in that, is there?"

' "You keep all your stock down there," I went on, "and more beside. I can see a hat-pin with a gold knob, that's not your wife's, and a pair of shoes with dandy silver buckles, that's not intended for your wife, nohow."

'At that Moss made a queer noise in his throat, and I thought he was going to have a fit. "What – what the devil are you talking about?" he gurgled.

' "I wish I had had you with me – then, Matt, for you could have doubtless summed up the woman to him – she was a blank to me – I only divined one had been there. "Yes, Mr. Mossy," I said, "you're a gay deceiver and no mistake! I know all about it!"

' "Do you," he said, eyeing me excitedly. "Do you know all about it? I'm not so sure, but in order to avoid running any risks, drop your voice a bit and have a cocktail with me!"

'He poured me out one, and I went on softly, "Well, boss Moss," I said, "we'll leave the female out of the question for the present. Underneath this cellar of yours, is a pit."

' "I'm damned if there is!" Moss snorted; "leastways, it's the first I've ever heard of it."

' "And in this pit," I said, "is the skeleton of a Spanish buccaneer called Don Guzman, who landed in this port on August 10, 1699, and after robbing and slicing up a family of the name of Hervada, who lived on the site of what is now the Copthorne Hotel, was hurrying off with all their money and jewels, when he fell into a pit, covered with brambles and briars, and broke his neck."

' "And you expect me to believe this cock and bull story," Moss growled. "Being out of a job so long has made you barmy."

' "It hasn't made me too barmy not to see through the way you deceive your wife, Moss," I said. "I'll bet she would think me sane enough if I were to tell her all I know. But I'll spare you if you will take me into your cellar and help me to do a bit of excavation there. But promise, mind you, that we will go shares in what we find."

' "Oh, I'll promise right enough," Moss replied. "I'll promise anything – if only to keep you from talking such moonshine."

'Well, in the end I prevailed upon him to accompany me, and we went into the cellar – just as I had depicted it – armed with a pick-axe and crowbar. Moss growling and jeering every step he took, and I, deadly in earnest.

' "It's under here," I said, halting over a flagstone in the corner of the vault. "But before we do anything you had better hide that hat-pin and these shoes, or your missis will find them. She'll hear us scraping and come to see what's up."

'Moss, who was in a vile temper all the time, made a grab at the things, pricking his finger and swearing horribly. In the meanwhile I had set to work, and, with his aid, raised the stone. We dug for pretty nearly an hour, Moss calling upon me all the time to "chuck it," when I suddenly struck something hard – it was the skeleton and close beside it, was the bag. You should have seen Moss then. He was simply overcome – called me a wizard, a magician, and heaven alone knows what, and fairly stood on his head with delight when we opened the bag, and hundreds of gold coins and precious stones rolled out on the floor. He wanted to go back on his word then, and only give me a handful; but I was too smart for him, and swore I would tell his wife about the girl unless he gave me half. When we were leaving the cellar, of course, he wanted me to go first, so that he could follow with the pick-axe, but here again I was too sharp for him— and I got safely out of the place with my pockets bulging. I went right away to Prescott's in Clay Street, and let the lot go for three thousand dollars. I wonder how Curtis has got on!'

They walked together to the hotel, and found Curtis busily engaged eating. 'I've worked hard,' he said, 'and now I'm in for enjoying myself. I've made them get out a special menu for me, and I'm going to eat till I can't hold another morsel. I've starved all my life and now I intend making up for it.'

'Been successful?' Hamar asked, winking at Kelson.

'Pretty well! Nothing to grumble at,' Curtis rejoined, pouring himself out a glass of champagne. 'First of all I went to Simpson's Dive in Sacramento Street, and started doing the tricks we discovered yesterday. Not a soul in the place could see through them, and I made about two hundred dollars before I left. I then had lunch.'

'Why you had lunch with us!' Hamar laughed.

'Well, can't I have as many lunches as I like?' Curtis replied. 'I had lunch, I say, at a place in Market Street, and there I read in a paper that Peters & Pervis, the tin food people, were offering a prize of three thousand dollars for a solution to a puzzle contained on the inside cover of one of their tins. I immediately determined to enter for it. I bought a tin and saw through the puzzle at once. Bribing a policeman to go with me to see fair play, off I set to Peters & Pervis'.

'"I want to see your boss," I said to the first clerk I saw.

'"Which of them?" the clerk grunted, his cheeks turning white at the sight of the policeman.

'"Either will do," I replied, "Peters or Pervis. Trot 'em up, time is precious."

'Away he went, but in a couple of minutes was back again, looking scared, "They're both engaged," he says.

'"Then they'll have to break it off," I responded, "and mighty quick. I'm here to talk with them, so get a move on you again and give that message."

'If it hadn't been for the policeman I don't think he would have gone, but the policeman backed me up, and the clerk hurried off again; and in the end the bosses decided they had better see me. They looked precious cross,

I can assure you, but before I had done speaking they looked crosser still.

'"You say you've done that puzzle" – they shouted – "the puzzle that has stuck all the mathematical guns at Harvard and Yale – you – a nonentity like you – begone, sir, don't waste our time with such humbug as that."

'"All right," I said, "give me some paper and a pen, and I'll prove it."

'"That's very reasonable," the policeman chipped in, "do the thing fair and square – I'm here as a witness."

'Well, with much grunting and grumbling they handed me paper and ink, and in a trice the puzzle was done; and it appeared so easy that the policeman clapped his hands and broke out into a loud guffaw. My eyes! you should have seen how the faces of Pervis and Peters fell, and have heard what they said. But it was no use swearing and cursing, the thing was done, and there was the policeman to prove it.

'"We'll give you five hundred dollars," they said, "to clear out and say no more about it."

'"Five hundred dollars when you've advertised three thousand," I cried. "What do you take me for? I'll have that three thousand or I'll show you both up."

'"A thousand, then?" they said.

'"No!" I retorted; "three! Three, and look sharp. And look here," I added, as my glance rested on some of the samples of their pastes they had round them, "I understand the secrets of all these so-called patents of yours – there isn't one of them I couldn't imitate. Take that 'Rabsidab,' for instance. What is it? Why, a compound of horseflesh, turnips and popcorn, flavoured with Lazenby's sauce – for the infringement of which patent you are liable to prosecution – and coloured with cochineal. Then there's the stuff you label 'Ironcastor,'" – but they shut me up. "There, take your three thousand dollars, write us out a receipt for it, and clear."'

'Nine thousand dollars in one day! We've done well,' Kelson ejaculated. 'What's the programme for to-morrow?'

'Same as to-day and plenty of it,' Curtis said, pouring himself out another glass of champagne and making a vigorous attack on a chicken. 'I think I'll let you two fellows do all the work to-morrow, and content myself here. Waiter! What time's breakfast?'

CHAPTER 7

SAN FRANCISCO LADIES AND DIVINATION

CURTIS was as good as his word. The following day he remained indoors eating, and planning what he should eat, whilst Hamar and Kelson went out with the express purpose of adding to their banking accounts.

In a garden in Bryant Street, Hamar saw a man resting on his spade and mopping the perspiration from his forehead. As he stopped mechanically to see what was being done, a cold sensation ran up his right leg into his right hand, the first and third fingers of which were drawn violently back. With a cry of horror he shrank back. Directly beneath where he had been standing, he saw, under a fifteen or sixteen feet layer of gravel soil – water; a huge cauldron of water, black and silent; water, that gave him the impression of tremendous depth and coldness.

'Hulloa! matey, what's the matter?' the man with the spade called out. 'Are you looking for your skin, for I never saw any one so completely jump out of it?'

'So would you,' Hamar said with a shudder, 'if you saw what I do!'

'What's that, then?' the man said, peering on the ground. 'Snakes! That's what I always see when I've got them.'

'So long as you don't see yourself, there's some chance for you!' Hamar retorted. 'What makes you so hot?'

'Why, digging!' the man laughed; 'any one would get hot digging at such hard ground as this. As for a little whipper-snapper like you, you'd melt right away and only your nose would remain. Nothing would ever melt that – there's too much of it.'

Hamar scowled. 'You needn't be insulting,' he said, 'I asked you a civil question, and I repeat it. What makes you so hot – when you should be cold – or at least cool?'

'Oh, should I!' the man mimicked, 'I thought first you were merely drunk; I can see quite clearly now that you're mad.'

'And yet you have such defective sight.'

'What makes you say that?' the man said testily.

'Why,' Hamar responded, 'because you can't see what lies beneath your very nose. Shall I tell you what it is?'

'Yes, tell away,' the man replied, 'tell me my old mother's got twins, and that Boss Croker is coming to lodge with us. I'd know you for a liar anywhere by those teeth of yours.'

'Look here,' said Hamar, drawing himself up angrily, 'I have had enough of your abuse. If I have any more I'll tell your employers. It is evident you take me for a bummer, but see,' – and plunging his hand in his pocket he pulled it out full of gold. 'Kindly understand I'm somebody,' he went on, 'and that I'm staying at one of the biggest hotels in the town.'

'I'm damned if I know what to make of you,' the man muttered, 'unless you're a hoptical delusion!'

'Underneath where I was standing – just here,' – and Hamar indicated the spot – 'is water. Any amount of it, you have only to sink a shaft fifteen feet and you would come to it.'

'Water!' the man laughed, 'yes, there is any amount of it – on your brain, that's the only water near here.'

'Then you don't believe me?' Hamar demanded.

'Not likely!' the man responded, 'I only believe what I see! And when I see a face like yours holding out a potful of dollars, I know as how you've stolen them. Git!' – and Hamar flew.

But Hamar was not so easily nonplussed; not at least when he saw a chance of making money. Entering the garden, and keeping well out of sight of the gardener, he arrived at the front door by a side path, and with much formality requested to see the owner of the establishment. The latter happened to be crossing the hall at the time, heard Hamar and asked what he wanted.

Hamar at once informed him he was a dowser, and that, chancing to pass by the garden on his way to the hotel, he had divined the presence of water.

'I only wish there were,' the gentleman exclaimed, 'but I fear you are mistaken. I have attempted several times to sink a well but never with the slightest degree of success. I have had all the ground carefully prospected by Figgins of Sacramento Street – he has a very big reputation – and he assures me there isn't a drop of water anywhere near here within two hundred feet of the surface.'

'I know better,' Hamar said. 'Will you get your gardener – who by the way was very rude to me just now when I spoke to him – to dig where I tell him. I have absolute confidence in my power of divination.'

The owner of the property, whom I will call Mr. B., assented, and several gardeners, including the one who had so insulted Hamar, were soon digging vigorously. At the depth of fifteen feet, water was found, and, indeed, so fast did it begin to come in that within a few minutes it had risen a foot. The onlookers were jubilant.

'I shall send an account of it to the local papers,' Mr. B. remarked. 'Your fame will be spread everywhere. You have increased the value of my property a thousandfold. I cannot tell you how grateful I am' – and he, then and there, invited Hamar to luncheon.

After luncheon, Mr. B. made him a present of a cheque – rather in excess of the sum which Hamar had all along intended to have, and could not have refrained from demanding much longer.

In the afternoon all the San Francisco specials were full of the incident, and Hamar, seeing his name placarded for the first time, was so overcome that he spent the rest of the evening in the hotel deliberating how he could best turn his sudden notoriety to account.

At ten o'clock Kelson came in, looking somewhat fatigued, but, nevertheless, pleased. He, too, had had adventures, and he detailed them with so much elaboration that the other two had frequently to tell him to 'dry up.'

'I began the morning,' he commenced, 'by accosting a very fashionably dressed lady coming out of Bushwell's Store in Commercial Street. Divination at once told me she was the popular widow of J. K. Bater, the Biscuit King of Nob Hill, and that she was carrying in her big seal-skin muff a gold hatpin mounted with an emerald butterfly, a silver-backed hair brush, a blue enamelled scent bottle, and a porcelain jar, all of which she had slyly "nicked," when no one was looking.

'I stepped up to her, and politely raising my hat said, "Good morning, Mrs. Bater. I've a message for you."

'"I don't know you," she said, eyeing me very doubtfully, "who are you?"

'"Forgotten!" I said tragically, "and I had flattered

myself it would be otherwise. Still, I must try and survive. I wanted to ask you a favour, Mrs. Bater."

' "A favour!" she exclaimed nervously, "what is it? You are really a very extraordinary individual."

' "I was only going to ask if I might examine the contents of your muff? I think you have certain articles in it that have not been paid for – and I believe I am right in saying this is by no means the first time such a thing has happened."

'She turned so pale I thought she was going to faint. "Why, whatever do you mean," she stammered, "I've nothing that does not belong to me."

' "Opinions differ on that score, Mrs. Bater," I replied, "you have a pin, a hair brush, a scent bottle and a jar," and I described them each minutely, "whilst in your house you have on your dressing table a silver-backed clothes brush, a silver manicure set you kleptomaniad – if you prefer to call it so – from Deacon's in Sacramento Street; a tortoiseshell manicure set, and an ivory card case you obtained in the same manner from Varter's in Market Street; a set of silver buttons, a glove stretcher, and a mauve pin-cushion – you likewise helped yourself to – from Selter's in Kearney Street; but I might go on detailing them to you till further orders, for your house is literally crammed with them. You have done very well, Mrs. Bater, with the San Francisco storekeepers."

' "Good God, man, what are you?" she gasped. "You seem to read into the innermost recesses of my soul, and to know everything."

' "You are right, madam," I said, trying to appear very stern and almost failing, she was so pretty. By Jove! you fellows, I wonder I didn't kiss her; she had such fine eyes, a ripping mouth and—'

'Oh! go on! go on with your story. Never mind her looks,' Curtis interrupted, 'I've got a touch of indigestion.'

'As I was saying,' Kelson went on complacently, 'I could have kissed her and I felt downright mean for upsetting her so.

' "Now you have found me out,' she said, "what do you intend doing? Show me up in there?" and she pointed shudderingly at the store.

' "No," I said, "not if you are sensible and come to terms. I will agree to say nothing about either this or any of your other – ahem! – thefts – if you let me escort you home, and write me out a cheque for a thousand dollars!"

'"Beast!" she hissed, "so you are a blackmailer!"

'"A black beetle if you like," I responded, "but I assure you, Mrs. Bater, I am letting you off cheap. I have only to call a policeman and your reputation would be gone at once. Besides, I know other things about you."

'"What other things?" she stuttered.

'"Well, madam!" I replied, "some things are rather delicate – er – for single men like me to mention, but I do know that – er – a lady – very like – remarkably like – you, has in her pocket at this moment a rattle which she bought and paid for in Oakland's late last night. And as, madam, Mr. Bater has been dead over two years – let me see – yes, two years yesterday – one can—"

'"Stay! that will do," she whispered; "come to my house and I will give you the thousand dollars. You must pretend you are my cousin."

'"I will pretend anything, Mrs. Bater," I murmured, helping her into a taxi, "anything so long as I can be with you."'

'You got the money?' Hamar queried.

'Yes,' Kelson said with a smile, 'I got the money – in fact, everything I asked for.'

There was a silence for some minutes, and then Hamar said, 'What next?'

'What next!' Kelson said, 'why, I thought I had done a very good day's work and was on my way back here to take a much needed rest, when I'm dashed if the Unknown hadn't another adventure in store for me. Coming out of a garden in Gough Street, within sight of Goad's house, was a lady, young and very plain, but rigged out in one of those latest fashion costumes – a very tight, short skirt, and huge hat with high plume in it. By the bye, I can't think why this costume, which is so admirably suited to pretty girls – because it attracts attention to them – should be almost exclusively adopted by the ugly ones. But to continue. I knew immediately that she was Ella Barlow, the much-pampered and only daughter of J. B. Barlow, the vinegar magnate; that she was in love, or imagined herself in love with Herbert Delmas, the manager of the Columbian Bank – a young, good-looking fellow, whom she had been trying to set against his fiancée, Dora Roberts. Dora is only nineteen, very pretty and a trifle giddy – nothing more. But this failing of hers – if you can call it a failing, was just the very weapon Ella Barlow wanted. She worked on it at once, and by sending Delmas a series of anonymous letters made him mad with jealousy. This resulted in a breach between Delmas and Dora, and Ella Barlow, much elated, at once tried to step into her shoes. She has been going out a good deal with Delmas, who is in reality still very much in love with Dora, and consequently exceedingly miserable. This morning Ella, anxious to show off a magnificent set of diamonds, given her by her father, telephoned to Delmas to take her to the Baldwyn Theatre, where she has engaged a box for this evening – hoping that the diamonds will bring him up to scratch, and that he will propose to her. When I saw her she was on her way to a notorious quack doctor and beauty specialist in Californian Street. She suffers from some nasty skin disease, and is in mortal terror lest Delmas should get to know of it, and also of the fact that all her teeth are false, and that two of her toes are badly deformed.'

'By Jupiter!' Hamar ejaculated, 'this divination of yours beats mine into fits – nothing escapes you!'

'No!' Kelson laughed, 'nothing! Ella Barlow, metaphysical and physical was laid before me just as bare as if the Almighty had got hold of her with his dissecting knife. I saw everything – and what is more I said to myself – here's plenty I can turn to a profitable account. Well! I didn't stop her – I let her go.'

'Let her go!' Curtis growled, his mouth full of almonds and raisins. 'You squirrel!'

'Only for a time,' Kelson said. 'I want to see Delmas!'

'Delmas!' Hamar interlocuted, 'why the deuce Delmas?'

'Impulse!' Kelson explained, 'purely impulse.'

'Yes, but impulse is often a dangerous thing,' Hamar said, 'it is essential for us three, especially, to be on our guard against impulse. What did you get out of Delmas?'

'Nothing!' Kelson said, looking rather shamefaced, 'but the matter hasn't ended yet. I'm going to the theatre after I've had something to eat. I'll tell you what happens, to-morrow.'

It was late ere Kelson came down to breakfast the following day, and Hamar and Curtis were comfortably seated in armchairs reading the *Examiner*, when he joined them.

'Well!' Hamar said, looking up at him, 'what luck?'

But Kelson wouldn't say a word till he had finished eating. He then lolled back in his seat and began:

'Arriving at the Baldwyn, I went straight to box one. A tall figure rose to greet me, and then an angry voice exclaimed, "Why, it's not Herbert! Who are you, sir? Do you know this box is engaged?"

' "I humbly beg your pardon, Miss Barlow," I said, "I do know it is engaged, but I came as Mr. Delmas' deputy and friend."

' "Came as Herbert's deputy and friend," Ella Barlow repeated – and by Jove the diamonds did shine – she was simply a mass of them, hair, neck, arms and fingers – and she had been so well faked up for the occasion that she was almost good-looking; but I thought of all I knew about her – and shuddered.

' "I will explain myself," I said, "Mr. Delmas telephoned to you this afternoon, did he not?"

'She nodded.

' "Saying that he very much regretted he could not leave business in time to escort you here. Would you mind very much going by yourself, and he would join you as soon as possible."

' "Yes," Ella Barlow said, "he told me all that."

' "Very well, then," I went on, "he rang me up some minutes later and asked me if I would take his place for the first hour or so, and he would be here by the end of the first act."

' "But it is most unheard of," Ella Barlow ejaculated, "I don't know you – I've never seen you before!"

' "That is, of course, very regrettable," I said, "but I will do all I can for the best. I've something to say that I'm sure will interest you. Have I your permission?" – and without waiting for her reply I sat next to her. The box was a big one, big enough to hold half a dozen people, and we sat in the extreme front of it. The lights were not full up, as the orchestra had not started playing. I kept her attention fixed on my face so that she was unaware what was taking place, immediately behind her.

' "What is it?" she said, "whatever can you have to say that can be of any possible interest to me?"

' "Why," I replied, "to begin with, I know something about your character!"

' "Then you're a fortune teller!" she exclaimed eagerly, "can you read hands?"

' "I can read everything," I said, looking hard at her, "hands, head, and feet. I am psychometrist, dentist, physician, metaphysician all in one!"

' "I don't understand," she said, looking queer, "what is the meaning of all this?"

' "It means," I said slowly, "that I have discovered who sent those anonymous letters to Herbert Delmas!"

' "Anonymous letters! how dare you!" she cried, "what have anonymous letters to do with me?"

' "A very great deal, madam," I replied, "shall I remind you of their contents and the occasions on which you wrote them?" I did so. I recited every word in them and told her the hour, day and place – namely, when and where each was written, and I summed up by asking what she would pay me not to tell Delmas.

'For some minutes she was too overcome to say anything; she sat grim and silent, her pale eyes glaring at me, her freckled fingers toying with the diamonds. She was baffled and perplexed – she did not know what course to pursue!

' "Well," I repeated, "what have you to say? Do you deny it?"

'She roused herself with an effort. "No," she said venomously, "I don't deny it. Denial would be useless. How did you find out? Through one of the maids, I suppose. They were bribed to spy on me!"

' "How I discovered it is of no consequence," I said, "but what is of consequence to you as much as to me – is the payment for hushing it up!"

' "Payment!" she cried, raising her voice to a positive shriek in her excitement, "pay *you* – you nasty, beastly, cadging toad. You—" but I can't repeat all she said, it would make you both blush! I let her go on till she had worn herself out and then I said, "Well, Miss Barlow, why all this fuss – why these fireworks! It can't do you any good. We must come to business sooner or later. If you don't pay me handsomely I shall tell Miss Roberts as well as Mr. Delmas."

' "Mr. Delmas won't believe you," she hissed, "you've no proofs at all!"

' "Perhaps not," I said, "but I've proofs of this. I know you have two deformed toes on your left foot, that all your teeth are false, and that you go to that charlatan, Howard Prince, in Californian Street, to be faked up. I must be brutal – it's no use being anything else to women of your sort. You've got a certain species of eczema, and you flatter yourself that no one but you and Prince are aware of it. What have you got to say now, Miss Barlow?" But Ella Barlow had fainted. When she came to, which I managed after vigorous application of salts and water – the effects of the latter on her complexion I leave you to imagine – I again broached the subject.

' "What is it you propose?" she said feebly.

' "Why, this," I said, "you hand me over all those diamonds, and your defects will – as far as I am concerned – always remain a secret. Refuse, and Miss Roberts and Mr. Delmas shall know all there is to be known at once."

'For some minutes she sat with her face buried in her hands – shivering. Then she looked up at me – and Jerusalem! it was like looking at an old woman. "Take them," she said, "take them! I shall never wear them again, anyhow. Take them – and leave me."

'Well, you fellows, I steeled my heart, and slipped every Jack one that was on her into my pocket.

' "You won't tell them," she whispered, catching hold of me by the arm, "you swear you won't." I won't try and remember exactly what I answered – but outside the door of the box Delmas joined me. He had been concealed within and had heard everything that passed.

' "I can't say how grateful I am to you," he said. "It's a bit low down, perhaps, but, then, we were dealing with a low-down person. You thoroughly deserve those diamonds – will you accept an offer for them from me? I should like to buy them for Miss Roberts and present them to her on our reconciliation." We came to terms then and there, and he 'phoned through to me an hour ago to say that he had made it up with Miss Roberts, that she was delighted with the diamonds, and that they are going to be married next month.'

'So out of evil good comes,' Hamar said, 'the maxim for us, remember, is – out of evil evil alone must come. What are you going to do to-day, you two?'

'Rest!' said Kelson, 'I'm tired.'

'Eat!' said Curtis, 'I'm hungry!'

'Now look here, this won't do,' Hamar remarked, 'you've earned your rest, Matt, but you haven't, Ed. You can't go on eating eternally.'

'Can't I?' Curtis snapped, 'I'm not so sure of that, I've years to make up for.'

'Then do the thing in moderation, for goodness' sake!' Hamar expostulated, 'and recollect we must, at all costs, act together. We have now twelve thousand dollars between us in the bank – that is to say, the capital of the Firm of Hamar, Curtis and Kelson represents that amount. It is our ambition to increase that amount – and to go on increasing it till we can fairly claim to be the richest Firm in the world. Now to do that we must work, and work hard, if we are to live at the pace Ed is setting us – but there is no reason why we should remain here, and I propose that we move elsewhere. I've got a scheme in my head, rather a colossal one, I admit, but not altogether impossible.'

'What is it?' Kelson asked.

'Yes, out with it,' Curtis grunted.

'It is this,' Hamar said, 'I suggest that we go to London – London in England – I guess it's the richest town in the world – and there set up as sorcerers – The Sorcery Company Ltd. We should begin with divination and juggling, and go on, according to the seven stages. We should of course sell our cures and spells, and there is not the slightest doubt but that we should make an enormous pile, with which we would gradually buy up, not merely London, but the whole of England.'

'That's rather a tall order,' Kelson murmured.

'A small one, you mean,' Curtis sneered, 'you could put the whole of England twice over in California, and from what I've heard I don't go much on London. I reckon it isn't much bigger than San Francisco.'

'Still, you wouldn't mind being joint owner of it,' Hamar laughed.

'No, perhaps not,' Curits said rather dubiously. 'I guess we could buy the crown and wear it in turn. Sam Westlake up at Meidler's always used to say the British would sell their souls if any one bid high enough. They think of nothing but money over there. When shall we go?'

'At the end of our week,' Hamar said, 'that is to say on Wednesday – in three days' time.'

'First class all the way, of course,' Curtis said, 'I'll see to the arrangements for the catering and berths.'

'All right!' Hamar laughed, as he filled three glasses with champagne. 'Here, drink, you fellows. "Long life, health and prosperity – to Hamar, Curtis and Kelson, the Modern Sorcery Company Ltd."'

CHAPTER 8

TWO DREAMS

'Do you believe in dreams?' Gladys Martin inquired, as, fresh from a stroll in the garden, she joined her aunt, Miss Templeton, in the breakfast room at Pine Cottage.

'I believe in fairies,' Miss Templeton rejoined, smiling indulgently as she looked at the fair face beside her. 'What was the dream, dearie?'

Gladys laughed a little mischievously. 'I don't quite know whether I ought to tell you,' she said. 'It might shock you.'

'Perhaps I'm not so easily shocked as you imagine,' Miss Templeton replied. 'What was it?'

'Well!' Gladys began, flinging both arms round her aunt's neck and playing with the pleats in her blouse, 'I dreamed that I was walking in the little wood at the end of the garden, and that the trees and flowers walked and talked with me. And we danced together – and, first of all, I had for my partner, a red rose – and then, an ash. They both made love to me, and squeezed my waist with their hot, fibrous hands. A poppy piped, a bramble played the concertina, and a lilac grew desperately jealous of me and tried to claw my hair. Then the dancing ceased, and I found myself in the midst of bluebells that shook their bells at me with loud trills of laughter. And out from among them, came a buttercup, pointing its yellow head at me. "See! see," it cried, "what Gladys is carrying behind her. Naughty Gladys!" And trees and flowers – everything around me – shook with laughter. Then I grew hot and cold all over, and did not know which way to look for my confusion, till a willow, having compassion on me said, "Take no notice of them! They don't know any better."

'I begged him to explain to me why they were so amused, and he grew very embarrassed and uncomfortable, and stammered – oh! so funnily, "Well, if you really wish to know – it's a bud, a baby white rose, and it's clinging to your dress."

'"A baby! A baby rose!" shrieked all the flowers.

'"And it means," a bluebell said, stepping perkily out from amidst its fellows, "that your lover is coming – your lover with a troll-le-loll-la – and – well, if you want to know more ask the gooseberries, the gooseberries that hang on the bushes, or the parsley that grows in the bed," – and at that all the flowers and trees shrieked with laughter – "Ta-ta-tra-la-la" – and with my ears full of the rude laughter of the wood I awoke. What do you think of it? Isn't it rather a quaint mixture of the – of the sacred – at least the artistic – and the profane?'

'Quite so,' said Miss Templeton with an amused chuckle, 'but I shouldn't ask for an interpretation of it if I were you.'

'Not for an interpretation of the trees and flowers?' Gladys asked innocently. 'I'm sure trees and flowers have a special significance in dreams.'

'Very well then, my dear, ask Mrs. Sprat.'

'What! Ask the Vicar's wife!' Gladys ejaculated, 'when I never go to church.'

'Certainly,' Miss Templeton replied, laughing again. 'Mrs. Sprat will quite understand. And I've always been told she is very interested in anything to do with the Occult. But hush! Here's your father. You'd better not tell him your dream. He's tired to death, he says, of hearing about your lovers, and agrees with me – there's no end to them.'

'Never mind what he says – his bark's worse than his bite,' Gladys rejoined, 'he doesn't really care how many I have so long as they keep within bounds, and I like them! Father!'

John Martin, who entered the room at that moment, went straight to his daughter to be kissed.

'I wish you wouldn't always select that bald spot,' he said testily, 'I don't want to be everlastingly reminded I'm losing my hair.'

'Where do you want me to kiss you, then?' Gladys argued, 'on the tip of your nose? That's all very well for you, John Martin, but I prefer the top of your head. But the poor dear looks worried, what is it?'

'I didn't have a very good night,' her father replied, 'I dreamed a lot!' Gladys looked at Miss Templeton and laughed.

'Did you?' she said gently. 'What a shame! I never dream. What was it all about?'

'Flowers!' John Martin snapped, 'idiotic flowers! Roses, lilac, tulips! Bah! I do wish you would have some other hobby.'

Gladys looked at her aunt again, this time with a half serious, half questioning expression.

'Shall I be a politician?' she cooed, 'and fill the house with suffragettes? You bad man, I believe you would revel in it. Don't you think so, Auntie?'

'I think, instead of teasing your father so unmercifully, you had better pour him out a cup of tea,' Miss Templeton replied. 'Jack, there's a letter for you.'

'Where? Under my plate! what a place to put it. That's you,' and John Martin frowned, or rather, attempted to frown, at Gladys. 'Why it's about Davenport – Dick Davenport. He's very ill – had a stroke yesterday, and the doctor declares his condition critical. His nephew, Shiel, so Anne says, has been sent for, and arrived at Sydenham last night! If that's not bad news I don't know what is!' John Martin said, thrusting his plate away from him and leaning back in his chair. 'It's true I can manage the business all right myself – and there's the possibility, of course, that this young Shiel may shape all right. I suppose if anything happens he will step into Dick's shoes. I've never heard Dick mention any one else. Poor old Dick!'

'I am so sorry, father!' Gladys said, laying her hand on his. 'But cheer up! It may not be as bad as you expect. Shall you go and see how he is?'

'I think so, my dear! I think so,' John Martin replied, 'but don't worry me about it now. Talk to your aunt and leave me out of it, I'm a bit upset. My brain's in a regular whirl!'

Undoubtedly the news was something in the nature of a blow: for Dick Davenport, apart from being John Martin's partner – partner in the firm of Martin and Davenport, the world-renowned conjurors, whose hall in the Kingsway was one of the chief amusement places in London, was John Martin's oldest friend. They had been chums at Cheltenham College, had entered the Army and gone to India together, had quitted the Service together, and, on returning together to England, had started their conjuring business, first of all in Sloane Street, and subsequently in the Kingsway. From the very start their enterprise had met with success, and, had it not been for Davenport's wild extravagance, they would have been little short of millionaires. But Davenport, though a most lovable character in every respect, could not keep money – he no sooner had it than it was gone. His house in Sydenham was little short of a palace; whilst, it was said, he almost rivalled royalty, in magnificent display, whenever he entertained. The result of all this reckless expenditure was no uncommon one – he ran through considerably more than he earned and – as there was no one else to help him – he invariably came down on John Martin. It was 'Jack, old boy, I'm damned sorry, but I must have another thousand;' or, 'Jack! these infernal scamps of creditors are worrying the life out of me, can you, will you, lend me a trifle – a couple of thousand will do it' – and so on – so on, *ad infinitum*. John Martin never refused, and, at the time of Davenport's illness, the latter owed him something like a hundred thousand pounds.

Fortunately John Martin, though far from parsimonious, was careful. He had an excellent business head, and, thanks to his sagacious share in the management, the business remained solvent. He knew Davenport's capacity – that nowhere could he have found another such a brilliant genius in conjuring – nor, apart from his thriftlessness, any one so thoroughly reliable. In Davenport's keeping all the great tricks they had invented – and great tricks they undoubtedly were – were absolutely safe.

Despite the fact that they had repeatedly offered big sums of money to any one who could discover the secret of how they were done, every attempt to do so had utterly failed. The Mysteries of Martin and Davenport's Home of Wonder, in the Kingsway, baffled the world. Of course one thing had helped them enormously – namely, they had no rivals. So colossal was their reputation, that no one else had ever even thought of setting up in opposition.

And now one of the two great master-minds, that had accomplished all these marvels and acquired such universal fame, was stricken down, checkmated by the still greater power of nature; and his colleague – the only other man in existence who shared his knowledge – was obliged to rack his brain as to what was now to be done – done for the continuance and prosperity of the firm.

After finishing her breakfast Gladys joined her aunt in the garden.

'To dream of flowers and trees evidently means bad news,' she said. 'But as I feel in a mood for a walk, I shall call at the Vicarage.'

'What, now! At this hour!' Miss Templeton cried aghast.

'Why not?' Gladys said imperturbably. 'I'm not going to pay a call. They haven't called on us. I shall say I've merely come to make an inquiry. Can she tell me of any one who interprets dreams? Come with me!'

But as her aunt pleaded an excuse, Gladys went alone.

The Vicar was in the garden in his shirt sleeves, and though obviously surprised to see Gladys, seemed quite prepared to enter into conversation with her. But Gladys was not enamoured of clergymen. Her ways were not their ways, and she had come strictly on business. Consequently she somewhat curtly demanded to be conducted into the presence of his wife, who received her very affably.

'Why, how very strange,' she observed when Gladys had stated the object of her visit. 'I was asked a similar question only yesterday. A Miss Rosenberg, who is staying with us, had an extraordinary dream about trees and flowers – only it took the form of a poem, which she kept repeating. There were several verses – quite doggerel it is true – but nevertheless rather remarkable for a dream. She wrote them down, and asked me if I could tell her whether there was any hidden meaning in them. Here they are,' and she handed Gladys two pages of sermon paper on which was written—

> 'In the greenest of green valleys,
> Aglow with summer sun,
> Lived a maiden fair and radiant,
> More radiant there was none.

> 'The flowers gave her their friendship;
> Her couch was on the ground.
> A happier, gayer maiden,
> Was nowhere to be found.

'The air was filled with music
Sung by the babbling brook.
Sweet lullabies with chorus clear
In which the flowers partook.

'The maiden knew not sorrow,
Until an evil day;
When riding lone across the moors,
A hunter lost his way.

'And chancing on this valley,
He met the maiden sweet.
Her beauty overwhelmed him;
He fell love-sick at her feet.

'Despite the fervent warnings
Of her friends the flowers and trees,
She listened to his courting;
And with him roamed the leas.

'The leas, far from the valley,
They rode the livelong night;
Till a heavy mist descending
Hid the roadway from their sight.

'Uprose, then, forms of evil,
From out the mocking gloom;
And seizing horse and hunter scared,
Left the maiden to her doom.

'Travellers now within those regions,
Through the nightly grey fog see
A woman's shade crawl slow along,
To a ghastly melody.

'And those who linger – follow
The phantom pale and wan.
O'er hill and dale, and rill and vale
It slowly leads them on.

'On till they reach the valley,
A valley grim and drear,
Where lurid things with fibrous arms
Their course through darkness steer.

>'And on the travellers palsied
>In frenzied crowd they pour.
>And those who view their faces,
>Are heard but seen no more.'

'Do you mean to say she dreamed all that?' Gladys evclaimed.

'Yes,' the Vicar's wife said. 'She told me so and I have no reason to doubt her. She doesn't romance as a rule, and is certainly not the least bit in the world poetical – on the contrary she is most practical and matter-of-fact. Her only hobby, as far as I know, is flowers.'

'Mine, too!' Gladys interrupted. 'Were you able to explain the verses?'

'No, I can't interpret dreams. I'm intensely interested in them; as I am in all things psychic. I was at a lecture given by Mrs. Annie Besant last night! She—'

'Do you know anyone who does interpret dreams?' Gladys asked.

'Why, yes! A firm, claiming to do all sorts of wonderful things – to tell dreams, solve tricks, divine the presence of metals and water, and so on, has just set up in Cockspur Street. I read a short notice about them in this morning's paper. I will get it for you.'

She left the room and in a few moments returned.

'Here it is,' she said. And under the heading of 'Sorcery Revived' Gladys read the following:

'There is really no end to the devices to which people resort nowadays to make money, but for sheer novelty, nothing, we think, beats this. Three Americans, Messrs. Hamar, Curtis and Kelson, fresh from San Francisco, California, have just bought premises in Cockspur Street, S.W., and set up there as Sorcerers!

'They style themselves "The Modern Sorcery Company Ltd.," and profess to interpret dreams, read people's thoughts, tell their pasts, solve all manner of tricks and detect the presence of metals and water. One wonders what next!'

'This paper evidently has its doubts,' Gladys commented. 'They are frauds, of course.'

'I dare say they are,' the Vicar's wife replied, 'though I believe in thought-reading and other things they say they can do. I advised Miss Rosenberg to see them about her dream. She went in by the nine o'clock train. Had you come a few minutes earlier you would have seen her.'

'Well, thanks awfully,' Gladys said, 'for telling me about these people. Very probably I'll go in to Town some time during the day and call at Cockspur Street. I must apologize again for calling at such an unearthly hour. Goodbye,' and Gladys smilingly took her departure.

CHAPTER 9

LOVE AT FIRST SIGHT

SHORTLY after Gladys reached home after her visit to the Vicarage, a young man with a serious expression somewhat out of keeping with his jaunty walk, entered the gate of Pine Cottage, and came to an abrupt halt.

'Well,' he ejaculated, 'this is a pretty place, and what's more – for dozens of houses and gardens are pretty – it's artistic!' In front of him stretched a miniature avenue of chestnut trees, which was rendered striking, even to the most casual observer, probably, not only on account of the irregular mounds of moss-covered stones that occupied its intervening spaces, but also, by reason of the masses of wild flowers (great clumps of which were springing up in the crevices of this impromptu wall) that lent to it an appearance half negligent, but wholly and entrancingly picturesque. Here, undoubtedly, was art. That did not astonish the young man. All avenues, in the ordinary sense, are works of art; and the mere excess of art he saw manifested did not surprise him; it was the character of the art that had brought him to a standstill and held him spellbound. And the longer he looked the more he became convinced, that whoever had superintended the arrangement of this scenery was an artist – an artist with a scrupulous eye for form.

The greatest care had been taken to keep the balance between neatness and gracefulness on the one hand and picturesqueness on the other. There were few straight lines, and no long uninterrupted ones; whilst at no one point of view did the same effect of curvature or colour appear twice. Variety in uniformity was the keynote.

At last tearing himself away from this one spot – where he felt he could have spent centuries – he turned to the right and then again to the left – for the path had now become serpentine, and at no moment could be traced for more than two or three paces in advance. Presently the sound of water fell gently on his ear, and in the shadiest of diminutive forests, amidst the interlacing branches of elm and beech, he caught the glimpse of a fountain. For an instant the wild thought of forcing his way through it, of plunging his burning forehead in its cooling spray, well-nigh mastered him. But his better sense conquered, and he kept to the path. Another turn, and he caught his first glimpse of a chimney; another – and the summit of a gable showed above the trees. The sun, which had been hitherto obscured, now came out, and suddenly – as if by the hand of magic – the whole scene was a brilliant blaze of colour. He had arrived at the end of the avenue, where the path forked; one branch turning sharply round in the direction of a side entrance to the house, whilst the other led with a gentle curvature to the front.

Facing the building was a broad expanse of velvety turf, relieved occasionally, here and there, by such showy shrubs as the hydrangea, rhododendron, or lilac; but more frequently, and at closer intervals, by clumps of geraniums, or roses – roses of every variety. There was nothing pretentious in the garden, any more than there was in the adjoining edifice. Its unusually pleasing effect lay altogether in its artistic arrangement; and one could hardly help imagining that the whole scene had, in reality, been called into existence by the brush of some eminent landscape painter.

The cottage itself was constructed of old-fashioned Dutch shingles – broad and with rounded corners – and painted a dull grey; a tint which, when contrasted with the vivid green of the tulip trees that overshadowed the entrance to the house, and reared themselves high above it on either side, afforded an artistic happiness perfectly intoxicating to its present visitor. The architecture of the cottage was – if not Early Tudor – something equally pleasing. Its roofs were divided into many gables; its windows were diamond paned and projecting, whilst oaken beams ran latitudinally and vertically over its grey shingle front. Encompassing the whole base of the exterior were masses of flowers – pinks, carnations, heliotrope, pansies, poppies, lilies, wallflowers, roses and jasmines; and besides the latter several other creepers had been planted beneath the walls, but had not yet attained to any height.

Shiel Davenport, for it was he, could not resist the temptation of peering in at the windows; and he saw that the interior of the cottage was artistry and simplicity itself. At the windows, curtains of heavy white jaconet muslin, not too full, hung in sharp parallel plaits to the floor – just to the floor. The walls were papered with French papers of rare delicacy – to match the seasons; (spring, summer, autumn and winter were all most effectively depicted), and the furniture though light, was at the same time costly. And here again was the same effect of arrangement – an arrangement obviously designed by the same brain that had planned the building and grounds. Shiel could not conceive anything more graceful. Flowers – flowers of every hue and odour were the chief decoration of the cottage. On almost every table were vases – in themselves beautiful enough – yet filled to overflowing with the finest roses. Ox-eye daisies, hollyhocks and forget-me-nots clustered about the open windows. And every puff of wind, every breath of air transmitted scent – the most delicious medley of scent imaginable.

The young man drew in deep draughts of it; he threw back his head, and, opening his mouth, revelled in the joy of feeling it steal softly down his throat and permeate his lungs. He was thus engaged when the sound of a voice brought him sharply back to earth.

In the open doorway of the house, an amused expression in her violet eyes, stood a girl – so wondrously pretty, that at the sight of her Shiel was again overcome, and could only gaze in helpless admiration.

'Do you want to see my father?' she inquired. 'He is getting ready to go out, but I daresay he will see you first.'

'I – I am sure he will,' the young man replied, 'I'm Shiel Davenport. I've come to tell him my uncle died at four o'clock this morning.'

'Oh, dear!' the girl exclaimed, 'I am so sorry – sorry for you, and for my father. I am sure he will be terribly upset. I'm Gladys Martin, perhaps you've heard of me – I knew your uncle.'

'Often,' Shiel said, 'And I think my uncle's description of you an excellent one.'

'His description of me!'

'Yes! he always spoke of you as the Queen of Flowers, and said you had a mania for all things beautiful, which was not surprising, seeing how beautiful you were yourself.'

'That was very nice of him,' Gladys said, looking amused again. 'Won't you come in? If you will wait here' – she led him to the drawing-room – 'I'll tell my father.'

She disappeared, and Shiel heard her run lightly up the stairs.

'By Jove,' he said to himself, 'she's the loveliest girl I've ever seen. From being so much among flowers, she has become one herself. Violets, roses, and heliotrope have all had a share in her creation! What eyes! what a mouth! what teeth! what hands! Surely I have found here, not only the perfection of all things beautiful, but the perfection of all things natural, the perfection of natural grace in contradiction from artificial grace. Moreover, she is a romanticist. There is an expression of romance, of unworldliness, in those deep-set eyes of hers, that sinks into my heart of hearts. "Romance" and "womanliness," and the two terms appear to me to be convertible, are her distinguishing features. She is an artist, an idealist, and, over and above all – a woman! Hang it! I'm in love with her!'

More he could not evolve, for his meditations were abruptly cut short by the entrance of a servant, who ushered him, straightway, into the presence of John Martin.

The latter though visibly affected by the news of his friend's death, was a man of the world, and, consequently, came to business at once. Much had to be discussed – arrangements for the funeral, the examination of correspondence relative to the firm, and plans for the immediate future.

'You don't know how my uncle's affairs stand, I suppose?' Shiel asked somewhat nervously.

'Yes,' John Martin said, 'I do. May I ask if you have any private means at all – or are you solely dependent on what you earn? By the way, what is your calling?'

'I am an artist,' Shiel said. 'No, I've nothing beyond what my uncle was good enough to allow me.'

'An artist!' John Martin murmured, 'how like Dick! Have you entertained the idea of inheriting a fortune? Have you any reason to suppose that your uncle was well off and had made you his heir!'

'I gathered so, sir, from the manner in which he lived and his attitude towards me.'

'Well! we won't talk it over now – leave it till after the funeral. Are you bent on continuing painting? There is very little remuneration in it, is there?'

'Not much,' Shiel answered gloomily, 'but I shouldn't care to give it up – unless of course it is absolutely necessary for me to do so.'

'Being an artist you wouldn't be much good in business.'

'None!'

'At all events you are candid. Well! I don't see any good in our dallying here – I had best go back with you to Sydenham. I've got a letter to write first, but I shan't be long.'

He was long enough, however, for Shiel to have another chat with Gladys. 'Do you believe in dreams?' she asked him. 'I had such a queer one last night, about trees and flowers; and, oddly enough, my father also dreamed of trees and flowers, and of the very same ones too. I am going into Town to-day to consult a firm that has just set up, called the Modern Sorcery Club Ltd. They profess to interpret dreams, and I am anxious to see whether they can.'

'In Cockspur Street, aren't they?' Shiel asked. 'I saw their advertisement in one of the papers. I presume you are not going there alone?'

'No!' Gladys laughed, 'I shall go with a friend, though I often do go into Town alone. I can assure you I am quite capable of looking after myself. In that respect, at least, I am quite up to date. Probably you are more accustomed to French girls?'

'Yes! I have spent most of my life in Paris,' Shiel said. 'But how could you tell that?'

'Oh! I guessed you were an artist – and had probably spent some time in Paris' – Gladys rejoined, 'by the way you looked at the house and garden. I could read appreciation in your eyes and gesture; such appreciation, as I knew, could only come from an artist. G. W. Barnett helped me in planning this cottage and the garden.'

'What! Barnett the landscape painter! I am a great admirer of his work. Were you a pupil of his?'

'Yes, he was one of the visiting R.A's at the Beechcroft Studio in St. John's Wood, where I worked for three years. We were then living in Blackheath – St. John's Park – a hateful place. Mr. Barnett was awfully good, when I told him we were moving, and that I wanted to live in really artistic surroundings – he suggested that I should be my own architect, and promised to do everything he could to assist me.'

'And your father hadn't a say in the matter,' Shiel commented, with an amused smile.

'Not in that,' Gladys said complacently, 'though there are one or two things in which he has a very decided say. Father can be very self-willed and obstinate, when he likes. But as I was remarking when you interrupted me—'

'I beg pardon!' Shiel murmured.

'Mr. Barnett promised to assist me. He came over here with me, and we chose this site.'

'Is he an old man?' Shiel inquired, a trifle anxiously.

'Not much more than middle aged – fifty perhaps!' Gladys said, 'though he looks much younger. He is still very good-looking. Well! he came over here – we chose this site, and—'

'Is he married?'

'No! Really, you seem very interested in him. Perhaps you will meet him some day: he comes here a good deal. As I was saying, we chose the site together, and he supervised the plans I drew up for the garden and cottage; I don't think, perhaps, I should have thought of that avenue if it hadn't been for him!'

'At all events it does you both credit,' Shiel remarked, 'for a more charming house and garden I have never seen. I should like to live here all my life. I should like—' but he was interrupted by John Martin. 'Come, it's time we were off,' the latter called out brusquely, 'time and trains wait for no man!'

'A young ass!' John Martin whispered in Gladys' ear, as the trio passed through the entrance of the railway station on to the platform, 'not a bit of good to me. Don't encourage him, whatever you do!'

'Encourage him!' Gladys retorted indignantly, seeing that Shiel, who had his ticket to get, was out of hearing. 'Do I encourage any one? All the same,' she added defiantly, 'I rather like him. It isn't every one's good fortune to be as smart as you, John Martin. Quick – hurry up! That's your train – and the guard's about to blow his whistle.'

With a vigorous push she hustled her father into the first compartment they came to, and Shiel sprang in after him as the train moved out of the station.

An hour later Gladys, looking extremely demure and proper, was rapping with a daintily gloved hand at the inquiry office in the great stone lobby of the Modern Sorcery Company's building in Cockspur Street.

'Have you an appointment, madam?' the commissionaire, in a bright blue uniform, asked.

'No,' Gladys replied. 'Is it necessary?'

'The firm are unusually busy,' the man explained, 'and unless you have made an appointment with them some days beforehand, it is doubtful whether they will be able to see you. However, if you will step into the waiting-room and fill in one of the forms you see on the table, I will take it to them. Which member of the firm have you come to consult?'

'I haven't the slightest idea,' Gladys said. 'I want to have a dream interpreted.'

'Then, that will be Mr. Kelson,' the man observed; 'he does all that kind of thing – tells dreams, characters, pasts, and reads thoughts. Mr. Curtis solves all manner of puzzles and tricks; and Mr. Hamar divines the presence of metals and water. There is a lady in the waiting-room now, come to have a dream interpreted. She's been there nearly an hour. This way, madam!' – and he escorted, rather than ushered, Gladys into a large, elaborately furnished room, in which a dozen or so well dressed people – of both sexes – were waiting, looking over the leaves of magazines and journals, and trying in vain to hide their only too obvious excitement.

Having filled in the necessary form, and given it to the commissionaire, Gladys looked round for a seat, and espying one, next to a strikingly handsome girl, she at once appropriated it.

There was something about this showy girl that had

attracted Gladys. She was one of those rare people that have a personality, and although this was a personality that Gladys was not at all sure she liked, nevertheless she felt anxious to become more closely aquainted with it. Both girls suddenly realized that they were staring hard at one another. The girl with the personality was the first to speak. With a smile that, while revealing a perfect set of white teeth, at the same time revealed exceedingly thin lips, she remarked, 'It's most wearisome work waiting. I've been here nearly an hour. I shouldn't stay any longer, only I've come from a distance. London is so hot and stuffy, I detest it.'

'Do you?' Gladys observed. 'I don't. I find it so full of human interest – indeed, of every kind of interest. Not that I should care to live in it, but I like being near enough to come up several times a week. I live at Kew.'

'Then you're lucky!' the girl said, 'I'd live at Kew if I could. But I can't – I'm one of those unfortunate creatures who have to earn their living.'

'I sometimes wish I had to,' Gladys remarked.

'Do you! Then you don't know much about it. It isn't all jam by a long way. I loathe work. I've been spending my holiday at Kew. I've just come from there.'

'Are you by any chance Miss Rosenberg?' Gladys asked.

'That's my name,' the girl replied with a look of astonishment. 'How do you know?'

Gladys explained. 'I've just been to the Vicarage,' she said, 'and Mrs. Sprat has told me about the verses. Did you really dream them?'

'Of course! I shouldn't have said so if I hadn't,' Miss Rosenberg replied angrily. 'I don't tell crams. Besides, I've never composed a line of poetry in my life. The verses were repeated to me in my sleep by some occult agency – of that I am quite certain. They were so vividly impressed on my mind that I had no difficulty at all in remembering them – every one of them, and I got up and wrote them down. Of course they must mean something.'

Gladys was about to make some observation, when the commissionaire, opening the door of the room, called out, 'Miss Rosenberg;' whereupon, with a sigh of relief, Miss Rosenberg took her departure.

CHAPTER 10

HOW THE DREAMS WERE INTERPRETED

'TELL Miss Rosenberg I'll see her now,' Matt Kelson said; and as he leaned back in his luxurious chair with that dignity of self-assurance only the man who is rich can maintain, it was hard to realize that he and the Matt Kelson of a year ago were the same. A year ago he had been a poor, underpaid, ill nourished pen-driver, with all the odious marks of a pen-driver's servility upon him. It was true he had been fastidious as to his appearance – that is to say, as fastidious as any one can be who has to buy clothes ready made and can only afford a few dollars for them; that he had sacrificed meals to wear white shirts – boiled shirts as one called them in San Francisco – and to get his things got up decently at a respectable laundry; but his teeth in those days did not receive the attention they ought to have received (he could not afford a dentist), the tobacco he smoked was often offensive; and there were to be found in him sundry other details one usually finds in clerks, and in most other people who literally have to fight for a living.

But now, all that was changed. Kelson was rich. He bought his suits at Poole's, his hats at Christie's, his boots in Regent Street. He patronized a dentist in Cavendish Square, and a manicurist in Bond Street. He belonged to a crack club in Pall Mall, and never smoked anything but the most expensive cigars. His ambition had been speedily realized. He had passionately longed to be a fop – he was one. The only thing that troubled him, was that he could not be an aristocrat at the same time. But, after all, what did that matter? The girls looked at him all the same, and that was all he wanted. He worshipped, he adored, pretty girls; and he was most anxious that they should adore him.

Consequently, his first thought, when he saw Lilian Rosenberg's name on the form the commissionaire presented him, was 'Is she pretty?' And the first thing he said to himself directly the door opened to admit her was, 'By Jove! she is.'

Then he assumed an air more suited to a partner in a big London firm, and flourishing a richly bejewelled hand, said, 'Pray take a seat, madam. What can I do for you?'

'I want you to tell me the meaning of these verses,' Lilian Rosenberg said, handing him two sheets of foolscap and then sitting down. 'They were suggested to me in my sleep – in other words, I dreamed them.'

'You dreamed them, did you!' Kelson said, noticing with approval that the girl had well-kept white hands, and that her clothes, though not particularly expensive, were *chic*, and up-to-date. 'Do you want me only to interpret this poem, or shall I tell you something about yourself first?'

'By all means tell me something about myself first – if you can,' Lilian Rosenberg said. 'I want to get as much as I can out of you. Your fees are exorbitant.'

'Very well, then,' Kelson rejoined with a smile. 'Don't blame me if I tell you too much. You were born at sea. Being a troublesome girl at home, you were sent to a boarding-school, where you distinguished yourself in various ways, and last but not least, by making the headmistress – a married woman – desperately jealous. This led to you being removed. Removed is a more delicate term than "expelled." Am I right?'

'Yes! I believe you are inspired by the devil.'

'Shall I go on?'

'Yes – I think so. Yes, go on, please.'

'You came home. Your mother died. Your father married again. You disliked your stepmother – you considered she ill treated you.'

'She did!'

'I won't dispute it. At all events you had revenge. You pretended to commit suicide, and wrote several letters – to the police among others – declaring that you were about to drown yourself owing to the cruelty of your stepmother. And so cleverly did you manage it, that every one believed you were drowned, and blamed your stepmother accordingly. Changing your name to Lilian Rosenberg you came direct to London. For some time you worked in a milliner's shop in Beauchamp Gardens, and then you set up as a manicurist in Woodstock Street. Among your clients was the wife of the Vicar of St. Katherine's, Kew, who took a great liking to you – you have extraordinary personal magnetism. Unable, however, to do more than pay your way at legitimate manicuring you—'

'That will do,' Lilian Rosenberg cried, a faint flow of colour pervading her cheeks. 'That will do! Explain the verses.'

'As you will!' Kelson said, 'but mind, I don't insist on the necessity of your paying the slightest heed to my explanation. According to the usual method of interpreting dreams, the valley of flowers is symbolical of innocence and self-restraint – of that path in life with which the goody-goodies say every young lady should be satisfied.

'The hunter is representative of the love of change and excitement; the horse – of self-indulgence. The misty moon means ruin, the metamorphosis into the crawling phantasm – death. Leave the path of virtue, and give way to self-indulgence and a craving for everlasting change and excitement, and a miserable ending will be your meed – and has been the meed of all others who have done the same thing.'

'Then the dream is a warning?'

Kelson was about to reply, when the door opened, and Hamar, with an apology for intruding, beckoned to him.

He spoke with him for several moments relative to a matter of some consequence, and then, glancing at Miss Rosenberg, and drawing Kelson still further aside, whispered, 'Let me caution you again, Matt. On no account let your soft feelings with regard to the other sex get the better of you. Remember it is imperative for us to do evil not good – to lead our clients into temptation, not out of it. I am doing my best to follow the injunctions of the Unknown, but we *must all* work in harmony – that is the most vital point in our compact, and you know if we do not keep the compact something frightful will happen to us. I can't impress this fact on you too much. Only yesterday I had to pull you up for giving good advice to a lady. Damn your good advice, give bad – bad advice, I say; anything that will do people harm – no matter whether they are ugly or pretty – and if you are not jolly well careful, pretty girls will be your – and our – undoing. I see you have a pretty girl here now – and from what I can read in her face, she is not a saint. Rub it in to her – rub it in to her well – persuade her to be a bigger sinner still. Now I can't wait to say more, I must go.'

'I asked you,' Lilian Rosenberg said, as Kelson resumed his seat, 'if the dream was a warning?'

'No,' Kelson said, 'I shouldn't take it as such. Despite the rather peculiar form it took, I am inclined to think it isn't a dream with any real significance – but merely a chance dream – a dream compounded of sayings and actions of the past that have come back to you all higgledy-piggledy, as they so often do in dreams. You learned a lot of poetry I suppose when you were at school?'

'Yes, but none like this.'

'No, I didn't suppose so, but the mere fact that your mind was at one time used to verses – acquainted with metre and rhythm, would account for the form adopted by your dream. I assure you it was purely chance – and that there is no significance in it! You are on the look out for work, is it not so?'

'I am,' Lilian Rosenberg said. 'Can you tell me where to get to it?'

'I am just thinking,' Kelson replied, 'I believe my partner, Mr. Hamar, wants a secretary. I can't, of course, say whether you would suit him. Do you type?'

'I can type and do shorthand,' Lilian Rosenberg replied eagerly, 'and I can correspond in German and French.'

'And the salary? Would two hundred a year do?'

'Yes,' after a slight pause, 'I could make it do. I should want one half-day holiday – from one o'clock – every week; and Sundays – and three weeks' holiday in the summer, and one at Christmas, and of course, the usual Bank Holidays.'

'I see!' Kelson said thoughtfully; 'you want plenty of time for amusement. Well! I will speak about it to Mr. Hamar, and if you leave me your address I will give it him. How nicely you keep your hands.'

'I manicure them every day,' Lilian Rosenberg said; then looking up at him from under the long lashes which swept her cheeks, she added, 'You won't forget to tell Mr. Hamar about me, will you? I am very anxious to get a post. You don't know what it is to be hard up, do you?'

The earnest, pleading expression in her long, dark eyes appealed to Kelson as nothing else had ever appealed to him. Since his arrival in London, he had seen many pretty faces, many beautiful eyes, but assuredly none so lovely as these. And what features! what teeth! what lips! what a chin! what a figure! It seemed to him that she was not like an ordinary girl, that she was not of the same composition as any of the girls he had ever met; that she was something hardly human – something elfish, something generated by the beautiful English woods and glades, filled with the soft glamour of the moon and stars. And all the while he was thinking thus, his heart rising in rebellion against the words of Hamar, the girl continued gazing up at him, and toying with the rings on her slender, milk-white fingers.

At last he dare look at her no longer, but stammering out his promise to do all he could to get her the vacant post, he pressed her hand gently, and bade her good morning.

Then he returned to his chair, and, leaning back in it, was seeing once again in his mind's eye the fair face of the girl who had just left him, when there was a rap at the door, and the commissionaire announced Miss Martin.

'Another of them,' Kelson said to himself. 'And about as pretty in her way as the last. Now I wonder what she wants.' He looked closely at her, but no past rose up before him – as far as this client was concerned his power of divination in that direction was nil – she was a blank.

'I've come to ask you the meaning of a dream I had last night,' she began, inwardly shuddering at the sight of so much pomade and jewellery.

'Yes,' he said with an encouraging smile, 'what was it?'

Of course she did not tell him all, but merely that she had dreamed of certain flowers and trees as, curiously enough, so had her father.

Kelson looked at her thoughtfully. Once he opened his mouth to speak and then checked himself; and it was some seconds before he actually broke silence.

'Taken separately,' he said at last, 'the ash tree portends an unexpected visit; a poppy, a visit from a man; red roses, falling in love; lilac, a present; a willow, kisses – heaps of them; bluebells, a proposal; brambles, difficulties in the way – for example, tiresome relatives; buttercups, a marriage; an ash tree, a son and heir – a dear little—'

'Thank you!' Gladys remarked, rising frigidly. 'Thank you! I will go now. What is your fee?'

'I trust, madam, you are pleased,' Kelson said in great distress.

'Will you kindly take your fee and let me out,' Gladys demanded, as he nervously placed himself in her way. 'Thank you. Good morning!'

And as she swept regally past him and down the stone passage, Hamar came out of his room and passed by her on his way to Kelson's office.

'Ye gods!' he exclaimed, eyeing the discomfited Kelson wrathfully. 'What in the world have you done to offend the lady? I never saw any one look so angry in my life. D—n it all! I hope you didn't insult her!'

'It was all your fault!' Kelson wailed. 'She asked me to tell her the meaning of a dream which was brimful of warnings against us.'

'Against us!'

'Yes, against us! I have never listened to such admonitions in a dream before. She must have some very friendly spirits watching over her. Well! what was I to do? I did my best. Mindful of what you said to me a short time ago, I put her entirely off the track; gave her an entirely misleading – and as I thought very pleasant – interpretation of the dream.'

'What did you say?'

Kelson told him.

'Jackass!' Hamar exclaimed. 'Jackass! You were far too broad. What pleases a San Francisco girl shocks a London lady. For goodness' sake have more tact another time, we don't want to get into hot water. I feel quite convinced that if any harm befalls us – if that compact is in any way broken – it will be through you. I wish to heaven the Unknown had given you some other power.'

'So do I,' Kelson groaned.

'At all events,' Hamar went on, 'the first three months is nearly at an end. Who was she?'

'Miss Gladys Martin!'

'Where does she live?'

'I don't know. I could divine nothing about her. She can't have any vices.'

'I don't suppose she has,' Hamar remarked dryly, 'Not from the look of her anyway. But there is time yet. Matt! I've taken a fancy to that girl and I mean to get hold of her somehow. I wonder if she is related to Martin – Davenport's partner! Jerusalem! What sport if she is!'

'Why? Why sport?' Kelson asked.

'Dolt! Don't you see! Martin is at our mercy. We are more than his rivals. We can drive him out of London any moment we like. His tricks indeed! Pshaw! Curtis can do them all right off the reel! And Curtis shall – we will show Martin up – make a laughing stock of him – ruin him! Unless – unless—'

'Unless what?'

'Great Scott! Don't look so alarmed! Unless – supposing that girl is his daughter – unless he gives me permission to pay my addresses to her!' – and Hamar laughed coarsely.

CHAPTER 11

LEON HAMAR CALLS ON THE MARTINS

'WHERE's Gladys?' John Martin asked as he rose with an effort, stiff and tired, from the remains of a meat tea.

In reply Miss Templeton merely pointed a finger – and went on crocheting.

Following the direction indicated, John Martin stepped out on to the lawn, and glancing round the garden called 'Gladys!' Then he listened, and there came to him snatches of a song, the words of which, full of arch sentiment, allied with (and to a large extent dependent on), a unique knowledge of and love of nature – would not have disgraced a Herrick or a Raleigh – the music – a Schubert, or a Sullivan. John Martin had spared no money in educating Gladys, and she did him credit. He thought so now, as exhausted from a hard day's poring over letters, he paused and leaned his back against a tree. A gentle breeze blew her notes to him, full of melody and mirth; fresh and young and tender – as tender as the rosebuds and violets that nestled at her bosom.

'By Jove!' John Martin murmured. 'Fancy my having a daughter like Gladys! I ought to be jolly well pleased. And so I am. The only thing I fear, is, that she'll marry some one who isn't half good enough for her! But who would be good enough for her! God alone knows! And God alone knows whether she or I ought to decide! Gladys!'

'Hulloa!', and the next moment a vision in pink emerged from the bushes.

'Gladys, I want to confide in you!'

'What's wrong, Daddy, dear?' Gladys said, thrusting an arm through his and walking him gently along with her through the glade. 'You weren't at all nice to me when we parted this morning, but you look so wearied that I'll be magnanimous and forgive you. What is it?'

'Why it's like this!' John Martin said, putting his arm round her and holding her close to him, as he used to do when, a little girl, she came sidling up to him for sugar-plums. 'Poor Dick's affairs are in a terrible muddle. Unknown to me he speculated right and left, and he has not only muddled through everything he had, but he has left a number of debts, and unfortunately I have to meet them.'

'You, Father! But why you?' Gladys cried.

'Because they were incurred in the name of the Firm. I can meet them all right, but it will be a big drain on my resources. That's worry number one. Worry number two is about young Davenport – Shiel. I don't know what to do about him. He was entirely dependent on Dick. His work as an artist doesn't bring him in enough to keep him in tobacco, and the worst of it is he doesn't seem capable of turning his hand to anything else; I can't see him starve, so I shall have to allow him something.'

'He seemed to me very intelligent,' Gladys observed, 'couldn't you take him into the Firm? Who are you going to have in his uncle's place?'

'That's the trouble!' John Martin replied. 'I do feel I want some one. I am getting on in years, my brain is not so vigorous as it used to be, and I can't go on inventing fresh tricks *ad infinitum*. Moreover, I need assistance in the purely business side of the concern. I want some one who is both business-like and inventive – some one young, brilliant and reliable.'

'You couldn't sell out I suppose?'

'No, not just at present. Thanks to poor old Dick the Firm is in rather a precarious condition! Another six months over, and we may be perfectly all right. No! I must stick on, and get another partner. And look here, Gladys, you know I let you do pretty nearly everything you like. But let me beg of you not to be too friendly with that young Davenport. I caught him looking very impressibly at you this morning, and I am quite sure, if he sees anything more of you, he will be falling head over ears in love. Which is the very last thing in the world I want!'

'That's making me out to be very attractive, Daddy,' Gladys said, looking round at him mischievously.

'And so you are, dear!' John Martin said. 'Wonderfully attractive! and none knows it better than yourself. But in this case you must think of consequences – consequences that might be disastrous to us all! Confound it all, who's this? What on earth does he want?'

Gladys gazed in astonishment. A young and very smartly dressed man was advancing towards them with a soft, cat-like tread. He was of medium height and slim build. His head disproportionately large; his right ear standing out, in proof that it had long been used as a pen-rest; his nose pronounced and Semitic in outline; his eyes, big, projecting and yellowish brown; his chin, retreating; his complexion, dark and saturnine.

Gladys shivered. 'What a horrible person!' she whispered, 'there is something positively uncanny about him. I feel cold all over and how he stares!'

'Yes – what is it?' John Martin demanded. 'Do you want to see me?'

'You're Mr. Martin, I reckon!' the stranger replied in the soft drawl, characteristic of California. 'I've come to have a little talk with you on business.'

'With me – on business!' John Martin cried. 'I don't know you! I've never seen you before!'

'You see me now anyway!' the stranger laughed, casting approving eyes at Gladys. 'My name's Leon Hamar, and I've come to talk over that show of yours.'

'D—n your impudence!' John Martin said, raising his stick threateningly. 'How dare you intrude upon me here on such a pretext.'

'Calmly, calmly, sir!' Hamar cried, his cheeks paling. 'I've come here with every intention of being civil. I am chief partner in the Modern Sorcery Company Ltd., and as conjuring figures prominently in our programme I thought you might prefer to have us as friends rather than rivals.'

'I'm sure my father need not fear your rivalry,' Gladys broke in, meeting Hamar's admiring gaze stonily.

Hamar bowed.

'If,' he said, 'you desire a proof of our ability to accomplish what we profess, I will give that proof without delay. With your per—'

'You have no permission from me, sir,' John Martin cried fiercely. 'Go!'

Hamar merely shrugged his shoulders. 'You ought not to get so heated,' he said, 'considering that exactly twenty feet below where you are standing is a spring. All you have to do is to mark the spot, and sink a well, and there will be no need for you to use the Company's water. As you are probably aware, spring water is a thousand times clearer and purer. Also,' he went on, stepping hastily back as John Martin again raised his stick, 'in the trunk of that elm over yonder is a hollow about eight feet from the ground, and if you look inside it, you will discover an iron box full of curios and jewellery. Shall I—'

'No!' retorted John Martin. 'If you don't go instantly I'll send for the police,' – and Hamar, coming to the conclusion that upon this occasion discretion was better than valour, hurriedly beat a retreat.

'You'll be sorry, John Martin!' he shouted from a safe distance, 'and so will Miss Gladys, charming Miss Gladys. But remember you have only yourselves to blame. Ta-ta!', and the next moment he was lost to sight.

'Well!' Gladys ejaculated, 'of all the beastly cads I have ever seen he fairly takes the biscuit. What colossal cheek! The idea of his coming here and speaking to us like that! Can't we prosecute him, Father?'

'Hardly!' John Martin replied, 'best leave him alone. I wish he hadn't come! He's upset me! My nerves are anyhow! Which was the tree he spoke about?'

'This one,' Gladys exclaimed, walking up to an elm, and patting it with her hand, 'but you surely don't believe what he said, do you? It was all rubbish from start to finish. Daddy, my dear old Daddy, I do believe you are worrying about it.'

'Hold my hat and stick a moment,' John Martin said, and making a spring, which for one of his age and weight showed surprising agility, he succeeded in catching hold of one of the nearest lateral branches. The elm being old, the bark had become very gnarled and uneven, and thus the difficulty of ascension lay more in semblance, perhaps, than in reality. Embracing the huge trunk, as closely as possible, with his arms and knees, much to the detriment of his clothes, seizing with his hands some projections, and resting his feet upon others, John Martin, after one or two narrow escapes from falling, at length wriggled himself into the first great fork, and paused to wipe his forehead.

'Oh, do take care, Father!' Gladys pleaded, 'you'll fall and break your neck. Do be sensible and come down now.'

But John Martin paid no attention, he went on groping.

'I've found it,' he suddenly shouted. 'That bounder was right, the trunk is hollow.' He was silent then, for some minutes, and Gladys could only see his boots. Then there was a muffled oath, a sound of choking and gasping, which made Gladys' blood run cold, and then – a great cry. 'There's something here, something hard and heavy. It's a box, an iron box! Take it from me.' And leaning as far down as he dared, he placed in Gladys' outstretched hands, a rusty iron box. Then there was the sound of scraping and tearing, and John Martin gradually lowered himself to the ground – his coat covered with green, and the knees of his trousers ripped to pieces.

Gladys ran indoors for a hammer and chisel, and, the hinges of the box being worn with age and exposure, it was but the work of a few seconds to break it open. It was full of gold and silver coins and jewellery; there were only a few gold pieces, the greater number of the coins were silver – the bulk Georgian – and their dates ranged from 1697 to 1750. The jewellery consisted of several massive gold bracelets, (two or three of very fine workmanship); some dozen or so plain gold rings; two silver watches, and a varied assortment of silver trinkets. All were more or less antique, but none – apart from the gold bracelets – of any great value.

'Well!' John Martn exclaimed, as they concluded their examination of the articles, 'what do you make of it?'

'Why that man put them there, of course,' Gladys said, 'can't you see the whole thing is nothing but a dodge to intimidate you into forming a friendship with him. I daresay he had heard that Mr. Davenport is dead, and thinks he sees an opportunity to be taken into partnership. He had a horrid face – sly and cunning, and his way of looking at me was positively disgusting. It makes me feel sick and horrid even to think of it.'

'What shall we do with these things?' John Martin asked, picking up one of the watches and eyeing it with curiosity.

'Are they ours?' Gladys replied.

'I certainly consider we've a right to keep them,' her father said, 'since we've found them ourselves on our own property, but I suppose, legally, they are treasure trove and ought to be given up.'

'Then surely the Government would pay us something for them, wouldn't it?'

'I should think so, at least a decent Government would. Anyhow, I think to give them up will be our best course. I doubt if the whole lot is worthy fifty pounds. Where was it he said there was water?'

'Good gracious!' Gladys exclaimed, 'you don't mean to say you are going to bother about that now!'

'It was here, I think,' John Martin went on, thrusting his stick in the ground, 'to the best of my knowledge – and I had experts' advice – there is no water anywhere near here. Had there been, I should not have gone to the expense of having pipes laid down to feed the pond.'

'Oh, Father, how can you be so silly,' Gladys cried, 'of course there isn't any water here. It's only a trick, a trick to frighten you – and I'm beginning to think it has succeeded.'

'I shall try here anyway to-morrow,' John Martin said grimly. 'Let us go in now.'

When Gladys went into the garden on the following morning she beheld an extraordinary sight. Her father, the gardener, and a man whom she did not recognize at first, as his back was turned towards her, but who, to her utter astonishment, proved to be Shiel Davenport, were hard at work, digging a pit.

Her father paused every now and then, and rested; but he did not allow the others a moment's respite. Every time they were about to slack, he urged them on. It was all very well for the gardener who was accustomed to it, but it was obviously killing work for Shiel Davenport, and

Gladys – as soon as she had overcome a preliminary outburst of laughter – gave vent to her sympathies.

'What a shame,' she exclaimed, 'Father how can you? Poor Mr. Davenport looks ready to drop. Take a rest, Mr. Davenport! Do – you have my permission.'

Looking very hot and exhausted, Shiel Davenport threw down his spade and attempted to make himself presentable.

'His clothes will be ruined, Father,' Gladys said, indignantly.

'They're not his clothes – he's wearing an old suit of mine,' John Martin explained, trying to appear unconcerned.

Shiel forced a laugh. 'I'm rather out of form, Miss Martin, I haven't had much exercise lately.'

'You're getting it now anyway,' John Martin chuckled.

'And it's blistered your hands horribly!' Gladys cried, pointing to several raw places. 'I will fetch you a pair of father's gloves – he's a brute!'

'Please don't trouble,' Shiel exclaimed, 'I'll use my handkerchief instead. Digging is even harder work than painting – in one way.'

'It's not fit work for you,' Gladys replied with another reproachful glance at her father. 'When did you arrive, I never heard you?'

'I 'phoned to him last night,' John Martin said, looking rather sheepish. 'I thought a day out here would do him good. He thought so too, and came on by the seven o'clock train. We've been digging ever since breakfast – but a bit of exercise won't hurt him, and I'll give him plenty of vaseline presently.'

They resumed work again; and Gladys retired indoors. At eleven o'clock John Martin let Shiel go. 'You can amuse yourself till luncheon with books and papers,' he said, 'you'll find plenty of them in my study. I'll join you later.'

But Shiel had other ideas of amusing himself, and as soon as he had washed and changed back into his own clothes, he followed the sounds of music until he reached the drawing-room.

'I'm sure you must feel dreadfully tired,' Gladys said, leaving off playing. 'It was too bad of Father to make you work like that.'

'I'm afraid your father thinks me a very useless article,'

Shiel replied, seating himself in an easy chair, and trying his hardest not to look too ardently. 'And an artist is not much good outside his profession.'

'Who is?' Gladys smiled. 'Shall you still go on painting?'

'Now that my uncle has died? It all depends – depends on whether he has been able to leave me anything in his will. From one or two things your father has said I fear he has not – in which case I don't quite know what I shall do. I could hardly expect Mr. Martin to take me into his firm.'

'Aren't you any good at invention?' Gladys asked, 'I know he wants some one who is – some one who can help him devise fresh tricks. This everlasting racking of the brains to think of something new is beginning to be too much for him.'

'I wish I could be of some use,' Shiel said, 'both for his sake and mine, and may I add yours. Anyhow I'll try. I have a certain amount of imagination – I suppose most artists have, and henceforth I'll devote it to trickery.'

'No, not to trickery!' Gladys said, 'to conjuring!'

'Well, to conjuring then – to planning something novel and startling in the way of a trick. And as they say, two heads are better than one, perhaps you will help me.'

'I,' Gladys laughed, 'why I've never invented anything in my life, barring a song.'

'Nevertheless I'm sure you would be of great help to me,' Shiel said; 'you would at least criticize my efforts, wouldn't you?'

'Oh, I should certainly do that,' Gladys laughingly rejoined, 'and probably do more harm than good.'

'You could never do any harm!' Shiel said, with so much eagerness that Gladys got up and began searching for a piece of music. 'I would give anything to paint you.'

'I have been painted – twice,' Gladys observed.

'For the R.A.?'

'Yes! I didn't much care about it, and I grew desperately tired of sitting.'

'Who painted you?'

'Heniblow painted me once, and Darker painted me once.'

'Then it's useless for me even to think of it. How did they treat you in their pictures?'

'Heniblow painted me in evening dress, and Darker

painted me in the character of Enid – you know, the Enid in the "Idylls of the King." '

'Yes. But I should like to paint you as "Melody in Flower Land." '

'I'm afraid I can't grasp it,' Gladys said.

'Can't you!' Shiel exclaimed, 'I can. The idea came to me when I heard you singing just now, and saw you sitting here, in the midst of flowers, and dressed like a rose. I should paint you clad as you are now – all in pink – seated in the garden singing; and all the flowers leaning towards you listening. I would give anything to paint it,' and he spoke with such enthusiasm that Gladys, remembering her dream, flushed.

'I think,' she said, 'we might go into the garden and see how the work is progressing.'

'I fear I can't do any more digging,' Shiel put in hastily, 'I willingly would if I could, but I really can't use my hands.'

'And you've not had any vaseline,' Gladys cried. 'I'll get you some,' and before he could prevent her she had gone.

She was back again, however, in a few moments with a tiny white jar and some linen bandages. 'I couldn't find my aunt,' she began, 'or she would bandage your hands for you.'

'Won't you?' Shiel asked. 'Do!'

He thrust his hands towards her as he spoke, and Gladys uttered an exclamation of horror – the palms and fingers were raw and swollen.

'I feel heartily ashamed of myself for being so thin-skinned,' Shiel said. But Gladys had disappeared. She returned almost immediately with a bowl of water.

'I'm sure they must hurt you dreadfully,' she exclaimed, as she gently bathed the hands. 'It makes me feel quite ill to see them.'

For the next few moments Shiel was in Paradise. The touch of her cool, white fingers on his hot and burning skin was far nicer than anything he had ever imagined. Her sweet-scented breath stealing gently up his nostrils soothed away all his care – even the remembrance of his recent loss.

With his whole heart and soul concentrated in his gaze, he watched her every movement – watched the waving and tossing of the stray wisps of hair over her temples and ears, as the breeze rustled through the open windows; and the gentle tightening and relaxation of her delicately moulded lips each time she breathed.

Shiel had always led a very solitary existence. Apart from his uncle he had no near relatives, and with the exception of the five or six weeks in the year he had always been in rooms. He had often felt lonely, but never quite so lonely as now – now that the only person he had known intimately and for whom he had entertained any real affection, was suddenly taken away. He was now absolutely alone in the world, and the poignancy of his position came home to him acutely.

It is a terrible thing to be lonely. Lonely men do all sorts of dreadful things – things they would certainly never dream of doing if they had companionship. And Shiel was doing a dreadful thing now. Every moment he was falling more and more desperately in love, despite the fact that he had no money, and worse still – no prospects of ever making any. And loneliness was in the main responsible for it.

Had he not been so lonely – had he not spent days and days, alone in lodgings, with no one to talk to – no one to care whether he were ill or dying; had this not been the experience he was even then undergoing, reason would have outweighed folly, and even though he might have realized that in Gladys Martin he had found his ideal of beauty – of womanliness, he would have been content only to admire.

As it was, he was in that very dangerous mood when the heart yearns for sympathy; when a plain woman's sympathy means much – and a pretty woman's more than much. It is no exaggeration to say that Shiel would have lain down and died for Gladys ten times over. For her sake – if only to see her smile, no mere physical pain would have been too excruciating for him to bear. And when she put the finishing touches to the bandages, and quite by chance, of course, their eyes met, he looked at her, as if he never meant to do anything else but look at her for all eternity.

Whether she understood as much or not, is impossible to say. Shiel asked himself the question over and over again before the day was out, and in his sleep, and during the next day, and for many days afterwards. Could she tell how much he admired her? How much he worshipped her? All that he was prepared to do for her sweet sake? All this he asked himself repeatedly, and went on thinking of her when he knew he ought never to have thought of her at all.

'I'm sure your hands are more comfortable now. Won't you go into the garden and see how the work is progressing?' she said. 'Or if you are afraid Father will want you to dig again, perhaps you would like to go into his study and read the papers.'

'I should like to stay here and listen to you singing,' he said. 'Mayn't I do that?'

'You might,' she said, 'but I have to go out.'

'Then I'll stay here till you return,' he said, 'I've never been in such a delightful room.'

'What do you think of Shiel Davenport?' Gladys remarked to her aunt a few minutes later. 'I don't think I've ever met such an extraordinary young man. He does nothing but stare at me, and when I ask him to do one thing he suggests doing another. He's the most difficult person to manage. In fact, I can't manage him at all.'

'Never mind about managing him, my dear,' Miss Templeton replied, 'so long as you don't let him manage you. Young men who do nothing but stare are not merely difficult – they are dangerous.'

CHAPTER 12

THE GREAT CHALLENGE

When John Martin came in to tea that afternoon, he gave Gladys a shock. Despite the fact that he had been in the sun all day and was much tanned in consequence he had never looked – so Gladys thought – so old and haggard.

'You dear old Daddy!' she said, hastening to pour him out some tea, 'you shouldn't work so hard – this silly digging has quite knocked you up! Haven't you finished?'

'Yes, I've finished!' John Martin said, catching his breath. 'I've found water!'

'Nonsense!'

'It's true all the same. We struck it at exactly the distance he said – twenty feet.'

'Then of course he knew.'

'How? How the deuce could he have known?'

'I can't say,' Gladys replied. 'All I know is, that he's not straight, and that there's some underhand trickery going on. But do have your tea now, and dismiss it from your mind. Anyhow, he can do you no harm.'

'Here's a letter for you, John,' Mrs. Templeton exclaimed, entering the room at that moment.

John Martin took it from her, and tore open the envelope curiously. It was a handwriting he did not know, and did not like – its characteristics were sinister.

'I knew it!' he cried; 'I knew the fellow was a scoundrel. What the deuce do you think he has the impertinence to do now?'

'He!' Gladys said, looking anxiously at her father. 'Whoever do you mean?'

'Why, that confounded young bounder who came here last night – Leon Hamar he signs himself. In this letter he declares that he can perform any of our tricks, and will accept the wager I offered for their solution some little time ago. He also says that unless I consent to see him, and to listen courteously to what he has to say, he will publicly announce his intention of taking up the wager, at our Hall, in Kingsway, to-night.'

'Do you think there is any possibility of his having discovered the secrets of your tricks?' Gladys asked. 'Could he have bribed any one to tell him?'

'I don't think so,' John Martin said. 'The only people who have any clue as to how they are done are my two attendants – both as you know natives of Cashmere, and men who, I feel certain, could not be "got at."'

'In that case,' Gladys remarked, 'I fail to see what there is to worry about. Your course is perfectly clear – take no notice of it.'

John Martin was silent – dazed. He did not know what to think or do! There was something painfully ominous to him in the discovery of the money and the water – something that accentuated the impression Hamar's sinister appearance had made on him. The man did not look ordinary – his manner, gestures, walk and expression were decidedly abnormal – in fact they put him in mind of the superphysical. The superphysical! Might that not account for his knowledge? Bah! There was no such thing as the superphysical. The man was extraordinary – but, after all, only a man – his knowledge only that of a man. And it must be as the shrewd Gladys conjectured – he had put the money in the tree himself and had learned of water through some subtle artifice – perhaps only guessed at it. He would defy him – let him do what he would!

This was John Martin's decision as he finished tea. An hour later he had changed his mind, and was speaking to Hamar on the telephone, expressing his willingness to grant him a brief interview if he came at once.

In rather less than an hour a motor drew up at the Martins' door and Hamar stepped out of it.

'Glad to find you in a more tractable mood, Mr. Martin,' he exclaimed on being ushered into the latter's presence. 'I reckoned you would sing to a different tune when you found that water. Would you like me to give you a few more samples of my skill, before we proceed to business?'

'Name your business at once,' John Martin replied gruffly; 'I haven't many minutes to spare.'

'No!' Hamar said, 'that's a pity; because part of what I have at the back of my brain may take more than a few minutes arranging. The situation in a nutshell is this. You have a pretty daughter, Mr. Martin?'

'How dare you, sir?' John Martin broke in, clenching his fist.

'Gently, gently, Mr. Martin!' Hamar observed, backing towards the door. 'Gently – you promised to give me a courteous hearing. I meant no offence. I say I admire your daughter immensely – she takes the shine out of our American girls.'

'The deuce she does!' John Martin foamed.

'She does, you bet!' Hamar went on. 'And I see no reason if she likes me, why we couldn't get engaged. I would do the thing handsomely as far as money goes. What do you say?'

'I say that unless you're very careful I shall break my promise and kick you.'

'I would pay you a big lump sum to take me into partnership,' Hamar went on complacently, 'and I would introduce a number of new tricks that would stagger

115

creation. I shouldn't be in any hurry to marry – the length of the engagement would be for you to decide.'

'Then it would be *ad infinitum*,' John Martin said grimly, 'for you'll never get my consent to a marriage.'

'Never is a long day – and even a John Martin may change. You want new blood and new capital in your Firm – you would have both in me. I assure you your show would boom as it has never boomed before!'

'And the only condition on which you offer me all this is my daughter?'

'You have said it – that is the one and only condition. Your daughter – my brains, my dollars.'

'I have decided!' John Martin said.

'Good!' Hamar exclaimed; 'I guessed you would! There's nothing like the almighty dollar, is there?'

'Yes!' John Martin rejoined; 'the almighty fist – and that's what you'll get if you don't clear out of this house instantly. And if you ever come skulking round here again, or write me any more letters I'll set my solicitor on to you.'

'Then it's war – war to the knife!' Hamar sneered. 'How melodramatic! But it won't last long. I shall be your partner – and I shall yet have Miss Gladys! *Au revoir* – I won't say good-bye!' and with a mock bow he hurriedly took his departure.

That night Messrs. Martin and Davenport's entertainment had progressed as usual for about half an hour when it suddenly came to a full stop. A man in the lower tier of boxes had risen and was addressing the audience in a loud voice: 'Ladies and gentlemen!'

In an instant all heads swung round and there were stentorian shouts of 'Silence!'

But Curtis – for it was he – was not easily daunted. 'Do you call this fair play!' he demanded; 'I am here to-night to make a sporting offer, and one which will afford you vast entertainment.'

Cries of 'Shut up!' 'Silence!' 'He's drunk!' 'Turn him out!' merging into one loud roar forced him to pause. Several uniformed officials now invaded the box, but Hamar – who, as well as Kelson, was with Curtis – fixing them with his big dark eyes that gleamed eerily in the half-lowered lights of the house – for the stage only at that moment was fully illuminated – held them in check, and they hung back not knowing what to do. This move of Hamar's took with a large section of the audience – some of whom were possessed with sporting instincts, whilst others were merely curious – and the somewhat premature cries of 'Turn him out!' etc., were soon lost in vociferous shouts of 'Let them alone!' 'Let them speak!' 'Let us hear what they have to say.' It was in the midst of this hubbub that John Martin in a great state of nervous agitation came to the front of the stage and inquired the cause of the commotion. The shouting still continued, and Gladys, who had come to the performance anticipating something of the sort, called to her father, from the wings, bidding him give Curtis permission to speak.

'You will lose all sympathy if you don't, Father,' she added; 'and besides you have nothing to fear. It's sheer bravado and impudence on their part.'

Thus advised, for Gladys was a level-headed girl, John Martin gave in; and the audience showed their approval by a vigorous round of clapping.

'I wish I were spokesman,' Kelson sighed, his eyes glistening at the sight of so many pretty upturned faces. 'Go on, old man!' he added, giving Curtis a nudge. 'Fire away, and show them you know a bit about elocution, for the credit of the Firm.'

Curtis needed no encouragement. What little bashfulness he had once possessed he had certainly left behind in San Francisco, for he leaned over the front of the box and smiled familiarly at the audience.

'I am Edward Curtis,' he said, 'one of the directors of the Modern Sorcery Company Ltd. Messrs. Martin and Davenport have so often boasted that no one outside their firm can perform their tricks that I have come here to-night resolved to disillusion them. I not only accept their offer of ten thousand pounds for the solution of their tricks, but I agree to pay them double that amount – cash down – if I do not do everything they do – from 'The Brass Coffin' to their world-famed 'Pumpkin Puzzle.' With Messrs. Martin and Davenport's permission I will explain one and all of their tricks to you to-night, and the only thing I ask of you, ladies and gentlemen, is to see that I get fair play.'

A spontaneous outburst of clapping followed this speech, and as soon as it had ceased one of the audience who had risen and was waiting to speak, said: 'I trust Messrs.

Martin and Davenport will accept this challenge, and allow the Modern Sorcery Company the opportunity here, in this hall to-night, of displaying their skill – or their ignorance, as the case may be. If Messrs. Martin and Davenport's tricks cannot be performed by any outsider – the Firm in accepting this challenge will merely be twenty thousand pounds the richer – and if – as is hardly likely, Messrs. Martin and Davenport should be outwitted, I am sure they themselves will be amongst the first to congratulate their successful rivals. I, for one, am quite ready to act as referee.'

'I too!' shouted a dozen other voices. 'Be a sport and accept his bet!'

'Ladies and gentlemen,' John Martin replied with dignity, 'you have given me no alternative, I accept the challenge. Perhaps those who have so kindly volunteered to act as referees will see that order is maintained whilst I go on with my performance, at the conclusion of which Mr. Curtis – I think that is the name of my rival – will be quite at liberty to try his exposition of my tricks.'

The performance then proceeded, and when it was over, Curtis, Hamar and Kelson, accompanied by six of those of the audience who had volunteered to act as referees, stepped on to the stage. Seats were provided for the referees – three on the one side of the stage and three on the other; and having seen that everything was fair and square John Martin retired to the O.P. wing, behind which Gladys was concealed.

A brief description of 'The Brass Coffin' trick, which was the first Messrs. Hamar, Curtis and Kelson proceeded to explain, will, perhaps, suffice.

A massively constructed brass-bound coffin is handed round to the audience, who carefully examine it, and being unable to discover anything amiss, pronounce themselves satisfied that it is genuine.

The operator then summons an assistant, jokingly refers to him as 'the corpse' – puts him into a sack, made to represent a winding-sheet, securely binds the sack with a piece of cord, and asks one of the audience to seal it. The sack and its contents are then placed in the coffin which is locked and corded. The operator then throws a sheet over the coffin, lets it remain there for a few seconds, and on removing it and opening the lid, the coffin is found to be empty. A shout from the front of the House makes every one turn round, when, to their amazement, 'the corpse' is seen standing up at the back of 'the Pit,' holding the sack with the rope and seal – intact– in his hand. Such was the marvellous feat which had been accomplished in Martin and Davenport's Hall night in and night out for years, the solution of which no one as yet had been able to discover. One can imagine, in these circumstances, the tremendous excitement of the audience at the prospect of seeing this notorious puzzle tackled – and tackled by a member of the Firm which was was already reputed to be doing all kinds of weird and extraordinary things. But, whereas it was quite obvious that John Martin was greatly perturbed (his eyebrows were working nervously, and his lips and fingers twitching), Curtis, on the other hand, was as cool as possible – he literally did not turn a hair.

'Now, gentlemen,' he said, turning to the referees, 'keep your eyes well skinned and observe everything I do. Ladies and gentlemen,' he went on, raising his voice, 'I am now about to show you how the coffin trick is done. Observe me – I'm "the corpse" – Mr. Kelson, here, is the operator—' and Matt Kelson, rather to Hamar's annoyance advanced, down the stage to take part in the proceedings.

'Watch me get into the sack!' He stepped into it as he spoke. 'Look at what I have in my hand,' he went on, holding up his right hand in full view of the audience. 'I have a plug of wood covered with the same material as this sack. As soon as I stoop down and the sack is pulled over me I shall thrust this plug into the mouth of it and Mr. Kelson will bind the sack round it. I shall then be put into the coffin. You think you know this coffin but you don't. See!' – and stepping out of the sack he tapped the head of the coffin, which was very broad and deep. 'Come closer!' and he beckoned to the referees, whose numbers were now augmented by three newspaper reporters – representatives of the *Daily Snapper,* the *Planet* and the *Hooter* respectively. 'Here is a secret panel worked by a spring. I will press, and you will press too.'

And amidst a breathless silence – the nine members of the audience on the stage following every movement – Curtis put his hand inside the head of the coffin and touched a very slight elevation in the wood. In an instant, by a wonderfully neat piece of mechanism, a panel slid back, leaving just sufficient room for a man of moderate dimensions to squeeze through.

Everyone now looked at John Martin – he was leaning back in his chair, breathing hard, his eyes starting out of his head, his cheeks white. Hamar saw him and grinned, grinned malevolently, but the smile died out of his face when he glanced at Gladys – the scorn in the girl's eyes made his blood boil.

'All right, Miss Martin,' he muttered between his teeth; 'you adopt that attitude now, but you will adopt a very different one later on! I'll win you body and soul, or my name is not what it is.'

He was interrupted in this amiable reflection by Curtis. 'I'm too stout to play the rôle of the corpse, and so is Matt,' Curtis said to him; 'you must undertake that part. Now!' he went on, 'take this plug and get into the sack,' and he whispered a few instructions in his ear. Then he tied the top of the sack – in reality tying it round the plug Hamar was holding – and one of the audience sealed the knot. Curtis and Kelson then lifted Hamar into the coffin, shut the lid and corded it. Then Curtis, turning to the audience, said:

'What is now happening inside the coffin is this – "the corpse" pulls the plug out of the mouth of the sack from the inside. The cord thus becomes loose and "the corpse" is able to open the sack. He at once touches the spring I pointed out to you in the head of the coffin, and the panel slides back – So!'

And as the audience looked, they saw the panel slide back, and first of all Hamar's head, and then his body, wriggle through the aperture thus made.

'The reason why you, audience, cannot see him make his escape is this,' Curtis explained; 'the head of the coffin is always turned away from you and placed against a mirror which you can't see, and which to you appears but the continuation of the stage. In this mirror exactly opposite the head of the coffin is an aperture, and it is through this "the corpse" makes his exit to the back of the stage. I will show it you. Here it is' – and beckoning to the referees to come quite close, he pointed to a glass screen, in the centre of the base of which was a glass trap-door, corresponding in height and girth to the head of the coffin.

'Here, corpse!' Curtis said, 'crawl through' – and Hamar, looking as if he by no means appreciated the undignified task of wriggling on his stomach before so many eyes, drew himself as tight together as he could, and squirmed through.

'Does that satisfy you, gentlemen?' Curtis inquired.

'Perfectly!' the referees answered. 'Nothing could be plainer. We see exactly, now, how the trick is done.'

At this there was a loud outburst of clapping, and Curtis bowed in the elegant manner in which he had been patiently and assiduously coached by Kelson.

He then proceeded to the second trick – 'Eve at the Window,' a trick almost, if not quite, as famous as 'The Brass Coffin,' and for the solution of which Martin and Davenport had frequently offered huge sums of money.

A large pane of glass some nine by six feet in area, and set in a frame, made to represent that of a window, is placed on the stage, about eighteen inches from the floor. Thirty-six inches from the ground a wooden shelf is placed against the window. An assistant – usually a woman – then mounts on the shelf and, looking out of the glass, proceeds to kiss her hand vigorously. The operator in a shocked voice asks her to desist. She refuses and, to the amusement of the audience, carries on her pantomimic flirtation more desperately than before. The operator pretends to lose his temper, and snatching up a screen places it at the back of her. He then fires a pistol, pulls aside the screen, and she has vanished. As the top, bottom and sides of the window, all in fact except the very middle, have been in full view of the audience, and as the window has been tightly closed all the time, the disappearance of the girl completely mystifies the audience.

Curtis explained it all. He pointed out that the keynote to the illusion lay behind the wooden shelf, which was so placed as to conceal the fact that the lower part of the window was made double, the bottom of the upper part being concealed from view by a second sheet of silvered glass placed in front of it. The shelf covers the line of junction and enables the window frame to be scrutinized by the audience.

As soon as the screen is put in front of the lady on the shelf – the glass pane slides up about a foot and a half into the top of the frame, purposely made very deep. The bottom of the window is cut away in the middle, leaving an aperture about two feet square, which was previously hidden from view by the double glass at the base. Eve makes her exit through this hole, and slides on to a board placed beneath the window in readiness for her. The pane of glass then slides down again, the screen is removed, and the window appears just as solid as before.

When Curtis concluded his verbal explanation he gave the audience a practical illustration of how the thing was done; he manipulated the screen and pistol, whilst Hamar posed as Eve, and directly he had finished there was another outburst of applause. Kelson dared not look at John Martin or Gladys. The brief glance he had taken of them at the conclusion of the giving away of the first trick had shocked him – and he purposely stood with his back to them. With Hamar it was otherwise – the joy of triumph was strong within him, and the picture of John Martin, leaning forward in his chair, with his mouth half open and a dazed, glassy expression in his eyes, only thrilled him with pleasure; he laughed at the old man, and still more at Gladys.

'That's the way to treat a girl of that sort,' he whispered to Kelson; 'scoff at her – scoff at her well. Let her see you don't care a snap for her – and in the end she'll run after you and haunt you to death.'

'I'm not so sure,' Kelson said. 'It might act in some cases, perhaps, but I don't think you can quite depend on it.'

'Pooh! You are no judge of women, in spite of all your experience,' Hamar retorted. 'I'll bet you anything you like she'll come round and make a tremendous fuss of me.'

'Supposing you fall in love with her, how about the compact?' Kelson said. 'You've warned me often enough.'

'Oh, but I'm not like you,' Hamar replied. 'There's nothing soft in my nature. I fall in love! Not much! Why, you might as well have apprehensions of my joining the Salvation Army, or wanting to become a Militant Suffragette – either would be just about as possible. No—! I shall make the girl love me – and we shall be engaged for just as long as I please. If I find some one that attracts me more, I shall throw her aside – if not, maybe, I shall marry her – but in either case there will be no question of love –

at least not on my part. She shall do as I want – that is all! Hulloa! Curtis is beginning again.'

There were five other tricks on the programme – all of which were world renowned. They were 'The Floating Head', 'The Mango Seed'; 'The Haunted Bathing-machine'; 'The Girl with the Five Eyes.' and 'The Vanishing Bicycle' illusion. As with the first two tricks, so Curtis did with the following five – he explained them, and then, aided by Hamar and Kelson, gave practical demonstrations of their solutions; and so thoroughly and clearly were these solutions demonstrated that the referees asked no questions – they were absolutely satisfied. Turning to the audience – at a sign from Curtis – they announced that the whole of Messrs. Martin and Davenport's tricks had been solved to their entire satisfaction, and that Messrs. Hamar, Curtis and Kelson of the Modern Sorcery Company Ltd. had, without doubt, won the wager.

'Have you anything to say?' Curtis asked, addressing John Martin.

'I acknowledge my defeat, though I do not understand it!' John Martin said with very white lips. 'I shall pay you the ten thousand pounds to-night.'

'Don't worry about that,' Hamar interposed; 'we don't want to take your money, all we wanted to do was to prove to you we could perform the tricks you believed to be insoluble.

'Ladies and gentlemen!' he went on, raising his voice, 'the Modern Sorcery Company Ltd. has given you some proof to-night of their capabilities in the conjuring line, and if you will give us the pleasure of your company to-morrow night – we invite you all free of charge for the occasion – we will give you a still further demonstration of our powers. May we count upon your patronage?'

A terrific storm of clapping was the reply, and as the audience slowly filed from the hall, John Martin staggered into the wing, reeled past Gladys ere she could catch him, and sank helplessly on to the floor.

CHAPTER 13

THE MODERN SORCERY COMPANY LTD.
GIVE A GRATIS PERFORMANCE

The days that followed were dark days for Gladys. Her father, whom she loved – and, until now, had never realized how much she loved – lay seriously ill. He had had a stroke which, although fortunately slight, must, as the doctor said, be regarded as a prelude to what would happen, unless he was kept very quiet. And to keep him quiet was not an easy thing to do. His mind continually reverted to what had just taken place, and he was for ever asking Gladys to tell him whether anything further had occurred in connection with it, whether there was anything about it in the papers.

Gladys, of course, was obliged to dissemble. She hated anything approaching dissimulation, but on this occasion there was no help for it, and what she told John Martin was the reverse of what she knew to be actually happening. The papers were full to overflowing with accounts of that fatal night's proceedings, and of the marvellous gratis exhibition given on the succeeding evening by the Modern Sorcery Company Ltd.

The *Hooter*, for example, had a full column on the middle page headed in large type—

EXTRAORDINARY SCENE

AT

MARTIN AND DAVENPORT'S

THE GREATEST CONJURING TRICKS

IN THE WORLD SOLVED!

Whilst the *Daily Snapper*, determined to be none the less sensational, began thus:

MYSTERIES NO LONGER!

'THE BRASS COFFIN TRICK' AND 'EVE AT THE WINDOW'

DONE AT LAST!

MARTIN AND DAVENPORT

LOSE THEIR PRESTIGE

This was bad enough, but the *Planet* published a paragraph that was even more galling, viz.—

'Now that Messrs. Martin and Davenport's great Illusions have been explained and their Hall in Kingsway, so long famous as the Home of Puzzledom, of necessity shorn of its glamour, one need not be surprised if those who delight in this kind of mystery, should turn elsewhere for their amusement. The British Public, which is above all things enamoured of novelty, will, doubtless, now resort to the Modern Sorcery Company, whose House in Cockspur Street bids fair to become the future home of everything uncanny. Their programme – to the uninitiated – presents possibilities – and impossibilities.'

So said the *Planet*, and as the number of attendances at Martin and Davenport's fell from 820 on the night of the challenge to 89 on the succeeding night, whilst the Modern Sorcery Company's Hall was filled to overflowing, there was every prospect of its prediction being verified. The solution of Martin and Davenport's tricks had taken place (Hamar had so planned it) on the last night the trio possessed the property of divination, and, consequently, on the night that terminated the first stage of their compact. The following night they would be in possession of new powers, such powers as would warrant them giving a gratis exhibition – an exhibition of jugglery absolutely new and unprecedented. That the exhibition was successful may be gathered from the following article in the *Daily Cyclone*—

'MARVELLOUS DISPLAY OF PSYCHIC PHENOMENA IN COCKSPUR STREET.

'The Modern Sorcery Company Ltd., in their new premises in Cockspur Street, gave the most remarkable display of Phenomena it has ever yet fallen to our lot to report. Indeed, the performances were of such an extraordinary nature that the huge audience, *en masse*, was scared; not a few people fainted, while every now and again were heard screams of terror intermingled with long protracted "Ohs!" '

A brief *résumé* of the entertainment ran as follows:

The first part of the Modern Sorcery Company's programme was carried out by Mr. Leon Hamar, solus, who, stepping to the front of the stage, announced that he was about to give a display of clairvoyance. Without further prelude he pointed to various members of the audience, and described spiritual presences he saw standing behind them. He did not say he could see a spirit, answering to the name of James or George – or some such equally familiar name – and then proceed to give a description of it, so elastic, that with very little stretching it would undoubtedly have fitted nine out of every ten people one meets with every day, but unlike any other clairvoyants we have known, he described the individual physical and moral traits of the people he professed to see. For example: To a lady sitting in the third row of the stalls, he said: 'There is the phantasm of an elderly gentleman standing behind you. He has a vivid scar on his right cheek that looks as if it might have been caused by a sabre cut. He has a grey military moustache, a very marked chin; wears his hair parted in the middle, and has light-blue eyes that are fixed ferociously on the gentleman seated on your left. Do you recognize the person I am describing?'

'I think so,' the lady answered in a faint voice.

'I will spare you a description of his person,' Hamar went on, 'but I should like to remind you that he met with a rather peculiar accident. He was looking over some engineering works in Leeds, when some one pushed him, and he was instantly whipped off the ground by a piece of revolving machinery and dashed to pieces against the ceiling. Am I right?'

There was no reply – but the sigh, we think, was more significant than words.

Mr. Hamar then turned to a lady in the next row. 'I can see behind you,' he said, 'an old dowager with yellow hair. She wears large emerald drop earrings, black satin skirt, and a heliotrope bodice of which she appears to be somewhat vain. She is coughing terribly. She died of pneumonia, brought about by the excessive zeal of – Ahem! – of her relatives – for the open-air treatment. Contrary to expectations, however, all her money went to a Society in Hanover Square – a Society for the Antipropagation of Children. I think you know the lady to whom I refer.'

Mr. Hamar had again hit the mark.

'Only too well!' came the indignant and spontaneous reply.

Mr. Hamar then turned to a man in the fifth row. 'Hulloa!' he exclaimed. 'What have we here – an Irish terrier answering to the name of "Peg." It is standing upright with its two front paws resting on your knees. It is looking up into your face, and its mouth is open as if anticipating a lump of sugar. From the marks on its body I should say it has been killed by being run over?'

Again Mr. Hamar was correct. 'What you say is absolutely true,' the gentleman replied; 'I had a dog named Peg. I was greatly attached to it, and it was run over in Piccadilly by a motor cyclist. I hate the very sight of a motor bicycle.'

After a brief interval of awestruck silence a voice from the gallery called out—

'You are in league with him!'

Then the man in the stalls stood up, and essayed to speak; but his voice was drowned in a perfect tornado of applause. He had no need – he was instantly recognized – he was J – B—. With a few more examples of clairvoyance Mr Hamar continued to entertain his audience for half an hour or so, by the end of which time, we have no hesitation in saying that every one was convinced that he actually saw what he said he saw.

The second part of the programme was entirely in the

hands of Mr. Curtis, who now came forward with a bow. 'Ladies and gentlemen,' he said; 'you all know that man is complex – that he is composed of mind and matter, the material and immaterial. I now propose to give you a physical demonstration of this fact. Will twelve of the audience kindly come up on the stage and sit around me, so that you may feel quite certain that I have here no mechanical devices to assist me?' – And amongst other well-known people who responded to Mr. Curtis's request, were Lord Bayle, Sir Charles Tenningham and the Right Hon. John Blaine, M.P. Having arranged these twelve volunteers in a semi-circle at the back of the stage, Mr. Curtis, standing in the centre of the stage, again addressed his audience. 'Ladies and gentlemen,' he said; 'the secret of separating the mind – or what Spiritualists, who love to bolster up their pretended knowledge of the other world by the invention of pretentious nomenclature, call the 'ethical ego' – from the body, lies in intense concentration. If you wish to acquire the power, practise concentration – concentrate on being in a certain place. If nothing happens at first, don't be discouraged, but keep on trying, and a time will come when you will suddenly leave your body, in a form, which is the exact counterpart of the body you have left. You will visit the place whereon you are concentrating. Perhaps the best method of practising projection is to put your forehead against a door or wall, and concentrate very hard on being on the other side. It may take weeks before you get a result, but if you persevere, you will eventually succeed in leaving your physical form and passing through the door, or wall, into the space beyond. Now watch me! I shall concentrate on projecting my immaterial body, and of walking in it, three times round my material body.'

Mr. Curtis closed his eyes, and for some seconds appeared to be thinking very hard. Then the audience witnessed a remarkable phenomenon – a figure, the exact counterpart of Mr. Curtis, stepped out, as it were, from his body, and slowly walking round it three times, deliberately glided into it, and apparently amalgamated with it. The twelve members from the audience who were within a few feet of the alleged ethereal body, as it walked past them, declared they saw it most vividly, and that feature for feature, detail for detail, it was the exact counterpart of Mr. Curtis, whose material body remained standing, upright and motionless, with its eyes tightly closed. Our representative questioned several of these eye-witnesses very closely, and they were all most emphatic in their belief that what they had seen was a *bona-fide* case of spiritual projection. At the request of a large part of the audience, Mr. Curtis repeated his demonstration, a further complement of men from the stalls joining those already on the stage to witness the operation.

Several tests were now applied to the ethereal body of Mr. Curtis, as it walked round his material body. One man, clutching at its sleeve, tried to detain it, but his hand passed through the sleeve, and held – nothing. Another man put out an arm to act as a barrier, and the projection, without swerving from its course, passed right through it; and, on the completion of the third round, disappeared as before.

In answer to inquiries, Mr. Curtis stated that the phenomenon might be taken as a good illustration of projections; and that he was prepared to project himself once again, in order to prove that it was erroneous to suppose that phantasms could not do all manner of physical actions. A deal table (upon which stood a tumbler and jug of water), a grandfather clock, and a piano were brought on to the stage, and Mr. Curtis once again projected his spirit form. The latter at once walked to the table, and, taking up the tumbler, filled it with water from the jug; after which it wound up the clock, and, sitting down on a seat in front of the piano, played 'Killarney' and 'The Star-spangled Banner.' And then, amidst the wildest applause – the first time assuredly 'a ghost' has ever received public plaudits in recognition of its services – it modestly re-entered its physical home.

Mr. Curtis then announced that not only could he project his ethereal body from his material body in the manner he had already demonstrated, but that with his ethereal body he could amalgamate with inorganic matter. He bade those on the stage approach the table in convenient numbers, *i.e.* two or three at a time, and listen attentively. He then took his stand on one side of the stage, about fourteen feet from the table; and the audience approaching the table and listening attentively, first of all heard it pulsate as with the throbbings of a heart, and then breathe with the deep and heavy respirations of some one in a sound sleep. The table then raised itself some three or four inches from the ground and moved round the stage; at the conclusion of which feat Mr. Curtis informed the audience that 'table-turning' – when not accomplished through the trickery of one of the sitters – was frequently performed by the work of some earthbound spirit – usually an Elemental – that could amalgamate with any piece of furniture, in precisely the same way as his own projection had amalgamated with the table in front of them. Elementals, Mr. Curtis continued, are responsible for many of the foolish and purposeless tricks performed at séances; and for the unintelligible and useless kinds of answers the table so often raps out. The best you can hope for, from an Elemental, is amusement – it will never give you any reliable information; nor will it ever do you any good.

With these words Mr. Curtis' share in the entertainment concluded. He retired to the wings, whilst Mr. Kelson stepping forward – begged those several gentlemen who, on Mr. Curtis' exit, had reseated themselves among the audience, once again to step up on to the stage.

'Be good enough,' he said addressing them in his most polite manner, 'to observe me very closely. I am about to give you a few further examples of what intense mental concentration can do, thus proving to you to what an unlimited extent mind can gain dominion over matter. You all know that will-power can overcome any of the internal physical forces; for instance, when you have tooth or ear ache – you have only to say to yourselves: "I shan't suffer" – and the suffering ceases. But what you may not know – what you may not have realized, is that will-power can over-rule external forces and principles – as for example – gravity. As a matter of fact, airships and aeroplanes are absolutely superfluous – and the time, money and labour they involve is prodigious waste. Any man with strong mental capacity can fly without the aid of mechanism. He has only to will himself to be in the air – and he is there. Look!' And to the amazement – the indescribable, unparalleled amazement of all present, Mr. Kelson knit his brows, as if engaged in intense thought, and, jumping off his feet, remained in the air, at a height of some four feet from the floor.

At his request members of the audience came up to him, and passed their hands under, over and all around him, to make sure there were no wires. He then struck out with his hands and legs after the manner of a swimmer, and moving first of all round the stage, and then over the stalls and pit, gradually ascended higher and higher, till he reached the level of the boxes, to the occupants of which he spoke.

Such an extraordinary spectacle – which apparently gives the lie to all our preconceived notions of gravity – has certainly never before been witnessed, and the effect it had on those who saw it, baffles description. When Mr. Kelson returned to the stage, and the terrific applause that greeted his arrival there had subsided, he gave the audience a few valuable hints as to how they, too, might accomplish this feat.

'Practise concentration,' he said, 'and develop your will power, if only by a very little, every day. Jump off a stool and begin with, saying to yourself as you do so: "I will remain in the air. I won't touch the ground," – and though you may fail for the hundredth time, if only you keep on trying you will eventually succeed. To keep your equilibrium on a bicycle is a feat which would have been pronounced utterly impossible by your ancestors of two hundred years ago; but just as that power came to you – after many futile efforts, all at once – so in the end, will flying come to you. See, I am now going to rise to the highest point in the building. Gravity pulls me back, but I say to myself: "I will rise – I will fly there" – and fly there I do!' – and, springing off the ground, he struck out with his arms and legs, flew swiftly and easily to the dome of the hall, which he touched – and then flew back again to the stage.

This completed the evening's entertainment. If only on the strength of its first performance, the Modern Sorcery Company, in our opinion, has more than justified its name; and although we understand they will give no more performances gratis, we feel confident in prophesying that, for many a long night, there will be no falling off in the attendance.

CHAPTER 14

SHIEL TO THE RESCUE

GLADYS did not feel too happy when she read notices such as these; she could not do other than see in them destruction to her father, and the worst of it all was she could do nothing to help him. Who could? Who could possibly invent anything as wonderful as the marvels of the Modern Sorcery Company Ltd.? And yet unless John Martin gave up altogether, that is what he must do. Nay, he must do more – he must not only equal the Modern Sorcery Company marvels, he must eclipse them. But after the affair of the challenge, it seemed to Gladys that there was no help for it – the Hall would have to be closed for a time. Now that Dick Davenport was dead, there was no one to take her father's place. On the night succeeding the catastrophe, she had persuaded one of the Indian attendants to undertake the rôle of operator, but his skill was not equal to the tax upon it, and the audience – a poor one – was very lukewarm in its applause. The following day she talked the matter over with her father. The latter was in favour of keeping the show on at any cost; Gladys, for closing it temporarily.

'A bad performance is worse than no performance,' she said, 'much better to close till you have invented some new tricks.'

John Martin groaned. 'I fear my days of invention are over,' he muttered. 'If I can read the papers and write letters, that will be about as much as I shall be able to do.'

'Couldn't you retire?'

'I would if I were not a Britisher,' John Martin replied, 'but being a Britisher I'd sooner shoot myself than give in to a d—d Yank!'

And Gladys, in terror lest her father should overexcite himself, promised she would see that the entertainment was carried on as usual, and that the Indian continued in the rôle of operator.

But when out of her father's presence, Gladys gave way

to despair. How could she – a woman – hope to cope with such a difficult situation? And she was racking her brains to know how to act for the best, when Shiel was announced.

A wave of relief swept over her. She could explain her difficulties to Shiel, in a way that she could not to any one who had no knowledge at all of her father's affairs – and she told him just how matters stood.

'Look here!' he exclaimed, when she had finished, 'why not let me take your father's place at the Kingsway? I have done a little amateur acting, and am not nervous at the thought of appearing in public. Your father confided in you so much – you must know all his tricks by heart – couldn't you coach me!'

Gladys looked at him critically.

'It wouldn't be half a bad idea,' she said. 'Supposing you come with me to the Hall, I can explain the tricks better if I show you the apparatus at the same time.'

Shiel thoroughly enjoyed that journey up to town. He knew it was wrong of him to think of his own pleasure, when the affairs of his companion were in such a critical condition. He knew he ought not to look at her in the way he did – as if she was the most precious thing in the world, and he would give her his soul if she wanted it – he knew that he – a penniless artist without any prospects – had no right to behave thus. But her beauty appealed to him with a force he was entirely incapable of resisting, and he went on looking at her in the way he knew he ought not to look at her, simply because he couldn't help it.

He lunched with her at her club in Dover Street, and then they taxied to the Kingsway.

The door-keeper, the only living creature in the building, saving themselves, seemed to share in the general depression hanging over everything – the great, empty front of the house with its gloomy, cavernous boxes and grim, grey gallery – the dark, dismal flies – the chilly wings – all hushed and still, and impregnated with the sense of desertion. But with this man beside her, who, she knew, would do anything he could to help, the place did not look quite so bad to Gladys as it had done the day before. There was a ray of light now where, before, ebon blackness had prevailed.

Without delay Gladys rang up the Indian attendants

on the telephone, and occupied the time prior to their arrival by describing to Shiel how each of the tricks was done.

Her pupil proved far more able than she had anticipated. After several rehearsals he was able to go through the whole performance without a hitch.

When they had finished, Gladys stretched out her hand impulsively. 'I don't know how to thank you enough,' she said. 'You are a brick, and if only you do half as well this evening as you have done now, we shall get on swimmingly – that is to say, as well as we can expect, until we can arrange a fresh programme. If only you were an inventor!'

'If only I were. If only I had money!'

'Why, what would you do?' Gladys asked curiously.

'Give it to you! Give you every halfpenny of it! – But as I haven't any, I mean to give you all the energy I possess instead.'

'Why me? My father you mean!'

'No, you!' Shiel said impulsively, 'both of you if you prefer it, but you first.'

'Me first! That doesn't seem very lucid – but I can't stay to hear an explanation now, for if I miss the four-thirty train I shall miss my dinner, which would indeed be a calamity!' And slipping on her gloves, she hurried off, forbidding Shiel to escort her further.

Left to himself, Shiel strolled along the Strand into the Victoria Gardens, where he bought an evening paper, and sat down to read it. The first thing that caught his eye was—

'MAGIC IN LONDON'

'This morning the West End received a shock. About twelve o'clock, a gentleman, fashionably dressed, turned into Bond Street from Piccadilly, and when opposite Messrs. Truefitt's prepared to cross over. The street happened just then to be blocked by a long line of taxis. The gentleman, however, had no intention of waiting till they had passed. Measuring the distance from one pavement to the other with his eyes, he jumped about fifteen feet into the air and cleared the intervening space without the slightest apparent effort –

a feat that literally paralysed with astonishment all who beheld it. On being remonstrated with by a policeman, who was highly perplexed as to whether such extraordinary conduct constituted a breach of the peace or not, the gentleman calmly leaped over the policeman's head, and striking out with arms and legs swam through the air.

'Continuing in this fashion, the cynosure of all eyes – even the traffic being suspended to watch him – he passed along Bond Street into Oxford Street, where he once more alighted on his feet. On being questioned by a representative of the Press, it transpired he was Mr. Kelson, one of the partners in the Modern Sorcery Company Ltd., whose wonderful performances at their Hall, in Cockspur Street, have already been reported in these columns.'

'I should well like to know how that flying trick is done,' Shiel said to himself. 'According to Kelson it is entirely a question of will power. I'll see if I can't develop my concentrative faculty and introduce a few of the same performances in our show. I'll go to the Hall and try them now.'

But his preliminary efforts were certainly far from successful. He jumped off chairs saying to himself 'I'll fly! I will fly,' and he struck out heroically each time, but the result was always the same – gravity conquered – he fell.

Had he not been so much in love with Gladys, he would have desisted; as it was, the more he bumped and bruised himself, the more determined he was to go on trying. In fact, flying with him became a mania; and according to the daily journals, his was by no means the only case. All over England people were trying to fly. An old lady, in Gipsy Hill, appeared in the Police Court to answer a charge of causing annoyance to her neighbours by practising flying, from off her bed at night. Her bulk being large and her will power apparently small, she yielded to gravity and landed on the ground with prodigious bumps, which set everything in the room vibrating, and which could be plainly heard in the adjoining houses, through the thin brick walls on either side of her room.

An old gentleman in Guilsborough had an extremely narrow escape. Being warned on no account to practise flying in the house or garden, lest his grandchildren should see him and want to do the same, he retired to the seclusion of an old, disused and dilapidated coach house. Here, in the upper storey, he practised by the hour together. He climbed on to a stool which he had taken there for the purpose, and when he fancied he had acquired the right amount of concentration, he sprang into the air, arriving, presumably through want of will power, on the floor. For two whole days he practised – bump – bump – bump – and the more he bumped, the more he persevered. At last, however, the floor gave way, and with loud cries of 'I will! I will!' he fell to the ground floor, ten feet below! He was unable to go on experimenting, owing to a broken leg and a fractured collar-bone.

In Aylsham, Norfolk, there had been a perfect epidemic among the children for trying aeronic gravity. Rudolph Crabbe, aged five, after listening to an account of the performances at the Modern Sorcery Company's Hall, which his father had read aloud, sprang off the dining-room table crying out 'I will fly! I will stay in the air.' Fortunately, he fell on the tabby cat, which somewhat broke the shock of concussion, and he escaped unhurt.

In College Road, Clifton, Bristol, an octogenarian thinking he would add novelty to the Jubilee celebrations at the College, leaped off the roof of his house, crying, 'I'll fly over the Close! I will fly over the Close!' – and broke his neck.

In St. Ives, Cornwall, where the treatment of animals is none too humane, a fisher-boy threw a visitor's Pomeranian over the Malakoff saying, 'You shall fly! You shall remain in the air;' whilst at Bath a girl of ten, snatching her baby brother from the perambulator, leaped over Beechen Cliff, calling out, 'We will fly together! We will fly together!'

These are only a few of the many similar cases Shiel read in the paper, and which he narrated afterwards to Gladys Martin.

'I am quite convinced,' Gladys said, 'that Kelson does his flying through supernatural agency. His assertion that it can be done through mere will power, is sheer humbug. It wouldn't be a bad idea to consult a clairvoyant. What do you think?'

Shiel thought it was an excellent suggestion. He saw in

it an opportunity of spending yet another afternoon in Gladys' company, and asked her to go with him to an occultist the very next day. When she assented, the pleasure of it tingled through every pore of his skin. Of course, Gladys assured herself there was no harm in her acceptance of Shiel's escort – that neither he nor she meant anything by it – that it was on her part merely a sort of an acknowledgment that he had been awfully good to her in her present predicament. Besides, if she needed further excuse, she had no reason for supposing Shiel to be in love with her – and had her father not spoken to her about it, she would not have remarked anything different in his glances, from the glances – for the time being, perhaps, earnest enough – bestowed upon her by other young men; which excuse, was, certainly, in Gladys' case, a more or less honest one.

They had some difficulty in selecting a psychometrist – so numerous were those who advertised, in an equally alluring manner – but they at length decided in favour of Madame Elvita, whose consulting rooms were in New Bond Street. When they arrived there, Madame Elvita was, of course, engaged. Shiel was delighted – it gave him an extra half-hour with Gladys. When Madame was free, she had much to tell them. First of all she spoke to them of Karmas, Kamadevas, Rupadevas, vitalized shells, etheric doubles, the Nermanakaya, and afterwards solemnly announced that she must relapse into a state of clairvoyance, in order to get in touch with Tillie Toot, a certain spirit from whom she could learn all that Gladys and Shiel wanted to know. Accordingly, in the manner of most other two-guinea clairvoyants, she composed herself in a graceful and recumbent attitude, made a lot of queer grimaces and still queerer noises, and spoke in a falsetto voice, which purported to be that of Tillie Toot, once a barmaid in Edinburgh, now one of Madame's familiar spirits. And the gist of what 'Tillie' told them was that Hamar & Co. derived their powers from Black Magic; and that the secrets thereof could only be learned from Madame, after a series of sittings with her – sittings for which Madame would only require a fee of fifty guineas: a most moderate, in fact trifling, sum, considering the wonderful instruction they would receive.

But Madame's magnanimous offer tempted neither

Gladys nor Shiel; and they abruptly took their departure.

Kateroski (*née* Jones) in Regent Street, whom Gladys and Shiel had agreed to consult in the event of a non-successful visit to Madame Elvita in Bond Street, also told them that Black Magic was the key to Hamar, Curtis & Kelson's performances. She advised them to get on the Astral Plane, where they would meet spirits who would give them all the information they desired.

Madame Kateroski's instructions were simple. 'It is really a matter of faith,' she said. 'All you have to do is to go to some secluded spot – the privacy of your bedroom will do admirably – sit down, close your eyes, look into your lids and concentrate hard. After a while you will no longer see your eyelids – your lids will fade away and you will be on the Astral Plane, and see strange creatures, which, although terrifying, won't harm you. When you get used to them, you will communicate with them, and learn from them all you want to know.'

'Shall we try?' Gladys remarked laughingly to Shiel, as they stepped into the street. 'But if faith is essential to success, I fear failure, as far as I am concerned, is a foregone conclusion. I know I shouldn't have sufficient faith.'

'Nor I either,' Shiel said. 'But, perhaps, we could acquire a necessary amount of it, if we were to experiment together. Supposing we try in that delightfully secluded copse in your garden.'

Gladys shook her head. 'I'm afraid it would be useless. Besides, if my father were to hear of it, he would fear worry had turned my brain, and most likely have another fit. No, we must think of something more practical. In the meanwhile, if you will keep on with the part you have so generously undertaken, you will be doing me an inestimable service.'

'Then I'll keep on with it for ever,' Shiel replied, and before she could stop him, he had kissed her hand.

CHAPTER 15

HOW HAMAR, CURTIS AND KELSON ENTERED
THE ASTRAL PLANE

In order to explain the manner in which Hamar, Curtis and Kelson were initiated into their new properties, I must now go back to the day preceding the gratis performance of the Modern Sorcery Company, that is to say the last day of stage one of their compact.

To Kelson the day had been one of surprises throughout. When he arrived at the building in Cockspur Street (he preferred living alone, and, consequently, rented a handsome suite of rooms in John Street, Mayfair), he was not a little astonished to meet Lilian Rosenberg on the staircase.

'I thank you so much!' she exclaimed, shaking hands with him most effusively. 'It is all owing to you I got the post.'

'Then Hamar has engaged you,' Kelson ejaculated.

'Why, yes! didn't you know!' Lilian said with a smile. 'I had a letter from him the very evening of the day I called here.'

'Did you! He never told me anything about it! How do you think you will get on?'

'Oh, splendidly! The work is interesting and full of variety. Moreover, I like the atmosphere of the place, it is so weird. I believe the three of you really are magicians!'

'If that be so,' Kelson said, 'then we have only acted in accordance with our character in engaging the services of a witch – a witch who has already bewitched one member of our trio. Now please don't go to the expense of lunching out: lunch with me instead. Lunch with me every day.'

'It is very kind of you,' Lilian Rosenberg replied, 'and I will gladly do so when I am not lunching with Mr. Hamar. But he has invited me to have all my meals with him.'

'That doesn't mean you are obliged to have them with him every day!' Kelson cried. 'Lunch with me this morning.'

'I am very sorry,' Lilian Rosenberg replied, looking at

Kelson with mock pleading eyes, 'please don't scold me, but I've really promised Mr. Hamar.'

'Have tea with me, then,' Kelson said.

'I've promised him that, too.'

'Supper then!' Kelson said, savagely.

'I'm awfully sorry, but I'm engaged all this evening, and practically every evening.'

'With Mr. Hamar?' Kelson asked suspiciously.

'Oh no! my own private business,' Lilian Rosenberg replied. 'Do forgive me. I should so like to have been able to accept your invitation. Now I must hurry back to my work,' and she gave him her hand, which Kelson held, and would have gone on holding all the morning, had he not heard Hamar's well-known tread ascending the stairs.

'Look here!' he said, as they entered his room together, 'I want Miss Rosenberg to have luncheon with me one day this week, and she tells me you have already invited her. Let her come with me to-morrow.'

'It is impossible,' Hamar said. 'Now I'll tell you what it is, Matt, I anticipated this the moment I saw you two together, and it's got to stop. You would genuinely fall in love with that girl – or as a matter of fact any other pretty girl – if you saw much of her – and love, I tell you, would be absolutely disastrous to our interests. You must let her alone – absolutely alone, I tell you. I have given her strict orders she is to confine herself to her work, and to me.'

'I think you take a great deal too much on yourself. I shall see just as much of Miss Rosenberg, when she is disengaged, as I please.'

'Then she never shall be disengaged. But come, do be sane and put some restraint on this mad infatuation of yours for pretty faces. Can't you keep it in check anyhow for two years – till after the term of the compact has expired! Then you will be free to indulge in it, to your heart's content. For Heaven's sake, be guided by me. Harmony between us must be kept at all costs. Don't you understand?'

'Oh, yes! I understand all right,' Kelson said, 'and I'll try. But it's very hard – and I really don't see there would be any danger in my taking her out occasionally.'

'Well, I do,' Hamar replied, 'and there's an end. To turn to something that may spell business. Just before I got up this morning I saw a striped figure bending over me!'

'A striped figure?'

'Yes! A cylindrical figure, about seven feet high, without any visible limbs; but which gave me the impression it had limbs – of a sort – if it cared to show them.'

'You were frightened?'

'Naturally! So would you have been. It didn't speak, but in some indefinable manner it conveyed to me the purport of its visit. To-night, at twelve o'clock, we are to go to the house of a Hindu, called Karaver, in Berners Street, where we shall be initiated into the second stage of our compact.'

'I hope to goodness we shan't see any spectral trees or striped figures – I've had enough of them,' Kelson said.

'Then take care you don't do anything that might lead to the breaking of the compact,' Hamar retorted, 'otherwise you'll see something far worse.'

Shortly before midnight, Hamar, Curtis and Kelson, obeying the injunctions Hamar had received, set off to Berners Street, where they had little difficulty in finding Karaver's house.

To their astonishment Karaver was expecting them.

'How did you know we were coming?' Curtis asked.

'A gentleman called here early this morning and told me,' Karaver explained. 'He said three friends of his particularly wished to be on the Astral Plane, at twelve o'clock this evening, and that they would each pay me a hundred guineas, if I would show them how to get there. I demurred. The secrets that have come down to me through generations of my Cashmere ancestors, I tell only to a chosen few – those born under the sign of Dejellum Brava.

'The stranger showing me the sign – written plainer than I have ever seen it – in the palm of his hand, I at once consented, and I had no sooner done so than he vanished. I knew then that I had been speaking to an Elemental – a spirit of my native mountains.'

'My nerves are not in a condition to stand much. Is there anything very alarming in this astral business?' Kelson asked.

'It depends on what you call alarming,' the Indian said coldly. 'I shouldn't be alarmed.'

'Don't be a fool, Matt,' Hamar interposed. 'I never saw

such a frightened idiot in my life. You ought to be ashamed of yourself. Think of what there is at stake.'

'Think of Lilian Rosenberg,' Curtis whispered, 'and be comforted.'

Karaver took them upstairs into a dimly lighted attic. In the centre of the carpetless floor was a tripod, around which the three were told to sit. Karaver then proceeded to pour into an iron vessel a mixture composed of: $\frac{1}{2}$ oz. of hemlock, $\frac{3}{4}$ oz. of henbane, 2 oz. of opium, 1 oz. of mandrake roots, 2 ozs. of poppy seeds, $\frac{1}{2}$ oz. of asafœtida, and $\frac{1}{4}$ oz. of saffron.

'Are these preparations absolutely necessary?' Kelson asked.

'Absolutely,' Karaver said. 'English clairvoyants will, doubtless, tell you they are not necessary. It is their custom, with a few slipshod instructions, to lead you to suppose that getting on the Astral Plane is mere child's play. It is not! It is extremely difficult and can only be done, in the first place, through the guidance of a skilled Oriental occultist.'

He then took a sword, and with it making the sign of a triangle in the air, afterwards scratched a triangle on the floor, over which, in red chalk, he superscribed a tree, an eye, and a hand. Then he heated the mixture in the iron vessel over an oil stove. As soon as fumes arose from it, he placed it on the tripod, crying, 'Great Spirits of the mountains, rivers and bowels of the earth, invest me with the heavy seal, in order that I may conduct these three seekers after knowledge to the realms of thy eternal phantoms.'

Immediately after this oration Karaver, dipping a twig of hazel in the fumigation, waved it north, south, east and west crying, 'Give me authority! Give me Ka-ta-la-derany;' and then kneeling down in front of the brazier, in a droning voice repeated these words:

'Green phantom figures of the air,
A ready welcome see that you prepare.
Black phantom figures from the earth,
Of friendly salutations see there is no dearth.
Red phantom figures of the furious fire,
For kindly greting change your usual ire.
Grey, grizzly googies from the woods and dells,

To gentle whisperings change your harrowing yells.
Flagae, Devas, Mara Rupas,[1] hie to the Plane, the Astral Plane,
And to these three poor fools, explain, explain
The secrets that they wish to learn, to learn!'

The mixture in the iron vessel was now giving off such dense fumes that Hamar, Curtis and Kelson felt their senses slowly ebbing away. The dark, lithe form of Karaver, his swarthy face and gleaming teeth receded farther and farther into the background, whilst his voice appeared to grow fainter and fainter. They were dimly conscious that he sprayed them all over with some sweet-smelling scent,[2] and that he whispered (in reality he spoke in his normal tones) these words: 'Darkona – droomer – doober – parlar – poohmer – perler. A – ta-rama – skata-rinek – ook – drooksi – noomig – viartikorsa.'[3] Then there

---

[1] According to Brahminical teaching there are seven main classes of spirits; some having innumerable sub-divisions. They are—

1. Arrippa Devas, with forms.
2. Arrippa Devas, without forms.

(Both Classes 1 and 2 are intelligent, sixth principles of certain planets. I style them Planetians, and classify them with all other spirits hailing from Jupiter, Neptune, etc.)

3. Mara rupas (identical with Vice-Elementals).
4. Pisaschas, *i.e.* male and female elementaries. (I have termed them Impersonating Elementals, since they consist of the astral forms of the dead, that may be utilized by Elementals.)
5. Asuras, *i.e.* gnomes, pixies, etc. (Corresponding to those I have designated Vagrarian Elementals.)
6. Monstrosities. (These I include among Vice-Elementals and Vagrarians.)
7. Kaksasas, viz. souls of wizards, witches, and of clever people with evil tendencies, scientists with cruel or harsh tendencies—such as vivisectionists and sophists. All these come under my division of 'earthbound phantasms of the dead'—spirits tied to this earth by passion or vices; and I should add to the list—militant suffragettes, strike agitators, hooligans, apaches, pseudo-humanitarians, religious bigots, misers, all people obsessed with manias, idiots, epileptic imbeciles and criminal lunatics. All such may at times be encountered on the lowest spiritual plane.

[2] Composed of 2 drachms of myrrh, $\frac{1}{2}$ oz. of sweet oil, 2 oz. attar of roses, $\frac{1}{2}$ oz. heliotrope and $\frac{1}{4}$ oz. of musk.

[3] These words are so arranged as to set in vibration and loosen the atmosphere, that keeps the spirit incarcerated in the physical body, and so set the latter free.

came a temporary blank, which was broken by a sudden burst of light. The light, at first, was so blinding that they involuntarily closed their eyes. It was quite different to any light they had been accustomed to – it was far more vivid, and was in a perpetual state of vibration. When they had got sufficiently used to this dazzling effect to keep their eyes open, they became aware that they were standing, apparently on nothing, that the atmosphere was not composed of air such as they knew, but of an indescribable something that rendered the act of breathing wholly unnecessary, and that all around them was no ground, no scenery, but only – space!

They had barely finished remarking on these facts, when there suddenly glided across their vision, forms – of every conceivable shape, *i.e.*, those resembling corpses of human beings and animals, with bloodless faces, glassy eyes and stiff limbs – some apparently just dead and others in an advanced state of decomposition, all possessed and propelled by Impersonating Elements; phantoms of earthbound people – misers, murderers, etc., several of whom approached the trio and tried to peer into their faces.

'For heaven's sake keep off!' Kelson shrieked, as the vibrating form of an epileptic imbecile, with protruding blue eyes and pimply cheeks, came up to him, and thrust its face into his.

'This is a bit thick,' Hamar said, vainly attempting to elude the phantom of a short, stout woman with a big head and purple face, who, putting out a large black, swollen tongue, leered at him.

'Curse you! D—n you!' Curtis screamed, throwing out his hands in a vain endeavour to beat off the phantoms of two idiot boys who were trying to bite him with their loose, dribbling mouths. 'A little more of this and I shall go mad!'

Seeing a tall, grey phantom with a man's body and wolf's head bounding up to them, Kelson would have run away, had not Hamar, whose presence of mind never quite deserted him, gripped him by the arm. 'If you leave us, Matt,' he said, 'we are lost. I feel our safety depends on our keping together. If I'm not mistaken this is a cunning dodge on the part of the Unknown to separate us. If that happens, I feel we may never get back to our bodies – and the compact will then be broken. We must hang on to each other at all costs.' So saying, he slipped his free arm through that of Curtis, and the three stood linked together.

Hamar clung on to the other two, until his hands grew numb, and the sweat stood on his chest and forehead in great beads. As figure after figure stealthily and noiselessly approached them, Kelson and Curtis writhed and shrieked; and, at times, it semed as if the chain must be broken. But alarming as were these harrowing types of Vice-Elementals – *i.e.*, nude things with heads of beasts and bodies of men and women; grotesque heads; malevolent eyes; mal-shaped hands; headless beasts, etc.; none had so dangerous an effect on the unity of the trio as the alluring type of Vice-Elementals, *i.e.*, shapes of beautiful women that smiled seductively at Kelson, and resorted to every device to entice him away with them. It was then that Hamar was taxed to the utmost, that he exhausted voice, strength, and patience, in holding Kelson back.

He was about to give in, when to his astonishment these Vice-Elementals vanished, and a phantasm, the exact counterpart of Karaver, only much taller, appeared before them, and commenced giving them instructions as to Stage Two.

'You,' he said, addressing Hamar, 'will possess the property of second sight, *i.e.*, the power to see, at will, earthbound spirits, conditionally, that you fumigate your room, for ten minutes every night, before retiring to rest, with a mixture composed of 2 drachms of henbane, 3 drachms of saffron, $\frac{1}{2}$ oz. of aloes, $\frac{1}{4}$ oz. of mandrake, 3 drachms of salanum, 2 oz. of asafœtida; that you abstain from animal food and wine, and give up smoking; that, three times every day, you bathe your face in distilled water, to which has been added three drops of the juice of the whortleberry, one drop of the juice of the mountain ash berry, 1 oz. of lavender water, 1 oz. of nitre, and $\frac{1}{2}$ oz. of tincture of arnica; and that, just before going to sleep, you look for three minutes, without blinking, at an equilateral triangle, transcribed in blood, on white paper, and composed of these letters and figures.' And he handed Hamar a piece of paper, on which were written these symbols: K.T.O.P.I.6.X.7.4.H.I.P.3.S.4.W.V.2.8.

'So long as you observe these conditions the power will remain with you. To-morrow, only, it will be awarded you without any preparations.

'You,' he went on, turning to Kelson, 'will possess the

property of projection, *i.e.*, the power of leaving your body, and of visiting, where you will, on the material plane. You will continue to possess the same, conditionally, that you carry out the same rules as Leon Hamar, with the exception that, instead of looking at a triangle before going to sleep, you will repeat these words. See, I have written them down for you.' And he handed Kelson a slip of paper, on which were transcribed 'Darkona, droomer, doober, parlar, poohmer, perler. A – ta – rama –skatarinek – ook – drooksi – noomeg – viartikorsa.'

'You,' he said, turning to Curtis, 'will be endowed with the property of overcoming gravity, *i.e.*, you will be able to fly, to jump great heights, and to lift and move prodigious weights; and this property will remain in your possession during the prescribed period, provided you abstain from all animal food, from smoking and from drinking alcohol; and observe the same rules with regard to fumigating your sleeping compartment, and bathing your face, as Hamar and Kelson. But, always, before you attempt to fly or to jump, it will be necessary for you to set in motion certain vibrations, in the ether, that counteract the attraction of gravity. You must repeat the words "Karjako Mandarbsa Guahseela," which I have written on this blue paper; and when you want to move or lift objects, you must first repeat the words "Perabibo Henlilee Okokokotse," which I have written on this green paper. Gravity, as you will see, is entirely dependent on sound – sound can move mountains. It did so in Atlantis, it did so in Egypt.'

Making the sign of a triangle, an eye, and a tree in the air, with the forefinger of his left hand, he slowly repeated the words 'Barjakva – ookpoota – trylisa,' and the concluding syllable was no sooner uttered, than the trio found themselves standing in Berners Street. But of Karaver's house – the house they had just quitted – there was no trace.

CHAPTER 16

HAMAR MAKES ADVANCES

THE doctors had stated that the tenth day would see the crisis of John Martin's illness; if he could tide over that period, he might go on for years without another attack. When the momentous day arrived, Gladys was simply eating her heart out with suspense. Not a sound was permitted in the house. The servants, tiptoeing about, hardly ventured even to exchange glances; the errand boys were waylaid and sent to the right-about, with a vague notion that if they opened their mouths their heads would be off; and some one was posted at the garden gate to deal, in a scarcely less summary manner, with visitors. Indeed, so fearful was Gladys lest her father should hear Shiel, who had managed to elude her outpost, that without meaning it, she greeted him curtly, and, more plainly than politely, gave him to understand that she wished him elsewhere.

'What have you been saying to Shiel Davenport?' Miss Templeton asked Gladys, when they met at lunch. 'I passed him in the road just now, and he looked so wretched that, despite his ineligibility, I felt quite sorry for him. I am sure he is very much in love with you.'

'Nonsense,' Gladys said, 'he is only a boy.' But boy though it pleased her to call him, she knew that he had played a man's part during her father's illness. Every night he had faithfully performed the rôle she had allotted to him, at the Kingsway Hall, and upon him she was forced to admit the success of the entertainment, in a large measure, depended. Without pushing himself, or being the least bit officious, he had ben equally helpful behind the scenes. He had held in check all those who, taking advantage of her father's absence, were disposed to dispute her authority and shirk their work – and he had also, on her behalf, successfully resisted their demand for higher wages. And, over and above all this, he had always considered her personal comfort. Her meals – which she could never bother about for herself, when engaged all day at the hall – were, thanks to him, brought to her as punctually, and served as daintily, as they would have been for her father; he had taken every care that she should not be disturbed when resting; and there was, in short, nothing he had not thought of doing to lighten the load, so unexpectedly laid upon her shoulders. The only fault she could find with him, was that he had not gained the good graces of her father.

The day slowly waned. Gladys had stolen into her father's room repeatedly to see how he fared, and to her his condition had seemed much about the same – he was as usual tired and peevish. But when, at six o'clock, she again stole in to peep at him, and found him lying back on his pillow absolutely still and motionless, and without apparently breathing, she was immeasurably shocked. Had he had another fit, or was he dead? Wild with grief and terror, she rushed from the room to telephone to the doctor, and met him on the landing.

'You need have no fear,' he said to her the moment he had looked at John Martin, 'he is sound asleep, and, when he awakes, the crisis will be past. To-morrow, he may go out for a bit, and, in a week, he will be himself again. Only you must take care that he does not use his brain too much.'

Gladys could hardly restrain her delight. She felt pleased with everything and everybody; and her greeting of Shiel, some two hours later, at the theatre, almost turned his brain. In fact it was owing to this pleasant surprise, that he made one or two stupid mistakes in his performance, and was sharply pulled back to earth by the ironic laughter of the audience. When the entertainment was over, and he was preparing to accompany Gladys as usual to her motor, the thought of her sparkling eyes and animated features again overcame him.

'What shall you advise your father to do?' he asked.

'I think he ought to lose no time in getting a partner,' Gladys replied, 'some one who can attend to the business side of the concern for him. It is essential he should not be worried with figures.'

'I suppose my services won't be required much longer?' Shiel said, speaking with rather an effort.

'Of course I can't answer for my father,' Gladys replied, 'but I should imagine he would be only too glad to employ you. The only thing is the salary. You can't live on air, you know, and with the poor attendances he gets now, I don't see how he can afford to pay much.'

'I would work for very little,' Shiel said. 'I should be awfully sorry to give up now. I wonder if you would miss me at all?'

'Of course I should!' Gladys retorted. 'You have behaved admirably, and I am most grateful to you.'

'You needn't be grateful to me. I have never enjoyed anything half so much as I have trying to help you. I am poor, penniless in fact, since my uncle left me nothing, but supposing – supposing I were to get some lucrative post, do you think – do you think there would ever be any possibility of—'

'Of what?'

'Of your caring for me! I am terribly in love with you.'

'I fear I must have given you encouragement,' Gladys said. 'I'm awfully sorry. You see I never thought of this, and I don't know what to say to you.'

'Won't you give me a chance, just a chance?'

'But my father would never hear of it. Unfortunately he seems to be prejudiced against you. Won't you wait a while, and then, if you are still in the same mind, speak to me again in – say – a year. By that time you will, no doubt, have made some sort of a position for yourself.'

'And in the meanwhile you will get engaged to some one else,' Shiel exclaimed.

'I don't think I shall,' Gladys said. 'Of course, I meet crowds of men, but you see I am not the marrying sort.'

'Do you think you could care for me just a bit?' Shiel asked eagerly.

'A tiny, tiny bit, perhaps,' Gladys said, 'but I'm not at all sure. I can think of no one now but my father, so that if you value my good opinion, or really want to prove your devotion to me, you must, for the time being, devote yourself to him. Who knows – it may lie in your power to do him some service.'

'I don't see how,' Shiel replied, somewhat despondingly. 'But no matter – after you, your father and your father's affairs shall be my first consideration. You will let me see you sometimes, won't you?'

'Sometimes,' Gladys laughed. 'Good-bye! Don't make any mistakes to-morrow. Your performance to-night was not as good as usual.' And, with this somewhat cruel remark, she stepped lightly into her motor, and drove off.

Shiel now gave way to despair. There are few conditions in life so utterly unenviable as penury and love – to be next door to starving, and at the same time in love. Day after day Shiel, who was thus afflicted, had revelled in Gladys' company, and had intoxicated himself with her beauty, fully aware that for each moment of pleasure there would, later on, be a corresponding moment of pain. It was only in romance, he told himself, that the penniless lover suddenly finds himself in a position to marry – in reality, his love suit is rejected with scorn; his adored one marries some one who has, or pretends he has, limitless wealth; and the despised swain ends his days a miserable and dejected bachelor.

All the same, Shiel determined that he would for once fare like the hero in romance – that he would either win the object of his affections or perish in the attempt; and no sooner did the fit of the blues, consequent on the conversation just related, wear off, than he set to work in grim earnest to discover some means of breaking up the Modern Sorcery Company Ltd., and of restoring to the firm of Martin and Davenport their former prestige.

In the meanwhile, affairs were by no means stationary, as far as Hamar and his colleagues were concerned. The appearance of their paper *To-morrow,* a morning journal, that chronicled faithfully every event of the following day, caused a tremendous sensation; and the sale of every other paper sank to nil – no one, naturally, wanting to buy the news that had happened yesterday, when, for the same money, they could obtain news of what would happen that very day. The stupid method of chronicling past events, Hamar announced in the first issue of his organ, was now obsolete. It was, perhaps, good enough for the Victorian era, but it was utterly out of keeping with the present age of hourly progress. Who, for instance, wanted to know that at 6 p.m., on the preceding evening, there had been a big fire in New York? Was it not far more to the point for them to learn, for example, that at 2 p.m., on that very day, Rio de Janeiro would be partially destroyed by an earthquake; that the Post Office in King's Road, Chelsea, would be broken into by thieves; that Nelson's Monument in Trafalgar Square would be blown up by Suffragettes; or something equally fresh and exciting? One cannot get thrills – at least not the right kind of thrills in reading of what has already taken place. To say to ourselves, or to a friend, 'Just fancy, we might have been in that railway accident,' or, in reading of a shipwreck, 'What a mercy we did not embark after all, is it not?' is not half as enthralling as to be wondering if, at eleven o'clock that night, when the terrific storm in which twenty-six people will be killed by lightning in various parts of England, we shall be among the fatal number. One is not much moved to find oneself alive when a danger is past, but one does get terribly excited in contemplating the risk we are bound to run of being killed. Within a week, the circulation of *To-morrow* had gone up from fifty thousand to ten million, and Hamar, inflated with success, said to himself, 'Now I will go and have another look at John Martin.'

When he arrived, Gladys was in the garden. His stealthy approach had given her no chance to escape.

'What is your business?' she asked, glancing nervously in the direction of the house, and dreading lest her father should see Hamar from his window.

'I've come to see your father,' Hamar said, his eyes resting admiringly on her face and then running leisurely over her figure. 'How is the old gentleman?'

'He is not well enough to see visitors,' Gladys said, with absolute hauteur. 'Perhaps you will state your business to me.'

'Well! I don't mind if I do!' Hamar replied. 'Let us sit down. It's more comfortable than standing.' And he dropped into a seat as he spoke. 'Now I've been noticing,' he went on, 'that your Show in the Kingsway is not getting on very well – that there are fewer and fewer people there every night, and I've no doubt it will soon have to dry up altogether. We, on the other hand, are doing better and better every night, and we shall go on doing better – there is no limit to our possibilities. We are worth half a million now – next year, we shall be worth ten times that amount!'

'You are optimistical, at all events,' Gladys said.

'I can afford to be,' Hamar grinned. 'Now, do you know what we intend doing before very long?'

'I haven't the least idea, and I am not in the slightest degree curious.'

'Aren't you? Well, you should be, since it concerns you. We mean to buy up the whole of Kingsway!'

'And later on, of course, the whole of Regent Street!'

'You are satirical. You are not alarmed at the prospect of having me for a landlord!'

'I don't understand you! The Hall in Kingsway is my father's own property.'

'If that is so then you have nothing to fear,' Hamar laughed, 'but I think it just possible you are mistaken. At any rate, I've been in communication with some one styling himself the landlord.'

'My father would have an agreement, anyhow!' Gladys said.

'Of course,' Hamar replied, 'and I've a pretty shrewd idea of the terms of it. But enough of this – let me come to the point. I intend buying the property, and I shall refuse to renew your father's lease, unless he agrees to give me what I want!'

'Of course a preposterous price?'

'No, you – only you!'

'Me!'

'Yes! I've never seen a girl I like more. I've limitless wealth and I'll give you everything you want – a steam yacht, motors, diamonds, anything, everything, and all I ask is that you should consent to be engaged to me on trial – say for fifteen months – just to see how we get on! What pretty hands you have.'

And before Gladys could draw them away, he had caught hold of them in an iron grasp, and, turning them over, cast admiring glances at the slim, white fingers with the long, almond-shaped and carefully manicured nails.

'I reckon,' he said, 'I shall never find any one prettier all through. What do you say?'

'Your proposition is impossible – monstrous! I detest you,' Gladys retorted, her cheeks white with anger. 'Leave go my hands at once, and never let me see you again!'

'I can't promise not to see you again,' Hamar said, 'but I'll let go your hands now, for I'm no more a lover of scenes than you. I anticipated a little fuss at first – it's the way all you women have – you are so modest, you don't appear too eager to snap up a good offer. You'll close with it right enough in the end. I'll call again in a few days. By that time you may have changed your mind.' And, before she could prevent him, he had again seized her hand and was kissing it over and over again.

With an ejaculation of the utmost indignation, she sprang away from him, and with all the dignity she could assume, walked to the house. What became of him she did not know. Some few seconds later she told the gardener to see him safely off the premises, but he was nowhere to be found.

A week later, Hamar turned up again at the Cottage, and, despite the vigilance of Gladys and the servants, caught John Martin alone.

When the latter, at last, came to the end of what had, at first, seemed an inexhaustible stock of invectives, Hamar stated his proposals with mathematical exactitude.

'I don't believe for one moment my landlord would be such a blackguard as to play into your hands,' John Martin spluttered.

'Oh, yes, he would!' Hamar replied. 'An Englishman will do anything for money, and I am prepared to offer him just twice as much as any one else for your Hall. Do you think he will refuse – not he!'

'But what on earth's your object? You've ruined me already.'

'Your daughter!' Hamar cried. 'Miss Gladys! I am prepared to go any lengths to get her. Refuse to give her to me and I'll turn you out of your Hall, I'll torment you with every kind of insect, I'll plague you with disease, I'll make your life hell. But give her to me – and I'll—'

'But I won't! And I defy you to do your worst, you – you—' and there is no knowing what would have happened, had not Gladys suddenly come in and dragged her father out of the room.

'How dare you?' she exclaimed, returning to the study to find Hamar still there. 'I've telephoned to the police, and unless you go instantly and promise not to come again, I shall give you in charge for annoyance.'

'Foolish of you – very foolish!' Hamar said, 'when I want to be friendly. Sooner or later you must give in, so why not end all this needless unpleasantness now, and receive me – if not with open arms – at least amicably. You are so awfully pretty! I must have just one —' but before he could kiss Gladys the police arrived, and Hamar once more retired – with somewhat undignified haste, and more than a little discomfited.

On arriving at Cockspur Street, Hamar's temper underwent a still further trial. Kelson, taking advantage of his absence, had gone off to tea with Lilian Rosenberg.

In ill-suppressed fury, he waited till they returned.

'A word with you, Matt,' he said, as Kelson tried to shuffle past him. 'So this is the way you behave when my back is turned. I suppose you've had a good time!'

'Delightful!'

'And you know the consequences!'

'Only that I'm looking forward to the same thing another day.'

'She'll go!'

'She won't,' Kelson chuckled. 'She is far too valuable. So there, old man! A month ago your threat might have held good. It won't now. You daren't – you positively daren't part with her – because, if you did so, you'd not only part with a good few of your secrets, but you'd part with me.'

CHAPTER 17

THE COURSE OF TRUE LOVE

'WHAT'S to be done with Matt?' Hamar asked Curtis, soon after the interview just recorded. 'He's as sweet on Rosenberg as he can be, and says if I dismiss her he'll go too!'

'Then don't dismiss her,' Curtis replied. 'Leave them both alone, that's my tip. I don't believe Matt's such a fool as to fall in love, and I'm quite sure the girl isn't. Why, she went to the Tivoli with me two nights ago, and to the Empire with another fellow the night before that. It isn't in her to stick to one, she would go with any one who would treat her. Don't worry your head over that. Matt might say "How about Leon and Gladys Martin."'

'So he might, but there's no danger there. The girl is deuced pretty – splendid eyes, hair, teeth, hands and all that sort of thing, and I've set my heart on a bit of canoodling with her, but as for love! Well! it's not in my programme.'

'Still, stranger things have happened,' Curtis said. 'Anyhow, I guess you're both mad and that I'm the only sane one. Give me a ten-course dinner at the Savoy, and you may have all the women in London – I don't go a cent on them.'

To revert to Kelson. From the hour he had first seen Lilian Rosenberg he had become more and more deeply enamoured. In the hope of meeting her, he had hung about the halls and passages of the building; had never missed an opportunity of speaking to her, of feasting himself on the elfish beauty of her face, of squeezing her hand, and of telling her how much he admired her.

'You really mustn't,' she said. 'Mr. Hamar has given me strict orders to attend to nothing but my work.'

'Oh, damn Hamar!' Kelson replied, 'if I choose to talk to you it's no business of his. You've not treated me well. I got you the post, and it is I you should go with, not Hamar.'

And in the quiet nooks and corners, perched on the window-sill, with one eye kept warily on the guard for fear of interruptions, he told her his history – all about himself from the day of his birth – told her about his parents, his childhood, his schooldays, his hobbies and cranks, his indiscretions, extravagancies, his carousals, debts, flirtations with just an excusable amount of exaggeration. He even went so far as to speak of a chronic rheumatism, of a twinge of hereditary gout, and of a slightly hectic cough with which, he suddenly remembered, he had at one time, been troubled.

'Don't you think,' Lilian Rosenberg said, with mock earnestness, 'you are somewhat rash! Have you forgotten that no woman can keep a secret – and you are not telling me one secret but many. Supposing in a fit of thoughtlessness or absent-mindedness, I were to divulge them! I should never forgive myself.'

'Would it distress you so much?'

'Of course it would. I should be miserable,' she laughed. And Kelson, unable to restrain himself, seized her hands and smothered them with kisses.

'Your fingers would look well covered with rings,' he said. 'I will give you some, and you shall come with me and choose. Only on no account tell Hamar.' And he kissed her – not on the hands this time – but the lips.

Hamar saw him. He watched him from behind the angle of the passage wall, but he said nothing – at least, nothing to Kelson. It was to Lilian Rosenberg he spoke.

'It is really not my fault,' she said. 'I don't encourage him, and if you take my advice, you will not interfere, for I am sure at present he means nothing serious. He is the sort of man who imagines himself in love with every one he meets. If you prevent him seeing me, you may actually bring about the result you are most anxious to avoid.'

'I'll risk that,' Hamar said, 'and I absolutely forbid you doing more than merely saying good morning to him. It is either that, or you must go.'

'Well, of course I will do as you wish,' Lilian said. 'I don't care a snap for him; and, after all, you ought to know your own business best! It is only natural that you should want him to marry some one who can bring money into the Firm.'

'I don't want him to marry at all, or anyhow, not yet. However, there is no necessity to discuss that point. We have definitely settled the line you are to adopt, and that is all I wanted to speak to you about. When next you feel inclined to flirt, come to me, and you shall have kisses as well as – rings.'

It was shortly after this *tête-à-tête* that Lilian Rosenberg was interrupted in her work, by a rap at the door.

'Come in,' she called, and a young man entered.

'I believe a clerk is wanted here,' he explained. 'I've come to apply for the situation. Can I see Mr. Hamar?'

'I'm afraid he's out. There's no one in at present,' Lilian Rosenberg replied, eyeing the stranger critically. 'If you like to wait awhile, you may do so. Sit down.' She signalled to him to take a chair and went on typing.

For some minutes the silence was unbroken, save for the tapping of fingers and the clicking of the machine. Then she looked up, and their eyes met.

'It's not pleasant to be out of work,' he said. 'Have you ever experienced it?'

'Once or twice,' she said. 'And I never wish to again. You don't look as if you were much used to office work.'

'No! I'm an artist; but times are hard with us. The present Government has driven all the money out of the country and no one buys pictures now; so I'm forced to turn my hand to something else.'

'I love pictures. My father was an artist.'

'Then we have something in common,' the young man

said. 'Would you like to see my work? I love showing it to people who understand something about painting, and are not afraid to criticize.'

'I should like to see it, immensely – though I won't presume to criticize.'

'May I enquire your name?' the young man asked eagerly. 'Mine is Shiel Davenport.'

'And mine – Lilian Rosenberg,' the girl said, with a smile.

'If I don't get the post, may I write to you sometimes, Miss Rosenberg, and ask you to my studio. I call it a studio, though it's really only an attic.'

Lilian Rosenberg nodded. 'I shall be delighted to come,' she said. 'I am afraid I am very unconventional.'

There was no time for further conversation, as Hamar entered the room at that moment.

'What do you want?' he asked curtly.

Shiel told him.

'You're too late,' Hamar said. 'I've engaged some one. If you'd called earlier, there might have been some chance for you, as you look tolerably intelligent. But it's no use now, so be off.'

As Shiel left the room he caught Lilian Rosenberg looking at him; and he saw that her eyes were full of sympathy.

The acquaintance, thus begun, ripened. She went to see his pictures, they had tea together, and they spent many subsequent hours in each other's company. And although Shiel saw in Lilian Rosenberg only a rather prepossessing girl from whom, after cultivating her acquaintance, he was hoping to learn the inner working of the Modern Sorcery Company Ltd., with her it was different.

In Shiel, Lilian Rosenberg saw the qualities she had always been seeking – the qualities she had almost despaired of ever finding – and which she had so often declared existed only in fiction. He only interested her, she argued; but she forgot that interest as well as pity is akin to love – and that where the former leads, the latter almost invariably follows.

'I don't believe you have enough to eat,' she said to him one day. 'You are a perfect shadow. How do you exist if you have no private means?'

'I just manage to exist, and that is all,' Shiel laughed,

and he spoke the truth, his present state of semi-starvation having resulted from the untoward events, which had happened prior to his application for the post of clerk to the Modern Sorcery Company Ltd., and his subsequent acquaintance with Lilian Rosenberg.

Whilst John Martin had been ill, and he had helped at the Hall in Kingsway, he had lived well. Gladys had taken care he was paid – not a big sum to be sure – but enough to keep him. But directly John Martin, in spite of Gladys' remonstrances, had resumed work, Shiel had been dismissed.

'I wish I could help you,' John Martin said to him, 'for I really feel grateful to you for all you have done, but to tell you the candid truth, I can't afford to pay any salaries. As you know, the receipts of the Hall are next to nothing; but the expenses continue just the same – rent, gas, and staff – all heavy items. Moreover, at your uncle's death, many of his creditors put in claims on the Firm for debts – debts he had incurred without either my sanction or knowledge – and it has been a serious drain on me to pay them off. In fact, my finances are now at such a low ebb that I cannot possibly do anything for you. If only the Modern Sorcery Company could be cleared off the scenes.'

'You would, I suppose, feel extremely grateful to whoever cleared them off?'

'I would,' John Martin replied, with a significant chuckle.

'Even though it were some one who had not stood very high in your estimation?'

'Even though it were the devil.'

'Now, look here, Mr. Martin,' Shiel said, trying to appear calm. 'I will devote all my energies and all my time to your cause – the overthrow of the Modern Sorcery Company, if only – if only, in the event of my being successful, you will give me some hope of being permitted to win your daughter.'

'I promise you that hope, and any other you may see fit to aspire to,' John Martin said, with a grim smile, 'since there isn't the remotest chance of your succeeding in the task you have set yourself. Believe me, it will take both money and wits to get the better of Hamar, Curtis and Kelson.'

'Anyhow, I have your permission to try. I shall do my best.'

'You may do what you like,' John Martin rejoined, 'so long as you don't talk to me again about Gladys till you've overthrown the Modern Sorcery Company. In the meanwhile, I must ask you to abstain from seeing her.'

'I am afraid I can't promise that.'

'Can't promise that,' John Martin cried, his eyes suffusing with sudden passion. 'Can't you! Then damn it, you must. I'm not going to have my daughter throw herself away on a penniless puppy. There, curse it all, you know what I think of you now – you're a bumptious puppy, and I swear you shall not come within a mile of her.'

'I shall,' Shiel retorted, drawing himself up to his full height. 'I shall see her whenever she will permit me – and since she is not at home at the present moment, I shall now await her return outside the house, and defy the savage old bull-dog inside it.' Leaving John Martin too taken aback with astonishment to articulate a syllable, Shiel withdrew.

True to his word, he waited to see Gladys. He paced up and down the road in front of the house from eleven o'clock in the morning, when his interview with John Martin had terminated, till eight o'clock in the evening, and was just beginning to think he would have to give up all hope of seeing her that day, when she came in sight.

'Really!' she exclaimed, after Shiel had explained the situation. 'Do you mean to say you have stayed here all day?'

'Of course I have,' Shiel answered. 'I told your father I would see you, and I meant to stay here till I did.'

'And what good has it done you?'

'All the good in the world. I shall sleep twice as well for it. I'm more in love with you than you think, and I mean to marry you one day. My prospects at present are absolutely Thames Embankmentish, but no matter, I've hit upon a capital way of ferreting out the secrets of the Modern Sorcery Company. I shall get employed by them' – and he told Gladys of the advertisement he had seen in the paper.

'Well! I wish you all success,' she said, 'but I'm afraid you've upset my father dreadfully, and the doctor says excitement is the very worst thing for him and may lead to another stroke. You must on no account come here again, until I give you leave.'

'But I may see you elsewhere?'

'If you're a wise man, you'll do one thing at a time. You'll discover the secret of the Sorcery Company first, and then—'

'When I have discovered it?'

'My father may forgive you. Have I told you I'm going on the stage? I know Bromley Burnham, and he's offered me a part at the Imperial. It is imperative now, that I should do something to help my father.'

'If you become an actress,' Shiel said bitterly, 'my chances of marrying you will indeed be small.'

'Not smaller than they are now,' Gladys observed. *'Au revoir.'* And with one of those tantalizing and perplexing smiles, with which some women, consciously or unconsciously, counteract – and sometimes, perhaps, for reasons best known to themselves – completely nullify the needless severity of their speech, shook hands with Shiel, and left him.

CHAPTER 18

STAGE THREE

THE weeks sped by. Gladys Martin went on the stage, and thanks to beauty and influence, rather than to talent – though in the latter respect she was certainly not wanting – she became an immediate success. Her photos, some taken alone, and some with Bromley Burnham, occupied a conspicuous place in all the weekly illustrateds, and in innumerable shop windows. People talked of her as they do of all actresses. Some said her father was a broken-down peer; some, a needy parson, and some, a policeman! Some said the Duke of Warminster was madly in love with her; others that Seaton Smyth, the notorious Cabinet Minister, was pining for a divorce on her behalf, and others, that she was seldom seen off the stage – she was entertaining the King of the Belgians.

'I've met her,' Lilian Rosenberg said to Shiel, as they stopped one evening to gaze at Gladys' portraits outside the Imperial Theatre. 'She came to our place to have a dream interpreted, and I thought nothing of her. I don't admire her the least bit in the world, do you?'

'I do,' Shiel replied, rather sharply.

'Why, you sound quite angry,' Lilian Rosenberg laughed. 'One would think you knew her. I wonder if Bromley Burnham is very much in love with her! He looks as if he were in these photographs! Do you think it possible for a man and woman to make love to each other every night on the stage, like they do, without one or other of them being affected?'

'I really couldn't say,' Shiel replied. 'I'm no authority on such matters – they don't interest me in the least.'

But this was an untruth – they did interest him – and very much, too. He seldom, indeed, thought of anything else. Had Gladys fallen in love with Bromley Burnham? Could she resist the fascinations of so handsome a man? He did not, of course, pay any heed to the gossip that coupled her name with dukes and other notorieties. He knew Gladys too well for that, but when he saw her thus photographed, clasped in the arms of Bromley Burnham, he had grave apprehensions. He longed to see her – to ask her if she were still free; but his every attempt failed. She always avoided him, and there was no other alternative save to further his scheme – his scheme for crushing the Sorcery Company – and to hope for the best.

And in these dark days of his life, when he was tormented by the yellow demon of jealousy, and at the same time endured hunger, Lilian Rosenberg was his solacing angel. Utterly regardless of appearances – she did not exaggerate when she said, 'I am not conventional; I don't care twopence for Mrs. Grundy.' She visited him in his garret, and she seldom went empty-handed.

'I don't want your things,' he rudely expostulated, when she loaded his table with cold chicken, jellies and potted meats. 'I'm not starving.'

'Yes, you are,' she said, 'and you've got to eat all I bring you.' And she made him eat. She made him, too, go for walks with her, and she insisted that he should go with her on Saturday afternoons for long rambles in the country, knowing all the time that Kelson was eating his heart out for love of her, and prophesying all kinds of terrible happenings to himself, unless she returned his affections.

Up to this point, at all events, Shiel did not allow his friendship with Lilian to blind him to the fact that he was cultivating her acquaintance with a set object. He frequently sounded her to see how much she knew of the inner workings of the Firm, and he satisfied himself that she knew very little.

'They never discuss their powers in my presence,' she told him, 'but I see them do very queer things. Mr. Kelson seldom walks to his room, he flies. He takes a little jump into the air, moves his arms and legs as if he were swimming, and flies upstairs and along the corridor. And what do you think happened the other day? Some men were carrying into the building a huge, oak chest and several large pictures that Mr. Hamar had bought at a sale, when Mr. Kelson arrived on the scene.

' "There is no need to lift these things," he said to the men, "put them down." He then made some rapid signs in the air and muttered something; whereupon the chest and pictures rose in the air, and followed him into the building, and up the stairs to their respective quarters.'

'The men must have been surprised,' Shiel said.

'Surprised!' Lilian Rosenberg ejaculated. 'They were simply bowled over, and looked at one another with such idiotic expressions in their bulging eyes and gaping mouths, that I nearly died with laughter.'

'And you've no idea how Kelson did that trick?'

'None, excepting, of course, that the signs he made, and what he said, must have had something to do with it.'

It was on the tip of Shiel's tongue to ask her, if she would try and find out for him, but he checked himself. Even at this juncture of their friendship he dare not appear too curious. He must wait.

To go back to Hamar. He had seen Gladys act; he had become more infatuated with her than ever; and his passion was stimulated by the knowledge that she was universally admired, and that half the men in London were dying to be introduced to her.

'Money will do anything,' one of Hamar's friends – they were all Jews – remarked to him. 'Offer the manager of the Imperial a hundred pounds and he'll do anything you like with regard to the girl. Every manager can be bought and every actress, too.'

The suggestion was a welcome one, and Hamar acted on it. But whether or not the exception proves the rule, he was immeasurably disconcerted to find that with regard to money and managers, his friends had deceived him. Far from being pleased at the offer of a bribe, the manager of the Imperial, an old Harrovian, raised his foot, and Hamar, who invariably paled at the prospect of violence, hurriedly withdrew.

On the eve of the initiation in Stage Three, the trio were very much perturbed.

'I hope to goodness nothing will appear to me,' Kelson said. 'My heart isn't strong enough to stand the shock of seeing striped figures. They should come to you, Curtis – a few jumps wouldn't do you any harm – you're fat enough.'

Agreeing each to sleep with a light in his room, they separated, and at about two o'clock Curtis, who had been suffering of late from his liver – the effect, so the doctor told him, of living a little too well – and could not sleep, heard a knock at his door. To his astonishment it was Kelson – Kelson, in his pyjamas.

'Hulloa!' Curtis exclaimed. 'What on earth brings you here, and however did you come?'

'The usual way!' Kelson said, in what struck Curtis as rather unusual tones. 'I flew here to tell you that we are now in stage three. Give me paper and ink. I want to write down the instructions I have received.'

Curtis conducted him into his sitting-room, switched on the lights and, giving him what he wanted, poured out a couple of tumblers of soda-and-milk.

'This will lower my temperature,' he said to himself. 'I shall know if I'm dreaming.'

He then sat by Kelson's side and observed what he wrote.

'The properties of walking on the water, and of breathing under the water are conferred on you during the forthcoming stage. You must refrain from red flesh and alcohol, but may eat poultry, fish, fruit, and vegetables in abundance.'

'The devil I may!' Curtis said in a fury. 'How very

kind! I would rather have roast beef than all the poulets and kippers in Christendom.'

Without noticing this interruption, Kelson went on writing.

'You must also concentrate for one hour every morning. Grade two in the scale of concentration, though sufficient for projection through ether, will not enable you to offer sufficient resistance to the pressure of water. You must reach grade three in the scale of concentration, before you can either walk on, or breathe under, the water. From six to seven a.m. you must fix your eyes on a glass of fresh spring water, and concentrate your very hardest on amalgamating with it, on passing your immaterial ego into it. At night, before you go to bed, you must drink a mixture composed of two drachms of Vindroo Sookum, one drachm of Harnoon Oobey, and one ounce of distilled water. Vindroo Sookum and Harnoon Oobey are a species of seaweed; the former of a pale salmon colour, the latter of a deep blue. They were formerly shrubs growing in the wood of Endlemoker in Atlantis, and are now to be found at a depth of two hundred fathoms, twenty miles to the north-east of Achill Island. These weeds must be well rinsed first; and when the prescribed amount of each has been carefully cut off and weighed, it must be boiled in the distilled water, and the compound, thus formed, allowed to cool before being drunk. This mixture renders the lungs immune to the action of fluid, and will enable you to breathe as easily in water as in air. There is still, however, the action of gravity to be considered, and this must be counteracted by sound. Before experimenting, these Atlantean words must be repeated aloud in the following order: Karma – nardka – rapto – nooman – K – arma – oola – piskooskte."'

'It's all very well to write all these directions,' Curtis said, 'but how am I to obtain the weeds? I can't go and fish for them.'

'You must engage the services of Mr. John Waley, formerly employed by the Brazilian Government in repairing marine cables. He will do all you want for the sum of £200.'

Kelson left off writing, and, wishing Curtis good-night, walked out of the room.

'You'll be deuced cold without an overcoat.' Curtis called out after him. 'Won't you have mine?'

But there was no reply, and though Curtis strained his ears to listen, he could catch no sound of a vehicle.

Kelson left Curtis at twenty minutes past two. At half-past two, Hamar, who had been sound asleep, was awakened by a loud rap.

'Kelson!' he gasped. 'How on earth did you get here? Are you a projection?'

'Don't worry me with questions,' Kelson replied 'I have come to give you instructions. A paper and ink, quick.'

Hamar obeyed with alacrity.

'On you,' Kelson wrote, 'is conferred the property of invisibility – a property common in Atlantis, and still possessed by the Fakirs of Hindoostan, the natives of Easter Island and certain tribes in New Guinea. You must reach grade three in the scale of concentration, by concentrating, from five to six o'clock, every morning, on amalgamating yourself with the ether. You must sit, with your head thrown back, gazing up into space – allowing nothing to distract your mind. Wholly and solely, your thoughts must be fixed on the ether. This property of invisibility can only be successfully practised when the third grade in the scale of concentration has been reached. Carry out these instructions, and, in a week's time, you will then be able to experiment – to become invisible at will. But before experimenting it will always be necessary to repeat the words "Bakra – naka – taksomana," and to swallow a pill, composed of two drachms of Derhens Voskry, one drachm of Karka Voli and one drachm of saffron. Derhens Voskry and Karka Voli are a crimson and white species of seaweed, that grows on the hundred-fathom level, thirty miles west-south-west of the Aran Islands, Galway Bay. Mr. John Waley, employed by the Brazilian Government for repairing cables, will procure these ingredients for you. To become visible, you've only to repeat the words, "Bakra – naka – taksomana," backwards.'

'But how about my clothes?' Hamar asked. 'Will they disappear too?'

'Everything!' Kelson answered. 'Hat, boots, tie and breeches. All you have on! Good-night!' And walking out of the room, he leaped into the air, and flew downstairs. But though Hamar listened attentively, he could not hear him leave the building – there was no sound of any door.

When they met the following mid-day in Cockspur Street, Kelson remembered nothing of his visits.

'All I know is,' he said, 'that the moment I got into bed, I fell asleep, and suddenly found myself standing in a kind of brown desert, talking to a tall man with most peculiar features and eyes, and a dazzling white skin. He informed me that he had been an animal-trainer in the State of Ballyynkan, Atlantis, and was ordered to give me instructions as to the taming of the present day wild beast.

' "You must obtain a stone called the Red Laryx," he said. "It is to be found in great quantities on the three-hundred fathom level, forty miles to the west-south-west of North Aran Island, and can be procured for you by the same man that gets the weeds for Hamar and Curtis. It is a blood-red pebble, covered with peculiarly vivid green spots, and cannot be mistaken. Sit with it pressed against your forehead for an hour every morning, and concentrate hard on amalgamating yourself with it – *i.e.* passing into it, and its properties will gradually be imparted to you. Do this regularly, for a week, and by the end of that time, you will be able to experiment with animals. All you will have to do, will be to hold the stone slightly clenched in your left hand, whilst, with your right, you make these signs in the air," and he showed me certain passes. "Stare fixedly into the animal's eyes all the while, and, by the time you have finished making the passes, you will find the animals are subdued. Pronounce these words 'Meta – ra – ka – va – Avakana,' holding up, as you do so, your right hand with the thumb turned down and held right across the palm, and the little finger stretched out as wide as it will go, and you will understand what any animal wishes to say."

'He ceased speaking, and approaching close to me, tapped my forehead; whereupon there was a blank; and on recovering consciousness, I found myself in bed, feeling somewhat exhausted and very cold.'

'You have no recollection of coming to see us, in your pyjamas, about two o'clock in the morning?' Hamar asked.

'Don't talk rot,' Kelson said. 'I'm in no mood for fooling, I've got a chill on my liver.'

'What was it, Leon?' Curtis inquired.

'A case of unconscious projection,' Hamar said. 'Clearly

the work of the Unknown. We must commence carrying out the instructions at once.'

At the end of a week, Hamar, Kelson and Curtis began to put in practice their newly acquired properties.

Hamar tested his, in a first-class railway carriage, on the London, Brighton & South Coast Railway.

'I'll go for a day's trip to Brighton,' he said, 'and cheat the Company. They deserve it.'

He went to Victoria, and ignoring the booking-office, calmly seated himself in a first-class compartment, where, amongst other occupants, sat a quite remarkably proper-looking clergyman, and a very handsomely dressed lady, with a haughty stare, and a typical *nouveau riche* nose!

When the ticket collector came round before the train started, Hamar waited, till every one else in the compartment had shown him their tickets, and then, just as the man was about to demand his, swallowed one of the prescribed pills, repeating immediately, in a loud voice, which caused considerable excitement among the other passengers, the words, 'Bakra – naka – taksomana!' The next moment he had disappeared.

'Strike me red!' the collector gasped, putting one hand to his heart, and grasping the door with the other. 'What's become of him? Was he – a – a – gho – st?'

'I don't – er –know – er, what to – to make of it,' the parson said, heroically preserving his Oxford drawl, in spite of his chattering teeth. 'I don't – er, of course – er, believe in gho – sts! He must – er, have been – a – a – an evil spirit. Dear me – aw!'

'Help me out of the carriage at once,' the lady with the stare panted. 'I consider the whole thing most disgraceful. I shall report it to the Company.'

'What's the matter, Joe?' an inspector called out, threading his way through the crowd of people, that had commenced to collect at the door of the compartment.

'I'm blessed if I know!' the collector said. 'The honly explanation I can give is that a gent who was seated here has dissolved – the hot weather has melted him like butter!'

At this there was a shout of laughter, the inspector slammed the door, the guard whistled, and the next moment the train was off.

As soon as the train was well out of the station Hamar

repeated the words he had used, backwards, and he was once again visible.

The effect of his reappearance amongst them was even more striking than that of his previous disappearance.

'Take it away – take it away!' the lady opposite him shouted, throwing up her hands to ward him off. 'It's there again! Take it away! I shall die – I shall go mad!'

'How hideous! How diabolical!' a stout, elderly man said in slow, measured tones, as if he were reading his own funeral service. 'It must be the devil! The devil! Ha!' and burying his face in his hands, he indulged in a loud fit of mirthless laughter.

'Why don't you do something? Talk theology to it, exorcize it,' a remarkably plain woman, in the far corner of the carriage said, in highly indignant tones to the clergyman. 'As usual, whenever there is something to be done, it is woman who must do it!'

She got up, and casting a look of infinite scorn at the clergyman – whose condition of terror prevented him uttering even the one telling, biting word – Suffragette – that had risen and stuck in his throat – raised her umbrella, and, before Hamar could stop her, struck it vigorously at him.

'Ghost, demon, devil!' she cried. 'I know no fear! Begone!' And the point of her umbrella coming in violent contact with Hamar's waistcoat, all the breath was unceremoniously knocked out of him; and with a ghastly groan he rolled off his seat on to the floor, where he writhed and grovelled in the most dreadful agony, whilst his assailant continued to stab and jab at him.

In all probability, she would have succeeded, eventually, in reaching some vital part of his body, had not one of the frenzied passengers pulled the communication-cord and stopped the train!

CHAPTER 19

A SERIES OF MISADVENTURES

WITH the advent of the guard, Hamar's assailant was dragged off him, and he was locked up in a separate compartment, 'to be given in charge,' so the indignant official announced, directly they got to Brighton. But Hamar ordained it otherwise. As soon as he had recovered sufficiently from the effects of the severe castigation the female furioso had inflicted on him, he became invisible, and when the train drew up at the Brighton platform, and a couple of policemen arrived to march him off, he was nowhere to be found! This was his first experiment with the newly acquired property. 'In future,' he said to himself, 'before I try any tricks, I'll take very good care there are no Suffragettes about.'

In London there was, of course, no need for him ever to pay fares. All he had to do, was to become invisible as soon as the taxi stopped, calmly step out of the vehicle, and walk away. As for meals, he was able to enjoy many – gratis. He simply walked into a restaurant, fed on the very best, and then disappeared. Of course, he could not repeat the trick in the same place, and cautious though he was, he was at last caught. It appears that a description of him had been circulated among the police, and that private detectives were employed to watch for him in the principal hotels and restaurants. Consequently, directly he entered the grill room at the Piccadilly Hotel, he was arrested and handcuffed before he had time to swallow a pill.

He was now in a most unpleasant predicament – the tightest corner he had ever been in. Supposing he could not escape – his sentence would be at the least two years' penal servitude – what would happen? Curtis and Kelson would never work the show without him. Curtis would give himself entirely up to eating and drinking, Kelson would marry Lilian Rosenberg; the compact with the Unknown would be broken; and after that – he dare not think. He must escape! He must get at the pills! The police took him away in a taxi, and all the time he sat between them, he struggled desperately to squeeze his hands through the small, cruel circle that held them. 'It's all right for Curtis and Kelson!' he said to himself, 'all right at least – now! They know nothing! They have never tried to think what the breaking of the compact means! Their weak, silly minds are entirely centred on the present! The present! Damn the present! They are fools, idiots, imbeciles who think only of the present – it's the future – the future that matters!' He scraped the skin off his wrists, he sweated, he swore! And it was not until one of the detectives threatened to rap him over the head, that he sullenly gave in and sat still.

The taxi drew up in front of the Gerald Road Police Station, and Hamar was conducted to an ante-room, prior to being taken before the inspector. Just as a policeman was about to search him, he made one last desperate effort.

'Look here,' he said, 'if I pledge you my word I'll not attempt to do anything, will you let me have my hands – or at least one of my hands – free a moment. Some grit has got in my eye and I cannot stand the irritation.'

'That game won't work here,' one of the detectives said. 'You should keep your eyes shut when there's dust about, or else not have such protruding ones.'

Hamar threatened to report him to the Home Secretary for brutal conduct, but the detective only laughed, and Hamar had to submit to the mortification of being searched.

'What are these?' a detective said, fingering the seaweed pills gingerly.

'Stomachic pills!' Hamar said bitterly, 'they are taken as a digestive after meals. You look dyspeptic – have one.'

'Now, none of your sauce!' the detective said, 'you come along with me,' – and Hamar was hauled before the inspector.

'Can I go out on bail?' Hamar asked.

'Certainly not,' the inspector replied.

'Then I shan't give you my name and address,' Hamar said. 'I shan't tell you anything.'

The inspector merely shrugged his shoulders, and after the charge sheet was read over, Hamar was conducted to a cell.

'This is awful,' he said, 'what the deuce am I to do! To send for Curtis and Kelson will be fatal, and it will be equally fatal to leave them in ignorance of what has happened to me. I am, indeed, on the horns of a dilemma. I must get at those pills.'

Up and down the floor of the tiny cell he paced, his mind tortured with a thousand conflicting emotions. And then, an idea struck him. He would ask to be allowed to see his lawyer.

'Cotton's the man,' he said to himself, 'he will get the pills for me!'

The inspector, after satisfying himself that Cotton was

on the register, rang him up, and after an hour of terrible suspense to Hamar, the lawyer briskly entered his cell.

They conferred together for some minutes, and having arranged the method of defence, Cotton was preparing to depart, when Hamar whispered to him—

'I want you to do me a particular favour. In the top right-hand drawer of the chest of drawers in my bedroom, in Cockspur Street, I have a red pill-box. These pills are for indigestion. I simply can't do without them. Will you get them for me?'

'What, to-night?' the lawyer asked dubiously.

'Yes, to-night,' Hamar pleaded. 'I'll make it a matter of business between us – get me the pills before eight o'clock, and you have £1000 down. My cheque-book is in the same drawer.'

The lawyer said nothing, but gave Hamar a look that meant much!

Again there was a dreadful wait, and Hamar had abandoned himself to the deepest despair when Cotton reappeared. He shook hands with his client, slipping the pills into the latter's palm. Whilst the lawyer was pocketing his cheque, Hamar gleefully swallowed a pill, and crying out 'Bakra – naka – takso – mana,' – vanished!

'Heaven preserve us! What's become of you?' Cotton exclaimed, putting his hand to his forehead and leaning against the wall for support. 'Am I ill or dreaming?'

'Anything wrong, sir?' a policeman inquired, opening the cell door and looking in. 'Why, what have you done with the prisoner – where is he?'

'I have no more idea than you,' the lawyer gasped. 'He was talking to me quite naturally, when he suddenly left off – said something idiotic – and disappeared.'

Hamar did not dally. He quietly slipped through the open door, and darting swiftly along a stone passage, found his way to the entrance, which was blocked by two constables with their backs to him.

'I'll give the brutes something to remember me by,' Hamar chuckled, and, taking a run, he kicked first one, and then the other with all his might, precipitating them both into the street. He then sped past them – home.

Hamar, by astute inquiries, learned that the police had decided to hush up the affair, not being quite sure how they had figured, or, indeed, what had actually occurred.

As to Cotton, the shock he had undergone, at seeing Hamar suddenly melt away before his eyes, was so great that he went off his head, and had to be confined in an asylum.

After this adventure Hamar shunned restaurants, and manipulating his new property sparingly, and with the utmost caution, warned Kelson and Curtis to do the same.

'I'll bet anything,' he said to them, 'it was a put-up job on the part of the Unknown – a cunning device to make us break the compact.'

'Oh, we'll be careful enough as far as that goes,' Curtis growled. 'It's this vegetarian diet that I can't stick. Fancy living on beans and potatoes, and only milk and aerated water to wash them down. It was bad enough in San Francisco, when we hadn't the means even to smell meat cooking – but with the money literally burning a hole in one's pocket, it's ten times worse! Whatever the Unknown has in store for us it can't be a worse Hell than what I've got now. What say you, Matt?'

'The same! Precisely the same!' Kelson said. 'Only it's love – not potatoes and beans that worries me. In the old days when I was penniless, I did get some consolation from knowing it was all hopeless – but now – now, when, as Ed says, "the money's literally burning a hole in one's pocket," and everything might go swimmingly – not to be allowed even to buy a bracelet – is more than human nature can endure. I certainly can't conceive a Hell to beat it.'

'Don't be too sure,' Hamar said, 'and for goodness' sake don't let the Unknown give you an opportunity of comparing.'

The night succeeding this conversation, Hamar, Curtis and Kelson introduced their new properties into the programme of their entertainment in Cockspur Street, and London got another big thrill. Hamar exhibited such startling proofs of his power of invisibility, that not only was the whole audience convinced, but from amongst certain prominent members of the Council of the Psychical Research Society, who were attending with the express purpose of unmasking Hamar, two had epileptic fits on the spot, and several, before they could get home, became raving lunatics.

At the commencement of the second part of the programme – the audience was still too flabbergasted to fully grasp what was happening. They saw on the stage a huge tank of water – with which they were told Mr. Curtis would experiment.

'What I am about to do,' Mr. Curtis – who now walked on to the stage – informed his audience, 'is quite simple. All you want is faith. Those of you who are Christian Scientists should be able to do it as easily as I. Say "I will! I will walk on the water!" and your faith – your colossal faith – faith in your ability to do it will actually enable you to do it.'

Curtis then repeated – in tones that could not be heard by the audience – the Atlantean cabalistic words – 'Karma – nardka – rapto – nooman – K – arma – oola – piskooskte,' and glided gracefully on to the surface of the water. Every now and then he sank slowly down to the bottom, where he strolled about, or sat, or lay down.

The audience was simply fascinated. Nothing they had hitherto seen tickled their fancy half as much. As an American, who was present, put it – 'To live under the water like a fish is immense – so hygienic and economical.'

Though the time apportioned to this part of the entertainment was half an hour, it was extended to over an hour, and even then the audience was not satisfied. They would have gone on watching Curtis – eating – drinking – jumping – skipping – singing and chasing gold fish – under the water all night, and when at length permitted to come out of the tank – exhausted and sulky – they gave him even heartier applause than they had given Hamar.

But the cup of their enjoyment was not yet full. The greatest treat of all was in store for them.

For the third and last part of the entertainment, a cage, containing a large Bengal tiger, was wheeled on to the stage.

'You look precious white,' Curtis remarked, just as Kelson was about to go on.

'I guess you'd look the same,' Kelson retorted, 'if you had to hobnob with a tiger. The Unknown always gives me the nasty jobs.'

'And in this case,' Curtis said with a low, mocking laugh, 'it also loads you with consolations. The house is full of ladies who adore you, and if you are eaten, just think of the sympathy welling up in their beautiful eyes! If that isn't sufficient compensation for you, I—' But the remainder of this encouraging speech was lost in a loud roar. The Bengal tiger shook its bars – the audience screamed, and Curtis flew.

With a desperate attempt to look calm, Kelson, clutching the red laryx stone in his left hand, walked on to the stage, whilst the tiger, rearing on its hind legs, tried to reach him with its paws.

There were loud cries of 'Oh! Oh!' from the audience, and Kelson's heart beat quicker, when a girl with wavy, fair hair and big, starry eyes, screamed out 'Don't go near it! Don't go near it!'

As soon as there was comparative quiet Kelson spoke.

'As you can see, ladies and gentlemen,' he said, 'this animal is genuinely savage! It is not like the tigers one sees in menageries, drugged and deprived of their natural weapons – teeth and claws. It comes direct from India, where its reputation as a man-eater is widespread. I am not, however, intimidated – its growls merely amuse me.'

Quaking all over, he approached the cage, and staring fixedly into the tiger's face, made the prescribed passes. In an instant, the whole attitude of the great cat changed. Dropping on to its fore-legs, it rubbed its head against the bars and purred. A low buzz of astonishment burst from the audience, and Kelson, now assured that the spell had worked, waved his disengaged hand, in the most gallant fashion, at the audience, and strutted into the cage. He shook paws with the tiger, patted it on the back, sat down by its side, and, whilst pretending to be on the most familiar terms with it, took every precaution to avoid coming in too close contact with its teeth and claws.

The audience was charmed – the men cheered, the ladies waved handkerchiefs, and the only disappointed persons present were a few belligerent and bloodthirsty boys, and a Suffragette, who severally, and for diverse reasons, would have relished the performances of a savage tiger, but had little sympathy with the performance of a tame one.

The next surprise that Mr. Kelson had for his audience, was the announcement that he could interpret the language of animals. At his invitation, a dozen members of the audience came on to the platform and stood near the cage. Looking steadily at the tiger he then pronounced the mystic words 'Meta – ra – ka – va – avakana,' holding up his right hand, with the thumb turned down and stretched right across the palm, and the little finger extended to the utmost. In an instant the great secret – the secret that Darwin had studied so strenuously for years – was revealed to him. The language of animals was olfactory. The tiger spoke to him through the sense of smell – through his nose instead of his ears. It regulated and modified the odour it gave off from its body, and which worked its way out through the pores of its skin, just as human beings regulate and modify the intonations of their voices. Indeed, so delicate are the olfactory organs of animals that the faintest of these language smells makes an impression on them, which impression is at once interpreted by the brain. If an animal wishes to leave a message behind it, it merely impregnates some article – a leaf or a root, or a clump of grass – or merely the ether with a brain smell, and any other animal happening to pass by the spot, within a certain time (in favourable weather), will at once be attracted by the smell, and be able to interpret it. That is the reason one so often sees an animal suddenly stop at a spot and sniff it – it is reading some message left there by some other animal. All this, and more, Kelson explained to his audience, who were exceedingly interested, many of them getting up to ask him questions. He also reported to them the tiger's conversation, which consisted chiefly of complaints against the management with regard to its food.

'To be everlastingly fed on scraps of horse-flesh,' it said, 'when there are dozens of plump young women sitting in the stalls, under its very nose, was tantalizing to a degree. Would Mr. Kelson kindly speak to whoever was responsible for such cruelty and negligence?'

A bear and a crocodile having been tamed in the same manner, and their remarks interpreted to the audience, the entertainment concluded.

The next day the papers were full of it.

The *Planet,* under the startling announcements—

'RECOVERY OF THE LOST SENSES.

MORE EXTRAORDINARY FEATS IN COCKSPUR STREET.

LEON HAMAR BECOMES INVISIBLE AT WILL,'

—narrated all that had occurred.

The *Monitor* – if anything more sensational – declared—

'The Language of Animals Discovered at Last!

The Problem of Breathing under Water—

SOLVED!

Dematerialization at Will established!'

And even the *Courier* – the steady, ever cautious old *Courier*, England's premier paper, created a precedent by the use of a quite conspicuously large type; *vide* the following—

'THE AGE OF MIRACLES REVIVED!

Actual Case of Subduing and Conversing with Wild Animals

Recovery of the Properties of Invisibility; of Walking on Water, and of Breathing under Water.'

As before, there were innumerable cases of imitation, many of them, unhappily, resulting in the death of the imitator. At Dover, for instance, a Congregationalist Minister, convinced that he had the requisite amount of faith, announced from the pulpit, that he intended walking on the water, in the Harbour, after service. Thousands flocked to see him, but despite the fact that he said 'I will! I will!' with the greatest emphasis, the unkind waves would not support him. Indeed, since they swallowed him, it might almost be said that the Rev. S— supported the waves.

For two whole days there were regular stampedes of experimenters to Hyde Park and Regent's Park, and the banks of their respective waters resounded with the words, 'I will walk! I will walk!' succeeded by splashes and cries for help.

Nor was the water feat the only one that induced imitators. Crowds flocked to the Zoological Gardens, and the various houses were literally packed with people trying to get into conversation with the animals; these attempts being also marked by a large proportion of fatal results. One old gentleman – a Fellow of the Royal Society – carried away in his enthusiasm to talk with a tiger, after making what he thought to be the correct signs, slipped his nose through the bars of the tiger's cage, and had it promptly bitten off – whilst a girl, in her endeavours to sniff the crocodiles, and so get in conversation with them, fell in their midst, and was torn to pieces before help arrived.

However, these fatalities only served as an advertisement to the firm, and hundreds of people, for whom there was not even standing room, were turned away from the house nightly.

But later on there were hitches. Curtis, whose dislike to vegetarian diet steadily increased, when dining one evening at his club, could no longer withstand the sight of roast beef. The smell of it tickled his palate unmercifully.

'Take this infernal mess away!' he said, pushing a plate of nut steak from him in disgust, 'and let me have a full course – entrée, soup, fish, meat, everything you've got – chartreuse and a liqueur, and bring it quick – I'm famished.'

He ate and ate, and drank and drank, until it was as much as he could do to rise from the table. And then, in excellent spirits, he repaired to Cockspur Street.

How he got on to the stage he could never tell. Everything was in a haze around him, until there was a dull crash in his ears, and he suddenly found himself drowning. No one, at first, noticed his helpless condition, but attributed his antics to part of the programme; and he most certainly would have been drowned, had it not been for Lilian Rosenberg, who, being quite by chance, in front of the house, perceived he was drunk, the moment he came on the stage. She flew to the wings, and, just in the nick of time, got two of the supers to haul him out of the tank. Of course, it was announced – with a pretty apology – by Mr. Hamar, that Mr. Curtis had been taken ill. Kelson immediately came on with his animals, and the audience departed without the slighest suspicion as to the truth.

Hamar was furious.

'You idiot!' he said to Curtis, 'that all comes of your making a beast of yourself – you would sacrifice Matt and me, for your insatiable craving for meat and alcohol. Can't you see it was a trick of the Unknown to make us break the compact? Had you been drowned, the partnership would, of course, have been dissolved – and it would have been your fault! You must obey your injunctions! Damn it, you must!' And Hamar spoke so fiercely that Curtis was for once in a way cowed, and solemnly promised that he would not repeat the offence.

Kelson was the next culprit; and his misdoings were indirectly associated with the foregoing incident. Lilian Rosenberg's action in saving Curtis's life, thrilled him to the core, and called into play all his ardent passion. He had seen her sitting in the front of the house, and had come upon the scene just as she was urging the supers to go to Curtis' assistance; and he then thought she had never looked so lovely.

'Come out with me to-morrow afternoon,' he whispered. 'Hamar's going out of town!' And before she could stop him he had kissed her.

Kelson hardly expected Lilian Rosenberg would accept his invitation, but on arriving at the place he had named, he was delighted beyond measure to find her there.

Nor could any one have been nicer to him. No girl, he told himself, who did not in some degree at least, reciprocate his sentiments, could have allowed him to stare into her eyes as she did, or squeeze her hands, as he did. He took her to the ladies' drawing-room of his club, where there were plenty of quiet, secluded nooks, and there, whilst she poured out tea for him, he once more related to her all his early deeds and ailments – real and imaginary – and all his ideals and aspirations.

Lilian Rosenberg was most sympathetic.

'You should have been a poet,' she said. 'There is something about you that it quite Byronic.'

And Kelson, who had never heard of Byron, was immensely flattered.

'Will you come to the jeweller's with me,' he said, 'and choose whatever you like best. Those fingers of yours are made for rings – rings of all sorts!' and he gave them a gentle pressure.

She let him escort her to Bond Street, and followed him gaily into Raymond's; but when it came to accepting a ring from him, she laughingly refused, and chose, instead, the most expensive diamond bracelets and pendants in the shop. Some of these she wore – the rest – unknown to him of course – she sold; sending the proceeds, anonymously, to Shiel Davenport – who was starving.

When Kelson went on the stage, that evening, his thoughts were so far away – planning for his honeymoon – that he entered the cage of a newly imported lion without having made the necessary signs, and would most certainly have been mangled out of recognition, had not one of the supers, perceiving how matters lay, rushed to his assistance, and kept the lion at bay with a pole, till further help could be procured. It had been a narrow squeak, and to Kelson the bare idea of continuing his performance was appalling. His nerves were, as he himself put it, anyhow, and he preferred retiring for the rest of the evening.

But Hamar would not hear of it.

'This is the second bungle we have had,' he said, 'and the reputation of the firm is seriously at stake. You must go on again and retrieve it.'

And Kelson, trembling all over, was obliged to reappear.

After it was all over, and he had bowed himself out into the wings, Hamar led him aside.

'Don't look so damned pleased with yourself,' he said, 'I don't half like the look of things. This is the third time the Unknown has tried to trap us – the fourth time it may be successful! Take care!'

CHAPTER 20

THE STAGE OF HAUNTINGS

MUCH to the relief of the trio, the end of stage three was at length reached – and, thanks to Hamar, reached without further mishap. To keep Curtis and Kelson up to the mark, Hamar had worked indefatigably. He had never relaxed his efforts in the strict watch he kept over them, and he had unceasingly impressed upon them the vital importance of obeying, to the very letter, the instructions they had received from the Unknown.

The part he had thus taken upon himself, the difficulties he had to encounter in this unceasing vigilance, had produced a new Hamar – a Hamar that was a personality; a personality so utterly unlike the old Hamar – the meek and servile clerk – as to make one wonder if there could possibly be two Hamars – outwardly and physically the same – inwardly and psychologically diametrically opposed. A year ago, Curtis and Kelson would have ridiculed the idea of being afraid of Hamar – such an idea would have struck them as simply absurd; but they were afraid of him now, they dreaded his anger more than anything, more even than the prospect of infringing their compact with the Unknown.

'We have made pots of money,' Curtis remarked one day. 'Why can't we give up work and enjoy it?'

'Because I say no!' Hamar hissed. 'No! We can't give it up – not, at least, until the last stage has been safely gone through. To give up now would be to break the compact!'

'Well, why not?' Curtis mumbled.

'Why not!' Hamar cried. 'Heavens, man, can't you understand! Can you form no conception of what failure to keep the compact means? Has the memory of that night – of that tree and all the foul things it suggested, passed completely out of your mind? It hasn't out of mine – it is as clear now as it was then. And often – mark this, both of you – often when I am alone in the night, I see queer luminous shapes – shapes of repulsive vegetable growths – of polyps – and of disgusting tongues that come towards me through the gloom and circle slowly round the bed, whilst the whole room vibrates with soft, mocking laughter! You know how mirrors shine in the moonlight. Well, the other night, when I looked at mine, I saw in it the reflection, not of a face, but of two light evil eyes that looked at me and – smiled! Smiled with a smile that said more plainly than words, "I am waiting!" and that is what the shapes, and the very atmosphere of the place at night always seems to say – "We are waiting! You are enjoying the joke now – we shall enjoy it later on!" If we knew exactly what was in store for us it wouldn't be so bad, but it is the vagueness of it, the vagueness of the horrors that the Unknown has hinted at, that makes it so appalling! We may die awful deaths – or we may not die AT ALL – the shapes, indefinite and misty no longer, but materialized – wholly and entirely materialized – may come for us and take us away with them! And it is to prevent this, that I am urging you, compelling you, to stick to the compact, and give the Unknown no loophole! Think of the tremendous rewards, if we succeed in passing through the last stage! As I have said before, Curtis need do nothing but eat, whilst you, Matt, can become a Mormon and marry all the pretty girls in London!'

This speech had the desired effect, and nothing more – for the time at least – was said about retiring.

'Do you think Leon is quite – er – like – er – like us?' Kelson said, when Hamar left them, after administering his admonition. 'At times he hardly looks human. His face is such a funny colour, such a lurid yellow, and his eyes, so piercing! He gives me the jumps! I can't bear to think of him at night!'

'Rubbish,' Curtis growled. 'You imagine it. There's nothing of the spook about Leon! He's of this world and nothing but this world.'

It was odd, however, that from that time he, too, began to have the same feeling – the feeling that Hamar was perpetually watching them – watching them awake and watching them asleep! Curtis awoke one night to see, standing on his hearth, a shadowy figure with a lurid yellow face and two gleaming dark eyes, which were fixed on him. He called out, and it vanished!

'Of course it's the nut steak!' And thus he tried to assure himself. But he was badly scared all the same.

Another night, he saw some one he took to be Hamar, peeping at him from behind the window curtains. He threw a slipper at the figure, and the slipper went right through it. If Hamar's phantom had been the only thing he saw, he would not have minded much; but both he and Kelson soon began to see and hear other things. Curtis frequently saw half-materialized forms, forms of men with cone-shaped heads and peculiarly formed limbs, stealing up the staircase in front of him, and, turning into his bedroom, vanish there. He heard them moving about, long after he had got into bed. Sometimes they would glide up to the bed and bend over him, and though he could never see their eyes, he could feel they were fixed mockingly on him. Once he saw the door of his wardrobe slowly open, and a white something with a dreadful face – half human and half animal – steal slyly out and disappear in the wall opposite. And once when he put out his hand to feel for the matches, they were gently thrust into his palm, whilst the walls of the room shook with laughter.

Kelson was equally tormented, though the phenomena took rather a different form. Alone in his bedroom at night, the shape of the room would frequently change; either the walls and ceiling would recede, and recede, until they assumed the proportions of some vast chamber, full of gloom and strange shadows; or they would slowly, very slowly, close in upon him, as if it were their intention to crush him to death. A feeling of suffocation would come over him, and he would gasp, choke, beat the air with his arms, be on the verge of losing consciousness, when there would be a loud, mocking laugh – and the walls and ceiling would be in their proper places again. At other times he would see strange figures on the wall – numbers of circles, that would keep on revolving in the most bewildering fashion. Then, suddenly, they would leave the wall and slowly approach him, increasing in circumference; and the same thing would happen, as happened with the wall and ceiling; he would undergo the whole sensation of asphyxiation, and be on the brink of swooning, when there would be a loud peal of evil, satirical laughter, and the circles would instantly disappear.

Sometimes the bedclothes would assume extraordinary shapes; sometimes the articles on his dressing-table; sometimes his clothes; and once, when he was about to put on his bedroom slippers, he found them already occupied – occupied by icy cold feet. Another time, when he put out his hand to take hold of a tumbler, he put it on the back of another hand – smooth, cold and pulpy!

Hardly a night passed without some sort of manifestation happening to one or other of the trio, and even Curtis – fat and stolid Curtis – began to lose flesh and look harassed.

On the eve of the initiation into stage four, the three, separating for the night, retired to their respective quarters in a far from pleasant state of expectation.

Hamar was undressing, when there came a loud ring at the telephone, outside his door.

'Holloa!' he called out, 'who are you?'

'Are you Mr. Hamar?' a voice asked, breathlessly.

Hamar replied in the affirmative, and the voice continued—

'I'm Mrs. Anderson-Waite, of 30 Queen's Mansions, Queen's Gate. I have been holding a séance here, with some of my friends, and most extraordinary things have happened, and are still happening. There are violent knockings on the wall and ceiling, and the table has become positively dangerous. It has repeatedly sprung into the air, and savagely assaulted several of the sitters. It has thrown one lady on to the floor, and despite our efforts to prevent it, has trampled on her so viciously that she is badly hurt, and the doctor who has just arrived thinks very seriously of it. We wanted to stop, but some strange power seems to be forcing us to go on. The table has rapped out your name and address, and says it has something important to communicate to you, and that unless you come here at once, it won't answer for the consequences.'

'All right!' Hamar said. 'I'll come. I'll be with you in less than half an hour.'

When Hamar arrived at Queen's Mansions, he found a terrified party of ladies awaiting him in the entrance to the flat.

'Thank goodness you've come!' they exclaimed, all together. 'We've been having an awful time. The table has driven us out of the drawing-rom – it is obsessed by a devil.'

'Let me have a look at it,' Hamar said, 'and I'll soon tell you.'

The leader of the party, Mrs. Anderson-Waite, very cautiously opened the drawing-room door, and Hamar peered in. In the centre of the room was a large, round, ebony table, that commenced to rock, in the most sinister fashion, the moment Hamar looked at it.

'It evidently wants to speak with me,' Hamar said; 'you had better leave me here with it for a few minutes.'

'Do take care,' Mrs. Anderson-Waite said, as she shut the door. 'It may want to murder you. If it does, ring this bell, and we will all come to your assistance.'

Hamar gave her an assuring smile, but he was by no

means as much at ease as he pretended to be. He stood staring at the table, too fascinated to take his eyes off it, and too afraid to move.

At length, however, pulling himself together, and convinced the table was the medium through which the Unknown wished to give him fresh instructions, he stealthily approached it. He addressed it, and it rapped out to him that he must at once obtain pen and ink and take down what it wished to say.

Obtaining the requisite materials from Mrs. Anderson-Waite, he sat down and was preparing to write on his knee, when the table told him to rub its surface briskly with his left hand, to trace on it the three Atlantean symbols, *i.e.* a club foot, a hand with the fingers clenched and the long pointed thumb standing upright, and a bat – and then – to place his paper on it, and transcribe what it had to say.

Hamar obeyed, and after sitting for exactly three minutes with his pencil between his fingers, he felt a cold, pulpy hand laid over his, impelling him to write with lightning-like rapidity. The script read as follows:—

'To Hamar, Curtis and Kelson – to the three of you in common – is given the knowledge of inflicting all manner of torments and diseases, of imparting all kinds of injurious properties, and of causing plagues.

'In the first place, you must understand that the essence of life, comprising the psychical, psychological and physical, permeates every part of the living corporeal body – and that any limb, or fragment of skin or flesh, cut off from the living corporeal body, retains the essence of life, comprising the psychical and physical in its full vigour and entirety. Consequently, if a person have grafted on to them a piece of skin or flesh, or be inoculated with the blood or veins of a tiger – then that person not merely becomes liable to all the physical infirmities of the tiger, but may – if the counteracting influences are not sufficiently strong – partake of all the tiger's psychological characteristics.

'Thus, if you give a person, in whom there is a latent tendency to drink, a drop of a drunkard's blood – in a glass of wine, or sweet, or pill, no matter what – that person will at once take to drink. Thus – mark you – people can be metamorphosed into libertines, suicides, idiots and murderers. This metamorphosis can also be produced by means of a magnet called the "magnes microcosmi," which is prepared from substances that have had a long association with the human body, and are penetrated by its vitality. Such substances are the hair and blood. Take either one of them, and dry it in a shady and moderately warm place, until it has lost its humidity and odour. By this process it will have lost, too, all its mumia – that is to say, its essence of life – and is hungry to regain it. It is now a magnes microcosmi, or a magnet for attracting diseases and properties, and if it be placed in close contact with a criminal or lunatic, it will be filled with his essence of life, and may then be used as a means of infecting other people with his pernicious qualities. Bury it under the doorstep of the person you wish infected, or hide it in his house, or mix it well with earth, and plant a shrub in the earth, and the vitality the magnet took from the criminal or lunatic will pass into the plant; and if the plant, or even flower of the plant, be given to any one, that person – unless he or she be a person absolutely free from the germs of vice – will be attracted to it, and greatly affected by it.

'Or again, the earth over the grave of a lunatic or criminal will contain his essence of life, *i.e.* his vitality, which impregnates everything around it, and if that earth be placed somewhere in the immediate presence of a person, in whom there are latent tendencies to vice – then that person will be affected by it.

'And through these methods of using the essence of life, that is impregnated with the disease you wish to inflict – you may infect people with all kinds of incurable ailments.

'But a quicker, and equally sure method of smiting people with disease, such as cancer, fever, epilepsy, apoplexy, etc.; of smiting them blind, deaf, dumb, lame, etc.; or bringing upon them all kinds of accidents, is to make an image of the person you wish to torment, and, setting it in front of you, preferably, at times when the moon is new, or in conjunction with Venus, Mars or Saturn, concentrate with all your will on whatever injury you wish to inflict. If, for example, you desire the person to become blind, stick a pin, or thorn, or nail in the eyes of the image; if deaf, in its ears; if maimed, cut a limb off the image; if to have a certain disease, will very earnestly that he or she shall have that disease. You may thus, too, torment the object of your aversion with plagues of insects and vermin.

'If you desire to bewitch your neighbour's milk, wine, or any food he or she has, you may do it by placing the mumia, *i.e.* the vehicle containing the essence of life of some criminal or lunatic, in the immediate vicinity of the food, etc.; or in the case of milk, by giving it to the cow to eat; or you may accomplish your design simply by means of concentration and an image.

'Always, however, whatever methods you employ, prelude them with this prayer: "I conjure thee, Great Unknown Power that is Antagonistic to man, that was at the Beginning, that is now, that always will be; by the winds and rain, and thunder and lightning; by the swirling rivers; by the Moon; by the sinister influence of the Moon with Venus, Mars and Saturn; help me obtain the perfect issue of all my desires, which I seek to perform solely for the furtherment of what is detrimental to humanity. Amen." And conclude them with the signs of the foot, the hand and the bat. If you desire to know anything further it will be unfolded to you in your dreams.'

The hand that had been laid on Hamar's was now removed. The writing ceased. The table rose several inches from the floor, and struck the latter three times in quick, violent succession. Then it remained quiet, and Hamar knew, by a subtle change in the atmosphere, that all occult manifestations – for that night at least – were at an end. The ladies were, of course, dying to know what had happened; and like most ladies who dabble in spritualism, were ready to believe anything they were told. Hamar, who had no intention whatever of telling them what had actually occurred, satisfied them admirably.

He went home delighted – far too delighted to sleep – for he had in his possession now the greatest of all weapons – the weapon to torment. And with it what could he not do! What could he not get! He could get – Gladys!

CHAPTER 21

THE SELLING OF SPELLS

THE period of stage four promised to be one of such a lucrative nature, that the trio set to work to profit by it at once. They bribed medical men to procure for them the mumia of people suffering from every kind of disease; of criminal lunatics; of idiots and epileptics; they obtained, by bribery also, the blood and hair of the most abandoned men and women – rakes, thieves, murderers. They bottled and labelled, and arranged and catalogued the mumia in a laboratory designed for the purpose; and, when all their preparations were complete, advertised—

SPELLS FOR SALE

THE MODERN SORCERY COMPANY LTD.

offer for sale every variety of spells –

love charms, sleep charms, etc.

In order to carry out the principal conditions of the compact, namely, to do harm, they made pseudo-love charms as follows :—

They procured the hair of a girl whom they knew to be an incorrigible, and, at the same time, heartless flirt; and, in the manner described (and related in the last chapter) made a magnes microcosmi of it. When ready for use, *i.e.* after it had been in immediate contact with the girl's flesh, so as to get it fully charged, they had portions of it set in rings, lockets and pendants. And the purchaser of any one of these trinkets had only to persuade the object of his (or her) affection to wear it, and his (or her) love would at once be reciprocated.

Had the magnes miscrocosmi been charged with real, deep-rooted love, the effect on the wearer would have been highly satisfactory, but charged as it was with the effervescent and fleeting fancy of a flirt, the effect on whoever wore it could not be more disastrous. The sentiments of the hopeful purchaser would be reciprocated for a time, which would probably lead to marriage – after which the affection his adored had professed would suddenly decrease, and before the honeymoon was over, would have vanished altogether.

During the week following the announcement of the sale of these spells, over a thousand were sold, the applicants being mostly shop girls, typists, clerks and servants; in the second week the sales rose to three thousand, and every succeeding week showed a still greater increase.

In charging the magnes microcosmi, the motive of the purchaser had always to be taken into account. If the love charm were wanted by a woman – a housekeeper may be, who desired some rich old man to fall in love with her, in order that she might come into his property; or by a woman – a companion probably – who, having wormed herself into the confidence of some eccentric old lady, was anxious that that lady should leave her all her money – Hamar took care that the magnes microcosmi should be charged with a lasting infatuation; and the sale of this love spell – the spell that was sought solely that the purchaser might inherit property to which he (or she) had no claim – far exceeded the sale of any other spell. Indeed, it was extraordinary how many people – people one would never have suspected – desired spells that would do other people harm.

Lady De Greene, the well-known humanitarian, who was indefatigable in getting up petitions to the Home Secretary, whenever the perpetrator of any particular heinous and inexcusable murder was about to be hanged, and who was universally acknowledged 'incapable of harming a fly,' called, surreptitiously, on Hamar.

'I understand,' she said, 'everything you do here is in strict confidence!'

'Certainly, madam, certainly!' Hamar said. 'We make it a point of honour to divulge – nothing!'

'That being so,' Lady De Greene observed, 'I want you to tell me of a spell that will hasten some very obnoxious person's death.'

'If you will give me an idea of their personal appearance,' Hamar said, 'I will make a wax image of them, and undertake they will trouble you no longer.'

But Lady De Greene shook her head. She had no desire to commit herself.

'Can't you do it in any other way,' she said, 'can't you let me give them an unlucky charm – the sort of thing that might bring about a taxi disaster?'

Hamar thought for a moment and then – smiled.

'Yes!' he said, 'I think I can accommodate you.'

Leaving her for a few minutes, he went to the laboratory, and from a tin box marked homicidal lunatic, he took a plain, gold ring. With this he returned to Lady De Greene, murmuring on the way the prayer he had learned from the table.

'Here you are,' he said, handing the ring to Lady De Greene, 'give it to the person you have mentioned to me – and the result you desire will speedily come to pass.'

Three days later, London was immeasurably shocked. It read in the papers that the highly accomplished Lady De Greene, beloved and respected by all for her strenuous exertions on behalf of humanitarianism, had been barbarously murdered by her husband (from whom – unknown to the public – she had been living apart for years), who had suddenly, and, for no apparent reason, become insane. Hamar, who was immensely tickled, alone knew the reason why.

This was no isolated case. Scores of Society women came to the trio with the same request. 'A spell, or charm, or something, that will bring about a fatal accident – not a lingering illness' – and the person for whom the accident was desired was usually the husband. And the trio often indulged in grim jokes.

Without a doubt, Lady Minkhurst got her heart's desire when her husband abruptly cut his throat, but alas, among those decimated, when the charm fell into the hands of one of the footmen, was her ladyship's lover.

Again, Mrs. Jacques, the beauty, who, at one time, wrote for half the fashion papers in England, certainly secured the demise of Colonel Dick Jacques, who tumbled downstairs and broke his neck, but as in his fall the Colonel alighted on one of the maids, who was not insured, and so seriously injured her that she was pronounced a hopeless cripple, Mrs. Jacques – with whom money was an object – had, of course, to maintain her for the rest of her life.

Likewise, Sir Charles Brimpton, in jumping out of the

top window of his house, besides pulverizing himself, pulverized, too, Lady Brimpton's pet Pekingese 'Waller,' without whom, she declared, life wasn't worth living; and Lord Snipping, in setting fire to himself, set fire to Lady Snipping's boudoir (which he had been secretly visiting), and thereby destroyed treasures which she tearfully declared were quite priceless, and could never be replaced.

Crowds of young married women were anxious to get rid of their rich old relatives, who clung on to life with a tenacity that was 'most wearying.'

'Can you give me a spell that will make my grandmother go off suddenly?' a girl with beautiful, sad eyes said plaintively to Kelson. 'Don't think me very wicked, but we are not at all well off – and she has lived such a long time – such a very long time.'

'You don't want her to be ill first, I suppose,' Kelson inquired.

'Oh, no!' the girl replied, 'she lives with us and we could never endure the worry and trouble of nursing her. It must be something very sudden.'

'This will do it,' Kelson said, giving her a locket containing the mumia or essence of life of a mad dog; 'fasten it round the old lady's neck, and you will be astonished how soon it acts.'

'And what is your fee?' the girl asked, her eyes brimming over with joyous anticipation.

'For you – nothing,' Kelson said gallantly. 'Only tell no one. May I kiss your hand?'

The firm's sale of spells for getting rid of husbands having risen one day to five hundred – and the sale of their spells for putting old people out of the way to fifteen hundred – even Hamar, who was no believer in the perfection of human nature, was astonished.

'My word!' he remarked. 'Isn't it a revelation? Who would have thought how many people have murder in their hearts? At least half Society would, I believe, become homicides if only there were no chance of their being found out and punished. Anyhow, if we go on at this rate there will be no old people left.'

And it did indeed seem as if such would be the case. For the moment the idea got abroad that old people could be thrust out of existence with absolute safety and ease, there was a perfect mania amongst men, women and even children, to get rid of them, and the deaths of people over sixty recorded in the papers multiplied every day. The following is an extract from the *Planet* of July 28—

BOLT.—On July 27, at No. — Elgin Avenue, S.W., Emily Jane, loved and venerated mother of Mary Bolt, M.D., in her 69th year. Drowned in her bath. And all the Angels wept!

CUSHMAN.—On July 27, at No. — Sheep Street, Northampton, Sarah Elizabeth, adored mother of Josiah Cushman, Plymouth Brother, in her 88th year. Run over by a taxi. Joy in Heaven!

TRETICKLER.—On July 27, at No. — The Terrace, St. Ives, Cornwall, Elizabeth, adored grandmother of Tobias Tretickler, Congregationalist, in her 91st year. Fell over the Malatoff. 'Oh, Paradise! Oh, Paradise!'

BROOT.—On July 27, at Charlton House, Queen's Gate, S.W., Jane, greatly beloved mother of John Broot, Labour M.P., in her 83rd year. Fell down the area. Peace, blessed Peace.

GUM.—On July 27, at No. — Church Road, Upper Norwood, Sophia, widow of the late Albert Gum, L.C.C., in her 85th year. Choked whilst eating tripe. Sadly missed!

PAVEMAN.—On July 27, at No. — Queen's Road, Clifton, Bristol, Anne Rebecca, dearly beloved mother of Alfred Paveman, grocer, in her 74th year. Accidentally burned to death! At rest at last.

But it must not be supposed from these few notices, selected from at least a hundred, that the applicants for spells were by any means confined to the upper and middle classes. By far the greater number of spells were sold to the working people – to those of them who, prudent and respectable, counted amongst their aged relatives, at least, one or two who were insured.

Nor was the sale of spells confined to adults; for among

the numbers, that flocked to consult the trio, were countless County Council children.

'Can you give me a spell to make teacher break her neck?' was the most common request, though it was frequently varied with demands such as—

'I'll trouble you for a spell to pay mother out. She won't put more than three lumps of sugar in my tea;'—or, 'Mother has got very teazy lately. I want a spell to make her fall downstairs'—or, 'Father only gives me twopence a week out of what I earn blacking boots; give me a spell to make him have an accident whilst he's at work.' And it was not seldom that the trio were petitioned thus: 'Please give us a spell to make our parents die quickly. Teacher says at school "perfect freedom is the birthright of all Englishmen," and we can't have perfect freedom whilst our parents are alive.'[1]

The statistics of those who died from the effects of accidents for the week ending August 1, of this year, in London alone, were – over sixty years of age, five thousand; between the ages of twenty-five and sixty, six thousand; and, for the latter deaths, children alone were responsible.

The greatest number of these accidents occurred in Poplar, West Ham, Battersea, and Whitechapel; and at length the working class applicants became so numerous that the Modern Sorcery Company could not cope with them, and were forced to raise their charges.

Among other customers, as one might expect, were many militant Suffragettes; whom Hamar and Curtis palmed off on Kelson.

'Give me a spell,' demanded a hatchet-faced lady, wearing a half-up-to-the-knee skirt, 'one that will cause the roof of the House of Commons to fall in and smash everybody – EVERYBODY. This is no time for half-measures.'

Had she been pretty, it is just possible Kelson might have assented, but he had no sympathy with the ugly – they set his teeth on edge – he loathed them.

'Certainly, madam, certainly,' he said, 'here is a spell

[1] Lest the reader should query this, let him consult the police in any of our big centres, and he will learn that crime and prostitution is immensely on the increase among children. In Newcastle it is estimated that there are over two thousand girls, of under fourteen years of age, voluntarily leading immoral lives, and making big incomes.

that will have the effect you desire,' and he handed her a ring containing a magnes microcosmi fully charged with the essence of life of an idiot. 'Wear it,' he said, 'night and day. Never be without it.'

She joyfully obeyed, and within forty-eight hours was lodged in a home for incurables.

Another woman, if possible even uglier than the last, approached him with a similar request.

'Let me have a spell at once,' she said, 'that will make every member of the Government be run over by taxis – and killed. They are monsters, tyrants – I abominate them. Let them be slowly – very slowly – SQUASHED to death!'

'Very well, madam,' Kelson said, carefully concealing a smile, 'here is what you want – wear it next your heart;' and he gave her a locket, containing a magnes microcosmi charged with the essence of life of a leper, which he had procured at considerable risk and expense.

'I consider your fee far too high,' the Suffragette said. 'You take advantage of me because I'm a woman.'

'Very well, madam,' he said, 'I will make an exception in your case, and let you have it for half the sum.'

With a good deal more grumbling she paid the half fee, and, fastening the locket round her neck, flounced out of the building. As Kelson gleefully anticipated, the spell acted in less than two days, and with such success, that he was more than compensated for the monetary loss.

Shortly afterwards, Kelson received a frantic visit from another Suffragette – a woman whose virulent sandy hair at once aroused his animosity.

'Quick! Quick!' she cried, bursting into the room where he was sitting. 'Let me have a spell that will blow up every Cabinet Minister, and their wives and families as well.'

'Such an ambitious request as that, madam,' Kelson rejoined, 'cannot be granted in a hurry. I must have time – to—'

'No! No! At once!' the lady cried, stamping her feet with ill-suppressed rage.

'—to consider how it can best be done,' Kelson went on calmly. 'I must have time to think.'

The lady fumed, but Kelson remained inexorable; and directly she had gone, he made a wax image of her, and taking up a knife chopped its head off. In the evening, he learned that a lady answering to her description had been run over by a train at Chislehurst – and decapitated.

'Look here,' he said, 'it's not fair. You and Curtis see all the decent-looking women and shelve all the rest on me. I'll stand it no longer.' And he spoke so determinedly, that Hamar thought it politic to humour him.

'Very well, Matt,' he said, forcing a laugh. 'I'll try and arrange differently in future. After to-day you shall have your share of the pretty ones – anything to keep the peace. Only – remember – no falling in love!'

CHAPTER 22

THE PERSECUTION OF THE MARTINS

HAMAR'S one great idea on reaching stage four was to utilize the torments as a means of getting Gladys. Though he saw crowds of pretty girls every day, none appealed to him as she did – and the very difficulty of getting her enhanced her value and stimulated his passions.

'I will give her one more chance,' he said to himself, 'and then if she won't have me I'll plague her to death.'

He went to the Imperial, and passing himself off as her father to the new official at the stage-door entrance, was shown into the ante-room (which led to her dressing-room). It took a great deal to scare Hamar, but he admitted afterwards that he did feel a trifle apprehensive whilst he awaited her advent; and his anticipations were fully realized.

'Why, Father!' she began, as the door of her dressing-room swung open and she appeared on the threshold, clad in a shimmering white dress, that intensified her fair style of beauty, 'what brings you—' The smile on her face suddenly died away.

'You!' she cried, 'how dare you! Go! Go at once! And if you dare come here again or attempt to molest me in any way, I'll prosecute you!'

Hamar, dumbfounded at such an exhibition of wrath, slunk out of the room without uttering a syllable.

'The vixen,' he muttered as soon as he found himself in the street. 'A thousand cats in one! Treated me like mud.

Jerusalem! I'll pay her out. And I'll lose no time about it either. She'll look differently at me next time we meet.'

He hurried back to Cockspur Street and going into the laboratory, threw himself into a chair and – thought.

The same evening at nine-thirty, in the interval between her first and second 'going on,' Gladys hastened to her dressing-room, and was preparing to partake of the light refreshments she had ordered, when – to her horror – she perceived crawling towards her, across the floor, a huge cockroach – a hideous black thing with spidery legs and long antennae that it waved, to and fro, in the air, as it advanced. It was at least double the size of any Gladys had hitherto seen, and her feelings can best be appreciated by those who fear such things – her blood ran cold, her flesh crawled, she sat glued to her chair, terrified to move, lest it should run after her. She screamed, and her dresser, startled out of her senses, came flying into the room.

'What is it, madam? What is it?' she cried.

Gladys pointed at the floor.

'Kill it!' she shrieked. 'Stamp on it! Oh, quick, quick, it is coming towards me.'

But the moment the dresser caught sight of the cockroach, she sprang on a chair and wound her skirts round her.

'Oh, madam,' she panted, 'I daren't! I daren't go near it. I'm frightened out of my life at beetles. And there's another of them' – and she pointed to the wainscoting – 'and another! Why, the room's full of them!'

And so it was. Everywhere Gladys looked she saw beetles crawling towards her – dozen upon dozens, hundreds upon hundreds – and all of the same monstrous size and ultra-horrible appearance.

'Look!' she screamed. 'They are climbing on to my clothes. One's got into my shoes, and another will be in them in a second. There's another – crawling up my cloak – and another on my skirt. Oh! Oh!' and her cries, and those of the dresser, speedily brought a troop of actors and actresses to the door. The instant, however, the cause of the alarm was ascertained, there were loud yells, and a wild stampede down the passages. The Stage Manager was called, but one glance at the floor was enough for him – he fled. And in the end three of the supers had to be fetched. Hot water, brooms, ashes, and quicklime were used, and although thousands of the cockroaches were killed, thousands more came, and so hopeless did the task of getting rid of them become, that the room eventually had to be vacated, and the cracks under the door securely sealed.

Before Gladys left the theatre, she was called on the telephone.

'Who are you?' she asked.

'Hamar,' came the reply, in insinuating tones. 'How do you like the beetles? You'll never see the end of them till—'

But Gladys rang off.

On her return home something scuttled across the hall floor in front of her. She sprang back with a scream. It was a gigantic cockroach. The hall was full of them. She summoned the servants, and they set to work to kill them. But they might as well have tried to stop Niagara, for as fast as they squashed one battalion, another took its place. They came out of cracks in the floor, from behind the wainscoting, from every conceivable place in the kitchens, and in a dense black ribbon some six inches broad, ascended the staircase. Gladys tried to barricade her room against them, but it was of no avail. They came from under the boards of the floor and poured down the chimney. They swarmed over the furniture, in the cupboards, chest of drawers, the washstand (where they kept continually falling into the water), in her clothes (her dressing-gown was covered with them), over the bed, and the climax was reached when they approached the chair she stood on. Too fascinated with horror to move, she watched them crawling up to her. She was thus found by her father. He had come to her assistance in the very nick of time, and after lifting her from the chair and taking her to a place as yet safe from molestation, returned to her room, where, with savage blows, smashing, equally, beetles and furniture, he remained till daybreak.

With the first streak of dawn the beetles decamped, and the fray ended. The work of devastation had been colossal. Corpses were strewn everywhere – and it took the combined household hours before all evidences of the slaughter were obliterated. As for Gladys, she had not slept all night and was a wreck.

'I can never go through another night of it,' she said

to Miss Templeton. 'Do you think we shall ever get rid of the horrible things?'

'We can but try, dear!' Miss Templeton said consolingly, and she accompanied Gladys up to town, where they inquired of doctors, and chemists, and all sorts of possible and impossible people; and returned to Kew laden with chemicals, and patent beetle destroyers. But though they tried remedies by the score, none were of use, and the beetles repeated their performance of the preceding night.

Gladys did not go to bed: surrounded with lighted candles, she sat on top of a wardrobe till daybreak. The following morning the house was fumigated with sulphur; and people were told off to kill the cockroaches, as they made their escape out of doors. By this means an enormous number were killed; but at night they were just as bad as before.

An engineer friend then suggested a freezing-machine. The temperature of the house was reduced to ten degrees below zero; the pipes froze (and burst next day), the milk froze, the housemaid's toes and the cook's little finger of the left hand froze, everything froze; and presumably the beetles froze, for there was not one to be seen.

However, it was quite impossible to resort again to this extreme measure. John Martin had the most agonizing attacks of lumbago. Gladys had neuralgia, and Miss Templeton – a slight touch of pleurisy.

When Gladys reached the Imperial that evening, she found that the staff had been battling with cockroaches all day, and that they had at last succeeded in getting rid of them with a fumigation mixture of camphor, cocculus, sulphur, bezonia and asafœtida – suggested to them by a Hindoo student.

For the next week not a beetle was to be seen at the theatre nor at the Cottage; and Gladys was beginning to hope that Hamar had ceased plaguing her (in despair of ever winning her), when the persecutions suddenly broke out again.

She had been in bed about half an hour, and was falling into a gentle and much needed sleep, when a tremendous rap at the wall, close to her head, awoke her with a start, and set her heart pulsating violently. Thinking it must be some one on the landing, she got up and lit a candle. There was no one there. The moment she got into bed again, the rapping was repeated, and it continued, at intervals, all night. This went on for a week, during which time Gladys was never once able to sleep.

A brief respite ensued; but it was abruptly terminated one morning, when Gladys awoke feeling as if some big insect were attempting to penetrate her body. Uttering a shriek of terror, she whipped the clothes from her, and sprang out of bed. Miss Templeton, who slept in the next room, came rushing in, and they both saw an enormous insect, half beetle and half scorpion, dart under the pillow. John Martin was fetched, but although he searched everywhere, not a trace of the insect could be found.

That night, directly Gladys got into bed and blew out the light, she heard a ticking sound on the sheets, and a huge insect with long hairy legs ran up her sleeve. Her shrieks brought the whole household to the room but the insect was nowhere to be seen.

She was thus plagued for nearly a fortnight. One insect only – never a number, but only one, of prodigious size and terrifying form – appeared to her in the least suspected places, *i.e.*, on the dressing-table or chimney-piece, in her shoes, or pockets; crawled over her in the dark; and could never be caught.

These perpetual frights, and consequent sleeplessness, wore Gladys out. She grew so ill that she had to give up acting and go into a home to try the rest cure.

Hamar then communicated with her, through a third person, and offered to leave off tormenting her, if she would agree to be engaged to him.

'I never will!' she said.

'Then I will never leave off persecuting you,' was his retort.

But he was wary. He had no wish to kill her or to damage her looks – so he let her get well and remain thus for a brief space. When she was once again in full vigour, acting at the Imperial, he recommenced his unwelcome attentions.

At first he confined his new plague to the servants at the Cottage. The cook was one day turning out a drawer in the kitchen dresser, when she was horrified out of her senses to find squatting there, a large, black toad, which stared most malevolently at her, and then sprang in her face. She shrieked to the housemaid to help her kill it, but before a weapon could be got, the creature had bounced through an open window, and disappeared.

After this incident the servants knew no peace. Their bedclothes were thrown off them at night, their dresses torn and bespattered with ink, their brushes and combs thrown out of the window, and the water they poured out to wash in was sometimes quite black, sometimes full of a bright green sediment, and sometimes boiling, when it invariably cracked both the jug and basin.

Unable to stand these annoyances the servants left in a body. Their successors fared the same, and worse. Besides having to endure the above-named horrors, pebbles were thrown through the windows, their chairs were pulled away as they were about to sit down (the cook, who was one of those upon whom this trick was played, thereby seriously injuring her spine), and all sorts of obstacles were placed on the stairs, so that those who ran down unwarily tripped over them and hurt themselves (two successive housemaids broke their legs, whilst another sprained her wrist).

The meat, too, was a constant worry – it went so bad that enormous maggots crawled out of it by the thousand and covered the table and floor; and the milk, of which a large quantity was taken daily, 'turned' in a very curious manner. After being deposited, in its usual place, in the pantry, it began to darken; first of all it became light blue, then deepened into an almost inky blackness, exhibiting curious zigzag lines; and, lastly, the whole mass began to putrefy and to emit a stench so overpowering that every one in the house retched, and the whole place had to be disinfected. This occurred day after day. Nothing would stop it. The dairyman who supplied the milk did all he could to counteract it. He had his dairies constantly cleansed, he saw that the cattle had a change of food, he bought an entirely new stock of dairy utensils, and no milk was ever sent to the cottage that he had not had carefully analyzed.

The troubles continued for three weeks, at the end of which period John Martin received a telephone call from Hamar.

'Hullo!' the latter said, 'I guess you've had about enough of it by this time. Wouldn't you like some sweet-smelling milk for a change, or do you prefer to go on till you all get typhoid? The remedy, you know, lies in your own hands. You've only to tell that daughter of yours to accept me, and I'll undertake all your troubles shall cease.'

'I'll see you hanged first, 'John Martin answered.

'Very well, then, you old mule,' Hamar shouted, 'look out for yourself – and Miss Gladys.'

CHAPTER 23

LOVE

To bring about plagues of insects Hamar had resorted to a very simple method. He had first of all made a wax image representing a cockroach – scorpion – centipede, or whatever other species came into his mind. Then, placing the image he had made in front of him, and repeating the prayer he had learned from the Unknown, through the medium of Mrs. Anderson-Waite's table, he had concentrated body, soul, and spirit on plaguing Gladys with the insect, which the image represented. When his concentration reached the highest degree, insects in their actual physical bodies were transported from the tropics;[1] but when he was unable to concentrate to the utmost, only the ethereal projections of the insects were obtainable; hence the hybrid – partly scorpion and partly beetle, that appeared and disappeared in Gladys' bed and bedroom.

To produce the rappings on the walls of Gladys' room, he had made a wax representation of a wall, and whilst concentrating to the very utmost, had struck it with his knuckles.

The plaguing of the servants Hamar had also accomplished by means of images and concentration.

But in order to bewitch milk, he had been obliged to resort to other means. He had converted the mumia of an idiot into a magnes microcosmi; and bribing the man who delivered the milk, he gave him instructions to soak

[1] There is no doubt that Moses inflicted the plagues, with which he tormented Pharaoh, in this way.

the magnes microcosmi, for a few minutes, in every portion that he left at the Cottage.[1]

At length Hamar having failed to gain his object by plaguing Gladys and the servants, set about tormenting John Martin. He made a wax image of the latter, and after pronouncing the necessary prayer, stuck the image full of pins, crying out as he did so 'John Martin, I hate you. John Martin, I curse you. John Martin, a plague on you.' And each time Hamar stuck a pin in the image he had made of John Martin, the real John Martin felt an acute pain in the region of his body corresponding to that in which the pin was stuck.

The doctor, who was called in, could make nothing of the malady, but, following the etiquette of the profession, cloaked his ignorance with a look of profound wisdom, and the pronouncement that he would tell them, in a day or two, what was the matter. In the meanwhile, he found it necessary and politic to prescribe a non-committal mixture of chalk and rhubarb, which, although disguised under the usual fanciful pharmacopœia appellation, did not, however, allay the pain. Sharp, agonizing pricks, now on the neck now in the chest, now in the most sensitive part of the knee-cap, now under the toe-nail, now – most painful of all – under the finger-nail – continued to torment John Martin, who, though as a rule fairly stoical, could not stand these attacks with any degree of composure. He screamed, and swore, and cursed, until the whole household was terrified – and Gladys, pretty nearly out of her mind.

During a lull – an interval, wherein John Martin enjoyed a brief respite, the telephone bell rang.

'Hulloa,' called a voice, 'I'm Hamar. Haven't you had about enough of it? Remember, you've only to say the word and I'll stop.'

'Tell him I'll do nothing of the sort,' John Martin said, 'that he'll never get the better of me this way.'

Miss Templeton gave the message, and Hamar replied 'Wait! Wait and see!'

He then thrust wool, pins, horsenails, straw, needles

---

[1] In stage two this might have been performed by ethereal projection, but Hamar could not resort to this method as the power of projection had now passed from him.

and moss into the mouth of the image, and John Martin had such frightful pains in his stomach that he went into convulsions; and, after an emetic had been given him, vomited up all the above-named articles, save the pins and needles which worked their way out through his flesh, causing him the most exquisite tortures.

Gladys, having given up going to the theatre in order to be with her father during these attacks, now declared that she could no longer bear to see him in such excruciating pain, whilst it was in her power to prevent it.

'Tell him,' she said, 'tell Hamar you'll accept his conditions. Don't think of me! I would rather do anything than see you suffer like this.'

'I can hold out a bit longer,' he groaned, 'at any rate I needn't give in yet.'

Every now and then there came a respite – perhaps for several hours, perhaps for several days – then the tortures recommenced. And always John Martin steeled himself to bear them. At last came the climax.

Hamar, infuriated that his efforts, so far, had proved fruitless, resolved, since time was pressing, to play his trump card and either win, or lose all. He rang up Gladys on the telephone.

'My patience is exhausted,' he said. 'I'll give you one more chance, and one – only. Agree to be engaged to me at once – or I'll smite your father with the most virulent form of cancer, and leave him to die.'

There was no question in Gladys' mind as to what she should do. Of all things in the world, she dreaded cancer most, and after the many evidences Hamar had given her of his skill in Black Magic, she did not doubt for one instant that he could, immediately he chose, carry out his threat.

'I have decided,' she said faintly, 'to – to – give in.'

'You accept me, then?' Hamar said.

'Y-yes!'

'When may I see you?'

'When you like.'

'Then I'll come at once,' Hamar replied. *'Au revoir.'*

But Hamar, when he arrived at the Cottage, did not realize any of the gleeful anticipations he had indulged in *en route*. Gladys was ill – so Miss Templeton informed him – at the same time begging him, if he really had any regard for Miss Martin, not to ask to see her for the next few days; and to this request Hamar, seeing no alternative, was obliged to assent. Shortly after he had gone, Shiel Davenport called, and found Gladys alone in the garden.

'I've been told that your father is ill,' he said, 'and should like to hear better news of him. How is he?'

'I think he's all right now,' Gladys replied, 'but he has suffered frightfully. Indeed, we've all had a terrible time.' And she told him what had happened.

'Then you've not been acting at the Imperial lately?' Shiel asked.

'Not for the past week,' Gladys replied. 'I couldn't leave father.'

'How has Mr. Bromley Burnham got on without you?' Shiel asked bitterly.

'I don't understand you,' Gladys said quietly. 'I have an understudy, and from what I am told she has given every satisfaction. I have some news which I fear won't be altogether welcome to you.'

Shiel turned a shade paler. 'What is it?' he faltered.

'I'm engaged to be married.'

For a few moments there was silence, and then Shiel exclaimed mechanically 'Engaged to be married! To whom?'

'To Leon Hamar! I couldn't help it.' And she explained the position.

'But he'll never keep you to it,' Shiel said. 'He couldn't be such a brute.'

'I'm afraid he will,' Gladys replied. 'He's shown pretty clearly that he's capable of anything. I've given him my promise – I must keep it.'

'Then it's good-bye to all interest in life – for me,' Shiel said, with a gulp. 'I've thought of no one but you since we first met. For you – in the hope of someday winning you, I've struggled on; I've reconciled myself to a bare existence. Now I've lost you, I've lost everything. I hate life. I shall—'

'You'll do nothing of the sort,' Gladys interrupted, 'unless you want me to regret ever having met you. I wonder that you say "I've nothing to live for" – when we can still be friends; and when you can, at least, win my respect, by putting your shoulder to the wheel, and exerting yourself to the utmost to get on.'

'And you – what about you?'

'Never mind me – I can well look after myself.'

'You'll live in Hell,' Shiel cried, her eyes goading him to madness. 'Even though you may not care for me, I do not choose to stand quietly by, whilst you spend your life in Purgatory. Hamar has won you through some diabolical trickery, and if I can't thwart him in any other way – I'll kill him. He shan't marry you.'

'He will,' Gladys sighed. 'No one can stop him. He is omnipotent.'

Apparently, Gladys' statement was more or less true; and ninety-nine men out of a hundred, in the same circumstances as Shiel, would have now recognized the hopelessness of the situation. But Shiel was abnormal. As he walked home from the Cottage that evening he kept on repeating to himself 'Gladys is my goal. I want only Gladys. I'll have only Gladys.' And having once made up his mind to get Gladys, it seemed to him, as if out of every obstacle, that lay between him and Gladys, he could and would merely make a stepping-stone. 'Since,' he argued to himself, 'all's fair in love and war, I'll win Gladys through another woman.'

And he straightway telephoned to Lilian Rosenberg to have tea with him.

The latter had already made an engagement for the afternoon; but, all the same, she accepted Shiel's invitation.

'Will you do me a favour?' he asked.

'If it is anything that lies in my power,' she said. 'What is it?'

'I want you to find out how Hamar works his spells. I asked you before.'

'I know you did and I've not forgotten,' Lilian said, 'but I have to be very careful. I've played the part of eavesdropper once or twice, and heard enough to confirm me in my suspicions that Hamar is in touch with evil, occult powers. I've heard him praying aloud to them on more than one occasion, and I've also a shrewd idea he performs, at least, some of his spells by means of wax images. But why do you want to know?'

'Only curiosity. I am intensely interested in the occult.'

'You don't want to start a rival show, do you?' Lilian asked jestingly.

'With a maximum capital of two pounds – and a minimum of knowledge!' Shiel laughed. 'Hardly. I wish I could. I would offer you the post of manageress.'

'Partner!'

'Well, partner, if you like. Would you take it?'

'Perhaps!' she said, looking at him with a sudden shyness. 'What a pity you are not rich. Can't you get a post that would bring you in about £200 a year for a start? I believe you really want something to stimulate you, to make you work in grim earnest – then you would succeed. There's grit in you – I love grit – but at present it's latent, it wants bringing out.'

'You are very kind,' Shiel said, 'but I'm afraid I'm a hopeless case, and, being such, have no business to be in your company. Will you come to the theatre with me?'

'The theatre! When you've no business to be in my company, and when it is as much as you can do to pay the rent of a back attic!'

'Oh, never mind that. I've had tickets given me. I've been doing odd bits of journalism lately, and a dramatic critic I knew has given me two stalls at the Imperial!'

'The Imperial!' Lilian Rosenberg ejaculated. 'That's where Gladys Martin is acting, surely! I can't bear her!'

'She's not the only person in the cast,' Shiel observed drily, 'and the play's a good one! Do come!'

With a little more persuasion Shiel gained her consent; and both he and she enjoyed the play, or more correctly speaking, the occasion, immensely. So long as Gladys was on the stage Shiel's eyes never once left her; whilst throughout the performance Lilian Rosenberg saw only Shiel, thought only of Shiel. The interest she had taken in him, the interest she had so confidently asserted was only interest, had grown apace – had grown out of all recognition. It needed only a fillip now to convert that interest into something warmer; and the fillip was not long in coming.

Shiel was seeing Lilian home to her lodgings in Margaret Terrace, a turning off Oakley Street, when a man knocked a woman down right in front of them. He was just the ordinary type of street ruffian – the whitewashed English labourer – and the woman, having without doubt been served by him in the same manner fifty times before, was probably well used to such treatment. But it was more than Shiel, who had spent so much time of his life where they treat women differently, could stand, and before Lilian Rosenberg had time to remonstrate, he had rushed up to the prostrate woman, and was holding the man at bay. A scuffle now began, in which the woman, whom Shiel had helped to regain her feet, joined. Both man and woman now attacked Shiel, who, placing himself with his back against the railings, defended himself as best he could.

The hour was late, there were no police about, and it seemed only too probable that the fracas would end in a tragedy. The labourer was a burly fellow, shorter than Shiel, but far broader and heavier, and any one could see at a glance that Shiel stood no chance against him. Lilian Rosenberg, at her wits' end to know what to do, ran into Oakley Street, and as there was no one in sight, she made for the nearest lighted house and rang the bell furiously. A man came to the door, whom, unheeding his expostulations, she caught by the arm and dragged into the street.

They arrived on the scene of action, just as the ruffian, breaking through Shiel's guard, struck him a terrific blow on the forehead, which sent him reeling against the railings. The newcomer (upon whom, both man and woman, seeing Shiel incapacitated, instantly turned) would probably have shared the same fate, had not the occupants of several of the neighbouring houses – amongst whom were some half-dozen athletic young men – roused by the noise, come out into the street, and the ruffian and his companion, seeing the odds were against them, decamped.

Shiel had not fully regained consciousness, when Lilian Rosenberg, regardless of propriety, led him into her sitting-room, bathed his forehead, dosed him with brandy, and making up a bed for him on the sofa, bade him rest there, till the morning.

When he took his departure, he had quite recovered, and Lilian Rosenberg had, at last, realized that she loved him.

CHAPTER 24

THE SUBPŒNA

A FEW days after the incident in Margaret Terrace, Shiel had an inspiration. He was lunching with an old schoolfellow whom, quite by chance, he had met in Lincoln's Inn, having previously lost sight of him for many years, and the conversation, which had at first been confined to the old days, had gradually drifted to what was ever uppermost in Shiel's mind – namely, the Modern Sorcery Company, *i.e.* Hamar, Kelson and Curtis.

'Did you know,' his friend remarked, 'that the old statute, introduced in Henry the Fifth's reign against sorcery, had never been repealed?'

'You don't mean to say so,' Shiel cried excitedly – a vague idea dawning on him. 'Tell me all about it.'

'Well, that's rather a long order. For one thing, it imposes all kinds of penalties from capital punishment to fines. For another, it was in force up to the beginning of George the Third's reign, where the last case of a person being burned for witchery in England occurred, and since then it has fallen into disuse.'

'Could it be revived?' Shiel asked, a sudden wild hope surging through him.

'For all I know to the contrary, it could,' his friend – who, by the way, was a barrister – replied. 'Of course no one could be burned or hanged under it, but they might be fined or imprisoned.'

'Then I wish to goodness you would file a case against the Modern Sorcery Company! I'd move heaven and earth to get the scoundrels sent to prison!' And he told his friend how matters stood between Gladys and Hamar.

The barrister – whose name was Sevenning – H. V. Sevenning, of T.C.D. and Cheltenham College renown – was keenly interested. It was not only that his sense of chivalry was stirred, but he saw sport. Consequently, the foregoing conversation resulted in a prosecution which, taking place some four weeks later, was reported in the *London Herald* as follows—

Extraordinary Charge Heard at the Old Bailey.

Revival of an Ancient Statute.

Yesterday, at the Old Bailey, before His Honour Judge Roshen, Leon Hamar, Edward Curtis and Matthew Kelson, of the Modern Sorcery Company Ltd., were indicted under the 23rd of Henry the Fifth, C. 15, which makes it a capital offence to practise and administer spells. The case for the prosecution promises to be a lengthy one. An enormous number of witnesses, who are most anxious to make statements, will be called; and it is anticipated that much of their evidence will be of a most extraordinary nature.

The accused are cited with having worked spells to the injury – which injury, in many instances, has been fatal – of a vast number of people, representative of every rank in life.

Hilda, Countess of Ramsgate, who appeared in heavy mourning, was the first witness called. In her evidence she stated, that it was owing to an advertisement she had seen in the *Ladies' Meadow*, that she had consulted the Modern Sorcery Company Ltd., with the object of buying a spell to prevent her Pekingese pet, Brutus, catching colds on his liver. She had hoped to see Mr. Kelson, as she had heard that he was more sympathetic, where ladies were concerned, than either Mr. Hamar or Mr. Curtis, but as Kelson was engaged, she had consulted Mr. Edward Curtis instead. The latter had given her a spell which he had assured her would have the desired effect, but directly she got home, her adored Brutus developed melancholia, and died raving mad, after having bitten her child, who, by the way, had died, too.

For the defence, Gerald Kirby, K.C., declared that the spell his client had given the Countess was perfectly harmless; that it could not possibly have produced either melancholia or madness. 'Can any dependence,' he said, 'be placed on a woman who obviously thinks more of her dog's death than that of her child!'

The Court was adjourned till to-morrow.

In the following day's paper, the evidence for the

prosecution was continued. Lady Marjorie Tatler, who, in the weekly and illustrated journals, for no other reason than her reputed beauty, was reintroduced over and over again to the long-suffering public, was the first to step into the witness-box.

She declared that Edward Curtis, instead of giving her a spell to make Florillda win the Derby, had given her a diabolical something that had brought out spots all over her face, and that she had to undergo a most expensive treatment before they could be got rid of.

In cross-examination, Lady Marjorie Tatler admitted that she had asked Edward Curtis for a spell that would cause all the horses running in that particular race, save Florillda, to be taken ill.

For the defence, Gerald Kirby, K.C., explained that his client was so disgusted at the immorality of Lady Marjorie's request, that he had purposely given her a spell that would have no effect upon a horse, and could not possibly bring out spots on her Ladyship's face. 'The spell Edward Curtis gave her,' Gerald Kirby said, 'was a mixture of hempseed and sago, flavoured with violet powder, and my client instructed her Ladyship to wear it next her heart.' (Loud laughter.)

Lady Coralie Mars, the next witness, who declared she had sought a spell to make the man, she was forced into marrying, fall into a trance, just before the marriage ceremony was to take place; and that, instead of bringing this about, the spell Edward Curtis had sold her had caused her to have St. Vitus' Dance, – was adroitly trapped into admitting that she had really wanted her fiancé smitten with paralysis. 'A wish,' Gerald Kirby announced, with a dramatic flourish of his hands, 'that so aroused my client's indignation that, instead of giving her the spell she wanted, he gave her one that would make her affianced husband more than ever hungry for the marriage hour to arrive. As for St. Vitus' Dance, would any woman, with an emotional and hysterical nature, such as obviously was that of Lady Coralie Mars, ever be free from such a complaint?'

The Hon. Augusta Mapple, who stated that she had visited the Modern Sorcery Company, for the purpose of obtaining a spell to bring about a defeat of the

Government, by afflicting the bulk of their supporters with such bilious attacks as would necessitate their absence from the House, and that, instead of giving her such a spell, Edward Curtis had given her one which had caused every member of her household to fall downstairs – admitted, under cross-examination, that she had asked for a spell that would make every supporter of the Government in the House be suddenly seized with tetanus. 'A diabolical request, your lordship,' Gerald Kirby said, 'and one to which my client could not possibly accede. Consequently, as a punishment for such cruelty, he sold her a spell that would result in her having a sharp attack of toothache. It could not possibly have produced any of the mishaps she attributes to it.'

It is unnecessary to quote further. By far the greater number of these witnesses, on being cross-examined by Mr. Kirby, who defended with an ability that has rarely, if ever, been excelled, were made to confess that they had wanted the spells for a far more subtle and dangerous purpose than they had previously stated; admissions which, of course, were highly prejudical to the case for prosecution.

Shiel lost hope. He had looked forward to the trial with an excitement that almost bordered on frenzy. It was never out of his mind. He thought of it at meals, he thought of it at his work, he thought of it out of doors, and, when he went to bed, he dreamed of it.

'I'll save you! I'll save you yet!' he wrote to Gladys. 'The trial can only result in one thing – the breaking up and imprisonment of the trio.'

But when he read the papers each day, and saw how, in almost every instance, evidence which ought to have been damning to the accused, had been twisted into their favour, his heart sank.

There was only one chance now – Lilian Rosenberg. She, of all the staff employed in the Hall in Cockspur Street, was best acquainted with the *modus operandi* of Messrs. Hamar, Curtis and Kelson.

'We must get hold of that girl at all costs,' H. V. Sevenning remarked to Shiel. 'You say you feel sure she likes you. Work upon her feelings to show the Firm up.'

'I don't much like the idea of it,' Shiel said, 'but I suppose the end justifies the means.'

'Of course it does!' Sevenning retorted. 'It's your only chance of saving Miss Martin.'

Acting on this suggestion, Shiel approached Lilian Rosenberg on the subject.

'What about the spells?' he asked her. 'Have you found out yet how Hamar works them?'

'I have only heard him muttering in his room again,' she said, her cheeks paling. 'And – you will only laugh at me – I have seen queer shadows hovering in his doorway and stealing down the passages, shadows that have terrified me. I never knew what real fear was before I came to Cockspur Street, and for the past few weeks I have been almost too afraid to open my door, for fear I should see something standing outside.'

'You have no doubt, I suppose, in your own mind, that the trio practise sorcery?'

'I certainly think they are helped in all they do by evil spirits.'

'Do you approve of such proceedings?'

'I don't think them right. I don't think we have any right to pry into the Unknown. Some day, undoubtedly, it will be given us to know, but until that day comes, we had far better leave it alone.'

'If you think like that,' Shiel said, 'how can you reconcile yorself to working for these people?'

'How can I help myself?' Lilian Rosenberg answered. 'Beggars can't be choosers. I am not responsible for what they do.'

'But supposing you knew they were about to commit a very heinous crime, wouldn't you feel it your duty to try and circumvent them?'

'That depends,' Lilian Rosenberg said. 'If I could stop them without running any risk of losing my post, then I would probably try to stop them, but if stopping them meant being "sacked," I most certainly shouldn't. It isn't so easy to get posts nowadays – especially good paying posts like this. What do you take me for, a fool!'

'Then you don't believe in self-sacrifice, even for a friend?' Shiel said slowly.

'That depends on the degree of friendship,' Lilian replied. 'If it were for some one I liked very much, then – perhaps!'

'Is there any one you like very much! I, somehow, couldn't fancy you being very fond of any one.'

'Couldn't you?' Lilian said, with a faint laugh. 'You don't think me capable of any deep affection. You forget, perhaps, that a woman doesn't always wear her heart on her sleeve.'

'I confess I don't understand women,' Shiel said, 'and I had best come to the point at once. I happen to know that the trio – or at least one of the trio – is contemplating doing something ultra-abominable – a cruel and shameful wrong, which I particularly wish to prevent. But I may not be able to do anything without your help! Will you help me?'

'How *can* I?' Lilian asked.

'Why, by finding out something which might be damning evidence against them, or by stating your opinion in Court. There is only one way of staying the trio from doing this dastardly thing, and that is by getting this case, which is now being tried, to go against them.'

'Well, and supposing, by some chance, the defendants should win! What would become of me?'

'Ah! that is where your self-sacrifice would come in! It would be a noble action.'

'How does this wrong, you say they are about to perpetrate, touch on you personally?'

'It touches on some one with whom I am personally acquainted.'

'Some one you like?'

'Yes!'

'A relation?'

'That I can't say.'

'Then I can't help you. I am naturally inquisitive; curiosity is, as you know, a woman's privilege. You must tell me all.'

'It's for a friend, then!'

'A man?'

'No,' Shiel replied, 'for a girl!'

There was an emphatic silence, and then Lilian Rosenberg spoke.

'Have I ever heard you mention her?'

There was silence again. Then Lilian Rosenberg said slowly—

'You surely don't mean Gladys Martin! I can think of no one else.'

'I do mean her!' Shiel replied, drooping his eyes. 'She is to be coerced into marrying Hamar.'

'The silly fool!' Lilian Rosenberg said. 'I would like to see any one trying to coerce me. And it is to serve *her* you want me to sacrifice myself.' And she turned away in disgust.

After this interview, Lilian studiously avoided Shiel; and despairing, at length, of ever winning her over, Shiel reported his failure to H. V. Sevenning.

'We must subpœna her,' said Sevenning.

'You'll never get her to speak that way,' Shiel said. 'If once she has made up her mind not to do a thing, nothing will ever compel her.'

'I have heard that said of people before,' H. V. Sevenning replied drily, 'but it's wonderful what the witness-box can do; it loosens the most mulish tongues in a marvellous manner.'

'It wouldn't hers,' Shiel maintained.

H. V. Sevenning, however, thought he knew best – what lawyer doesn't? Moreover, it was all part of the game – the great game of becoming notorious at all costs. He served the subpœna.

Like most modern girls, Lilian Rosenberg was wholly selfish; and for this fault only her parents were to blame. She had been brought up with the one idea of pleasing herself, of saying and doing exactly what she thought fit; and no one had ever thwarted her. Now, however, the unforeseen had happened. She was smitten with the grand passion and confronted for the first time in her life with the startling proposition of 'self-sacrifice.' She loved Shiel. She wouldn't marry him for the very simple reason he had no money – but that only added piognancy to the situation. She loved him all the more. She knew Shiel loved Gladys Martin. Whether he could ever marry Gladys was another matter – but he loved her all the same. And the proposition, that had been so abruptly thrust upon Lilian Rosenberg, was that she should sacrifice herself, not only to save Gladys Martin from marrying Hamar, but to pave the way for Shiel, supposing Gladys could reconcile herself to penury, to marry her himself. In other words she had been called upon to give up what was, at the moment, dearest to her in the world, and to court all the inconveniences and worries of being thrown out of employment – for if she gave evidence that would in any way tend to damage the firm of Hamar, Curtis & Kelson, she would undoubtedly lose her post and, in all probability, never get another – at least not another as good – for the sake of a woman whom she did not know, but, nevertheless, hated.

Yet there was in her, as there is in almost every girl, however up to date, a chord that responded to the heroic. A short time back she would have scoffed at the very thought of self-sacrifice; but now, she actually caught herself considering it. She kept on considering it, too, until the trial was well advanced, and had practically made up her mind to denounce the trio and go to the wall herself, when the subpœna was served.

CHAPTER 25

CURTIS IN A NEW RÔLE

In an instant, Lilian Rosenberg had decided the course she would adopt.

'What a disgusting thing to do,' she indignantly exclaimed. 'I wouldn't have believed it of Shiel. The idea of forcing me to give evidence – of forcing me to save the situation for the sake of the woman he thinks he loves! I shan't do it!'

And she proved as good as her word. Apart from her importance as a witness, considerable interest attached to her on account of her appearance – she was infinitely more attractive than any of the women who had hitherto appeared in the witness-box – though many of them were so-called Society beauties.

'You were wrong,' was the look which Shiel read in H. V. Sevenning's eyes, as Lilian Rosenberg took the oath. 'She is on our side.'

But simple as Shiel was in many ways, he knew women

better than the lawyer, and the exceedingly sweet expression Lilian Rosenberg had assumed, and which he knew to be quite foreign to her, filled him with misgivings. Nor was he mistaken. The evidence she gave was entirely in favour of the trio.

The case for the prosecution was concluded. For the defence, Gerald Kirby, K.C., resorted to satire. He characterized the whole proceedings as the most absurd in any Court for the past two centuries, and wondered, only, that it had been possible to procure a counsel for such a ridiculous prosecution.

'Even though,' he remarked, 'spirits such as have been specified by the prosecution do exist – which is extremely dubious – there has never yet been produced any reliable corroborative evidence respecting them, and the Prosecution has wholly failed to prove, that it is through the medium of these spirits, that the Modern Sorcery Company have worked their spells. The marvellous feats that we have all seen performed in Cockspur Street have been accomplished – as the defendants have all along stated – through will – sheer will power and nothing else; and I intend producing evidence to show that the secret of the wonderful efficacy of all the charms and spells sold by the Sorcery Company, lies in will power also. Whenever they have been consulted with regard to the purchasing of a spell, the Firm have invariably pointed out this fact to the purchasers, carefully explaining at the same time that the rings, lockets and other articles sold to them were merely to assist them in concentration. It is ridiculous to suppose that such trivial articles could have produced, of themselves, such calamities as the witnesses for the prosecution attributed to them. But, of course you did not believe the statements of such witnesses. How could you? How could you expect anything but falsehood from women who, upon cross-examination, had owned that their object in obtaining the spells was a far more dangerous object than they had at first led you to suppose. They sought spells that would do evil, and that evil was not accomplished. Now, I ask you, if the Firm worked their spells through the instrumentality of evil spirits – for it is assuredly only evil spirits that are associated with Sorcery – would not the spells they sold naturally have brought about the sinister results for which they were required? Undoubtedly they would! And they failed to produce the desired effect, simply because their efficacy depended, not on spirit agency, but on human will power; which power one could only too plainly see the society ladies – who had witnessed for the prosecution – did not possess.

'It may be asked, why these defendants, if they do not accomplish their spells through Black Magic, style themselves "The Sorcery Company" – and so mislead the public? Obviously they do so purely for advertisement. "The Sorcery Company" is an attractive title, a "catchy" title, and for this reason, which is surely a legitimate one, since it is strictly in accordance with the prevailing custom of advertisement – the firm of Hamar, Curtis and Kelson adopted it. They did not expect – they were not so extraordinarily foolish as to expect – any one would take them literally. They thought – as you and I think – that sorcery cannot be taken seriously – that it is confined to fairy tales – and that, as a fairy tale, it is potent only in the nursery.'

This was the gist of counsel's speech for the defence. A number of witnesses then gave evidence for the defendants; and when the prosecuting counsel rose, it was only too evident that he was pleading for a lost cause. The Court with ill-concealed derision barely accorded him a hearing.

Two hours later the *Meteor*, always the first in the field when sensations crop up, headed the first column of their front page with—

Collapse of the Sorcery Case

Crushing Speech by Gerald Kirby, K.C.

Acquittal of the Defendants

'The Judge' – so the *Meteor* reported – 'expressed himself in absolute agreement with the defending counsel. "The action," he said, "ought never to have been brought – it was sublimely ridiculous to accuse any one of being in league with forces in the existence of which no sane person could possibly believe."'

Shiel was in despair. All chance of saving Gladys seemed to be fast disappearing. He telephoned to her, and was answered by Miss Templeton.

Gladys, she said, had gone out with Hamar, who had motored down to the Cottage the moment the trial was over and the verdict known.

'I wish to God we had won the case,' Shiel observed.

'So do I,' Miss Templeton replied, 'and so did Gladys – she regards her position now as absolutely hopeless!'

'Tell her not to lose heart,' Shiel answered hurriedly. 'If I can't find any other means, I'll—' but Miss Templeton rang off, and he spoke to the wind.

Full of wrath against Lilian Rosenberg, he went round to see her, and met her, just as she was entering her house.

'I've come to see you for the last time,' he announced. 'After the way you behaved in Court, we can no longer be friends.'

'I don't understand,' she said in rather a faltering voice. 'What have I done?'

'Only perjured yourself,' Shiel retorted. 'The tale you told the judge was very different to the tale you told me, therefore it is impossible for us to continue our friendship. I could never have anything to do with a woman whose word I can't rely upon – whose character I scorn, whom I despise – and—' he was going to add, 'detest,' but checked himself, and unable to trust himself in her presence any longer, he gave her a glance of the utmost contempt, and wheeling round, walked quickly away.

As in a dream, Lilian Rosenberg went upstairs to her room, and throwing herself on the bed, buried her face in the pillow and indulged in a fit of crying. It was not the thought of losing Shiel that was so painful to her – she might have grown reconciled to that – it was the thought of losing his esteem. Most people would agree with her – would assure her she had done the right thing in looking after number one. 'What, after all, is perjury?' she argued. 'Nearly every one in this world perjure themselves at one time or another – certainly all women.'

But it was not the opinion of the majority she cared about – it was the respect of the one; the respect she had wilfully and spitefully sacrificed.

Was it too late to recover it?

With regard to Gladys she was very sceptical. The reluctance to accept Hamar as her future husband she still believed to be all pretence, and she felt convinced that Gladys, in her heart of hearts, was only too glad to get the chance of marrying any one so rich. This being so, she could not bring herself to think she had done Shiel any actual wrong. Gladys would never marry him. The only person she had harmed was herself. She had lied, and Shiel was not the sort of man to condone an offence of that sort easily. Still, weeping would do no good; it would only make her ugly. She got up, had tea, and went out. She could think better in the open air – it soothed her. For some reason or other – custom perhaps – she strolled towards Cockspur Street, and there ran into one of the few people she particularly wanted to avoid – Kelson.

He was delighted to see her.

'It's nectar to me to be out again,' he said. 'Jerusalem! – it was awful in the Courts. Have supper with me.'

It was a fine starlight night – the air cool and refreshing, and a wild abandonment seized Lilian Rosenberg. She would have supper with the devil had he asked her.

'I've nothing to lose now,' she said to herself. 'Nothing! I'll have my fling.'

'Where shall we go?' she asked. 'It must be somewhere entertaining.'

'Why not to my rooms?' he said. 'We can talk better there – we shall be all alone!'

She raised no objection, and they were about to step into a taxi, when Hamar and Curtis suddenly put in an appearance.

'Matt!' Hamar cried, seizing his elbow. 'I want a word with you.'

'Not now,' Kelson protested, looking hungrily at Lilian.

'Yes, now!' Hamar said. 'At once! I shan't keep you more than five minutes' – and he dragged Kelson away with him.

The moment they had gone, Curtis, who was obviously the worse for drink, addressed Lilian.

'Kelson won't come back,' he said. 'Hamar is mad with him. He says if he ever sees you two together again he'll sack you. Let me take his place!'

A sudden inspiration came to her. There were one or two things she badly wanted to know – and with a bit of coaxing, Curtis, in his present state, might tell her anything. She would try.

'All right,' she said. 'I'll come.'

They got into the taxi and Curtis, as far as his fuddled senses would allow, made violent love to her.

After supper – they had supper in his rooms – he grew a great deal more amorous. She let him sit close beside her, she let him put his arm round her waist; but before she let him kiss her, she struck her bargain.

'No!' she said, thrusting him away. 'Not just yet. That can come later – if you are good. I want you to tell me something first. About this marriage of Mr. Hamar and Miss Martin – is it likely to come off?'

'Ish it likely!' Curtis said with a stupid leer. 'Ish it likely! Not much. Leon means nothing! He only wants the fun of being engaged to a pretty girl – like I wantsh fun with you. Nothing more.'

'Then he'll throw her over after a while.'

'After he gets what he wantsh to get.'

'And suppose she proves different to what he expects?'

'After he pashes stage seven – that will be all right!' Curtis said giving her waist an emphatic squeeze. 'Everybody will be all right then. You and Matt – for exshample – and I and – and – whishky!'

'Stage seven! What do you mean?'

'Why don't – you know!' Curtis gurgled – and then a sudden gleam of intelligence coming into his watery eyes, he added. 'Then I shan't tell you – nothing shall make me. It's a shecret!'

'I won't kiss you till you do!' Lilian Rosenberg said.

'I'll make you.'

'Oh, no, you won't,' Lilian Rosenberg cried, disengaging herself from his grasp, and rising. 'Don't you dare touch me. I'm going.'

Curtis watched her with a helpless grin. Then he suddenly cried out, 'Come back! Come back, I shay!'

'Well, will you do as I want?' Lilian Rosenberg said.

'I'll do anything – anything to please you – if only you shtay with me.'

She sat down, and his arm once again encircled her.

'Now,' she said, pushing his face away. 'Tell me!'

Bit by bit she drew out of him the whole history of the compact with the Unknown, how in stage five, the stage they were about to enter, they would have fresh powers conferred upon them – their present power, *i.e.* of working spells and causing diseases, being then cancelled; how they would obtain supreme power over women when they reached the final stage – stage seven; and how the compact would be broken and their ruin brought about, should either of them marry, or should anything happen before this final stage was reached, to disunite them.

Lilian could account for a great deal now. The uncanny feeling she had always experienced in the building; the curious enigmatical shadows she had seen hovering about the doorways and flitting down the passages; the extraordinary nature of the feats and spells; Hamar's mutterings and his fury, whenever Kelson spoke to her – were no longer wholly unintelligible. But she must know all. She must be most exacting.

Finally, she got from Curtis everything there was to be got from him, and she laughed immoderately, when he excused himself on the grounds that it was all Leon's doing – Leon had told him to offer her a little compensation for the loss of her escort.

'And you have compensated me more than enough,' Lilian Rosenberg said. 'Now you shall have your reward,' and she kissed him – kissed him three times for luck.

'But you're not going?' he said, staggering to his feet and attempting to hold her. 'You're not going till the roshy morning sun shines shaucily in on us.'

'Oh, yes, I am,' she said. 'I've had quite enough of you! Good-bye!'

And before he could prevent her, she had run to the front door and let herself out.

CHAPTER 26

IN HYDE PARK AT NIGHT

BUT now that Lilian Rosenberg was possessed of all this information respecting the trio, she was once again in doubt how to act, or whether to act at all. Supposing she were to attempt to warn Gladys Martin against Hamar, how would Gladys take the warning? Would she pay any attention to it? The odds were she would not; that having set her heart on marrying Hamar for his money, she would blind herself to his faults and resolutely shut her ears to anything said against him. Also there was the very great possibility of Gladys being rude to her — and even the thought of this was more than she could bear to contemplate. If only Shiel were reasonable! If only he could be made to see how utterly ridiculous it was for him to think of winning such a girl as Gladys — Gladys the pretty, dolly-faced, pampered actress, who had never known a single hardship, had always had a well-lined purse, and would never, never marry poverty! Then back to Lilian Rosenberg's mind came her parting with Shiel — she recalled his intense scorn and indignation. A liar! He did not wish to have anything to do with a liar! It's a good thing every man is not so fastidious, she said to herself bitterly, or the population of the world would soon fizz out. She laughed. He had never questioned her morals in any other sense — perhaps, in his innocence or assumed innocence, he had thought them spotless — at all events he had most graciously ignored them. But a liar! A liar — he could not put up with. And why! Because the lie had touched him on a sore point. When lies do not touch a sore point, they, too, are ignored.

She walked to the Imperial and looked again at Gladys' photographs. How any man could fall madly in love with such a face, was more than she could conceive. It was a mincing, maudlin, finicking face — it irritated her intensely. She turned away from it in disgust, yet came back to have another look — and yet another. God knows why! It fascinated her. Finally she left it, fully resolved to let its odious original go to her fate — without a warning. Soon after her return to the Hall in Cockspur Street, she was sent for by Hamar.

'Didn't I tell you,' he said, 'that you were on no account to encourage Mr. Kelson?'

'You did!' Lilian Rosenberg replied.

'Will you kindly explain, then,' Hamar said, 'why you have disobeyed my orders?'

'How have I disobeyed them?' Lilian Rosenberg asked.

'How!' Hamar retorted, his cheeks white with passion. 'You dare to inquire how! Why, you were on the point of accompanying him to his rooms last night to supper, when I stopped you! I have overlooked your disobedience so many times that I can do so no longer. Your services will not be required by the Firm after to-day fortnight.'

'Won't they?' Lilian Rosenberg replied, her anger rising. 'I think you are mistaken. I know a great deal too much to make it safe for you to part with me. I know – for instance – all about your Compact with the Unknown!'

'You know nothing,' Hamar said, his voice faltering.

'Oh, yes, I do!' Lilian Rosenberg answered. 'I know everything. I know how you first got in communication with the Unknown in San Francisco; I know how you receive fresh powers from the Unknown every three months (the old powers being cancelled). I know the penalty you will undergo should the Compact be broken – and – what is more – I know how the Compact can be broken.'

'How the deuce have you learned all this?' Hamar stammered.

'Never you mind. Am I to remain in your service or leave?'

'I think,' Hamar said, stroking his chin thoughtfully, 'it is better that you should remain – better for all parties. I owe you some little recompense for your loyalty to the Firm, and for the admirable way you spoke up for the Firm in Court. I will make you out a cheque for a hundred pounds now – and your salary shall be doubled at the end of this week. Promise to keep out of Mr. Kelson's way in future – for the next six months at any rate – after that time you may see him as often as you like – and I will give you as a wedding present a cheque for twenty thousand pounds!'

'Twenty thousand pounds! You are joking!'

'I'm not. I vow and declare I mean it. Is that a bargain?'

'I will certainly think it well over,' Lilian Rosenberg said, 'and let you know my decision later on.'

From what Curtis had told her she knew it was the last day of stage four, that the trio that evening would be initiated into stage five – the Stage of Cures, and a mad desire seized her to witness the initiation. But how would the Unknown manifest itself on this occasion – and to which of the trio? She could not keep a close watch on the three of them. If only she had been friends with Shiel, they might, in some way, have worked it together.

Curtis had carefully avoided her since the supper; but she had seen Kelson, and he had looked at her each time he met her as if he yearned to fall down at her feet and worship her. Should she attach herself to him for the evening – and run the risk of another quarrel with Hamar? She dearly loved risks and dangers – and the danger she would encounter in defying Hamar appealed to her sporting nature. It was easy to secure Kelson – one glance from her eyes – and he would have followed her to Timbuctoo.

'Charing Cross – under clock – after show to-night,' she whispered as she flew hurriedly past him. 'I want to speak to you.'

Now it so happened that Hamar had given Kelson orders to return to his rooms, directly the performance was over, and to remain in them till morning, in case he was wanted in connection with the initiation. But he might have spared himself the trouble. It was Lilian, and Lilian only, that Kelson now thought of – it was Lilian, and Lilian only, that he would obey. The idea of meeting her – of having her all to himself – of being able to do her a service – filled him with such uncontrollable delight, that he hardly knew how to comport himself so as not to arouse Hamar's suspicions. Directly the performance was over he sneaked out of the Hall, and pretending not to hear Hamar, who called after him, he jumped into a taxi, and was whirled away to the trysting-place. Lilian Rosenberg, who arrived a moment later, was dressed in a new costume, and Kelson thought her looking smarter and daintier than ever.

'You shall kiss me at once,' she said, 'if you promise me one thing.'

'And what is that?' he asked, looking hungrily at her lips.

'I want you to let me see the Unknown when it comes to you to-night,' she said.

'Good God! What do you know about the Unknown!' he exclaimed, his jaws falling, and a look of terror creeping into his eyes.

'A great deal,' she laughed, 'so much that I want to learn more' – and of what she knew she told him, just as much as she had told Hamar. 'And now,' she said, 'I repeat my promise – you shall have a kiss – think of that –

if only you will hide me somewhere so that I can see the Unknown or its emissary.'

'I would do anything for a kiss,' Kelson said, 'but I fear it is impossible to fulfil the condition, because I haven't the remotest idea where or when the Unknown will appear. Besides, it is just as likely to go to Hamar or Curtis as to come to me; and up to the present I haven't felt the remotest suggestion of its favouring me. Is this the only condition I can fulfil, so that you will let me kiss you?'

'Certainly,' Lilian Rosenberg replied. 'I am not in the habit of being kissed. Such an event can only happen in the most exceptional and privileged circumstances – such, for example, as exist at the present moment, when I ask you to put yourself to some considerable trouble – if not actually to incur danger – in order to accomplish what I wish.'

'And yet I remember kissing you unconditionally,' Kelson commented.

'Memory is a fickle thing,' Lilian Rosenberg replied, 'and so is woman. Times have changed. I'll leave you at once, unless you promise to do your very utmost to grant my request.'

Kelson promised, and – after they had had supper at the Trocadero, suggested that they should take a stroll in Hyde Park.

'I hope you are not awfully shocked?' he inquired rather anxiously, 'but a sudden impulse has come over me to go there. I believe it is the will of the Unknown. Will you come with me?'

'We shan't be able to get in, shall we, it's so late?' Lilian Rosenberg said. 'Otherwise I should like to – I'm rather in a mood for adventure.'

'They don't shut the gates till twelve,' Kelson said, 'and it's not that yet.'

'Very well, let's go, then. I'm game to go anywhere to see the Unknown,' and so saying Lilian rose from the table, and Kelson followed her into the street.

They took a taxi, and alighting at Hyde Park Corner entered the Park. It was very dark and deserted.

'It's nearly closing time,' a policeman called out to them rather curtly.

'We are only taking a constitutional,' Kelson explained. 'We shall be back in five minutes.'

They crossed the road to the statue, and were deliberating which direction to take, when they heard a groan.

'It's only some poor devil of a tramp,' Kelson said. 'The benches are full of them — they stay here all night. We had better, perhaps, turn back.'

'Nonsense!' Lilian Rosenberg replied. 'I'm not a bit afraid. There's another groan. I'm going to see what's up,' and before he could stop her she had disappeared in the darkness. 'Here I am,' she called; 'come, it's some one ill.'

Plunging on, in the darkness, Kelson at last found Lilian. She was sitting on a chair under a tree, by the side of a man, who was lying, curled up, on the ground.

'He's had nothing to eat for two days, and has Bright's Disease,' Lilian Rosenberg announced. 'Can't we do something for him?'

'Two gentlemen told me just now,' the man on the ground groaned, 'that if I stayed here for a couple of hours — they would pass by again and guarantee to cure me. I reckoned there was no cure for Bright's Disease, when it is chronic, like it is in my case; but they laughed, and said, "We can — or at least — shall be able to cure anything."'

'What were the two gentlemen like?' Kelson asked.

'How could I tell?' the man moaned. 'I couldn't see their faces any more than I can see yours — but they talked like you. Twang — twang — twang — all through their noses.'

'Sounds as if it might be Hamar and Curtis,' Kelson remarked.

'That's it!' the man ejaculated. "Amar. I heard the other fellow call him by that name.'

'How long ago is it since they were here?' Kelson asked.

'I can't say, perhaps ten minutes. I've lost count of time and everything else, since I've slept out here. They talked of going to the Serpentine.'

'We had better try and find them,' Kelson said.

'If you had the money couldn't you get shelter for the night,' Lilian Rosenberg said. 'It must be awful to lie out here in the cold, feeling ill and hungry.'

'I dare say some place would take me in,' the man muttered, 'only I couldn't walk — at least no distance.'

'Well! here's five shillings,' Lilian Rosenberg said, 'put

it somewhere safe – and try and hobble to the gates. If they haven't closed them, you will be all right.'

'Five shillings!' the man gasped; 'that's – it's no good – I can't count. I've no head now. Thank you, missy! God bless you. I'll get something hot – something to stifle the pain.' He struggled on to his knees, and Lilian Rosenberg helped him to rise.

'How could you be so foolish as to touch him,' Kelson said, as they started off down a path, they hoped would take them to the Serpentine. 'You may depend upon it, he was swarming with vermin – tramps always are.'

'Very probable, but I run as much risk in a 'bus, the twopenny tube, or a cinematograph show. Besides, I can't see a human being helpless without offering help. Listen! there's some one else groaning! The Park is full of groans.'

What she said was true – the Park was full of groans. From every direction, borne to them by the gently rustling wind, came the groans of countless suffering outcasts – legions of homeless, starving men and women. Some lay right out in the open on their backs, others under cover of the trees, others again on the seats. They lay everywhere – these shattered, tattered, battered wrecks of humanity – these gangrened exiles from society, to whom no one ever spoke; whom no one ever looked at; whom no one would ever own that they had seen; whose lot in life not even a stray cat envied. Here were two of them – a man and a woman tightly hugged in each other's embrace – not for love – but for warmth. Lilian Rosenberg almost fell over them, but they took no notice of her. Every now and then, one of them would emerge from the shelter of the trees, and cross the grass in the direction of the distant, gleaming water, with silent, stealthy tread. Once a tall, gaunt figure, suddenly sprang up and confronted the two adventurers; but the moment Kelson raised his stick, it jabbered something wholly unintelligible, and sped away into the darkness.

'A scene like this makes one doubt the existence of a good God,' Lilian Rosenberg said.

'It makes one doubt the existence of anything but Hell,' Kelson said. 'Compared with all this suffering – the suffering of these thousands of hungry, hopeless wretches – the bulk of whom are doubtless tortured incessantly, with the pains of cancer and tuberculosis, to say nothing of neuralgia and rheumatism – Dante's Inferno and Virgil's Hades pale into insignificance. The devil is kind compared with God.'

'I believe you are right,' Lilian Rosenberg said, 'I never thought the devil was half as bad as he was painted. The Park to-night gives the lie direct to the ethics of all religions, and to the boasted efforts of all governments, churches, chapels, hospitals, police, progress and civilization. There is no misery, I am sure, to vie with it in any pagan land, either now or at any other period in the world's history.'

'True,' Kelson replied, 'and why is it? It is because civilization has killed charity. Giving – in its true sense – if it exists at all – is rarely to be met with – giving in exchange – that is, in order to gain – flourishes everywhere. People will subscribe for the erection of monuments to kings and statesmen, or to well-known and, often, richly-endowed charitable institutes, in exchange for the pleasure of seeing, in the newspapers, a list of the subscribers' names, and themselves included amongst those whom they consider a peg above them socially; or in exchange for votes, or notoriety, they will give liberally to the brutal strikers, or outings for the poor.'

'I suppose, by the poor, you mean the pampered, ill-mannered and detestably conceited County Council children,' Lilian Rosenberg chimed in. 'I wouldn't give a farthing to such a miscalled charity, no – not if I were rolling in riches.'

'And I think you would be right,' Kelson replied. 'But for these really poor Park refugees it is a different matter. Obviously, no one will make the slightest effort to work up the public interest on their behalf, simply because they are labelled "useless." They belong nowhere – they have no votes – they are too feeble to combine – they are even too feeble to commit an atrocious murder; consequently, for the help they would receive, they could give nothing in return. By the by, I doubt if they could muster between them a pair of suspenders – a bootlace – a shirt-button, or even a—'

Lilian Rosenberg caught him by the arm. 'Stop,' she said, 'that's enough. Don't get too graphic. What's the matter with that tree?'

They were now close beside the banks of the Serpentine; the moon had broken through its covering of black clouds, and they perceived some twenty yards ahead of them, a tall, isolated lime, that was rocking in a most peculiar manner.

CHAPTER 27

THE RIGHT GIRL TO MARRY

THOUGH the wind was nothing more than the usual night breeze of early autumn, the lime-tree was swaying violently to and fro, as if under the influence of a stupendous hurricane. Lilian Rosenberg and Kelson were so fascinated that they stood and watched it in silence. At last it left off swaying and became absolutely motionless. They then noticed, for the first time, that there were three figures standing under its branches, and that one of the figures was a policeman.

'Hide quickly,' Kelson whispered, 'those two are Hamar and Curtis. Quick, for God's sake – or they will see you.'

Lilian Rosenberg hid behind an elm.

'Hulloa!' Kelson called out, advancing to the group.

'Why it's you, Matt!' Curtis cried. 'Hamar said you would come!'

'Said I would come! How the deuce did he know?' Kelson exclaimed. 'I didn't know myself till the moment before I started.'

'I willed you,' Hamar explained; 'as soon as I got back to my rooms after the Show, a voice said in my ears – I heard it distinctly – "Be at the Serpentine – the south bank – underneath a lime-tree – you will know which – at twelve to-night." I looked round – there was no one there. Naturally, concluding this was a message from the Unknown I hastened off to Curtis, who was in his digs – and needless to say – eating, and having dragged him away with me in a diabolical temper – I then sought you. Where were you?'

'Taking a walk. I felt I needed it.'

'Alone! Are you sure you weren't out with some girl.'

'I swear it.'

'It seems as if I'm not the only liar!' Lilian Rosenberg

said to herself in her place of concealment. 'What would Shiel say to that?'

'Humph! I don't know if I ought to believe you,' Hamar remarked. 'Did you feel me willing you to come here?'

'Rather!' Kelson said. 'That is why I came. I seemed to hear your voice say. "To Hyde Park – to Hyde Park – the Serpentine."' Then sinking his voice he whispered, 'What's up with the policeman, he looks deuced queer?'

'He's in a trance. We found him like this,' Hamar said. 'He is undoubtedly under the control of the Unknown. I expect it to speak through him every moment. Get ready to take down all he says, I've come prepared,' and he handed Kelson and Curtis, each, a pencil and a reporter's notebook.

He had hardly done so, when the policeman – a burly man well over six feet in height, who was standing bolt upright as if at 'attention,' his limbs absolutely rigid, his eyes wide open and expressionless – began to speak in a soft, lisping voice that the trio at once identified with the voice of the Unknown – the voice of the tree on that eventful night in San Francisco.

'The great secret of medicine – the secret of healing – will now be revealed to you,' the voice said. 'Pay heed. In cases of tumours and ulcers take a young seringa, lay it for half an hour over the stomach of the afflicted person, then plant it with the mumia, *i.e.* either the hair, blood, or spittle of the sick person, at midnight. As soon as the seringa begins to rot, the ulcer will heal.

'In phthisis pulmonalis, the mumia of the sick person should be planted with a cutting of the catalpa, after the latter has been subjected for some minutes to the breath of the diseased person. As soon as the cutting shows signs of decay, the sick jerson will be cured.

'In diabetes, plant the mumia of the patient with a bignonia, and as soon as the latter begins to rot, the diabetes will go.

'In appendicitis, cover the stomach of the sick person with a piece of raw beef, until the sweat enters it. Then give the meat to a cat, and as soon as the latter has eaten it, the patient will recover.'

'What becomes of the cat?' Kelson asked.

'The appendicitis is transferred to it,' the voice explained. 'It should be killed at once.

'In cancer take the sea wrack Torrek Mendek – a weed of deep mauve colour streaked with white. It must be boiled in clear spring water (3 ozs. of wrack to half a pint of water), and then let to cool. When quite cold, a dessert-spoon of it should be taken by the sufferer every four hours – and at the end of two days the disease will have completely disappeared. The wrack is to be found at the twenty fathom level, six miles west-south-west of the Scilly Isles.

'In Bright's disease, the mumia of the afflicted should be planted at 1 a.m., with a cutting of sassafras, after the latter has been slept on, for one whole night, by the sufferer. As soon as the sassafras begins to rot, the patient will be cured.

'In dropsy, place a hare, that has been strangled, over the diseased portion of the body, and let it remain there for one hour. Then bury the hare, together with the mumia of the sick person, as soon as the hare begins to decay, the patient will recover.

'In jaundice and liver diseases (apart from sarcoma), plant the mumia of the afflicted, at 2 a.m., with a cutting of black walnut, and as soon as the latter begins to decay, the sufferer will get well.

'In all skin diseases, the mumia of the patient must be planted, at midnight, with a cutting of hickory, and when the latter begins to rot the disease disappears.

'In all fevers, the mumia must be planted, at 3 a.m., with laurel cuttings, after the latter have been placed under the bed of the patient for one night. As soon as the cuttings show signs of rotting, the fever abates.

'In acute inflammations, diseases of the heart, rheumatism, and lumbago, the mumia must be buried, at midnight, with a raven that has been drowned, and placed on a chair by the left side of the patient for one night. As soon as the raven begins to rot, the patient will be fully restored to health.

'In cases of insanity, hysteria, and nervous diseases the mumia of the sufferer must be planted, at 2 a.m., with a cutting of white poplar, and as soon as the latter shows evidences of decay, the afflicted will get well.

'In cases of hypochondria, and melancholia, the mumia

of the sufferer must be planted, at 4 a.m., with a crocus, and as soon as the latter begins to rot, the disease will depart.

'In every case it will be necessary to prelude the performance with the following invocation—

' "Oh most powerful and prescient Unknown, before whom the greatest of the Atlanteans prostrate themselves. That was in the Beginning, that is now and always will be. I conjure thee by the magic symbols of the club-foot, the hand with the fingers clenched, and the bat, in this the magical year of Kefana, to extend to me thy wonderful powers of healing. Rena Vadoola Hipsano Eik Deoo Barrinaz." '

The lisping voice ceased, and, with a convulsive start, the policeman came to himself.

'Hulloa!' he said, in his natural gruff tones, rubbing his eyes. 'I must have "dropped off." Who are you? What are you doing in the Park at this time of night?'

'We've been watching you!' Hamar said. 'It is a bit of a phenomenon to see a London bobby asleep on his beat.'

'And to hear him talking in his sleep too,' Curtis added.

'I didn't know I was talking,' the policeman muttered. 'It all comes of being too many hours on duty. What have you got those note-books out for? Not been taking down anything about me, have you?'

'Show us out of the Park and you'll hear no more about it,' Kelson chimed in.

'Follow me then,' the policeman said. 'I'll take you to one of the side entrances.'

'Matt!' Hamar exclaimed as they passed the tree behind which Lilian Rosenberg was hiding, 'I smell scent – and what is more I recognize it. It is *Violette de mer* – the scent that – Rosenberg uses! You were with her this evening!'

'I swear I wasn't!' Kelson replied. 'I bought some scent in Regent Street this afternoon.'

'Humph,' Hamar grunted. 'I have my doubts.' They walked on in silence till they came to a small iron gate, where the policeman left them, whilst he went to the lodge for the keys; and all the while Kelson was in terror, lest Hamar should catch sight of Lilian Rosenberg, who had kept close behind them, and was now standing, but a few yards away, trying to conceal her identity and escape notice.

But the policeman on his return with the keys called out to her, and Kelson, fearing that she might be either taken in charge for loitering there, in apparently suspicious circumstances, or made to remain in the Park all night – neither of which contingencies he could possibly permit – at once came forward, and explained that she was a friend of his.

The policeman was satisfied. The sight of another half-sovereign had rendered him more than polite, and, without saying a word, he let them all out together.

The moment they were in the street, Hamar turned on Kelson, white with passion.

'So,' he said, 'I was right after all – liar! fool! You would risk all our lives for a few hours' flirtation with this silly girl.'

'If it's only flirtation, Leon, what does it matter?' Curtis interposed. 'For goodness' sake shut up wrangling and let's get home. I'm starving.'

'I shall have something to say to you to-morrow morning,' Hamar remarked, in an undertone, to Lilian Rosenberg.

'And I to you,' was the furious reply. 'I shall not forget the disrespectful way in which you have just spoken of me, in alluding to the scent.'

She signalled to a taxi, and giving Kelson a friendly good-night, jumped into it and was speedily whirled away.

On the whole, the evening had been a disappointment. She had wanted to see the Unknown – the awful thing that had inspired Kelson and his colleagues with such unmitigated horror – and instead she had seen only an obsessed policeman – a cataleptic 'copper' – who, had he not spoken in a strangely uncanny voice, would certainly have seemed to her absolutely ordinary.

With regard to Hamar's displeasure, she was not in the slightest degree disturbed. He would never dare say anything to her. And after all that had occurred he would never venture to sack her. All the same she hated him. There was just sufficient in her conduct to make the name he had called her by applicable – therefore her bitterest wrath and indignation were aroused against him. He had behaved unpardonably. She could kill him for it.

'I'll just show him,' she said to herself, 'what that uncivil tongue of his can do. He shall see that it can do him infinitely more harm than all Kelson's love-making. For one thing I'll spoil his chances with Gladys Martin; and — I wonder if I could make use of what I know about him, as a means of getting friendly again with Shiel. At all events I'll try.'

With this object in view she went round to Shiel's lodgings, and was informed by the landlady that Shiel was ill.

'Nothing serious, I hope?' she asked.

'It has been,' the landlady replied, 'but he is better now. It all came through his not taking proper care of himself.'

'May I see him, do you think?' Lilian Rosenberg inquired.

'I don't know,' the landlady grumbled. 'He's in a very touchy mood — no one can do nothing right for him. But maybe there won't be any harm in your trying,' she added, her eyes wandering to the half-crown in Lilian Rosenberg's fingers.

She opened the door somewhat wider, and Lilian Rosenberg entered. Shiel was immensely surprised to see her. Illness and solitude had very considerably subdued him, and though at first he showed some resentment, he speedily softened under her sympathetic solicitation for his health. She put his room straight and dusted the furniture, got tea for him, and when she had completely won him over by these kindly actions, and made him beg her pardon for ever having spoken harshly to her, she broached the subject all the while uppermost in her mind — the subject of Hamar and Gladys.

'He hasn't the slightest intention of marrying her,' she said. 'All he wants is to make her his mistress, so as to be able to throw her over the moment he gets tired of her, and then marry some one of title. He is tremendously taken with her of course — her physical beauty, which he had the impudence to tell me surpassed that of any other woman he had seen, appeals strongly to his grossly sensual nature. If she won't give in to him now, she will be obliged to do so in six months' time.'

'I don't understand you,' Shiel said feebly; 'why in six months' time?'

Lilian Rosenberg then told him what she knew about the compact.

'So you see,' she added, 'that if the final stage is reached no woman will be safe – the trio will have any girl they fancy entirely at their mercy.'

'How inconceivably awful!' Shiel exclaimed. 'Surely there is some way of stopping them.'

'There is only one way,' Lilian said slowly, 'the union between the three must be broken – they must quarrel, and dissolve partnership.'

'You may be sure they will take good care not to do that.'

'Don't be too sure,' Lilian Rosenberg replied. 'Matthew Kelson is very fond of me. With a little persuasion he would do anything I asked.'

'Then do you think you could bring about a rupture between him and Hamar!' Shiel asked eagerly.

'I might!'

'And you will – you will save Gladys Martin after all!'

Lilian did not reply at once.

'Do you think she is the sort of girl who would marry poverty,' she said, evasively, 'poverty like this!' and she glanced round the room.

'I won't ask her to!' Shiel exclaimed. 'Whilst I have been lying in bed, ill, I have thought of many things – and have come to the conclusion I have no right ever to think of marrying. It is difficult for me to earn enough to keep one person in comfort – and I've lost all hope of ever earning enough to keep two.'

'Well, if you don't ask her,' Lilian Rosenberg said, 'there's one thing, she will never ask you. And I think you are remarkably well out of it. If you do ever marry, marry a girl that has grit – a girl that would be a real "pal" to you – a girl that would help you to win fame!'

CHAPTER 28

WHOM WILL HE MARRY?

HAD Lilian Rosenberg been able to see the effect of her conversation upon Shiel after she had left him, she would have been disappointed. He had, prior to this interview with Lilian Rosenberg, as he told her, made up his mind to abandon all idea of marrying Gladys Martin; and there is a possibility that had her name not been mentioned, had she not been recalled so vividly to his mind, he would have adhered to that resolution – at all events so long as he refrained from seeing her. But such is human nature – or at least man's nature – that directly Lilian Rosenberg had left him, Shiel's love for Gladys burst out with such wild, invigorated force that it swept reason and everything else before it. Gladys! He could think of nothing else! Every detail in her appearance, every word she had spoken, came back to him with exaggerated intensity. Her beauty was sublime. There was no one like her, no one that could inspire him with such a sense of ideality, no one that could lead him on to such dizzy heights of greatness. It was all nonsense to say, as Lilian Rosenberg had said, there were just as many good fish in the sea as had ever come out of it – there was only one Gladys. Hamar should never marry her – he would marry her himself. She must be told at once of Hamar's infamous designs. A mad desire to see her came over him, and disregardful of the doctor's orders that he should remain in bed several more days, he got up, and dressing as fast as his weak condition would allow him, took a taxi and drove to Waterloo.

On reaching the Cottage, at Kew, he found Gladys at home, and to his great joy, alone.

There is nothing that appeals to a woman more than a sick man, and Shiel, in coming to Gladys in his present condition, had unwittingly played a trump card. Had he appeared well and strong she would probably have received him none too cordially – for she was very tired of men just then; but the moment her eyes alighted on his thin cheeks and she saw the dark rings under his eyes, pity conquered. This man at least was not to blame – he was not of the same pattern as other men, he was not like so many men whose adulation had grown fulsome to her, and – he was totally unlike Hamar.

In very sympathetic tones she inquired how he was, and on learning that he had been sufficiently ill to be kept in bed, asked why he had not told her.

'Auntie and I would have called to see you,' she said, 'and brought you jelly and other nice things. Who waited on you, had you no nurse?'

Fearful lest he should give her the impression he was speaking for effect, or trying to trade on her feelings (Shiel was one of those people who are painfully exact), he told her as simply as he could just how he had been placed.

'But why come here,' Gladys demanded, 'when you were told to stay in bed till the end of the week? It is frightfully risky.'

Shiel then explained to her the purport of his visit.

'Then it was to warn me, to put me on my guard against Hamar, that you disobeyed the doctor's orders,' she said.

Shiel nodded. 'You are not displeased, are you?' he asked nervously.

'I am displeased with you for thinking so little of yourself,' Gladys said, 'and more than obliged to you for thinking so much of me. You know I only consented to marry Mr. Hamar to save my father – and you say he no longer has the power to work spells?'

'I believe that to be a fact,' Shiel replied.

'Then he lied to me!' Gladys observed. 'He threatened that unless I saw him as often as he wished, and went with him wherever he wanted, and a good many more things, he would inflict my father with every conceivable disease. You are quite sure your information is correct?'

'Absolutely!'

'Then, thank God!' Gladys said with a great sigh of relief, 'I shall know how to act now.'

'You will break off your engagement?' Shiel inquired eagerly.

'No! I can't do that!' Gladys said sadly. 'I've promised to marry Mr. Hamar, and, therefore, marry him I must.'

'Promises made under such conditions are mere extortions, they don't count.'

'I fear they do,' Gladys replied. 'I've never yet broken my word.'

'Then there's no hope for me,' Shiel gasped. 'I must go – it maddens me to see you the affianced bride of that devil.'

He rose to go, but had hardly gained his feet, when his strength utterly failed and he collapsed. Gladys helped him into a chair, and then flew for some brandy. In the hall, she met her aunt, who had just returned from an afternoon call. In a few words she explained what had happened.

'Poor young man,' Miss Templeton said. 'I thought he looked very ill the last time I saw him. And he came here solely to benefit you! Well, you have a good deal to answer for, and your face is not only your own misfortune, but other people's too. But it will never do for your father to see Mr. Davenport. He went off in a very bad temper this morning, and if he comes back and finds him here, there'll be a scene.'

Miss Templeton and Gladys consulted together for some minutes, and then decided to send for a taxi and have Shiel conveyed back to his rooms, Miss Templeton accompanying him.

Miss Templeton knew that Shiel was poor, but like most people who have lived in comfortable surroundings all their lives, she had no idea of what poverty was like – the poverty of a seven-and-sixpence a week room in a back street; and when she saw it she nearly swooned.

'Why, this is a slum!' she ejaculated as the taxi stopped next door to a fried fish shop in a narrow street swarming with children sucking bread and jam, and rolling each other over in the gutters.

'I don't wonder the man is ill here!' she said to herself, as the door of the house they stopped at opened and she snuffed the atmosphere. 'The place reeks – and – oh, gracious! is this the landlady?'

Yet the woman was ordinary enough – the type of landlady one sees in all back streets – greasy face, straggling hair, dirty blouse, black hands, bitten fingernails, short skirts, prodigious feet, a grubby child clinging on to her dress and every indication of the speedy arrival of another.

'I suppose you're 'is mother, hain't you, mum?' she said, gaping at Miss Templeton's rather fashionable clothes in open-mouthed wonder. 'I told 'im 'e ought not to go out, but 'e never 'eeds what I say.'

Miss Templeton, though not particularly flattered at being taken for Shiel's mother – since, like most ladies of mature age, she wished to be regarded as much younger – nevertheless, thought it better not to disillusion the woman. The poor, she told herself, often have very decided views on propriety. With the woman's aid she got Shiel upstairs, and, as he was too feeble to undress himself, despite his protestations, helped to disrobe him. She had thought, when she first saw the slum, of returning to Kew at once, but she did no such thing. She stayed with Shiel; persuaded the landlady to make him some gruel (which proved to be a sorry mess, but had at least the advantage of being hot), and bribed one of the children to fetch the doctor. Shiel nearly died. Had it not been for the careful nursing and good food provided by Miss Templeton, who visited him every day, he would never have turned the corner.

'The poor boy is terribly fond of you,' Miss Templeton said to Gladys. 'In his delirium he talked of nothing but saving you from Leon Hamar – from that devil Leon Hamar – and if one can place any reliance at all on the ravings of a sick man, a devil Leon Hamar undoubtedly is. What a pity it is Shiel hasn't money.'

These remarks were naturally not without effect on Gladys, and she could not help growing more and more interested in the man, whose love for her had proved so deep-rooted and ideal, that he had practically sacrificed his life, in an attempt to serve her. Finally, she found herself awaiting her aunt's daily report of his illness with an anxiety that was almost acute.

In the meanwhile, John Martin came home one evening in a rare state of excitement.

'What do you think?' he exclaimed, throwing a bundle of letters on the table, 'one of Dick's speculations has turned out trumps, after all. He had invested several thousands of pounds – in Shiel's name – in enamel-ivorine, the new stuff for stopping teeth, which looks exactly like part of the teeth. I remember I thought it an absurd venture at the time, but for once in a way I was wrong—'

'Ahem!' interrupted Gladys.

'There has been a sudden boom in the patent, every dentist is using it, and, as a consequence, the shares have risen enormously. I've heard from Dick's lawyer to-day that Shiel is now worth fifty thousand pounds!'

'Good heavens!' Miss Templeton ejaculated, 'and Gladys has bound herself to Hamar! I suppose,' she said afterwards, when John Martin and she were alone together, 'that you would not have any objection to Shiel now, if Gladys were free to marry him.'

'Certainly not!' John Martin said, 'certainly not, I

always liked Shiel. A fine manly young fellow, very different to the type one usually meets nowadays. I only wish Gladys were free!'

'You would raise no obstacle to her becoming engaged to Shiel?'

'None whatsoever! But what's the good of talking about an impossibility. Gladys is stubbornness itself – when once she has made up her mind to do a thing, nothing in God's world will make her not do it.'

'Wait,' Miss Templeton said, 'wait and see. I think I can see a possible way out of it.'

She had learned much from Shiel in his 'wanderings.' He had constantly alluded to Hamar, Curtis and Kelson – and Lilian Rosenberg; to the great compact, and to the one possible way of breaking that compact – namely through the instigation of a quarrel between the trio. From several of the statements he had made, Miss Templeton deduced that Kelson was greatly under the influence of Lilian Rosenberg – and it was from these statements that she finally received an inspiration.

Miss Templeton saw deeper than Shiel – it had always been her custom to read between the lines. 'Now,' she argued, 'if Kelson were so easily influenced by Lilian Rosenberg, who was young and attractive, it was almost a *sine quâ non* that he was in love with her, and as marriage was one of the eventualities strictly forbidden to the trio in the compact – "they must neither quarrel nor marry," Shiel had explained – here was their chance. Kelson must marry Lilian Rosenberg, and by so doing, break the compact and overwhelm the trio in some sudden and dire catastrophe. But the marriage must take place within six months' time. How could that be arranged? Could Lilian Rosenberg be bribed or persuaded into it? for of course Miss Templeton being a woman – albeit an old maid – had at once divined that Lilian Rosenberg was in love with Shiel – that she did not care a straw for Kelson, and that to marry the latter she would need some very strong inducement. And the only inducement she could think of was Lilian's genuine love for Shiel.

'Yes, it is upon this one weakness of Lilian's that I must work,' she said to herself. 'It is the only way I can see of saving Gladys.'

Resolved at any rate to experiment upon these lines, she lost no time in seeking out Lilian Rosenberg, who received her very coldly and was distinctly rude.

'What have my affairs to do with you? Who sent you here?' she demanded.

'Humanity!' Miss Templeton replied. 'I have come entirely of my own accord to plead the cause of one who is seriously ill – possibly dying!'

'Seriously ill! – possibly dying!' Lilian Rosenberg said incredulously, nevertheless, turning pale. 'Mr. Davenport is surely not as bad as all that!'

'When did you see him last?' Miss Templeton asked.

'A fortnight ago,' Lilian Rosenberg replied. 'I have been inundated with work the past two weeks.'

'Then you've not heard that he's had a relapse,' Miss Templeton said, 'and is now in a most critical condition! He has something on his mind, and the doctor assures me that whilst he is still worrying over that something, there is no chance of his recovery.'

'Do you know what it is – the something?' Lilian Rosenberg asked, the white on her cheeks intensifying.

'Yes!' Miss Templeton said slowly, and trying to appear calm. 'He is very worried about Miss Martin's engagement to Mr. Hamar.'

'And why, pray?'

'Because he knows all about Mr. Hamar – and the compact.'

'He has told you?'

'I have gleaned it from what he has said in his delirium.'

'Has he been as ill as that?'

'Yes, he has. He had a temperature of a hundred and four the day before yesterday.'

For a few moments there was silence. Then Lilian Rosenberg said, 'Can you believe what a man says in delirium?'

'In this instance I feel sure you can,' Miss Templeton replied.

'Why should Miss Martin's engagement be of such interest to Mr. Davenport?'

Miss Templeton thought for a moment. 'Because,' she said at last, 'he is in love with her.'

'Are you sure of it?'

'Absolutely!'

'Do you think she cares for him, even as much as that?' and she snapped her fingers.

'I think she may care for him a very great deal some day – she has begun to care for him already!'

'But she would never dream of marrying any one as badly off as Mr. Davenport. He is practically starving.'

'He was – but he's not now. He's come into money.' And she explained about the fifty thousand pounds.

'I see!' Lilian Rosenberg said after a prolonged pause, 'that accounts for her having just begun to care for him. Supposing there was some one who had been fond of him all along – in the days when he hadn't a halfpenny to his name, and every one else shunned him!'

'I should feel very sorry for that person,' Miss Templeton said, 'but setting aside the sacrifice of his happiness – it would be wrong for him to marry her if his heart was fixed elsewhere.'

'Which you say it is.'

'Which I am sure it is!'

'Well, supposing it is – what does it concern me? Why tell me all this?'

'Because it lies in your power to put an end to the Compact and bring about the catastrophe the Unknown threatened.'

'I think you credit me with rather too much. I do not quite see how I can accomplish all this?'

'But I do,' Miss Templeton said, briskly. 'I believe I am right in saying Mr. Kelson is in love with you – that you can make him do pretty well anything you please. Well, all you have to do is to lead him on to propose and insist on his marrying you at once – or at all events before the expiration of the Compact. If you succeed in doing this the Compact will be broken!'

'That may be,' Lilian Rosenberg exclaimed, 'but where, pray, should I come in? Why on earth should I marry a man I don't care a snap for?'

'Why!' Miss Templeton replied, slowly, 'why, because by marrying a man you don't care a snap for, you would save the life of a man – I am quite sure, you care a very great deal for.'

CHAPTER 29

THE END OF 'THE BEYOND'

It took Lilian Rosenberg some time to make up her mind.

'It's extraordinary,' she said to herself, 'how fond I am of Shiel. I used to think it an impossibility for me to be really fond of any one. . . . The question is, however, am I sufficiently in love with him, to give him up to that soft little cat – Gladys Martin! If it weren't for his illness – if I could only persuade myself that he isn't as ill as Miss Whatever-her-name-is – said, I shouldn't think twice – I should let things be – but as I feel sure he is really ill – dangerously ill – and the only chance of his recovery lies in the possibility of his marrying Martin – I must deliberate. Shall I or shall I not? If it were any other woman I shouldn't so much mind – but – Gladys Martin! I can't endure her. There is one hope, however, namely – that if he marries her, he will soon tire of her – and – and come to me. What a tremendous score off her that would be! But, no! I wouldn't do that! Because – because – well there – just like my infernal luck – I love him. Could I marry him, I wonder, even if there were no Gladys Martin? It is doubtful! Yet I believe I could. But what is the good of conceiving impossibilities! There is a Gladys Martin – and – I can never have Shiel. The only question I have to settle is – Shall she have him? Shall I marry Kelson so that Martin can marry Shiel?'

Lilian Rosenberg turned this question over in her mind for a whole day and night, sometimes arriving at one decision, sometimes at another. In the end – very elaborately dressed, and looking daintier than she had ever done in her life, she waylaid Kelson and asked him to have tea with her.

Any pretty face, accentuated by all the allurements of a large mushroom hat and hobble skirt, was enough for Kelson; but when that face belonged to the one girl for whom, above all other girls, he had a colossal weakness, he simply could not feast his eyes enough on it.

'Have tea with you? Of course I will,' he said. 'But

we must be careful. Hamar is about. If you walk on up the Haymarket, I'll follow in a taxi, and pick you up, directly I get to a safe distance.'

'I see you are as much in awe of Mr. Hamar as ever,' Lilian Rosenberg laughed. 'I'm not! I've found him out – he's all talk. But do as you will – get your taxi and I'll walk on – we'll have tea in my new flat.'

Kelson was so delighted he hardly knew if he stood on his head or his heels. 'You are prettier than ever,' he said, as the taxi-door shut and they sped away. 'I declare there seems no limit to your beauty.'

'Only because you're partial,' she said. 'I shall grow ugly one day. Perhaps – soon.' With a savage energy, she set to work to completely overcome him. With a languishing expression in her eyes – eyes, which she made use of mercilessly, without giving him a moment's respite – she watched his whole being vibrate with love and adoration.

They had hardly entered the drawing-room of her flat when he threw himself at her feet, and poured forth his worship of her in the most extravagent phrases.

'Look here, Mr. Kelson,' she said at length, withdrawing the hand it seemed as if he would never leave off kissing, 'this is all very well; but I daresay you make love to countless other girls in this same fashion. How can I tell if you are really serious?'

'Don't I look as if I am?' he cried.

'One can never judge correctly by looks,' she replied; 'they are terrible deceptive. You are very emphatic in your avowals of love, but you say nothing about marriage.'

'Then you do care for me! Jerusalem! How happy I should be if only I thought that!'

'Think it, then,' Lilian Rosenberg said, 'and let us come to an understanding. Can you afford to keep a wife – keep her, as I should expect to be kept – plenty of new dresses, jewellery, theatres, balls, motors, Ascot, Henley, Cowes?'

'I reckon I could do all that,' Kelson replied. 'I've just over a hundred and fifty thousand pounds in the bank, and with this "cure" business, I'm taking on an average ten thousand per week. I would settle a hundred thousand on you, and make you a handsome allowance – a thousand a week – more if you wanted it.'

'Well!' Lilian Rosenberg said after a slight pause, during which Kelson had again seized her hand and was kissing it convulsively, 'to quote one of your Americanisms – I reckon I'll fix up with you. On one condition, however.'

'And that,' Kelson murmured, still kissing her feverishly.

'That we marry a week to-day!'

Kelson dropped her hand as if he had been shot. 'We can't!' he cried 'The Compact!'

'Oh, damn the Compact!' Lilian Rosenberg said coolly. 'You marry me then – or not at all!'

'You are joking – you know what the Compact means!'

'I know what you think it means. For my own part I don't see that you have the slightest reason to fear. The Unknown cannot really harm you. All you have to do is to turn religious. Anyhow you must risk it – that is to say, if you want me.'

'It will lead to a quarrel with Hamar,' Kelson said desperately. 'The Firm will dissolve – and I shan't get a cent more money.'

'I'll be content with what you have in the bank now. We can live on the interest of fifty thousand. The hundred thousand you will, of course, settle on me at once.'

He was silent. She taunted him, she ridiculed him; she at last lost her temper with him – whereupon he succumbed. The marriage should take place at a register office within the week.

'There'll be no time for a trousseau!' he said.

'Oh, hang the trousseau!' she said. 'I shall have a hundred thousand pounds. And now for a word of advice. Be sure that you do not let Hamar get any inkling of our approaching marriage, and be most careful to avoid doing anything that might arouse his suspicions. It isn't that I'm afraid of him – but I don't want rows – I'm sick to death of them!'

'You can rely on me to be careful, darling!' Kelson said, kissing her on the lips. 'I'll be discretion itself,' and so he meant to be. All the same – as is the case with every lover – every lover worthy of the name of lover – who loves with all the full, ripe vigour of genuine passion, his heart played havoc with his head; and he was blind to everything save visions of his beloved. In other circumstances this would not have mattered very much, but with Hamar's lynx eyes continually watching him, it was certain to lead to disaster.

'Ed!' Hamar said to Curtis one day. 'Matt's been getting into mischief. I know the symptoms well. He can't look me in the face, and every now and then, when he fancies my attention is attracted elsewhere, I catch him peeping furtively at me as if he were frightened out of his life I should ferret out some secret. It would be deplorable if now that we have got so near the end of the Compact, we should be held up by some idiotic blunder – some nonsensical love affair of his. I wonder whether it's Rosenberg or some other girl. Will you find out?'

'How can I?' Curtis growled. 'I'm not his keeper.'

'I know that!' Hamar said. 'Come, be reasonable. You want to be a Crœsus – so that you can eat and drink your head off – don't you! Well! You will! You will be one of the three wealthiest men in the world – you will have the world at your feet, if only you stick to me for the next seven months: till we have passed the seventh stage. If you don't – if either you or Matt deliberately quarrel with me, or marry – then, as I've dinned into your ears a thousand times, the Compact will be broken, and – not only that, but some frightful catastrophe will wipe us off. Now will you do what I ask? Come – a dinner with me every night this week at the Piccadilly – champagne – and no vegetables!'

'All right,' Curtis said sulkily, 'for the good of the cause I suppose I must, but I hate spying.'

Two nights later in a private room at the Picadilly, after dinner, when the champagne and liqueurs had got into Curtis's head and he was leaning back in his chair smiling and silly, Hamar suddenly said, 'Ed! you remember what I told you – about watching Kelson. Have you discovered anything?'

'Shupposing I have,' Curtis replied, 'shupposing I haven't – whatch then?'

'Ah, but I know you have,' Hamar said, striving to hide his eagerness. 'Come, tell me, another liqueur – I'll square it with the Unknown – it won't hurt you!'

'Won't it!' Curtis gurgled. 'Wont'ch it! I'll tell you everything. No – nothingsh, I mean.'

But Hamar when once he had smelt a rat, was not easily put off. He coaxed, and coaxed, and eventually succeeded.

'Leonsh!' Curtis said, with a sudden burst of drunken confidence. 'Leonsh! it's worse than either you or I shuspected. I caught them alone this morning – in my offish.'

'Them! Rosenberg and Matt!'

'Yesh, of course, shilly! I told Matt I was going out. He thought I had – so into the room I came – quite unshuspected, unobsherved. She was sitting on hish knees, cuddling – and he was putting a ring on her finger. "Four more days, darling," shays he, "and we are married! Jerushalem! Damn the Compact and damnsh Hamar!" "Hamar doesn't shuspect, does he?' Rosenberg shays. "Not a bit – not in the slightest," old Matt replieshes, "why it is I who amsh brave now." Then he kisshes her, and fearing they would detect my presence, I slipsh quietly out.'

'Will you swear this is true?' Leon said, his voice trembling with excitement.

'I'll swearsh it!' Curtis answered, 'but you look crossh. Whatsh the matter, Leon? *God! What's the matter!*'

An hour later, as Kelson was rising from his chair in front of the fire to gaze, for the hundredth time that evening, into the eyes of Lilian Rosenberg's portrait on the mantelshelf, the door of his room flew open and in staggered Curtis – white, wet and bloated.

'Great heavens!' Kelson cried. 'What the deuce have you been doing to yourself? You look a perfect devil!'

'I am one!' Curtis groaned. 'I am one, Matt! I've given your show away.'

'My shów away! What, what the deuce do you mean?'

In a string of broken sentences Curtis explained what had happened. 'I'm damned sorry, Matt, old man,' he pleaded. 'It was the drink that did it – I didn't know what I was saying till it was too late – till I saw Leon's face – and that cleared my brain – brought me to myself. It was hellish. I remember the moment I mentioned the word marriage – he sprang up from his chair, and as he hurried out, I heard him mutter, "I'll go to her straight – I'll—" Matt, old man, he meant mischief. I'm certain of it. Come with me to her flat – for God's sake – COME.' And catching hold of Kelson, who leaned against the mantelshelf, dazed and stupefied, he dragged him into the street.

To revert to Hamar. Curtis information had transformed him. He was, now, another creature. Prior to his conversation with Curtis, he had suspected, at the most, that Kelson might be contemplating a secret engagement to Lilian Rosenberg – but a hasty marriage – a marriage in a few days' time – he had never dreamt that Kelson could be as mad as that. It was outrageous! It was abominable! It was sheer wholesale homicide! At all costs the marriage must be stopped. And mad with rage, Hamar dashed out of the hotel, and calling a taxi, drove direct to Lilian Rosenberg's flat.

He found her alone – alone – and with a strange expression in her eyes – an expression he had never noticed in them before. She was in the act of examining a magnificent diamond ring.

'You're quite out of breath,' she said coolly, 'didn't you come up by the lift?'

'I've come to talk business,' Hamar panted. 'It's no use looking like that. I know your secret.'

'My secret!' Lilian Rosenberg replied, opening her eyes and simulating the greatest unconcern, 'what secret? I don't understand.'

'Oh, yes, you do!' Hamar said, 'you understand only too well – you deceitful minx. Had I only been smart – I should have given you the sack months ago. This marriage of yours with Kelson shall not come off.'

'My marriage with Mr. Kelson!' Lilian Rosenberg said, turning a trifle pale. 'I really don't know what you are talking about.'

'You do!' Hamar shouted, his fury rising. 'You do! You know all about it. You were seen sitting on his knee this morning, and all your conversation was overheard. I have found out everything. And I tell you, you shan't marry him.'

'I shan't marry him!' Lilian Rosenberg said with provoking coolness. 'Whoever thinks I want to marry him?'

'He does – I do!' Hamar shouted – his voice rising to a scream. 'You've hoodwinked me long enough – you hoodwink me no longer. You've encouraged him from the first – made eyes at him every time you've seen him – taken advantage of my absence to prowl about the passages to waylay him – had him round to your rooms and visited him in his. You've no sense of shame or honour – you've broken your promises to me – you're a liar!'

'Anything else Mr. Hamar!' Lilian Rosenberg said, her

eyes glittering. 'When you've quite finished, perhaps – you'll kindly go and leave me in peace.'

'Go! Leave you in peace!' Hamar shouted. 'Damn you, curse your impertinence! Go! I'll not budge an inch till I wring from you an oath – a solemn binding oath, that you'll break off your engagement with Kelson at once.'

'Really, Mr. Hamar!' Lilian Rosenberg said, 'I cannot put up with quite so much noise. Will you go or shall I ring for the porter to turn you out?'

She moved in the direction of the bell as she spoke, but before she could touch it Hamar had intercepted her.

'Stop this foolery!' he said catching hold of her wrist, 'I'm in grim earnest – the lives of all three of us are at stake – jeopardized through you – through your infernal greed and selfishness. Do you hear!'

'Please let go my wrist,' she said quietly.

'I won't!' he shouted. 'I'll squeeze, crush it, break it! Break you, too, unless you swear to break off your marriage!'

'I'll swear nothing,' Lilian Rosenberg said faintly. 'You're a brute. Let me go or I'll cry for help.'

She screamed, but before she could repeat the scream, Hamar had her by the throat – and then blind with passion and before he fully realized what he was about, he had shaken her to and fro – like a terrier shakes a rat – and had dashed her on the floor.

For some minutes he stood rocking with passion, and then, his eyes falling on the inanimate form at his feet, he gave a great gasping cry and bent over it.

'God in Heaven!' he ejaculated, 'she's dead! I've killed her!'

He was still bending over her – still feeling her lifeless pulse, still trying to resuscitate her – feebly wondering how he had killed her, feverishly debating the best course to pursue – when Curtis and Kelson burst in on him.

At the sight of Lilian Rosenberg's lifeless body both men started back. 'Great God! Hamar!' Curtis gasped. 'What have you done to her?'

'Nothing!' Hamar said, turning a ghastly face to them. 'I – I found her like this!'

'Liar!' Kelson shouted beside himself with fury. 'Liar!

We heard her scream. Look at your hands – there's blood on them! You've killed her!'

Before Curtis could stop him he sprang at Hamar, and the next moment both men were rolling on the floor.

'Call for the police, Ed!' Kelson gasped, 'the police – or—' But before he could utter another syllable, walls, floor and ceiling shook with loud, devilish laughter. There was then silence – enthralling, impressive, omnipotent silence – the electric light went out – and the room filled with luminous, striped figures.

The Time/Space Series from Sphere

Sphere books now has a bestselling time/space series, presenting the many theories about man's origins and potentials.

WE ARE NOT THE FIRST   Andrew Tomas   35p

Is all of modern science a mere rediscovery of ancient knowledge?

BEYOND THE TIME BARRIER   Andrew Tomas   35p

Can the past be photographed? How can the time barrier be broken? A fascinating study of the possibilities of time travel.

ATLANTIS: FROM LEGEND TO DISCOVERY   35p

Andrew Tomas
There are many instances of evidence of progressive scientific concepts in antiquity. What was Atlantis?

GODS AND SPACEMEN IN THE ANCIENT EAST   35p

W. Raymond Drake
In literature and legend there is a tradition that spacemen from other planets guided mankind in the distant past ...

MY LIFE AND PROPHECIES   Jeane Dixon   35p

Jeane Dixon is the famous American clairvoyant who has predicted many important events and here she explains her powers and makes forecasts for the future.

A Science Fiction and Science Fantasy Collection edited by Michael Moorcock

Making its first appearance in paperback book format, Britain's foremost science fiction quarterly magazine, New Worlds. 'The essence of good science fiction' *New Scientist*.

NEW WORLDS 1		25p
NEW WORLDS 2		30p
NEW WORLDS 3		30p
NEW WORLDS 4		35p
NEW WORLDS 5		40p
NEW WORLDS 6	with Charles Platt	40p

A Selection of Gothic Fiction from Sphere

THE GOLDEN VIOLET	Margaret Campbell	35p
THE SPIDER IN THE CUP	Margaret Campbell	35p
THE SPECTRAL BRIDE	Margaret Campbell	35p
BLANCHE FURY	Margaret Campbell	35p
THE THIRD WOMAN	Jean-Anne de Pré	35p
THE HAUNTED WOMAN	Melissa Napier	35p
THE TWISTED CAMEO	Katheryn Kimbrough	35p
THE HOUSE ON WINDSWEPT RIDGE	Katheryn Kimbrough	35p

A Selection of General Fiction from Sphere

THE TAMARIND SEED	Evelyn Anthony	30p
DANDO SHAFT!	Don Calhoun	30p
VENUS IN INDIA	Charles Devereaux	40p
THE ONE-EYED KING	Edwin Fadiman	45p
COME IN, NUMBER ONE, YOUR TIME IS UP	Derek Jewell	45p
TRESPASS	Fletcher Knebel	40p
THE CIRCLE GAME	Joel Leiber	40p
CONFESSIONS FROM THE CLINK	Timothy Lea	30p
SATYR	Robert de Maria	30p
GOLDENGROVE	Darryl Ponicsan	40p
THE PRINCESS AND THE GOBLIN	Paul Rosner	50p
STEWARDESSES DOWN UNDER	Penny Sutton	30p
THE PHOTOGRAPHS	Vassilis Vassilikos	30p
KILLING ZONE	William C. Woods	30p
JOHN ADAM IN EDEN	Christopher Wood	30p

A Selection of Crime Thrillers from Sphere

ASSASSIN	James Anderson	30p
THE ALPHA LIST	James Anderson	35p
VICTIMS UNKNOWN	Richard Clapperton	30p
THE ABDUCTION	Stanley Cohen	30p
ONLY WHEN I LARF	Len Deighton	35p
THE WHITE LIE ASSIGNMENT	Peter Driscoll	35p
A COLD FRONT	Bridget Everitt	30p
SUPERFLY	Philip Fenty	30p
ACROSS 110TH STREET	Wally Ferris	35p
CZECH POINT	Nichol Fleming	30p
SHROUD FOR A NIGHTINGALE	P. D. James	35p
UNNATURAL CAUSES	P. D. James	35p
KLUTE	William Johnston	30p
LINE OF FIRE	Roger Parkes	30p
TOLL FOR THE BRAVE	Harry Patterson	30p

The Dennis Wheatley Library of the Occult

In this paperback series we propose to include novels and uncanny tales by:

Majorie Bowen, John Buchan, Ambrose Bierce, R. H. and E. F. Benson, Brodie-Innes, Balzac, Algernon Blackwood, F. Marion Crawford, Wilkie Collins, Aleister Crowley, Dickens, Conan Doyle, Dostoyevsky, Lord Dunsany, Guy Endore, Dion Fortune, Kipling, Le Fanu, Bulwer Lytton, Walter de la Mare, A. E. W. Mason, Arthur Machen, John Masefield, Guy de Maupassant, Oliver Onions, Edgar Alan Poe, Sax Rohmer, Bram Stoker, W. B. Seabrook, H. G. Wells, Hugh Walpole and Oscar Wilde.

****

Also books on:
Palmistry, Astrology, Faith healing, Clairvoyance, Numerology, Telepathy, etc.

****

For particulars write to Sphere Books Ltd, 30/32 Gray's Inn Road, London WC1X 8JL.

All Sphere Books are available at your bookshop or newsagent, or can be ordered from the following address: Sphere Books, Cash Sales Department, P.O. Box 11, Falmouth, Cornwall.

Please send cheque or postal order (no currency), and allow 7p per copy to cover the cost of postage and packing in U.K. or overseas.

Black Magic titles by Dennis Wheatley published by Arrow Books

THE DEVIL RIDES OUT
GATEWAY TO HELL
THE HAUNTING OF TOBY JUGG
THE KA OF GIFFORD HILLARY
THE SATANIST
STRANGE CONFLICT
THEY USED DARK FORCES
TO THE DEVIL – A DAUGHTER
A serious study of the Occult, fully illustrated
THE DEVIL AND ALL HIS WORKS

If you would like a complete list of Arrow Books, including other Dennis Wheatley titles, please send post card to:

P.O. Box 29, Douglas, Isle of Man, Great Britain.